A DEMON BOUND

DEBRA DUNBAR

❀ Created with Vellum

DEDICATION

To Dr. Hadley Tremaine (1939-2001), Chairman of the Department of English, Hood College, Frederick, Maryland, who taught me that there is great treasure to be found in what others consign to hell.

CHAPTER 1

I parked down the street from the bail bond office and pretended to fuss with some papers on the passenger seat as I watched two boys race toward me out of the corner of my eye. They were hauling ass, and one darted across traffic in a daring effort to cut the other off.

"Wait for it, wait for it," I muttered as they sped toward the car.

One, two, three, open. I flung the car door out to its full width and a wave of satisfaction rolled through me as I heard a thump and felt the door vibrate against my hand. The boy toward the outside had managed to dive out of the way, missing the door by inches and rolling expertly as he landed on the ground. The inside boy wasn't so lucky. He'd bounced off the door with the thump I had felt and hit the cement sidewalk with a meaty thwack.

"Yeah," yelled the outside boy as he hopped to his feet. He punctuated the word with an exuberant fist pump. I got out of the car and gave him a high five.

"All yours, Roberto," I told him.

I paid a twenty to any kid who watched my car while I

took care of business. That normally wouldn't have been a good deal. A Corvette in this neighborhood would attract a lot of attention, and a kid watching it wouldn't necessarily deter theft. But my car was well known. All the kid needed to do was inform anyone looking to lift the tires that this was my vehicle, and let me know if anyone was stupid enough to do so anyway. Well worth the twenty.

I turned to the other kid, who was staggering to his feet from the pavement and wiping a bloody nose.

"Maybe next time, Dante," I said. He nodded, pinching the bridge of his nose and staggered off.

I had a moment of panic as I shut the car door and thought that Dante may have dented it. Humans were soft and squishy, but he'd hit with a good bit of force. I lucked out this time, though. No dent, just a bit of blood and snot that I wiped off with the side of my arm. Fuck! That was close. I don't always think things through before I do them, and it would have really sucked if he'd damaged my car.

"Are you going to evict Old Man Larson, Ma'am?" Roberto asked me.

"Nope, just collecting rents," I replied.

Most people would rather have been home by the pool with a cold beer on a hot day like today, but I actually liked collecting rents. I'd spent the morning taking cash from those tenants who didn't trust the mail system, or who found it impossible to obtain a checking account. This was my last visit of the day with one particular tenant who needed an in-person, see-the-light kind of call.

I'm a slum lord. Commercial, residential, it doesn't matter as long as the building is cheap, squeaks by code and I can rent it. About seventy percent of my tenants pay promptly. I've been told that's an incredible percentage with these types of properties. The others shove cash-stuffed envelopes at me as soon as I ring the bell.

I'm also a demon, which is probably why I have such a high compliance rate on my rent collections. We demons usually live in another realm and pop over here to vacation. Low ranking demons save for centuries to pay someone for safe passage. Ones with status in the hierarchy come over whenever they feel like it. Of course, it is still risky trying to get through the gates undetected, and to hustle your ass back before your fun activities bring death down on your head. The more often you come over, the greater the chance is that you'll be caught and killed by the angels.

I've been here over forty years on a sort of extended vacation, which is unheard of among my kind. I've managed to stay alive by laying low and posing as a human, with as little energy usage and bad behavior as possible for a demon. So far I've succeeded in remaining undetected.

I walked the block down to the apartment building feeling the heat from the broken sidewalk right through my shoes, and kicked an empty whisky pint out of the way to ring the doorbell. My tenant should have been waiting for me since I pulled some favors and had a friend arrange a drug buy. Otherwise he would most likely hide in the back and pretend he was not home. When that happens, I have to sneak around the place peering in windows and eventually breaking in to confront the tenant. I hate that. These houses are all over one hundred years old and the windows aren't standard size. It's very difficult to get them repaired. My tenant was expecting a buyer and not a landlord, so I hoped I didn't have to break any windows to get in this time.

After a few moments, I heard some shuffling near the door and sensed someone looking out the peephole. I tried to look around nervously like I was a proper yuppie addict. I'm a terrible actress, so I was actually a bit surprised when he opened the door and ushered me quickly in. He looked me over and visibly relaxed. Humans are sometimes uncomfortable around me, but once they really look at me, and their eyes tell them I'm an average sized woman with average features, their brain squashes any fearful instincts. I go out of my way to look harmless. Not covered in tattoos, not pierced all over, no punk hairdo. No big warts, bulging muscles, glowing eyes, horns, etc. (could these two lists go together?) Just a nice normal, middle aged, rather plain woman.

"Are you Brad?" I asked him while looking around the place.

The inside looked like a frat house with old pizza boxes and beer cans carelessly tossed on coffee tables or stacked on the rather dirty beige carpet. I eyed it in distaste. I'd have to clean that carpet when their lease ended. I'd charge them double for it too. A plaid second-hand couch sat in front of a huge flat screen TV on the wall. Two guys sprawled on the couch with pistols visible in their waistbands. They were big, but flabby with wrinkled dirty clothes and longish hair. They looked pretty stoned and rather unaware of my presence.

"Yeah," he replied "what are you looking to take home?"

"The rent." I gave that a moment to sink in. "I'm actually the landlord, not a buyer."

That announcement was greeted with laughter from Brad. The guys on the couch didn't budge, still slumped with their eyes fixed on the TV. At least they weren't lunging at me with guns drawn at this point.

If the stoned guys on the couch managed to somehow achieve a miracle and hit me, I could repair almost any wound. It would hurt, and it might take a while, but I wouldn't die. Or I could convert the bullets before they reached me.

When demons convert, we dissect the molecules or atoms of something and rearrange them into something else. Transmutation, as the human alchemists called it. That is the big 'magic' of demons. Sometimes conversion works out neatly and you end up with all your atoms and molecules used and accounted for. Sometimes you have spare shit that you have to figure out what to do with. Some of that shit isn't particularly stable on its own, leaving you to borrow atoms out of other things around you to stick together. All this has to occur in fractions of a second because that's usually all you have before something explodes, or there is chlorine gas, or worse.

In the bullet scenario before me there were some troublesome atoms to deal with. You could do pretty much anything with carbon, but iron was the atom demanding attention when a bullet was speeding at you. Not a big deal when viewed on a world disaster scale, but kind of messy to deal with on the fly like this. And *any* conversion action on my part could possibly be messy enough to attract notice of the angels, who dedicated their existence to noticing these kinds of things and coming down with holy fury on our heads.

I could weld the steel triggers of the guns. Just shoot a blaze of energy across the room and melt the guns, burning half their pants off in the process. Back home, no one cared if you set the guys on fire welding triggers. Back home, no one would even bother with welding triggers, just shoot a big flashy burst of something and cook them all dead. Problem solved.

I couldn't afford to be too flashy though, since I was living under the radar as much as I could. I would bet that a small amount of energy from me wouldn't set off alarm bells with the angels, but why take the chance? Plus, I kind of got off on the risk of handling these situations without any energy usage at all. It was a real adrenaline rush. A bullet to the head or a vital organ would most likely kill me in this form, contrary to mythology.

"Come on, cough it up," I told him. "You owe it, I'm here. Just pay me the three months rent and no one gets hurt."

I had a premonition someone was going to get hurt. Might be me. Definitely would be Brad.

Brad sneered. If I had been a human, I probably would have been shaken. It was a good sneer. Very dramatic. Very Hollywood.

"You are the only one likely to get hurt, babe," he said. "And you're not leaving here with a dime."

Brad then proceeded to look me over like I was a steak on the grill and added an addendum. "Maybe the guys and I could enjoy some quality time with you to repay us for time wasted on this bogus deal you set up."

To bring his point home, he took a menacing step toward me.

Now this is when the fun starts for me. I live for the day this sort of thing happens. I smiled at Brad and let my mean out.

"All three of you?" I asked. "I haven't had that kind of pleasure in a long time. I prefer to leave my tenants alive and functioning so they can pay their rent, but if you're offering this in lieu of cash payment I am very tempted. I get a little carried away with the rough stuff though, so I can't guarantee that any of you'll survive."

I didn't see how the guys behind me reacted, but Brad looked unnerved for a brief second before he pulled himself together. He must have been made of tough stuff or perhaps sampling his own wares since he took the remaining three steps toward me, well within my zone of personal space, and gripped my chin in his hand. I locked eyes with him and froze him to me. Stupid human. To meet a demon's gaze like that was to give them control.

I smiled, convinced that I had him and was shocked when he punched me in the face. It was a good uppercut to the chin that knocked me on the filthy stinking carpet. I was reminded of Dante as I felt blood drip down my chin, although mine was from my mouth. Fucker had made me bite hard into my tongue. What had happened? Why couldn't I lock him in place? Was he legally blind or something? Maybe his drugs had blurred his vision? Did I suddenly suck at this particular skill?

"You are one sick psycho, freak," Brad told me. "Maybe you'll be less cocky with a few broken bones."

He went to kick me in the side and I rolled out of reach, scrambling in an embarrassing fashion to my feet. I was pissed enough to want to just blast him through the front of the building, but instead held back and assessed the situation. I backed up to a table and glanced quickly at the two on the couch. They sat still as statues, so thankfully all I needed to deal with was Brad.

Brad dove at me, and I spun out of his reach, putting the table between us. This wasn't working out like I'd planned. He had greater strength than me in my human form, and I wasn't exactly skilled in human fighting methods. I was reluctant to use any of my demon energy, but it would really suck if he pummeled me. My reputation would suffer.

We circled the table a few times. Brad looked smug. It pissed me off further. Pissed me off enough that I reached down and used some energy to snap a leg off the table, hoping it wasn't enough to be detected by any angels. The table remained improbably upright, so I kicked it over with my foot and dove at Brad, swinging.

His visual impairment wasn't so severe that he couldn't see a table leg coming at his head. He backed up, ducking and dodging as I chased him into a corner, and I finally connected the thing with his stomach. He doubled over and presented me with a lovely opening to whack him on the head. He dropped, but I gave him a few more swats to his kidneys just to make sure before I rolled him over and really locked him in this time. Fucking bastard. I should kill him. I should Own him.

It had been so long, and the urge to Own was beginning to gnaw at me with an annoying regularity. It would be risky, though. Owning is our process of gathering the essence of a being into ourselves. Of course, the physical body dies, and it's not pretty either. Humans have their spirits so deeply imbedded in the flesh that there is a lot of shredding that happens when we Own. That's part of the appeal, honestly. The pain, screaming, thrashing about, terror as you rip them from their very cells, it's very stimulating to a demon. And the fun continues because they live on inside you to play with and enjoy as long as you live. Brad didn't look like he'd be worth the risk though. Sad, since I haven't had the joy of Owning a human in several decades. Killing him would be almost as much fun. I didn't like to kill tenants who paid though. And I was hoping he'd pay.

"Perhaps you'd rather just pay the rent?" I asked him as he stared up at me.

CHAPTER 2

Moments later I left the row house with the back three months rent, plus four months forward on their lease. I really don't understand why Brad would have let those two stoned guys on his couch have guns since they were far too impaired to use them. How they were supposed to join in on a threesome rape in that condition was beyond me. It was all rather anticlimactic.

I headed toward my car and grabbed my cell phone. It was just after noon, and I was pleased that I had wrapped this up so early. "Michelle, I'm done and three fifty one is paid through December."

Michelle is my property manager. I've been through quite a few property managers over the last four decades, but Michelle is a keeper. Our partnership has profited her, too, and she now owns her own company — although she still continues to manage my properties personally.

"Woohoo!" Michelle cheered. "Are you coming by? We can grab lunch."

Michelle's eagerness to see me had less to do with our

friendship and more to do with the fact that she got an under-the-table cut of all cash payments. A large amount of my business was off the books, and Michelle wholeheartedly supported this.

"I can't," I told her. "I'm going to just grab a bag of tacos and get home in time to ogle the lawn service."

"You go girl!" Michelle said. "It's Friday, meet us at The Wine Room for happy hour. You know, your hottie neighbor will wrap up mowing early so he can hit the clubs tonight."

I hated The Wine Room.

"Wait," I hesitated. "Will they let me in? After last time?"

"Yes, they will let you in," Michelle sighed. "But no more groundhogs. That thing bit a waiter."

"It wasn't me," I lied. "I told you it wandered in off the street."

I'm a terrible liar. I don't think she believed me.

"All the girls will be there, and a real estate agent who's been pestering me to meet you. She's handling that block by the canal on the south side," she said. I was grateful she dropped the groundhog subject.

Most of Michelle's friends didn't like me but she always asked me to join her for social events. Our friendship gave a gritty edge to her very businesslike reputation, but this time I was sure she just wanted her cash before the weekend. No hurt feelings on my part. I'd show up dressed inappropriately, and see how many people I could make uncomfortable in an hour or so. The real estate agent was a mild draw, too. I really wanted this block of canal houses.

"Sheesh, Michelle," I complained. "I don't want those dilapidated pieces of crap. And you know the bank will want fair market value because they loaned some idiot twice that five years ago on spec".

"Come anyway," she said. "She'll buy you a Cosmo to try

and get on your good side, and you can scare all the suits at the bar."

I hated Cosmopolitans with a passion, but agreed to be there at five.

"Any problems, Roberto?" I asked my young car watcher.

"Some weirdo was giving it the eye, but they left when I told them it was Satan's car," he said.

It was a huge stretch to refer to me as Satan. The appropriate term would have been Ha-Satan, The Iblis, or The Adversary, but no one had held that title in over a million years and my actual level in the hierarchy was far below that. Ah well, whatever got the job done was okay with me.

Roberto took in the growing bruise on my chin and the red staining my shirt. "You have some trouble, Ms. Martin?"

"Nah," I told him as I looked carefully over my precious car. "I bit my tongue. You should see the other guy though. He'll be pissing blood for days."

I thanked him and handed him a twenty.

The noontime sun was intense and the pavement shimmered in front of my car with the radiated heat as I slowly edged my way through downtown traffic. A jay walker darted across the road and I swerved, barely hitting her big purse with my rear view mirror. It sucked that I hadn't hit her properly, but my mind was on other things. I kept thinking about the energy I used to break off the table leg. It wasn't much. It wasn't like I'd converted or anything. It probably wasn't enough for any angels to sense. Hopefully.

The city gave way to farms interspersed with one-street towns. Cows huddled under scrub trees to escape the heat, and the crops drooped in the blistering sun. I was hoping there would be some heat lightning this afternoon. Enjoying the gorgeous day, I cranked the air conditioning with the windows open as my tacos made a mess on my lap.

In thirty minutes I was pulling carefully down the long rural lane toward my house. I passed by my neighbor, Wyatt's house on the left. Wyatt had bought the place a few years back when it had gone up for tax auction. I'd bid on it, but he was willing to pay a bit more than I was. It was one of those old, Cape Cod-style houses that had suffered from fixed income elderly owners, and neglect. Wyatt hadn't done much to fix it up, but he didn't seem to have a lot of money. He constantly played computer games and did odd jobs to keep him in Ramen noodles. That's how he came to be in charge of my lawn mowing, stable care, and pool care.

When I saw what an incredible specimen of maleness had moved in next door, I had promptly trotted over a basket of baked goods along with a six pack of beer and introduced myself. We'd struck up a friendship based on my continued bribes of alcohol and food, and my willingness to let him treat my house and property as his own. Early on he had offered to do barn work and it had progressed from there. He tended to do the lawn mowing without his shirt on, so I ensured he had to do it several times a week. Everywhere else lawns languished in the drought, but my grass grew like it was on steroids. Wyatt never mentioned how unusual this phenomenon was.

I'd razed the old farmhouse when I bought this place. Instead I'd built a sweeping contemporary with stone and cedar. There was a seldom-used front porch with Adirondack chairs and lots of glass windows that looked mirrored from the outside and clear from the inside. It was around the back of the house where I spent most of my time. Huge two-story windows and sets of double French doors looked out from the kitchen and bedrooms to a lovely patio and pool. From the front and back of the house, wide pathways led to the barn, horse pastures, and a little landscaped garden with a fountain and private spot to sit. I'd become really fond of this home. Especially the pool.

I parked in front of the house and headed around to the barn, hoping I hadn't missed the lawn mowing peep-show entertainment of the afternoon. Wyatt was pushing in an empty wheelbarrow as I walked over. He had on cut off shorts and a wife-beater. His dirty blond hair was sun streaked and hung around his ears in front and in back to his shoulders. Wyatt always looked like he was a few months late for a haircut. It was a good look for him. His was the sort of broad shouldered, lean musculature that comes from lifting hay bales, not dumbbells. He grinned as he saw me and I caught my breath at his fineness.

"Hey, Sammy," he called. "I mucked the stalls, but am waiting to let the horses out to pasture until later since it's so hot. I'll put a round bale in the feeder, then I'll weed-eat." He peered at me closer. "What happened? I thought you were just collecting rents, today. Did someone give you a hard time?"

"I bit my tongue." I really needed to fix my wounds. My jaw was throbbing and my tongue hurt so bad that I couldn't eat or drink without pain. Eating tacos on the ride home had been an agonizing experience.

"Looks like you took a face plant into someone's fist."

"Yeah, that too. I beat the shit out of him, though." I turned to walk into the house. "I'm going to chill by the pool with a beer. Come join me when you're done."

I had only taken a few steps when he called out.

"Sam, have you seen Boomer? He hasn't been around all day."

Boomer was my Plott hound. He hunted at night and pretty much slept in the barn all day. Wyatt was always after me to contain him somehow, to curtail his nighttime wanderings. He was worried that Boomer would wind up a stray collected by Animal Control, or possibly full of buckshot from a neighborhood farmer. I knew my hound could take care of himself. I reassured Wyatt that he'd be back eventually, and ran in to change out of my taco-stained jeans and into a swimsuit. First I stopped by the kitchen to throw some beers and ice into a cooler, and then headed up the stairs, stripping as I went.

Throwing on my itty bitty powder blue bikini, I raced out to the pool. The water looked cool and inviting on the hot day, but I didn't want to miss the entertainment by swimming. I'd pop in later. Outdoor piped music on, cooler with beers beside my lounge chair, shades on. I strategically placed my chair to watch a shirtless Wyatt weed-eat and hoped he didn't wonder why my back was blocking the sun.

I was closer to Wyatt than I was with any other human. After he'd moved in, he'd immediately started doing odd jobs for me, but he also came around all the time to just hang out. He was over every day, sometimes several times a day. It wasn't unusual for him to be hanging out in my kitchen, or swimming in my pool. Every now and then I'd ask him to do some handyman kind of work, but most of the time he'd just take the initiative to do stuff like mulch the garden or clean out the fountain. Then we'd sit by the pool and drink, or cook something up in the kitchen, or relax and watch TV. He was over here a lot and I liked that.

Of course, I'd wanted to have sex with him the moment I saw him, but I waited. Demons are not usually so patient. Humans have such short lives and they tend to crank through them quickly. It seems that in a blink of an eye they are dead and gone. So if you want one, you've got to grab him or her quick.

There was also that pesky age thing. Wyatt was mid twenties in age and I was closing in on one thousand. If I did the math, he was slightly older than me in demon years. As

Samantha Martin, I was in my forties, but for humans in this day that kind of age difference didn't seem to matter much.

I saw women come and go from Wyatt's house without a repeat appearance and I knew he was a player. That wasn't something that bothered me at all. What did bother me was that I wanted our close friendship, I wanted sex with Wyatt, but I also wanted more. I liked him; I wanted him to be with me. I fantasized about having him for eternity; about Owning him.

Maybe after I became bored with him, I'd Own him. The prospect was exciting, but then I'd think about our friendship and have doubts. I liked hanging out with him by the pool, talking about our day, listening to him go on and on about some video game he was playing. If I Owned him, all that would be gone. The thought of losing his friendship was a painful ache in my middle.

Done with the trimming, Wyatt skimmed out the pool, then dropped his cutoffs and dove in for a cool down swim in his boxer briefs. I watched him swim long laps under water, my head moving back and forth like at a tennis match. How transparent would those boxer briefs be after a swim? They were pretty clingy before he dove in and I'd had a nice profile look and a breathtaking view of his tight ass before he hit the water.

Finally cooled off, Wyatt rose from the water in front of me like a Greek god and flung himself in the lounge chair beside me dripping streams of water in a path from the pool. Silently, I handed him a beer and he used the edge of the chair to pry off the cap. All this without one word to each other. I can't begin to describe the amazing warm contentment and sexual tension that I felt that afternoon. It was perfect. Better than anything I had back home.

"You're looking better," Wyatt broke the silence with his

cheerful voice. He reached over with a finger and touched my jaw. "Swelling and bruising are totally gone."

"My tongue is healed too, see?" I stuck my tongue out and he leaned over to get a closer look. Romantic, I know.

"Amazing how fast you heal," Wyatt drawled. "And your grass needs cutting every two days too. It's like everything is on hyperspeed at your house, Sam."

"I'm special," I told him.

"Yeah, I think so," Wyatt said. I felt all sorts of happy inside at the compliment. "You heading out tonight?" he asked.

"Wine Room." I grimaced. Wyatt wrinkled his nose in sympathy. "I've got some business I need to do, and an agent wants to unload some bank-owned properties on me. It's those canal row houses I told you I was interested in, so I probably need to meet her. You?"

"I really need to work, too. Some zombies need killing," he said, referring to one of his video games. "I may hit the club early for some fun and kill zombies on an all-nighter."

"Techno music, Ecstasy, and a curvy blonde?" I asked ignoring the video game part of his comment. If zombies ever invaded the realm, I'm guessing Wyatt would save the world. He would totally be my go-to guy if I found an animated corpse wandering around my pasture.

"I hate X," he replied, "but the dance club and the curvy blonde sound good to me." He reached over and tapped my beer bottle with his own.

What the hell was that about? I really didn't understand the subtleties of human interaction sometimes. I liked curvy blondes too, but was this action on his part supposed to mean that we were doomed to be only platonic buddies? Or that I was equally the player? Or that he thought I was a lesbian? Humans were so confusing, so hard to read. The anticlimactic afternoon with Brad had me craving sex, and having Wyatt so close was tempting beyond belief. I could take him now. Sex, body and mind, Own him as part of me forever. Then run like crazy for the nearest gate home, and hope I made it out of here before an angel caught me and tore me to bits. Instead, we sat for a moment in silence and drank our beer.

"Hey, do you want to ride the horses tomorrow morning? Early, before it gets hot?" Wyatt asked, turning to me.

"Sure you'll be up to it, with your blonde and zombie all-nighter?" I asked, more than a bit of bitterness creeping into my voice.

"I have amazing stamina," he said grinning and wiggling his eyebrows suggestively. "I'll be here at six to tack up. Think you can drag your lazy butt out of bed that early?"

"Doubtful," I told him, taking a swig of my beer.

"If you're not there, I'm gonna come up and get you," Wyatt teased. "And yes, I know you sleep naked. You've told me repeatedly."

Maybe there was hope for consensual sex, after all. I daydreamed for a moment about Wyatt and I having sex in a field with the horses grazing nearby. Or maybe in the tack room on top of the saddle pads. Or maybe we'd never get out of my bedroom.

We finished our beers, and Wyatt headed back to his house, announcing that those zombies weren't going to kill themselves. I went inside and studied my wardrobe to see what outfit might shock all the movers and shakers at The Wine Room. I decided to go with comfort and pulled on my faded skinny jeans with the strategic worn patch on the upper thigh. I made sure I had on a good push up bra for maximum cleavage then, thinking of Wyatt with his wife beater, I yanked a thin, tight, white tank top over my head. The scooped neckline barely covered the lacy edges of my bra. I added some worn cowboy boots, a blingy belt, and *voila*! Sexy country girl. I never bother with my hair or make-up, but for some reason tonight I went all out. Thick mascara, sweeping eyeliner, and deep pink lip stain. I piled my shoulder length brown mane high up on my head and let pieces escape to hang straight along my face and at the nape of my neck. I was very happy with the overall look. It was like one of the Petticoat Junction girls had come out of a good romp in the hay.

I thought about driving my Suburban to complete the look, but parking that thing downtown was a pain in the ass. I only drove it when I was hauling the trailer or picking up feed. The Corvette was my true love.

The Wine Room was as pretentious as you could get. It was purposely small, so it was always packed. Crowds of hopefuls waited to get in the door. Huge panes of glass covered all the exterior walls, so you could see and be seen. It was especially a nightmare to try and eat there since the bar crowd was inches away from the dining tables. Nothing was worse than trying to eat your eighty dollar prime rib with a gin-drinking lawyer six inches away and staring at your plate.

The guy at the door recognized me and nodded me in once he checked to make sure I didn't have a large bag with a groundhog in it. Not that it mattered much. They normally ended up kicking me out within an hour of my entering, even without a groundhog.

Michelle and her posse were in the usual spot. Theirs was the best location, and one they would have had to arrive unfashionably early and fight for to score. From their special spot, they could see and be seen by passersby on Main Street. It was hard to see them from the door, but I knew they'd be there and wove my way among all the navy and black suited business people with their ties and sensible pumps. I made sure I rubbed my boobs and hands over everyone I could on the way back.

Michelle had done her hair different. She normally had a mess of long black braids intricately arranged around her head, but she had taken the extensions out and had a pixie-looking straight do. I'm sure it was twenty times cooler in this heat than her usual style. She was tall and thin with high cheekbones and dark eyes in her ebony face. She grinned when she caught sight of me. She had a slight gap between her blazing white teeth that I found totally sexy. She was beautiful in an exotic, angular kind of way.

"Samantha." She drawled out my name in a slight island accent as she took in my cowgirl attire. Michelle's mom was Jamaican or something. I could never remember. "Were you out riding that neighbor of yours? Where are your spurs, girl?" She gave me a hug.

Spurs. Yum, what a visual.

"I wish. Hey, you have any gum? I had tacos for lunch." I rooted in her bag without waiting for her reply, pulling out a stick of gum and placing the fat envelope full of cash under her wallet.

As I stuffed the gum in my mouth, Michelle winked at me and on impulse reached over to kiss my cheek. Michelle was straight. Not that that mattered. I'd considered many times assuming a male form and picking her up some night, but good business associates were hard to find. Especially property managers. I wasn't about to jeopardize that relationship for a night of sex. Besides, a conversion of that scale would be like sending up a flare for the angels to see.

I turned to look at her friends. A few were trying hard not to notice me. Two stared at me in amazement, taking in my casual outfit and my bold freedom with Michelle's purse. I picked out the real estate agent right away. She was a walking stereotype. In a sea of drab suits, she had on a bright yellow skirt suit of all things, with a flowered shirt peeking out the jacket. Her blonde hair fluffed out in a big wave. She was the most immaculately groomed person I'd ever seen. I met her eyes expecting to see vacuous excitement and got a shock. Shrewd brown eyes met mine in calculating appraisal. She wandered her eyes over the rest of me taking in the ripped blue jeans with a raised eyebrow and a twitch of her bronze lips before raising her eyes back up to meet mine.

"Candy Star," she announced, reaching to shake my hand.

I almost burst out laughing. It was a stripper name. What kind of bimbo mom names their kid Candy Star? She must have been horribly teased in school. Why in hell hadn't she changed it? I glanced at her left hand. Maybe Star was her husband's name. I never could understand the whole human thing of taking your husband's name, and this would have been a good reason to break that custom.

"Hi Candy, I'm Samantha Martin," I replied in a bored tone. I didn't want her thinking I was excited to meet her. "I'm getting a drink, can I get you something?"

"Oh, I was going to get you a Cosmo," she bubbled back, channeling a perky real estate agent personality that was in direct contrast with those shrewd brown eyes.

"I hate Cosmos," I told her as I edged toward the bar.

"Me too," she muttered under her breath and eyed the one in her beautifully manicured hand with disgust.

I discreetly threw my gum on the floor where someone would be sure to get it all over their three-hundred-dollar shoes and squeezed between two half-drunk lawyers at the bar. I brushed my hand and boobs against the one, and my rear across the other out of habit. They eyed me appreciatively. I seriously needed to take this much care with my appearance more often. I'd probably get laid a whole lot more.

Standing up on the rail under the bar that you rested your

feet on as you sat, I sprawled the upper half of my body across the gleaming mahogany showing cleavage to the front and sticking my rear out in the back. The bartender practically knocked down a waitress in his rush to ask my boobs what they would like to drink.

The only redeeming quality of this place was that it offered a wide choice of quality vodkas, and did some cool infusions. Vodka was amazing. It was one of the best human inventions, ever. Back home, everyone drank dull old wine, sometimes warmed up, sometimes cold. It was okay. Nah, who am I kidding, the stuff sucked big time, but — whoo-boy! — vodka was the shit.

"Two shots of Van Gogh Double Espresso Vodka. The stuff in the freezer," I told him.

The bartender poured the shots into equally chilled shot glasses, all the while managing to keep an eye on my breasts. No doubt in case one escaped and burst into full view. I tipped him well and made my way back to Candy and the other girls.

"Here's to our future partnership," I said, handing her one of the shots. She looked at it nervously, grimaced, and tossed it down. Her eyes watered and she choked a little, sipping the Cosmo in her other hand in desperation. It was a shame because up until that moment I had thought she was kind of cool. Chasing the very elixir of life with that swill, how could she? Disappointing.

I looked around the bar at the ocean of black and navy and thought about going home and watching *X-Files* reruns. Normally, I'd be inspired to start some trouble, but I just didn't seem to have it in me tonight. I was still worried that my energy usage earlier today may have exposed me. I was missing Wyatt and wondering if he'd found a curvy blonde. Besides, this place really sucked. They got all stuffy and bent out of shape if you broke a bottle on some guy's head or threw your steak knives at the wall.

Just as I lifted my glass to drink my vodka, I heard Michelle say in a soft worshipful voice "Ohhhh, look there. Just look at him."

I glanced toward the door, because that tone was the most un-Michelle-like I'd ever heard. And I saw the angel.

CHAPTER 3

I'm not sure how I knew right away that he was an angel, but I knew. I drew a ragged breath, choking on the vodka and dove behind one of Michelle's friends. The pudgy one who was luckily wearing a floaty muumuu thing. It should have been embarrassing, cowering behind a fat girl like that, but I was more concerned about my probable death.

Panic was throwing my heart around my chest and beading sweat on my forehead. Shit. Shit, shit shit. No, fuck, fuck, fuck, actually. Was he here for me? Stupid, of course he was! He must have been close enough to sense the small amount of energy I'd used to break off that table leg and brain Brad. Why else would he be here? I'd been so careful for all these years. I snuck through the gate with great skill, and had performed no conversion in decades; nothing but the tiniest of energy which I'd carefully covered up. The biggest display I'd made was when I'd taken and Owned Samantha Martin, but that had been so long ago. If that had alerted him, he'd have been on me twenty years ago at the latest. It had to have been today, and he must have been close to sense it. Damn my lousy luck.

I crawled across the surprisingly clean floor as far as I could from the angel, making sure I avoided my discarded gum. You'd think he wouldn't take me out in a crowded place like this since angels were supposed to be all goodness and light, but truth was I'd heard they didn't much care about collateral damage. The stupid humans didn't even notice me crawling and scooting between their legs, they were so enraptured.

I'd only had a quick glance at him before my dive to the ground, but he definitely stood out in a crowd. Tall. Like way taller than anyone in the room tall. Big chestnut curls on his forehead and touching the top of his ears. His skin was a strange white tone and texture. He was like a walking marble statue; a Greek god come to life. I hadn't seen his eyes and didn't want to. From the noises in the bar and the migration toward the door, I could only assume the humans were mobbing him. Probably pawing him all over like he was a unicorn or something. I wondered how he'd react to that.

Thankful for the crowd and the distraction, I reached the fire door. Very carefully, I put my hand against the bar to open it, and my other hand near the door catch. Gently, I sent a small trickle of energy into the door, completing the alarm circuit around the latch. Pushing the door, I quietly tiptoed out of the bar. I hoped that hadn't been enough for him to sense. Luckily, the humans had tons of energy flying around with their microwaves and cell phones, and that masked quite a bit.

As I turned to make sure the door closed without a sound, I saw a quick hand hold the door open. In my panicked state, I brought every speck of energy I had within reach to the surface, ready to deflect and defend. Luckily, I noticed the beautifully manicured nails and tennis bracelet before I started blowing things up. Candy slipped out behind me and pushed the door shut before turning to face me. We stared at each other. I know I didn't look exactly human at that moment, with such a massive amount of energy humming out all my pores and my eyes glowing, ready to strike. Candy, though, was unfazed as she surveyed me thoughtfully. She met my eyes for a moment, nodded as if I had confirmed something, then turned on her heels to walk with purpose down the street.

I didn't waste any time. I raced down the block and ducked into an alley. I wasn't sure what to do. Part of me wanted to go back and watch the angel leave to see what he was doing and where he was going. Not knowing what he knew about me and my assumed life was the most fearful part of this whole situation. I was terrified to get that close to him, though, in case he could somehow sense me near.

Should I head for the closest gate and get the hell out of Dodge? The most reliable gate was near Baltimore, but everyone used it. The angels kept a close eye on the area and a guardian routinely took out any who tried to use it. There was a small wild gate west near Sharpsburg, but wild gates were very dangerous and I didn't have time to study and master it. I didn't know where it went to, anyway.

I had come in through a gate in Seattle, but I wasn't sure I could make it all the way across the country. Plus, I really didn't want to run and abandon all I had worked to build over the last forty years. I had emergency procedures in place to protect my assets in case I had to make a quick break for it, but I hated to leave the life I loved. It's not like I could take my Corvette through the gate with me. Or Wyatt, unless I Owned him first.

I was too afraid to even peek around the corner toward The Wine Room. Was he still there? He could be walking down the street toward me right now. My heart thudded away and I gasped in air.

"Hey," I hissed at a young guy walking past the alley. He

looked startled, but not terribly alarmed. Happy hour downtown was fairly safe, even if someone was accosting you from the shadows.

"Yeah, you," I insisted. The guy took a step towards me, curious. "Look down the street and tell me if you see an angel."

He looked around the alley for hidden video cameras.

"I'm serious. Down that way." I pointed helpfully.

He looked at me quizzically, but backed a few steps out of the alley and looked down the street. "Yeah, I see one."

I freaked. "Where? Is he coming this way? Is he glowing? Oh fuck! Oh fuck!"

I was making my new friend nervous. "No, it's that painting on the side of the building. You know, the one that looks like an old guy leaning out a window, but he has shadowed wings behind him. I thought that's what you meant."

"This is not *I Spy*," I shouted at him. "I need to know if a real angel is anywhere on the street, if you can see one. I really don't want him to kill me."

"I'll walk down here a bit and check," the guy said in a placating voice as he backed slowly out of the alley. "Just stay right here. I'll look for killer angels and be right back."

I knew better. The guy walked quickly toward a more populated area of downtown while I snuck around the block to my car to make my escape. He'd either sic the cops on me or send the angel my way.

I thought about my situation as I drove toward home. If I was going to die tonight, I was going to do it in my own house, surrounded by the things I loved. My mind whirled, and I had to finally set the cruise control as my speed was fluctuating wildly between the legal fifty-five and well over a hundred miles per hour.

The angel hadn't locked right in on me at the bar, so my energy usage must not have been strong enough for him to have an absolute fix on me. He hadn't come running when I'd opened the fire door or, more importantly, when I pulled a bunch of energy to the surface for defense. Maybe I would be okay. If I could just keep things absolutely minimal, fly even more under the radar, maybe he would give up and go kill some other, more careless, demon.

I was so distracted with my thoughts that I was three miles past my road before I even noticed. I pulled into a little local bar to turn around and stopped. I needed to calm down and focus. And I was suddenly afraid to go home and be there alone waiting for death to possibly find me. At least here I had a chance of blending into the crowd.

The Eastside Tavern was a local's hangout. The narrow front parking lot was packed with trucks and bikes. People milled about the fenced deck beside the front door, smoking cigarettes in the cooler evening air. I edged my way between the carelessly parked cars and around the back, searching without success for a parking spot. The place *was* packed. I finally found a parking spot way out at the rear lot, past the dumpster, by a little wooded area. The Corvette might not have fit in with the motorcycles and trucks, but I did with my jeans and boots. I got out and set the car security. There were a few people around back here too, smoking or talking.

"Nice car," a bearded man said waving his smoke at it. "I have a Corvette too, but it's not as nice as yours."

I smiled at him in acknowledgement. There were wooden steps leading up to a back entrance that appeared to open to a dining area or perhaps some kind of banquet room. I walked around to the front of the building and headed up the wooden stairs past the smokers' deck. The front door was a slab of heavy glass, reinforced with metal bars. I wrestled it open and paused to take the place in.

Everything in The Eastside Tavern was cheap and fake. I don't know if this was so it would be inexpensive to replace when patrons trashed it, or if the owners didn't give a shit about even pretending to run a classy joint. Probably both. The floors were Fiberboard with a photo of wood grain laminated on top. The long u-shaped bar had the same wincingly artificial wood as the floor. The tables were cheap metal and Formica topped with metal rims. Torn vinyl-covered metal chairs were scattered around each table. The owners had dispensed with any kind of ceiling and instead had hung old license plates and plastic light fixtures resembling deer antlers from the exposed floor joists of the second story.

The tables were full of people gleefully smashing crabs and picking out meat with knives and fingers. Dismembered carcasses piled high on the brown paper protecting the Formica, or spilled onto the floor in a mess of broken shells and Old Bay Seasoning. Observing all of this with placid faces were the only non-fake things in the bar: a plethora of mounted deer heads; pheasants, foxes, and boars decorated the walls side by side with aluminum sports signs and neon beer advertisements. I loved humans' affection for taxidermy. Killing something, and then displaying its dead body in a prominent place to show everyone what a successful and powerful killer you were was near and dear to my heart. I envisioned humans eyeballing each other's kills and suffering from antler envy. We weren't so different.

I headed around next to the pool table so I could look out across the expanse of the bar and the people eating their crabs. I wouldn't have a clear exit if an angel stormed the front door, but at least I'd see him first and have a brief moment to hide. The pool balls crashed behind me and I heard the cheers and smacking palms of a good break. The guy beside me flicked his eyes to me, and then turned his gaze back to the TV screen above the bar. He had dried mud on his work boots that extended almost a foot up his jeans. There wasn't a navy suit in the place.

Two women worked behind the bar, hustling primarily beer for the customers. I really wanted a drink, and thought about draping myself across the bar as I did at The Wine Room. I reconsidered when I realized I'd only piss off the women on the other side. Instead, I flagged a bartender down with some help from the guy next to me. I didn't rate any attention, since I was clearly not a regular, but the guy next to me certainly did and she came promptly over when he bellowed for her.

"Do you have any vodka in the freezer?" I asked.

She looked at me, as if she were waiting for the punchline of the joke. I wasn't about to drink warm generic vodka, so I ordered a bottle of Bud Light.

Another guy had joined the muddy dude on my side of the bar, flanking me between them. Muddy guy had a plate of food covered in gravy plopped in front of him, and proceeded to ignore everything but his meal. Nobody was paying any attention to me at all. I looked around behind me at the men and women engrossed in their pool game and realized no one seemed uncomfortable with my presence. Relaxing, I took a swig from the cold beer bottle and looked around.

There was a group of bearded guys by the smokers' door trying to pick up a shapely girl with legs a mile long; an overweight couple stealing fries off each other's plates and laughing; several rowdy groups gleefully smashing crabs and clinking beer mugs; a Latino guy in a construction logo hat who looked like he'd been up since before the sun; a really hot blond guy with some blonde girl rubbing her boobs on his arm. Hey. Our eyes met across the room. Pleasant warmth spread down my body as I smiled into Wyatt's beautiful baby blues.

He made a beeline for me, practically dragging the curvy blonde hanging onto his arm.

"Sammy," he said, clearly delighted to see me. "I didn't know you ever came here."

"I haven't been here before. I was on my way home and thought I'd stop in." I looked around. "I like it here," I said honestly.

There was a sense of calm I got from the place. Not that it appeared to be a mellow, chilled out kind of bar. It was just familiar. I felt I could relax and maybe be a little bit myself without getting thrown out every time I came in. Or at least I'd get thrown out with others hitting the dirt beside me.

"You...you look *really* nice," Wyatt said, his eyes traveling down me, as if he hadn't seen me almost naked this afternoon.

I caught my breath and stared at him in amazement. Could this day have any more wild swings between shit and great? Where had this come from? Had someone slipped something into his drink? Had I transformed from his older, scary, moderately attractive, neighbor buddy into a potential friends-with-benefits candidate?

"Thanks," I replied. "I need to do the make-up and hair thing more often. Maybe then I'd have sex more than once a decade."

"The gravity defying boobs are pretty eye-catching, too." Wyatt grinned. "Honestly, Sam, if you'd at least pretend to be normal you might get laid more. You scare all the girls and boys away."

I knew he was teasing, but I think he meant it, too. Hopefully he meant the boob part.

"If I get horny enough I'll just whack someone over the head with a pool cue, duct tape them in place and have my way with them." I was only partially kidding.

Wyatt laughed. The woman on his arm tugged slightly,

clearly wanting to move Wyatt away from me and my duct taping ways.

"Are you scared of me?" I asked him suddenly. I hoped not. I'd hate to have to eventually resort to duct tape with Wyatt. He'd be a whole lot more fun with his hands free.

"Absolutely terrified," he said.

I wondered if both Wyatt and I had been waiting for the other to make a move, like in those sappy movies on Lifetime. I appraised the woman hanging on his arm. Wyatt hadn't introduced me. In fact, Wyatt was rudely ignoring her existence. Not that I had a problem with that. She was pretty. Nice figure. She looked like a boring fuck to me. I was going for it, and blondie wasn't going to get in my way.

"The waitress just brought our beers out," Wyatt said, disengaging with great difficulty from his blonde albatross. "I'll go get them and be right back."

The second he turned his back I snapped my eyes to the girl and glared at her. She shook a little, and then raised her chin in defiance. Ooo, putting up a fight, was she? Well, I didn't have time for this nonsense since Wyatt would be back in a short moment.

"Get out right now," I snarled at her, throwing every bit of mean I had into it.

Her eyes widened in terror and, without delay, she took off out the door.

"Woman, you really *are* scary," the muddy guy next to me said in admiration before turning back to his chicken fried steak. Yep, I liked this place.

I chugged down my beer as I saw Wyatt approach, shoving the empty on the bar.

"Your friend left." I snagged the second beer out of his hand and took a swig. "She won't be coming back."

Wyatt raised an eyebrow and I was relieved to see he looked amused.

"I like this one better anyway, Wyatt," said the guy next to me.

Thumbs up from Mr. Chicken Fried Steak. I wasn't sure whether that was a good thing or not.

Wyatt's smile reached his eyes and we talked in that comfortable, easy way we always did. He'd nixed his original dance club plans for the night pretty soon after he turned out my horses for the evening. Instead, he had popped in here for a few beers, intending to go straight back home to kill the zombies.

I told him about my Wine Room experience, leaving out the angel, of course. Wyatt made sympathetic noises when I described my outrage at the vodka abuse Candy had perpetrated. I told him I'd left early and never really got to discuss those canal properties with her. We chatted comfortably as the evening drew late and I felt myself relax fully. After we finished several beers, I reluctantly told him I needed to head back home. I intended to hide all night under my bed from the angel. Maybe he'd keep me company.

"I'll walk you to your car", he said.

The summer bugs were making a deafening racket in the wooded area behind the bar. The smokers had migrated closer to the door, and a few said goodbye to Wyatt, addressing him by name. I beeped the alarm off the Corvette and turned my back to the driver's door. After two years of flirting and friendship, Wyatt suddenly became a guy of action as far as I was concerned. He swooped down for a kiss, wrapping one arm around my back to curl me up against him and reaching the other up to brush his hand along my neck and up to gently hold the base of my skull. Smooth. Unexpected. Dreamed about many days and nights for a very long time.

I love kissing in human form. Their lips are so full and soft. You can bite down on them with your dull human teeth, or run your tongue across them, or suck on them. So many nerve endings and so many senses at play. You can be a little rough, too, without worry of slicing anything off with razor sharp teeth, or asphyxiating someone with a two foot tongue down their throat. Humans don't get off on that sort of thing. At least, not the ones I'd met to date.

Wyatt was feather-light to the point of frustration. Lips, tongue, teeth, even his thumb rubbing along my jawline were just barely at the point of contact. Every nerve ending in me quivered as if they were trying to reach out and complete the connection. I'm not good at the whole delayed gratification thing. I grabbed his shirt on either side of his waist with both hands and spun him around so I was pressing his back into the car.

Wyatt gave a muffled laugh and kissed more firmly. Just to make sure he knew where this was going, I straddled one of his legs, and rubbed my thigh up against his crotch. He returned the favor, easing his hand from my waist to cup my ass and hold my hips in an optimal tilted position. Heat scorched through me, and my breathing turned ragged. Nothing existed outside him at this moment. I could no longer hear the million bugs singing in the night, or catcalls from any smokers who might be watching. I could no longer smell the mix of cigarette smoke, fried foods, and dumpster garbage that was the parking lot. I didn't think about Wyatt's belt potentially scratching my beloved car. And I most definitely did not think about the angel.

I stretched all my human senses as far as they could go and filled them with Wyatt as my hands yanked his shirt up and roved up his bare sides. It was so much, but it wasn't enough. I'd had purely human sex with hundreds of men and women throughout the centuries, but this particular human pulled forth very conflicting desires. I wanted so much more, but if I Owned him, our relationship would change forever.

I'd still have him with me, but not in this physical way, and definitely not the warm friendship I'd grown to enjoy so much. *No, no Owning*. Not with an angel so close, and especially not Wyatt. Not Wyatt.

Unable to resist exploring beyond human limitations, I carefully sent tiny gentle feathers of my personal energy into him, touching, seeking, and gathering knowledge of him without taking. No Owning, just checking things out. No Owning. Wyatt pulled his mouth from mine and gasped, his pupils huge in his blue eyes.

"Oh my. What are you doing?"

He didn't sound fearful, or in pain. Actually he sounded turned on beyond belief, which ratcheted up the desire on my end as well. I added more feathers of my personal energy, and focused them on his neural pathways. Wyatt shuddered in obvious pleasure, and bent to kiss me again, running his lips over my jaw and down my neck. I'm ashamed to admit it, but at this point I just lost it. It's hard enough to maintain control when your flesh in this form is so stimulated. It had taken lots of practice and the guidance of my foster brother, Dar before I could have human sex without killing my partner. And here I was, wanting that human orgasm so bad, and at the same time right on the edge of Owning him completely. I tightened the feathers within him, and I pulled.

"Mine," that familiar voice deep within me announced in silence. It was a word that carried power, that announced claim. It was my way of marking my territory and enveloping what I would soon Own.

Wyatt went rigid and with a sharp breath pulled back. We began an escalating tug of war deep inside him that would have been funny had it not been so deadly. Want, want, want. I was firmly attached and nothing he could do could shake me off. His tugs started to take on a feel of desperation. I pulled steadily, making slow progress only to be halted as he dug in with all his might.

We were at an impasse. I could take him against his will, but I would need to rip him free of his body. It would be even more bloody and messy, and a clear act of violence to anyone who would be watching. It also would result in my head being lopped off by that angel before I could complete the act.

The sexual stimulation had ended with Wyatt's insistence on not becoming dead. His unwillingness to proceed and give his whole self over was like a splash of sanity on my desire and I relaxed slightly in my grip. What the fuck was I doing? No Owning. And no Owning Wyatt. How could this have gone so wrong?

"Wait," I told him in what I hoped was a reassuring voice. "I'm pulling free, but I need to do it slowly so you don't rebound and go into convulsions or start hemorrhaging". Okay, maybe that wasn't so reassuring.

"Don't pull back hard. Just hold your ground and gently ease back. Don't panic."

I'd never done this before. I'd never had an unsuccessful Own, or stopped part way like this and backed out. I was a little worried that I'd screw it up and end with Wyatt dead. I took a calming breath and began disengaging the feathers one at a time, with great care. When they were barely touching, I gently drew them back through Wyatt a few at a time. It was taking forever, but Wyatt held very still. I'm surprised he trusted me, but I guess he really didn't have any other option. His breath hitched as I pulled my energy back within me and I paused worried he was going to panic and injure himself.

Slowly I continued, pulling the last of my energy out of him and stepped back. It felt almost cold after all the heat our closeness had generated. Wyatt stared at me but I couldn't read him in the darkness of the parking lot.

"What on earth were you trying to do? What *are* you?" he said, his voice firm now that he wasn't fighting for his life.

"I'm sorry," I said, my voice a pitiful whine. I wasn't sure what to say. "I lost control. I'm so very sorry. It won't happen again."

"What are you?" he repeated, careful not to touch me. "Normal people don't do whatever it was that you were doing. I've always thought there was something weird about you, but you've been my friend so long that I just ignored it."

I squirmed. I really didn't want to tell him. Either way this was probably the end of any potential sex with Wyatt. This was probably the end of anything with Wyatt.

"Wyatt, you've known me for two years," I pleaded. "I don't want to lose you as a friend. Please forgive me. I promise it will never happen again. Never."

"Are you some kind of alien? A witch? Are you the devil, like that Jehovah's Witness guy said this spring? You need to tell me what you are right now or this friendship is definitely over."

I sighed, closing my eyes. "Your kind would call me a demon. I'm not like you think, though. I don't run around mildewing the global crop harvest, or trying to enslave the human race. I just want to have a normal life, like everyone else."

"A... A demon?" He sounded rather panicked. "As in Satan demon? You take people's souls and condemn them to hell? You like to tear people's limbs off and torture them before you kill them?"

I winced. Yeah. Although it sounded so much worse when he said it.

"No, no, not at all," I assured him. "I'm just an imp, no

more than a cockroach in the scheme of things. I'm still me, Wyatt. The same me that I've always been."

He looked undecided. But undecided was better than hating me, or never wanting to see me again.

"I never wanted to hurt you. I'm sorry. Once I realized what I was doing, and that you didn't want it, I stopped. You're okay, I swear. And I will never do it again. I promise."

"Were you trying to kill me? How is that not hurting me? How in the world would you think I'd want that?" The indecision was teetering in an unfavorable direction.

"I would never kill you, Wyatt," I told him, my eyes beseeching him to forgive me and go back to the way things were between us. "I just got carried away. It's been a really weird day. I would never hurt you, never kill you." I was lying. There was a good chance that I would eventually lose control and hurt him, probably would eventually kill him.

Silence stretched on between us. I smelled the dumpster nearby, listened to the bugs singing. I wished Wyatt would say something, or hit me, or knock my head against my car. Anything. I couldn't even leave since he was blocking the door of my car. This fiasco ranked right up on par with the angel showing up tonight. I'd never see Wyatt again after this. No relaxing conversations by the pool. No sex. No Owning. I was a stupid fucking idiot and I just wanted to go home.

Wyatt stared at me in silence for what seemed like eternity, and then he stepped aside and opened my car door for me. I felt like my guts were going to drop out of me when he did that. It seemed so dismissive, so final. I slid by him and bent to crawl into the seat.

"Get some sleep, Sam," he said in a calm, tired voice.

I drove right home. And I didn't really care if the angel showed up and killed me in my sleep or not.

CHAPTER 4

I had a restless night and was just starting to get back to sleep when my cell phone rang.

"Ugh," I grunted into it, not able to focus on the screen enough to see who was calling me at such an ungodly hour on a Saturday.

"Get your lazy rear out of bed and get down here. I've already tacked up your horse." Then a click.

I stared at the phone fully awake and perplexed. Wyatt. And he sounded downright cheerful. Was this how humans dealt with conflict that involved someone nearly killing you? How they dealt with finding out their neighbor and best friend was a demon? True, he wasn't in my bedroom dragging my naked ass out of bed, but he was still intending to keep our riding date. With a spark of hope, I leapt out of bed and pulled on jods and a polo shirt. I grabbed my field boots by the door and ran barefoot out to the stables. Wyatt tossed my helmet at me as I dashed in.

Piper, my big bay gelding, stood ready with his English saddle and bridle. Piper was a Thoroughbred Shire cross. He was tall and solid with a placid, unshakable disposition.

Horses don't like demons, and they especially don't like me. It had taken me years to get Piper to let me put a saddle on him, let alone ride him. I loved riding, though, and the time it took to gain the horse's trust was time well spent in my book.

Wyatt had saddled up Vegas for himself, a chestnut Quarter Horse gelding with an impressive pedigree. He was smaller than Piper, and less muscular, but full of heart with a silly sense of humor. Wyatt must have suspected I bought Vegas for him when I brought the horse home last year. I don't ride Western, and have never been into Quarter Horses. I spent a fortune on this horse hoping Wyatt couldn't resist and would ride with me. It had worked. Since Vegas arrived we tended to go out a few times a week when weather allowed.

I eyed Wyatt as he finished with Vegas. He looked the same as usual. Well rested, freshly showered (unlike me), cheerful. Had last night not happened at all? If I'd realized my neighbor was some strange powerful being who wanted to fuck me and kill me at the same time, I don't think I would be out riding horses with her the next day. Well, maybe I would, but I'm not a human.

I hopped around the aisle of the barn in an undignified manner, putting on my boots as Wyatt tightened Vegas' girth. We hadn't spoken a word and I wasn't sure how to break the ice while managing to carefully avoid mentioning the last six hours. I strapped on my helmet, then smiled and tossed Wyatt one off the rack.

"Catch."

He caught it and scowled playfully.

"You must be joking. Since when have you ever seen me fall? Cowboy hat, maybe; riding helmet, no."

I have this argument with Wyatt every time we ride. I'd done the whole "my stable my rules" and "my horse my rules" thing. He argued, but always gave in. And it's true he never fell. The guy rode like he was Krazy-glued to the saddle.

"Accidents happen, Wyatt. And I can't put your brains back in your head".

Wyatt looked at me speculatively.

"Can't you? You seem to be able to heal yourself. To what extent can you do it with others?"

"I don't technically have the ability to heal," I explained. "I can fix myself, but I usually screw it up when I try to fix someone else. Besides, I'm not good with brains. They're really tricky."

Wyatt thought a moment. "Okay, why are brains so hard? As opposed to, say, a liver or an amputated limb?"

"The actual physical formation of the brain isn't an issue; it's all the neural pathways." I loved explaining this sort of thing, and it was kind of nice to have this conversation with Wyatt.

"You have no idea the number of neural connections in the human brain. Plus, they change from moment to moment. You're literally not the same person you were a few seconds ago, each experience changes the connections in slight ways. I could do a decent job, only to have you missing half your life experiences or a significant change in your personality. One little missed connection has huge consequences."

Wyatt looked at the helmet with new respect.

"If you were a flatworm, I'd say 'go for it'. I'd be pretty confident I could fix your neural network and you'd still be fairly close to the flatworm you were before the accident. Since you're a human, I can pretty much guarantee I'd fuck it up big time."

I was very serious. Wyatt seemed to realize that and put on the helmet without further argument.

We rode for hours without a word, just like we always do.

Fast. Through woods, and over coops into adjoining fields and the public trails that snaked all through this section of Maryland. Normally we'd meet the occasional mountain biker or four wheeler, but today it was just us and nature.

I'm a terrible rider. Couple that with the fact that horses don't like me or my kind much, and it means I spend a lot of my time in the dirt, on my ass, staring up at the horse. I only fell off once that morning, losing my balance over a coop. Piper stopped as soon as I hit the ground and looked at me reprovingly.

"Sorry, boy," I told him, then looked around for a log, fence, rock, something to get me up high enough to climb back into the saddle. Piper was a big boy. After trying a few things unsuccessfully, I clambered up the coop, but couldn't get Piper close enough. Wyatt rolled his eyes at me and finally hopped off to throw me back into the saddle.

As we cooled down the horses on a walk back toward my barn, Wyatt looked over at me cautiously.

"So, do you demons possess people? Like in *The Exorcist*?" he asked.

I shuddered. Possessing involves putting yourself in a human body with the human still in there. It is stupid and dangerous. You have maybe ten percent of your power, and it announces your presence like a bullhorn. Demons who regularly do possessions don't last a fortnight.

"No. Only the very lowest demons do that. Not me." Well, not since that time a few centuries back when a priest yanked me out and stuck me in a pig body instead. Pigs don't appreciate that sort of thing.

We hopped off of our horses in the stable yard and walked in together. Wyatt still looked rather nervous. I could see the fear in him, even though he struggled to hide it. I wished I could show him that I was still the same person he grilled steaks with Thursday night. The same girl he pitched into the pool headfirst last week. I hated that he looked scared of me.

Tossing his saddle pad in the corner, Wyatt took his saddle into the tack room while I brushed Piper. I hoped he could move past this. I hoped we could at the very least still be friends. No doubt I'd see a for-sale sign in front of his house within the week.

"Sam? You need to come in here," Wyatt called.

I walked into the tack room carrying my saddle and saw Wyatt standing over Boomer. My hound was sprawled on the floor, his brindle fur covered with bites, cuts and blood. He thumped his tail and panted as he saw me. I bent down and examined his wounds carefully. This couldn't have been the angel. If it were, Boomer would have been dead and disintegrated. I couldn't imagine what could have attacked him. No dog would have gotten a tooth on him, let alone tore him up this bad. A fox wouldn't have taken him on. There were coyotes around, but even cornered and fighting for their life they wouldn't have caused this kind of damage. The Allegheny Mountains used to be home to Eastern Panthers, but they were no more. A few had been sighted down south, but not up here. A bear maybe? A black bear defending her cubs may have done this. There did seem to be more claw marks than bites, which would indicate a bear. Boomer wasn't one to back down from a fight either, stupid dog.

"Uhhh Sam? You're, uhhh, leaking," Wyatt said observing me cautiously.

I looked down and realized that I had let some of my raw energy creep up to the surface where it was glowing across my skin like a sheen of sweaty light. An opalescent drop fell to the floor and sizzled like acid. I discreetly neutralized it. I never leak. It was a point of pride with me. How embarrassing. Just one more slip I couldn't afford to make with an angel so close.

"Sorry. I was trying to think what could have done this. Boomer is smart, and much stronger than he looks."

"I'd speculate big cat," Wyatt said, bending down to look closer. "Or grizzly, but not in this part of the country. We really need to get him into the emergency vet."

"No, he'll be okay," I assured him. "It's not that bad."

Wyatt looked at me in disbelief.

"Let me at least carry him into the house and do first aid from the vet kit."

"He *stinks*," I countered. "I'm not letting him my house like this."

Wyatt glared at me. It was a good glare. We stood that way for a while in a silent contest of wills.

"Okay!" I threw up my hands. "I'll fix him." I couldn't say no to Wyatt. Especially now that our friendship was teetering on the edge.

"I thought you said you weren't good at that when it wasn't yourself. Let's just take him to the vet," Wyatt urged.

Wyatt had enough to freak out about without my explaining that Boomer wasn't a normal dog. That would have to wait.

"I can do Boomer. He'll be fine. Really."

I picked up a rubber handled screwdriver and looked around. Crickets and spiders were too small. The barn cat hadn't had her kittens yet, or I would have used one of them. Ah, there was a big mouse over behind the feed tub. I locked eyes with it holding the animal in place as I carefully moved the feed tub. Then I impaled him with the screwdriver.

"Here," I said handing the squirming bleeding mouse-on-a-stick to an incredulous Wyatt. "Take this and stick him in the bug zapper."

"Can't we just take him to the emergency vet?" Wyatt asked, holding the mouse with an admirably firm grip.

"The mouse?" I asked confused. "He's almost dead. I don't

think they can do anything for him."

Wyatt sighed in exasperation and left the room with the mouse.

I surveyed Boomer, and when I heard the distinctive sound of the bug zapper, I put my hands on him. Before I fixed him, I wanted to check out his damage and make very sure that he hadn't been in close contact with an angel. I couldn't imagine an angel would scratch and bite, but just in case I sent energy down inside the wounds to explore. No angel or demon energy. Just plain old bites and scratches, thankfully. Satisfied, I pulled my energy back and readied myself to fix my dog.

One way I can fix is by driving cell reproduction into overdrive and accelerating the natural healing process. It involves minimal energy, but has its issues. You're making a copy of a copy of a copy, and those cells aren't as stable as what they originally were. For a really good heal, you need to recreate and that involves conversion. The resulting cells are solid and perfect. Better than they were before injury in most cases.

Unfortunately conversion has a very specific energy signature. Any angel who senses conversion (and they have very acute senses for this) knows exactly what he is dealing with and usually can track the energy to its source. So basically, what I was about to do to Boomer was like sending up a flare. I hoped that the energy of the bug zapper electrocuting the mouse would mask my own energy. Human energy usage often did, if the energy I used was small enough. Still, it was a risk. I was a fucking idiot risking myself like this just to make Wyatt happy.

It took seconds. I fixed everything at once. Cracked bone, chipped rib, torn muscle, veins, nerve connections, skin cells, regrew hair. He'd had a bowel perforation which was just disgusting. I had to recreate the section of intestine, and then search throughout his abdomen taking out bacteria and microorganisms that had no business outside the digestive system. As I stared down at the newly whole Boomer, I realized that Wyatt was still electrocuting the mouse.

"Okay, I'm done. You can stop now," I called.

Wyatt came running in and handed me the screwdriver with a blackened, reeking lump of burnt mouse on the end. I looked at him in astonishment. What did he expect me to do with it? Eat it? It looked like a macabre shish kabob.

"I thought you needed that," he explained. "For a magic spell or something to heal Boomer."

His voice trailed off as he noticed Boomer was whole and standing beside me thumping his tail.

"Oh yes, worked great," I told him tossing the mouse and screwdriver into the metal trash can. "Thank you."

I wasn't about to go into lengthy explanations of how I hoped the electricity would cover up my quick fix of Boomer. How I hoped that I didn't have an angel bearing down on me right now.

We finished with the horses and turned them out to pasture for the day, then stood awkwardly looking everywhere but at each other. Neither one of us knew what to say; how to end the morning.

"I'm going to grab a nap. I'm having some friends over for a gaming party tonight and we'll probably be up all night," Wyatt said looking at the rafters.

"Me too. Nap I mean, not the gaming party. So, see you around?"

He nodded, still looking at the rafters. We each paused a moment, then left. One step forward, two steps back. At least he was still talking to me.

I made a ham sandwich, showered, and curled up for a long nap. I had a busy evening ahead, and unfortunately it didn't involve crashing Wyatt's gaming party.

CHAPTER 5

I languished in bed a good chunk of the day, curling up in the feather pillows and indulging in some much needed sleep. Late afternoon, I hauled myself up, showered, and ate some leftover Chinese food from my fridge while in the nude. I saw the blinking light on my cell phone telling me I missed a call from Michelle.

"Hey girl," I said as she picked up. "Sorry I left last night without saying anything."

I was undecided what excuse to give. I couldn't very well tell her that I was running for my life, or that I had a date to suck the life force out of my sexy neighbor. Luckily Michelle herself supplied a plausible alibi.

"No problem, I know you and Candy had business to discuss."

Ahhh, right. Candy had left when I did. I was surprised she hadn't stayed and pawed the angel with everyone else. She must have really wanted to sell me those canal properties to follow me out the back door like that.

"Were you there when that movie star arrived?" Michelle asked.

For a second I was confused, and then I realized she must mean the angel.

"I'm pretty sure he was in that action flick from this spring with the runaway train. They're filming some Civil War romance out at Antietam battlefield this week and he must be in it. He was so nice. Everyone mobbed him and he didn't get angry or snotty or anything. Huge guy, built like a tank and just gorgeous. All those curls, and his eyes were black. I mean black. They were darker than mine. He signed a few autographs. Jeff thought he was that wrestler, but this guy had longer hair and was older than him."

Yeah, much older. I listened to Michelle continue to speculate on what movie star the angel might have been.

"Did he mention where he was staying or how long he'd be in town?" I asked. Or if he was hunting down a demon?

Michelle didn't know where the angel was holed up, or if he was still in the area or not. She didn't seem to know much and I wondered if angels had the ability to wipe memory or influence emotion. I wished I could do that. It would be a very useful skill.

I hung up with Michelle without much more knowledge than before, and with an unsettling hunch that I would probably see this angel again. Finally, around dusk, I threw on some running clothes and laced on my shoes. Boomer was waiting for me on the doorstep.

Boomer isn't a full blooded Plott hound. He was what humans would have called a hellhound. One of my kind had impregnated a female dog, and the result was Boomer. It's really not as disgusting as it sounds. We have sex with just about anything we can catch. Breeding, though, is a different matter that requires intent on our part, even cross species breeding. Spawning a hellhound wasn't cause for embarrassment, but it would get you teased a bit. Producing animal hybrids could be very lucrative, as there was a good market for them. So, some of us put up with the teasing and earned a good living through hybrid breeding.

I hadn't sired Boomer, I'd actually won him off another demon in a bet. Back home, there was a certain enhancement to my reputation in having him in my household. Unfortunately, I'd had to lock him down tight when I'd brought him here and he was not as useful as I wished. I don't have the best impulse control, but Boomer has none at all.

The first time I'd brought him here, we'd had to run for our lives hours later. Several times, I'd experimented with different degrees of reduction of his powers, but I'd ended up having to practically neuter him to keep him from being detected. He was little more than a regular dog in his current state, and that made me feel a bit guilty about his injuries. If he'd been at his full strength, nothing shy of an angel or one of my kind could have hurt him. Of course, I was a little pissed at him too for not backing off and retreating before he was so dangerously injured. A normal dog would never had made it home in that state, but Boomer had enough minimal use of his energy to keep himself going and drag himself home.

"Take me there, boy," I told Boomer softly, and he headed down our lane toward the main road.

As we passed Wyatt's house, I saw the cars lined up all over his grass with people laughing and cheerfully carting boxes of electronics toward the front door. Wyatt jogged out to the road when he saw me. Boomer eyed him, then wiggled up to him and nudged his hand for petting.

"You hump his leg and I'll rip your head off," I told him. I meant it.

"Me or the dog?" Wyatt asked in good humor. "You're going for a run this late?"

"Yeah, I slept all afternoon and my internal clock is out of whack," I said.

Wyatt looked up. "Should have some decent moonlight. Come over when you're done to help us kill insurgents and protect the homeland. We'll be going until the wee hours."

I nodded, and Wyatt broke away to answer one of his guests' questions regarding cable compatibility. He seemed more comfortable with me. Almost like before. I felt an ache of hope and longing as I watched him carry a box in his house. If I got back early enough, I think I might just go kill some zombies.

Boomer and I reached the end of the lane, close enough to hear the cars on Route 26. Boomer looked at me expectantly and broke into a trot. We headed west weaving through country roads and cutting across fields. Although I appreciated the efficiency of as-the-crow-flies travel, I struggled to get over barbed wire fences and undetected through people's lawns. The terrain was hilly with rather treacherous footing given the dim light. We crossed from Carroll into Frederick County and I wondered how far Boomer had been ranging. Finally, about five miles from home, we paused at the fence line of a mowed hay field. There was a tiny, one-story ramshackle house at the back edge of the field. Boomer again looked at me expectantly.

There were no lights leading up to the house, and no porch light, although the lights in the house indicated someone was home. I wasn't sure what was going on. Boomer's injuries didn't look like they were caused by any guard dog that this human might have. I couldn't imagine this homeowner having a bear or a mountain lion as a pet. Finally. I just walked up to the front door and knocked, figuring I'd ask the resident if he'd had any bear trouble lately.

The door swung open on its hinges from the weight of my knock. You would have thought with all the movies I'd watched that I'd know better than to walk in. In every cop show, in every horror movie, bad things happened when the door was ajar like this and the hero/victim walked right on in. I wasn't used to considering myself as either a hero or a victim, so walk in I did. And I got knocked sideways into the wall. A dirty, unshaven, vagrant-looking man glared at me. Then, I did my second stupid thing. I pulled out my mean and ordered him to back off.

I should have realized he was bumfuck nuts. Insane. Mentally unstable. Mean works great on just about everyone except crazy people. They are very sensitive to my kind as it is. They recognize us, and they won't back down ever. No matter what you throw at them, what you do to them, they will not back down. They will vocally and physically fight you with every whacked out insane skill they have. They will out you to everyone they see. Luckily, no one believes them most of the time. Insane people have followed me all over downtown and for blocks informed all passerby that I was a fire-breathing, plague-spreading devil come to kill them all and end the world. The only thing you can do is look embarrassed and hope the cops come to haul the guy away.

"Demon," this particular crazy guy shrieked at me in a pitch so high it hurt my ears. "You send your hellhound to spy on me, and here you are to take my soul. You will not succeed."

He started grabbing random things and throwing them at me. He was very accurate in his aim. I deflected the pillows and shielded myself from the bottles and books. I ducked and dodged while running around the room trying to get in a good position to dive at him, or to force him into a place with fewer potential projectiles. He didn't seem to be running out of ammunition anytime soon, so I dropped to the floor and dove under a table. This crawling on the floor thing was beginning to be a habit.

"Could use some help here, you fucking worthless cur," I

shouted at Boomer who peeked in the door and laughed at me.

The house was like a damn hoarder's, I thought as I hid behind chair legs and avoided picture frames, headphones, lamps and ashtrays. Ashtrays. Who the hell smoked in the house anymore? All the while, the guy continued to shrill accusations about my kind and my supposed intentions. According to him, I had been stalking him for decades and was planning on forcing him to eat his own eyeballs while I gnawed on his spleen.

This could go on all night, and the guy could easily overpower me if he found an opening and grabbed me. I knew the risks involved, but didn't have much choice. I shot a burst of electricity at him converting so I could get it past the air's resistance. It wasn't much, only twenty-five thousand volts, but I kept the amperage low and the burst short. Hopefully it was just enough to throw him off balance and get him calm enough to tell me where the bear was.

The guy screamed and dropped to the floor clutching his heart. Drama queen. There was no way that did more than shock his skin. I darted from under the table and held him in place with a chair. I knew better than to try and touch a crazy person. I should have known better than to shock one.

"Have you had a problem with any bears? Maybe raiding your garbage? Or perhaps someone around here has an exotic pet? A big cat?" I felt like a total fool asking someone these questions while I was pinning him to the floor with a chair.

Imagine my surprise when, with an inhuman roar stinking of garbage breath, the guy flung both me and the chair across the room and against the wall. Things got blurry for a few seconds. As the guy ripped the chair away and went to slap me, I raised my arm in defense and was again surprised when his nails tore through my arm, raking strips of flesh and muscle down to the bone. Finally focusing, I realized that instead of hands he had claws. And an elongated jaw with sharp teeth. Very unfortunate and unattractive deformities.

I felt the claws dig into my side, and was flung once again across the room, to skid on the floor and into the couch. Pain ripped through my side, but I was relieved to realize he hadn't punctured my liver or any other important organ. This was really enough. I wasn't about to fight like a human while he tore me into jerky strips. I breathed in and threw a much larger bolt of electricity at him. About one hundred amps worth. It was a small amount, but still overkill when converting it through the air between us and pushing it through the skin's natural resistance directly into his chest cavity. I was capable of producing at the level of lightning, but I didn't feel like setting the house on fire. A billion volts and a hundred thousand amps would be hard to control too as it blew through the human and out through the wall behind him.

The guy convulsed as the current crashed his heart, seized his diaphragm, and burned out organs as it exited down his back. He danced like this for a few seconds while I was sure to keep the current going steady. In electricity, it's important to keep a constant stream as humans have been known to survive short intermittent bursts even at very high levels. It really sucks when you think someone is dead, only to have them get up and stagger at you a few moments later. Finally, he collapsed with a smell of burnt hair and skin.

I walked over and lay my hands on the man, letting my energy explore him. He was dead, which given the oddness of my last twenty-four hours I wasn't taking for granted. He was also weird. DNA is mostly the same among all mammals, but there are slight differences. This guy had human DNA, but there were anomalies. The areas I noticed were similar to those humans with Hypertrichosis, although it was more than the X-chromosome link, and he didn't seem furry enough. Perhaps he indulged in laser hair removal? He didn't look like he could afford that kind of thing, especially since it would have had to be extensive. Hypertrichosis also didn't explain the extended jaw and elongated strengthened nails.

Reluctantly, I pulled away from the man. Curiosity killed the cat, but I couldn't let it kill me. I had to get out of here. With an angel so close and presumably on the hunt for me, I was worried that my energy burst, even one so commonplace as electricity, would be investigated. I looked around at the wreckage of the house, and headed home.

Easier said than done. Five miles with deep lacerations on your forearm and waist, plus a concussion and bruises was not a cake walk. I jogged when I could, and walked a lot. In some spots I needed to go around entire fields as it was too much for me to get over the fencing. The whole way home I cursed Boomer, who had hid outside the door during the entire fight and was without a scratch. The trip in had taken an hour max; the trip back over three hours. I limped by Wyatt's house at past three in the morning in considerable pain and longing for my bed. His yard was filled with cars, and his house lit up with flashing lights of video games and sounds of shooting, screaming, and laughing. People milled around the porch with the deep hum of conversation. I know I was invited, but there was no way I was popping in to visit Wyatt and meet all his friends dirty, sweaty and covered with blood and gashes. I paused and looked longingly at his house, then walked on by.

Boomer got another scolding as I locked him in the barn. There's nothing a hellhound likes more than eating corpses, and I didn't want him heading back out to snack on the dead guy, or getting in any more trouble. I was thinking of sending him back home for my household to care for if this was the kind of bullshit I'd have to deal with. Bad, bad dog.

Giving one more longing look toward Wyatt's house, I headed in. Running attire went into the trash, and I showered, nearly passing out in pain as the hot water hit my wounds. I had slowly begun fixing the damaged flesh, but I was taking a very long time to avoid any excess energy use, which might give me away. I'd done way too much in the past few days as it was, and I could hardly keep frying mice or causing power surges in my house. I would just have to deal with injury and pain and make this a slow project.

Finally clean, I dug around in my bathroom and carefully bandaged my side and arm. They were healing nicely, but I didn't want to take the chance of anything breaking open and oozing blood on my sheets. I have absolutely no experience in first aid, and the tape pulled uncomfortably on my skin. I tossed and turned in bed for a while before giving up and heading down to doze off watching TV.

CHAPTER 6

Sunday was another scorcher. I was in my usual spot by the pool with fluffy towel and a mug of hot sweet coffee. It had been a rough night of sleep, partly due to the invasion of Anime from the TV into my dreams. My injuries were healing, but were still angry red welts across my arm and waist. Ugly, even if they did match the red kiss marks on my bikini. Not that it mattered. No one was likely to see me sweating alone by the pool.

Taking a swig of the hot coffee, I rolled onto my stomach. The heat on my back was intense, even this early, and drops of sweat tickled as they rolled across my back and down my sides. James Brown shouted in my ears and I just let my mind wander. That guy last night was so weird. And not just his mental state either. I wished I could have brought him back here and taken him apart at my leisure; tease apart his genetic sequence and see what his body told me. I toyed with the idea of going back and seeing if I could stuff his body into the Suburban. I'd need to hide it from Boomer while I played with it though. Otherwise he'd eat it.

I wondered what the authorities would think when his

body was discovered. Electrocutions did happen, although you'd usually expect to see a fire, or at least a burnt out socket or appliance. It clearly looked like there had been a fight in the place too. House trashed and resident apparently killed with a burst of electricity to the chest. I'd probably left some of my blood behind and that would be puzzling too. I can hold my blood to strictly human parameters, but under stress or when I'm using energy, my own signature mixes in along with energy. It would totally fuck up their analysis, I thought with amusement.

A shadow touched my thigh and moved up to block the sunlight on my back. I rolled over and thought how incredibly sexy this was to be lying here sweaty and nearly naked, squirming as I shifted on the lounge with Wyatt standing over me. Wyatt's eyes roved and I adjusted the bikini top making sure to give the girls a good jiggle. My eyes roved too and I really liked what I saw at this angle.

Wyatt's eyes stopped and he frowned.

"What on earth did you do to yourself?" he asked, horrified at the raised red welts in slashes across my body and arm. At least they weren't oozing any more. "Did you have a fight with some barbed wire last night? Or that bear that tore up Boomer?"

"I should have stuck with the treadmill," I said, skirting the topic.

"They look awful," he continued, clearly not willing to let go of this one. "I know how quickly you heal; you must have been practically cut in half to still look like that."

"I'm fixing them very slowly," I confessed. "I kinda need to lay low and watch it, so I'm going to look nasty until later tonight. It wasn't that bad, really."

"Why do you need to lay low?" he asked.

Ugh. Why couldn't he just stand there and look sexy?

"I'm a demon, Wyatt. If I make my presence here too obvious, there are things that will come to take me out."

That scared look flashed across his face, again. My gut tightened in reaction; here we go again.

"What things? You're a demon, what in the world would be able to take you out?" he asked.

"I'm not immortal. Damage this body enough and I won't have time to fix it or create another before I die."

"Humans wouldn't come after you for healing yourself," he persisted. "What would?"

"Angels," I admitted. "If they detect us, they come and kill us."

Wyatt stared at me a moment. "Angels."

I wasn't sure what to say, so I just let the word hang in the air.

"So, how did you get these injuries?" Wyatt finally said, breaking the silence.

"Barbed wire," I lied. No sense in making him an accessory after the fact.

Wyatt studied the cuts in silence and nodded.

"Do I need to burn up another mouse for you? Or something larger, like a squirrel perhaps?"

Ha, ha. Very funny. Actually I was relieved that he was somehow beginning to take all this horror film weirdness in stride.

"Nah, I'm good. I've got fresh coffee in the kitchen. Grab yourself a mug and pull up a chair."

Wyatt looked amused.

"It's got to be one hundred degrees out here and you're drinking hot coffee?"

"I like it hot." I told him. "Throw some ice in it if you want though."

Wyatt disappeared into the house. I loved that he was so comfortable around and inside my place. Like he belonged here. He'd know right where the coffee mugs were, where in the fridge I kept my special stash of cream. I wished he was as familiar with the upstairs portion of my house as the downstairs.

I heard him return with his coffee and the scrape of the lounge chair he pulled up.

"I've got to go over to Mom's this evening for a family dinner," he said conversationally. "Amber's home from college. Her birthday is Tuesday and we're celebrating."

"Amber is your younger sister, right?" I asked. I could never remember human family relationships. Back home, no one knew or cared who their parents or siblings were. We were raised in group homes and didn't have these complicated family trees to keep track of.

"Yeah, she's nineteen," he paused for a moment as if considering whether to continue. "I did have an older sister, but she died before I was born. Rachel was three when she drowned in a neighbor's pool. I wasn't born until five years later, and Amber was born five years after me."

"Your folks are divorced?" Humans always seemed to get divorced. I couldn't figure out why they got married at all.

"No, Dad died when I was ten. He was installing a two-twenty line in the garage for a dryer hookup, and he somehow electrocuted himself."

Okay, that was really freaky, given all the electrocution occurring yesterday. Clearly, it was a coincidence since it had happened fourteen years ago.

"Anyway," Wyatt continued, "have any ideas on what to get a nineteen year old girl?"

I moved down my sunglasses so he could clearly see my raised eyebrows.

"Okay, I guess it's gift card time."

"How about those stuffed animal pillows I see on TV?" I suggested with amusement.

Wyatt laughed. "Amber isn't the cheerleader, pink, cutesy toy kind of girl. She's more geeky-Goth wannabe." He paused and grinned. "A gift certificate for body piercing and a tramp stamp?" he laughed. "Mom would kill me."

In the end, he decided the gift card was the safest option.

I enlisted his help in giving Boomer a much needed bath, and then we brought the horses in from the heat and made sure water buckets were fresh and hay bags were full. Wyatt headed off, and Boomer and I ordered pizza and settled in to watch TV. Watching one show at a time was pretty boring, so I had installed four TVs next to each other on the wall in a square arrangement. Wyatt said it looked like something from *A Clockwork Orange*.

I watched each channel's news simultaneously, but there was no report on a dead man found in his house in eastern Frederick County. The guy did look like a vagrant, so it could possibly be weeks or even months before anyone discovered his body. He didn't look the type to have social commitments where his presence might be missed. I decided I should just forget about it and relax.

CHAPTER 7

My Monday morning always starts with the six o'clock Zumba class at the gym. It's packed because the instructor looks like a Latin god. Everyone loves to get in their early-morning eye candy, and they desperately try to attract his attention with their spasmodic hip thrusts. I try to never miss the Zumba class since I believe comedy is a great way to start your week.

This class, I positioned myself amid a group of tittering soccer moms. It was great fun, although I had to hold myself back from turning it into a giant mosh pit slam dance. Last time I did that, they kicked me out for a month. Today, I enjoyed watching an eighty-year-old lady — with a cane no less — shimmy, her boobs flying like weapons around her waist.

After the class, while everyone else lined up to flutter their eyelashes and thank the hot instructor in rusty high school Spanish, I headed out and did my real workout. There was a flyer for a Judo class and I fantasized for a moment about taking it and beating everyone into a bloody mess. I'm so competitive though that I know I'd be sparring and lose control and pop someone's head off. That would be a lot of fun, but it wouldn't be a good thing for my continued life in this realm. No Judo for me.

I was joining Michelle for lunch and meeting her at an end-of-lease walk through, so I actually showered and pulled on the clean shorts and tank top from my bag. I just watched while she inspected the oven, fridge, and carpet. I can't remember the last time I did a walk through. Usually Michelle only called me in if she thought the tenant might get violent. This guy was harmless. Short skinny balding guy on government disability supplements. He was moving in with his daughter. His eyes flickered to me every few seconds, and if I moved, he jumped in alarm. It was kind of funny actually, so I made a point of moving a lot.

"The toilet paper holder came off the wall, but I put a new one on," the tenant pointed out, practically shaking with anxiety. Did he think we were going to yank it off the wall and shove it up his ass? We just wanted a decent apartment and money, not his personal pain and suffering. Sheesh.

We ended up deducting a carpet cleaning and some drywall repair from his security deposit. No one gets out for free. We'd find something to charge even Martha Stewart for. Hot glue mark or excess faux stained glass on the lighting fixtures. The guy didn't argue, and in fact thanked Michelle and me profusely as Michelle handed him a check and collected the keys.

"Mexican?" Michelle asked as we locked up and walked toward the commercial area of downtown. This apartment was actually in a decent neighborhood close to the trendy eateries. I think I could get fifty more a month for it now.

"No way. I need a salad or I won't be able to shit for a week," I replied.

"Lovely visual there, Samantha."

I got my salad. Michelle had a reuben and enough fries to

feed a small nation. I don't know where she put it. She always ate hearty, never seemed to work out, and was thin as an international model. I guess good genetics and height made all the difference. Michelle and I discussed work, as we usually did on our lunches. We debated trying a new plumbing contractor, talked about upcoming leases and who might renew versus who might move out. We commiserated about the tenant who was always losing his keys. We charged him for the copies at an exorbitant rate, but keeping spare sets and having someone run them over at very inconvenient hours was wearing on us. I wondered if one of those numerical locks would help. He'd probably forget the number, but at least we could just tell him over the phone rather than having to run over there in the middle of the night. Maybe we could still charge him each time he called for the code. Finally, as we were finishing up, I approached the topic I really wanted to discuss.

"I've got a relationship issue and want your advice," I said.

Michelle stared. We seldom discussed personal stuff. I didn't even know if Michelle had a steady boyfriend right now or not.

"What, like someone tried to spend the night? Or actually had the nerve to want more than a hook-up in a dark alley? You need to know my advice on where to dispose of the body?"

Okay, that was hitting a bit close to home.

"Wyatt and I made out Friday night, but I freaked him out and things didn't end well. He's still coming by my house and we seem to still be friends. Do you think I've ruined my chances and we're only platonic now?" Crap, I sounded like one of those whiny, desperate letters women wrote to magazines.

Michelle squealed like a murdered rabbit.

"You guys made out? Finally? I want details. Details, girl, details!"

Great. Now I regretted saying anything at all. I imagined having this conversation with my foster brother, Dar. He'd laugh his head off, then advise me to haul Wyatt into my basement, tie him up, and do whatever I wanted until I got bored with him. He'd think my extended vacation was making me weak and vulnerable. There are no girlfriend talks at home, and this was making me kind of squirmy.

"We were kissing outside a bar, up against my car, and things got a bit intense. I really freaked him out. "

"Was he into it at first? What freaked him out? How did he react?"

Hmmm, how to explain this one.

"I was doing some stuff to him that he had never done before. He was into it at first, but then I got a little carried away and it was too much for him. I could tell he wanted to stop, so I did. After I stopped he didn't seem as scared. He seemed angry, but not smash-my-head-against-the-car angry." How was that for vague?

Michelle sighed. "You're not going to give me the details, are you?"

"Nope," I told her.

Michelle looked disappointed.

"Girl, I always figured you were into the really kinky stuff, but Wyatt seems to be more of a bread and butter guy if you know what I mean." She wiggled her eyebrows. I wondered if Michelle was into the really kinky stuff. Probably not the same kinky stuff as I was.

"What happened after?" she prodded. "Before you guys left to go home. You said he's still coming over?"

"We talked a few moments. I tried to explain things. I apologized over and over like a damned broken record and swore up and down it would never happen again. He called to wake me up Saturday morning and tell me to get my lazy rear down to the barn for our ride. He seemed cheerful, but cautious and nervous at times."

"Have you guys talked about what happened since then?"

"No, but when something comes up that reminds him, he still gets that scared look. He's starting to tease me a bit about it though. Is that a good sign?" I was pitiful. The other demons would never let me live this one down if they found out.

Michelle nodded thoughtfully.

"I think you should be a little flirty with him. Make a comment, then back off and don't pursue it. Let him know you're interested still, but let him make the move. But give him lots of openings where he *can* make a move, though. He needs to be the one to initiate it, so he feels like he's the man."

I had no idea what the hell she was saying, but I smiled and nodded and swore to myself I'd never do this again. Be flirty, but not too flirty. Give him openings to initiate sex, but not too obvious. Fuck this. If I had to do all this crap just to have Wyatt, I might as well fall back on my traditional approach. The one Dar would advocate.

I ran a few errands and headed back home late afternoon to see Wyatt heading down my driveway. I pulled alongside and thought about incapacitating him, stuffing him in the Corvette's tiny trunk and dragging him into my basement. I didn't have any decent rope, but I did have a lot of duct tape.

"Hey," I said to him, restraining my impulses.

He leaned into the car resting his forearms on the window edge. Seven inches away. I could lean over and kiss him. Or grab him. But I was supposed to let him make the moves per Michelle, the love doctor.

"What are you doing tomorrow morning?" he asked.

"Eating oatmeal. Reading the paper. Taking a shower. Naked. With a loofa sponge."

Was that flirty? Or too flirty? Shit, I didn't know how to do this thing. Wyatt did laugh though, so maybe it was the right thing to say.

"Come over to my place around nine. I want to teach you how to shoot."

"With a gun?" I was a bit confused. I couldn't imagine why I'd ever need to shoot a gun.

"Yes, with a gun," he said.

"Because I clearly need some way to defend myself?" Did he think I was in need of human technology for protection of my person? After everything that happened between us?

Wyatt reached in the window and ruffled my hair. It was the first time that he'd touched me in an affectionate manner since our 'incident'.

"No, I just thought it would be fun. "

"I didn't even think you shot real guns. Just the computer game ones." Maybe that was insulting, I though too late.

"How do you think I killed those groundhogs last fall? The ones you asked me to get rid of?" He laughed. "Did you think I stabbed them with a screwdriver, or caused them to spontaneously combust?"

I hadn't considered *how* he killed them. They were there, putting big, horse-tripping holes in my pasture, and then they were gone. How they got gone never crossed my mind.

"Okay, I'll be there" I told him. Didn't Michelle say I should take an interest in his hobbies? At least this was more palatable than sitting on a couch, waving some little plastic thing around in front of the TV.

The next morning, I locked Boomer in the barn to be out of the way of any bullets that might loop around the house and whizz onto my property. Satisfied that he was safe, I proceeded to walk down to Wyatt's.

Up close, the dilapidated Cape Cod looked like a damned shack. The paint was peeling, and the window sills and eaves showed signs of significant rot. One broken window had a plywood board nailed over it from the inside. Was Wyatt so poor that he couldn't make even basic repairs to his house? He never complained about needing money, or doing without, but his house was in shambles. From the outside, it looked like he hadn't done a thing in the two years since he'd bought it. Perhaps his home repairs had started on the inside? It would take a lot to fix this place up, so maybe he was just doing a little at a time? Either way, the place made me feel anxious inside, like I should find a way to sneak Wyatt more money, or arrange for a contractor to show up free of charge. How could I manage this without offending his pride, I wondered? Then I wondered why I gave a shit about Wyatt's falling down house or his pride. That wasn't like me at all.

It was just as bad in the back yard. There was a dangerously rickety deck off his kitchen, gray with age and full of splintered, bowed planks. He had an equally rickety card table set up on the ground in front of the deck with a target out in my back field. There were cigarette burns, and bottle rings on the card table. An assortment of guns was laid out like a flea market sale.

I'd seen guns in movies before but had limited experience with them up close. I remembered a huge long gun about two hundred years ago when I had popped over here for some fun. It was a stupid weapon. It took forever for the guy to get it ready, and then it was just as likely to explode in his face as fire. It never seemed to hit its mark either. I'd pretty much written them off after that. They looked awesome on TV, but I know the liberty producers take with reality.

Wyatt introduced me to the guns. No really, introduced me. Like we were at a cocktail party. I got to meet Mr. Shotgun. I learned about smooth-bore barrels, the difference between gauges and calibers. This particular one was a 12-

gauge, which was supposed to be the most common and thus easier to find and purchase ammunition. It was also a pump action which, according to Wyatt, was more reliable than the semi-automatics, whatever they are. Evidently, I was going to get up close and personal with Mr. Shotgun (whose first name was Remington) before I got to meet the other weapons at the party this morning.

Wyatt handed me Remington and I just looked at him. The gun I mean, not Wyatt. I stuck the butt end under my arm and grabbed the barrel with my left hand, my right hand on the bottom of the gun holding the trigger.

"Here, let me show you," Wyatt said moving behind me. "It's not loaded."

I think I stopped breathing when Wyatt put his arms around me. He moved the butt of the shotgun to the hollow in my shoulder, putting his left hand on mine and moving it back to the appropriate position. We stood there with his arms and hands against mine, the entire front length of his body pressed against my back and rear, and his lips so close to my ear that my hair moved with his breath. A slow warmth built low in my abdomen and eased down between my thighs. Maybe we could stay this way all morning.

"Sam?"

Oh, crap. He'd been giving me some kind of directions and I was supposed to respond. I had no idea what he'd said.

"Yep. Okay."

I hoped that would suffice. Wyatt gave a low chuckle against my ear.

"Should I go over that again?"

I said no. If we kept this up I was going to have to take matters into my own hands. I wished that I'd brought some duct tape.

Wyatt loaded the gun and commented that he was out of bird shot, so we were using slugs. I gleefully envisioned cramming slimy slugs into a shotgun and blowing them out the barrel. That would be so cool. Someone should invent that. Everyone would want one.

Carefully, I racked the gun and placed my left hand on the forearm and my right on the grip behind the trigger where Wyatt had positioned my hands before. Pointing it at the target, I pulled the trigger. Nothing happened.

"Take off the safety," Wyatt said, pointing to the appropriate part when I looked at him blankly. "And don't forget to seat the gun against your shoulder".

I clicked off the safety and pulled the trigger. There was a roar, and a slam of pain, and I was on my ass sprawled into the dirt of Wyatt's back yard.

"Ow, motherfucker!"

"It's a 12-gauge," Wyatt said, helping me to my feet. "And we're using slug ammo. You need to get it positioned solidly on your shoulder, with your cheek against it to sight it better. You're strong, there's no reason you can't shoot this gun".

I dusted my rump off and Wyatt assisted in cleaning me off, even licking a finger and wiping a smudge from my forehead.

"Let me see," he said pulling aside my tank top and bra strap to look at my shoulder.

"Ouch. You'll have a bruise."

I was feeling anything but pain as he ran a finger across my collarbone.

"Are you okay to shoot it again? Do you want to fix your shoulder first?"

"I'm fine. It's not bad."

Mr. Remington Shotgun may have won this round, but I'd be damned if I let him get the best of me.

"Did I hit anything?" I asked Wyatt.

"No, and if we're lucky you missed the neighbor's cows."

I really didn't give a shit about the neighbor's cows, but I had Wyatt show me again how to position the shotgun properly. This time, I tried hard to concentrate on what he was saying and less about his body pressed to mine. I wasn't entirely successful.

Five rounds later I was managing not to get knocked on my ass, but still didn't seem to be shooting anywhere near the target. My shoulder was killing me, but there was no way I was going to give in. Wyatt finally threw in the towel for me and suggested we bypass the rifle and move on to the pistols instead.

There were three pistols at the table. Wyatt picked up the shiny one first and showed it to me.

"This is a 9mm, which refers to the ammo. It's a Beretta. This is pretty much your standard, common-use pistol. It holds fifteen rounds in the clip, so you can get a good number of shots off before needing to put in a new clip."

Wyatt showed me how to load the clip and the bullets inside it. Next up was what appeared to be a gun for a toddler. Wyatt called it a "pocket gun" and said it was a Colt Magnum Carry which was a six-shot revolver. It was evidently an ideal back-up weapon that you could strap to your calf or carry in a purse and use if something happened to your larger pistol. I still liked the idea of preschoolers packing, but I could see this had its uses for adults too.

"I have another revolver, too. My father's Colt Peacemaker. It was used in the army back in the late 1800s and is what you would have expected to see gunslingers carry in the Wild West. It was mainly a cavalry gun, but it was very popular outside the military at the time. It's a reliable gun, and even though it is single action, you can do that move you see in the westerns where the sheriff pulls the hammer back with his palm and lets it go to fire the gun rapidly without using the trigger. That's called fanning. My father taught me to shoot with that gun."

I quickly calculated human life expectancies.

"But your Dad wouldn't have been alive when that gun was made and these new guns are so superior. Why would he have bought such a relic and used it?"

Wyatt smiled.

"History is important to us, to me, and to humans in general. It links us to our ancestors and makes us see the totality of our achievements instead of just what we can accomplish in our short lifetimes."

He picked up the Beretta and looked at it fondly.

"We wouldn't have these firearms, or even the amazing weaponry in our military, without exploding cannons in the sixteenth century and generations of people dedicated to improving them. Keeping historic items around, it helps connect us with our past and allows us to feel like we can individually contribute to a chain of knowledge and advancement that builds our future."

I can't really describe how I felt hearing him say this. Humans mentally were like amoebas compared to us. The simplest things took them forever to think out and put together. I knew humans learned from each other, but this was the first time I realized the sum total of their advancements. They were mental midgets individually, but collectively and over time their intelligence and their accomplishments grew exponentially complex. Who knew what they'd be in a few thousand more years.

"I've grossly underestimated you," I said. I meant the human race as a whole, but I think Wyatt took this as a personal compliment because he beamed at me. I tucked this away to contemplate it later, and looked at the last pistol on the table. It was a huge ugly hunk of metal. I think I was in love.

"What this one?"

"This," Wyatt announced as if he were presenting me to

the queen, "is a Desert Eagle .50-caliber. It has a gas operating repeating system with rotating pistol locks."

Wyatt went on to describe the firing mechanism that produced enormous pressure in the barrel, and some other stuff about backward slide movement and recoil springs. I picked it up and the sucker was heavy. About seventy-two ounces heavy. It was blocky, ugly, big, and held only seven rounds, but I fell in love just as Wyatt clearly had. It was such unbelievable overkill. I did love overkill.

I picked up one of the bullets and let my energy explore it. Brass casing with bullet inside, gunpowder, and a chemical mixture of lead, sulfide, and barium nitrate at the back end. I could envision the process of ignition in the primer, subsequent ignition of the powder, and combustive pressure ejection of the bullet. Brass is soft, so the powder combustion would push the cartridge case against the inside walls of the barrel, sealing the sides and allowing maximum pressure to propel the bullet with the expanding gas. Simplistic and still inefficient since, by my quick calculations, only about twenty-six percent of the energy created by the combustion would propel the bullet. The rest would be wasted in heat or unused energy. Clever, though.

I got to shoot the Beretta. Wyatt had me shoot it two handed with the butt of the gun resting in my left palm. One handed was supposedly ideal since you could turn your body and present a smaller target to your opponent, but using both hands stabilized the gun, especially for inexperienced shooters, and allowed for greater accuracy. I could have had four arms like the goddess Kali and I still wouldn't have hit the target. Five rounds with the shotgun and fifteen (a whole clip) with the pistol and the target stood there pristine and mocking me. I was tempted to just reach out and blow it to bits. That would have not only been accurate, but very efficient in energy usage. I decided that indulging in my urge to show off might send the tentative and rather promising advances in our relationship back a few paces.

Wyatt wasn't so humble. He slapped a new clip in the pistol and, with one hand, pounded out five shots in rapid succession. He didn't even look like he was aiming. In fact, he was holding the gun at some strange crooked angle which was in direct contradiction to his instructions earlier. We walked over to look at the target which had a nice cluster of holes where the drawing indicated a head should be.

"I think you killed him," I said, admiring the grouping. I wanted so badly to add that I could easily do this without a gun, while doing Sudoku and playing piano at the same time, but I figured that he knew that and I didn't want to rub it in.

I helped him put the guns back in his safe where I saw several others he hadn't trotted out for our session. The card table and target went under the dilapidated deck.

"Come have lunch with me," Wyatt said putting a hand on my shoulder and sliding it down my arm to squeeze my hand.

I'd never been in Wyatt's house beside my journey to the gun safe just a few moments ago. It seemed strange that we'd known each other these two years, and he was so free with my place, yet I'd never been in his home. I hoped this offer of lunch indicated some trust on his part.

The house inside was just as bad as it was on the outside. Furnishings were sparsely scattered around on the chipped linoleum and worn carpets. Wood paneling covered most of the walls, except for a strange wallpapered photograph mural in what must have been the dining room depicting a green forest scene. The furniture all looked to be hand-me-downs or thrift store, and the appliances didn't match. Wyatt clearly spent every dime of his earnings on his computer equipment and TV which took up the entire living room in a humming sprawling mess of boxes and cables. I reached into the lemon yellow refrigerator to get the iced tea and the door nearly fell off in my hands.

"Shit, Wyatt. Your damned fridge door is falling off its hinges. I know what I'm getting you for Christmas."

Wyatt shrugged unconcerned and told me I'd need to lift it a bit when closing it to make sure it sealed tight. The shape of his home didn't seem to embarrass him at all. In fact, he seemed oblivious to its dilapidated condition.

We made Paninis for lunch. Wyatt didn't have a Panini press, so we used an old waffle iron instead. What he lacked in modern, functioning appliances, Wyatt made up for in the contents of his fridge. I expected a case of beer and cold Ramen noodles, but he had almost as many gourmet foods on his broken shelves as I did. We fixed turkey Paninis with gruyere, artichoke, and roasted red pepper. They were amazing. I'd not cooked before coming to this realm, but luckily many of those I Owned did know how to cook and I could call on their memories. Otherwise, I would have been at the mercy of take-out for forty years. Still, this was really good and beyond what I usually managed on my own. I told Wyatt he should come over every day and cook me dinner on my decent stove. He thought I was joking.

I hated to leave, but I had some zoning documents I needed to review this afternoon. The city was trying to extend the historic district to encompass a few blocks where I had five apartments. Having to comply with their regulations would seriously cut into my profits and just piss me off in general. I was covering the bribery and threatening bases, but it still was good to explore their logic and reasons in case I needed to rebut this in a more civilized manner. These documents would be boring as hell, but I needed to buckle down and plow through them.

Wyatt walked me to the door and as I turned to say good bye he planted a kiss on me. It wasn't passionate. It was gentle and tentative. I pushed back my raging hormones, kept my hands to my sides, and my tongue in my mouth.

"Wow, I didn't die," Wyatt said in amazement.

"And you didn't shoot me," I added.

Wyatt laughed.

"Are we okay?" I asked.

"Sam, you're my best friend," Wyatt said softly. "I can't just throw that away."

He kissed me again this time with greater intensity. I kept my hands fisted and firmly locked to my sides and kept myself in check. It wasn't easy as he held himself under no such restrictions and brought his hands up to cup my face, his fingers in my hair. I really wanted to press myself against him, but held back, even as he ran his tongue over my bottom lip. He stepped back and looked at me appraisingly.

"I'll call you later tonight," he said.

"Okay," I told him breathlessly and headed down the lane toward my house. Hmmm. A lot to think about and absolutely no desire to peruse zoning documents and historic district guidelines.

I let Boomer out of the barn and flicked on the radio and outdoor speakers by the pool. Maybe the documents would be more palatable if I read them outside. Pop music blared from the speakers, pumping out a Rihanna song. Walking over to the water I slipped off a sandal and dipped in a foot. What the hell. Work could wait. I pulled off my clothes, throwing them haphazardly around the patio and dived naked into the pool, reveling in the feel of the cool water against my skin. I did laps, and then sprawled on the inflatable lounge for a while. Fuck zoning, this was too nice a day to read that crap. I rolled off the lounge and did more laps.

As I came up for a breath of air, I saw a pair of high heels walking across the patio. They stopped a few feet from the edge and I swam to them. Pushing the hair from my eyes, I looked up and saw an immaculate Candy Star before me. Her blonde poof of hair was pulled tightly back, and she daringly wore white capris and a crisp tan and white button down shirt. I would have had dirt or coffee spilled on that outfit within seconds of putting it on. I wondered if she had a dirt repelling force field surrounding her pants. Or maybe some other kind of repelling force field, I thought humorously.

I knew I didn't have an appointment with her, and it was pretty ballsy to come out to my home uninvited to discuss business deals. I stared at her silently, not giving her the courtesy of a greeting.

"I have a rather unfortunate matter that I need to discuss with you," she said.

CHAPTER 8

Okay, now I was curious. I couldn't imagine the canal row houses being an "unfortunate matter". Candy was at the bar when I saw the angel. I was hoping *that* wasn't the "unfortunate matter" she was referring to.

I swung myself up and over the side of the pool, noticing Candy's uneasy expression when she realized I was swimming in the buff. I decided to expand on this by pulling myself upright to stand square in front of her, and wringing out my hair onto the patio. I didn't know whether she was more alarmed at the prospect of getting pool water on her gleaming white capris or the full frontal view.

"What's up?" I asked as she looked around unsuccessfully for a towel to hand me.

"I am a representative for Bobby Winegarten" she said, giving up her search and deciding to only look at me from the neck up.

She said this like I should know who the hell Bobby Winegarten was. He can't have been important or I would have remembered his name. Although I was really bad at names in general.

"Is he one of the county commissioners?" I guessed. "The one who dated the previous mayor?"

"No," she said watching me carefully with those shrewd brown eyes of hers. "Bobby Winegarten was found dead in his house on Rosecrest Lane off Old Annapolis Road last night. I'm here because he was part of my pack. As head of his pack, I represent him."

Oh fuck. The electrocuted unwashed crazy guy. It wasn't on the news last night or this morning though. And what was a pack? Why was Candy even here? Did real estate agents moonlight as crime scene investigators? Was she undercover FBI with license to deviate from the bland clothing? She'd have to be better than Spencer Reid to trace this back to me, especially in such a short time.

"I don't know him," I said casually. "Did he leave me money or something?"

Candy sighed.

"No. You killed him and I'm here to claim weregeld as the head of his pack."

I understood weregeld. We don't have family so to speak, but we do maintain households and those in our households are our property. If one is murdered, accident or not, it's not a big deal. The killer does need to pay a price to the owner, though. If not, it calls their status into question and they could be knocked down in the hierarchy, or even killed themselves. If Candy was the head of this Bobby's household, whatever she called it, then I did indeed owe restitution. I'd gladly pay it, but only if she could prove I did it. Another demon would have been able to read my energy signature and pin this on me, but I doubted this human had a video tape of me doing the deed or something equally incriminating. A murder with no evidence was no murder at all.

"If this man was murdered why aren't the police investigating it?" I asked.

"Do you really want the police investigating this?"

I shrugged and smiled. I'm not afraid of the human law enforcement officers.

"Well *we* don't like to involve others in our matters. Our kind prefers to handle this on our own. I went to check on Bobby after he missed an appointment yesterday. I found his house in disarray; clear evidence of a fight and a struggle. Bobby was dead apparently from some kind of high voltage strike to the chest."

I walked over to a lounge chair and sprawled into it making sure I flashed Candy all the good parts. She winced and darted her eyes back to my face. She didn't want to involve the police, and her rambling about her "pack" sounded a little off the deep end. I was beginning to figure she was in the Klan or with some subversive terrorist group. I could take her. And no one would find the body. I shot a quick glance at Boomer, who casually got up and stretched before wandering off to guard against intruders.

"What makes you think I killed your friend?" I asked. "Is there a super high-powered defibrillator in my car with my prints all over it?"

Candy looked at me carefully as if she understood the gravity of her situation.

"Bobby came to me last week as his pack leader and advised me that a hellhound was spying on him. To be honest, Bobby had his struggles with reality and was always concerned that someone was trying to follow him or even kill him. I told him to continue to report on this hellhound, but not to engage it in a fight. I didn't want him tearing up the neighbor's Rotti and have to deal with covering that up.

"Late Friday night, Bobby called me and told me that the hellhound had broken into his house and he had severely injured it trying to defend himself. He was terrified that the demon who owned the hound would retaliate. I had a strong suspicion what you were after we met in The Wine Room, so I didn't want to just dismiss his claims. I met with him Saturday morning, but couldn't get a good scent on this hell-hound Bobby was talking about. I could clearly smell the neighbor dog, though. Since Bobby was uninjured and there were no unusual smells I figured he was having one of his psychotic episodes. I had him take his pills and told him I'd check back with him on Tuesday. When I didn't hear from him before then, I thought he'd regained some sense of reality.

"I went over there this morning and found him dead. He apparently died late Saturday night. There were very clear scents in the house. I recognized your scent from the bar, and this time I did pick up the scent of your hound on the door sill."

"And what do my dog and I smell like," I said. This woman was clearly off her rocker. She had nothing on me, and I was looking forward to killing her.

"Your dog smells like hot chocolate and wet dog."

Yum. Well, except for the wet dog.

"You smell like dark burnt chocolate — that's very strong. You also smell like the human form you have now, and behind all that I can smell wisps of hundreds of humans and animals. I can't differentiate the humans and animals. You have the most complex smell I've ever known, and the most distinctive."

"It's nice that your nose is so acute," I said in a bored tone. "You're quite the human Bloodhound." It was time to wrap this up because I suddenly wanted some pudding. The kind you cook on the stove so I could eat it warm right out of the pot.

Candy looked at me as if deciding what to do. Slowly she began unbuttoning her shirt and slipping off her heels. I watched her disrobe with interest. She clearly wasn't aflame with desire. I could only assume that maybe she felt she would negotiate restitution better if we were both on an equal, naked playing field.

Candy obviously worked out. Hard. Her body rippled with lean muscles, and her breasts were small and natural with a slight gentle droop that comes from age and childbirth. Her belly showed confirmation of childbirth too. Low down on the six pack abs she had soft folds of skin and a cesarean section scar pale above her light brown curls of pubic hair.

She carefully folded and placed her clothes on a dry lounge chair. Facing me, her muscles began rolling under her skin like a thousand tennis balls, and her bones twisted and turned. I shot up out of my chair and stared in horror.

"Fuck! Fuck! Oh shit! Fuck!" I shouted as her body twisted and turned beyond the capabilities of the human flesh she wore.

Now to put this into perspective, I don't gross out easily. I think Texas Chainsaw Massacre is a comedy. Pain and suffering doesn't bother me, but this was brutal. Watching her spend ten minutes contorting her body, changing small sections at a time as she converted was agonizing. I can't imagine how painful this must be, and I wondered how she didn't pass out. Finally she was done and a huge wolf stood before me panting with eyes a little glazed from the difficulty of the transition. She was gray, with black tips on the edges of her coarse fur. The same shrewd brown eyes looked back at me as I admired her.

It was a good conversion. Excellent control and command over the details of the body. Solid, well formed. A bit bigger in the fore body than I would have done, but powerful and imposing nonetheless. The wolf took a deep breath and began to transform back with the same agonizing slowness. No, it actually took longer and it looked like some portions got stuck and had to be forced into the correct form. I winced quite a few times. This would clearly win a torture contest back home. I made a mental note.

Candy stood naked before me and slowly sat down on the chaise trying not to look weakened. She didn't need to prove herself any further to me; I was impressed all to hell.

"Holy shit on a stick!" I shouted at her. "Why the fuck did you take so long to do that? You didn't have to make it last that long to impress me. You are one tough bitch, girlfriend."

Candy looked at me puzzled.

"You're not surprised that I'm a werewolf? Like something out of a horror movie? I doubt you've ever seen one of us before, since we need to keep it hidden to be in compliance with our existence contract."

"Hell, yeah I'm surprised you're a werewolf. I thought that dead guy had some mutated form of Hypertrichosis, but I didn't realize he could convert. Can you only convert to the two forms? And why did you take so long to change form? Damn that must have hurt like a motherfucker!"

Candy stood up a bit wobbly and put on her clothes.

"We are only able to assume the two forms. I don't think it's the same kind of form change that you can do. It can take anywhere from ten to twenty minutes to do a full change. It's also very difficult to change back so quickly."

When I convert, I change everything simultaneously. It takes less than a second. Basically, I hold my core personal energy, my spirit, along with any raw energy I have stored, explode out all the other molecules and structures, and then collapse them back in the form and order that I need. There are times when I do a slow conversion or a modification. Like when I want to scare the piss out of someone by having horns on my head. It's much more effective to "grow" them by extending them out of my skull slowly. Flash, bang, instant horns isn't as scary. It hurts to form them slowly like that, but it's manageable. Slowly converting my entire form over up to twenty minutes was something I've never wanted to do.

"It must suck when you're attacked and it takes ten minutes to change your form." I commiserated.

"If the wolf form is optimal, we try to prepare beforehand. With today's weapons technology, though, we mainly use our wolf form only for the joy of hunting and socializing with our pack. We're strong and we have some special skills in both of our forms. If we're really in a tight spot we can change and hold a partial form for a brief time to get out of danger."

That explained the claws and elongated jaw on the dead guy. I sat back down on the lounge. Candy had earned my respect. I'd admit guilt if a demon detected my energy signature at a crime, and as a werewolf, Candy's nose was in the same category. I was ready to pay my weregeld. Just not too much.

"So, how much was the life of this psychotic troublemaker worth to your pack?" I asked.

Candy began to speak, then paused gesturing at me.

"Can you please put on some clothes? Or at least a towel."

I met her gaze then slowly reached up and pinched my nipples. Candy turned bright red and looked up at the sky shaking her head.

"Fine. It's not money I am requesting, but a service."

This was so fun, flustering her like this. I was tempted to lean over and lick one of my nipples, but she did have a legitimate petition here and I needed to be serious.

"I can't accept or decline until I know what sort of service you require."

I'd expected a dollar figure, or a request to pay an inflated price for the row houses. Judging from compensatory damage awards in lawsuits, humans put a dollar value on everything. This service request was unusual and more in the nature of what a demon would have asked.

"What do you know about angels?" she asked keeping her eyes firmly above my neck.

I went cold. What did *she* know about angels? Humans thought of them as a vague manifestation of their deity. They bought hideous, kitschy decorative figurines depicting pious winged figures, supposedly what the angels looked like. I had no idea why the humans associated those benevolent statues with the creatures I'd heard about back home.

"Not much. Few demons still around were alive during the wars. Since the separation treaty took effect, no demon has ever survived an encounter with one. We usually pop over here for some short-time fun, then get the hell out of Dodge before they kill us. They can sense us when we convert, although no one is really sure how much energy usage or how close they need to be for us to show up on their radar. Once they lock in on our energy signature, it's difficult to come back. Pretty much game over if one is on your trail."

Back home, we didn't talk much about the angels or the wars. I know we used to live together in Aaru, what the humans called heaven. We'd always had strong philosophical differences though. Angels are all about self control. They hold to their spiritual form and only become corporeal when absolutely necessary. When they are in physical form, they endure it by holding themselves apart from the form and denying themselves the experience of the flesh as much as possible. They believe that physical manifestation sullies their purity and dims their capacity for enlightenment. We on the other hand feel that experiencing everything we can in the physical realm, diving deep within the sensations of the flesh, is a necessity of life. How can one possibly be whole without feeling, touching, knowing everything one can?

I knew that these differences set the stage for the war and eventual separation. I suspected there was more to the war than philosophy, but either no one remembered or no one spoke of it. It's not like we could just walk up to an angel and discuss it. The treaty completely separated our kind. And if we met one over here, we were dead. Not much time for an enlightening conversation.

Candy waited to make sure I was done, and then dusted off a lounge chair, sitting down and putting her elbows on her knees as she leaned forward toward me.

"By our count, there are about fifty angels in this realm at any given time. I don't know what a lot of the angels do, but there are groups that are enforcers. There's one in charge of werewolves, and one is a liaison to the vampires."

Vampires. I hadn't seen one of those in six hundred years and I'd assumed they'd died out. Candy continued.

"These enforcers catalog everyone in their group. They ensure everyone acts within the parameters of the existence contract and kill anyone who violates the contract. Basically, werewolves all exist at the whim of the angels. This isn't a paternal kind of relationship."

"Wow, sucks to be you," I told her cheerfully. I couldn't imagine having an angel breathing down my neck every second, waiting for one to pop out of nowhere and lop your head off because you forgot to put the cap on the toothpaste or something.

She ignored my comment. "The angel in charge of enforcing the werewolves is named Althean. A few years ago, he started killing werewolves, and we knew the kills weren't justified under the contract. Lately, he's escalated."

"So why is he killing you off? Why now?" I asked suspiciously. "If he's just gone off the deep end, can't you report him up the chain of command? He's got to have a boss. They all have bosses."

Candy looked uncomfortable.

"Some of the angels hold the opinion that we're Nephilim. I'm not sure how far up this goes. It could be that Althean's boss approves of his actions."

"What's Nephilim?" I asked. It sounded like a type of cookie.

"The offspring of Fallen angels and humans. Back when humans were just starting to evolve, a group of angels began having sexual relations with them. They had supposedly spawned a whole race of hybrid beings before the rest of the angels found out and came down on them with holy fury. There were no werewolves prior to this event, so many angels figure that we were the product of this joining: the Nephilim."

No way. She had to be making this one up. Angels hated being in the flesh. They would never have lowered themselves to reproduce with humans.

"Others think we were just a random event of evolution," she continued. "If we're Nephilim, then we're condemned to extermination as a reminder of how even angels can go wrong. If we're a product of evolution, then we fall under the protections and privileges that the human race holds."

Angels took forever to decide these kinds of things. It was likely this guy was just some vigilante, but he could have supporters who agreed with him, who were likely to turn a blind eye to his actions.

"Wait," I interjected. "Is this Althean the angel we saw in the bar?"

Maybe the angel in the bar was looking for Candy and not me. That would make my life so much better.

"No, based on my information, I suspect that the angel in the bar is one named Gregory."

I let that sink in. I knew where this was going.

"So who is this Gregory angel?" I asked with a growing sense of doom. Cue the scary music.

"He's over all the enforcers and takes on anything serious that's beyond the lesser angels." She looked at me sympathetically, "He's the angel who takes out the demons. If the others sense a demon presence they think they can't kill, they defer to Gregory to handle it. Gregory has killed pretty much every demon that *has* been killed in the last eight thousand years. From what I've been told, he has a sword he uses to kill demons. The sword sucks the power from them and reduces them to a pile of sand."

I felt rather sick.

"What does any of this have to do with the service you are requesting?" Hopefully if we changed the subject I wouldn't be dwelling on the ever-increasing likelihood of my being turned into a pile of sand.

"I want you to kill Althean."

I stared at her. This was not within a mile of what I'd expected. What an insane request.

"You're fucking kidding me. My eliminating an angel, which no one has done since the war, somehow equates to the life of a crazy vagrant?"

"It's genocide. He's on a rampage to kill off our species. If he's not stopped, we'll all die."

"And that matters to me why?" Did I look like the Lone Ranger or some kind of super hero? Demon Zorro to the rescue?

Candy switched tactics.

"You've got Gregory on your trail right now. He was there in the bar for you. You know this. You're going to need to go home real soon. Imagine going home with this feather in your cap. What would this do to your position in the hierarchy? There's a reason the angels end up deferring to Gregory when it comes to demons. None of them can handle more than the weakest among you. You could take Althean out and go home a legend."

Now, that *was* tempting. It was also absolutely insane to even dream that I'd be strong enough to take out an angel. Plus, I was hoping I could lay low and Gregory would go hunt down some other demon. A huge battle with another angel wasn't exactly laying low.

"We'd be blameless, and there wouldn't be any retaliation on us. That's important because we have to live here. You can go back and forth. You can take the blame and the fame. And the other angels would believe it was you who took out Althean and not us because they truly fear you. That's why you were banished."

We weren't really banished. It was a stalemate with a division of realms. Kind of like North Korea and South Korea.

"You'll just get another angel assigned to you," I told her. "Maybe a worse one. If this is their grand plan to exterminate your species, this will only delay that not prevent it."

Candy looked pained.

"I hope that the other angels don't care as long as we follow the rules. If this is a segment of a larger campaign though, then killing Althean will buy us time. Give some of us a chance to try and go underground or prepare to take as many of them out as we can until we're dead. I'm hoping the former."

I snorted. This whole thing was insane.

"What makes you think I could possibly take out an angel?"

Candy smiled grimly. "You've got the talent and power to do this." She looked at me speculatively with those shrewd eyes. "You're smart. Most demons could never be here this long posing as a human and remain undetected. Clever and enterprising. I think you've got great power, but you may be rusty since you haven't used it in so long."

She was good. Flattery to butter me up, then subtle insults to manipulate me into doing what she wanted. I was full of admiration. And I was NOT rusty.

"Even if I could, that Gregory guy is nearby. He would be on me like flies on shit. He'd probably kill me before I could finish the job. No deal. Think of something else for weregeld. Maybe I buy those canal properties at fair market value?" Michelle would kill me for paying so much for those things. Ugh.

Candy took a breath and looked at me cautiously.

"I've let every pack leader in North America know about you. Your appearance, your financials, your smell signature, everything. It just takes one call and the angels will have you. They'll kill you, disburse your assets, eliminate the humans you've marked as yours."

I winced. I normally don't care about humans, but Wyatt…

"If you leave, we'll let the angels know about you and wipe clean everything you've put together," she continued. "You'll never be able to return, either. They'll be on the lookout for you, and we will too. Doesn't matter what form you take, we can smell you and turn you in."

Fucking bitch. I might only be an imp, but I'm still a demon. I envisioned Candy in my basement with duct tape, her skin hanging in strips from an oozing body. Of course, I'm sure every werewolf in the nation knew exactly where she was. One werewolf I could take, more than five, probably not.

"He was there," she added. "At Bobby's house. The angel. Not Althean, Gregory. He's closing in on you. He sensed your energy usage, and he's coming for you. Any day now, he'll be sniffing around your house. You'll come home and find him standing over your dead dog, waiting for you."

I felt my heart pound. I'd used a small amount of energy

at the tenant's house, plus what I'd done to heal Boomer, and the electricity at the werewolf house. On their own, they might not have brought attention, but all together and with an angel close by… I was so fucked.

Either way, I was dead. One, I go after Althean and go out in a blaze of glory. The other, I run and hide under rocks until this bastard, Gregory, finally hunts me down. I was so tired of being just an imp, a lowly cockroach.

Candy leaned forward, her face sympathetic and friendly. "We can cover for you. Give you time to get away. You can probably still remain here, too, if you keep your energy usage low. We'll offer you friendship with the werewolves. We'll always cover for you and run interference between you and the angels. Think. You'll have the status of taking out an angel, you'll satisfy the weregeld, and you'll have valuable allies that will be duty-bound to have your back."

I thought furiously about how this might work. I could make the kill with as little energy usage as possible. If the werewolves stalled any other angels, and I held my energy tightly to myself, I'd probably have a few hours before they tracked me down even in the worst case scenario. That would give me time to get to a gate and get out.

"You need to vow to protect Wyatt, too," I told her. "I'm under no illusions that I'd be able to stay after this. I don't want the angels taking their fury out on him. I need to know that he'll be safe."

"Who is Wyatt?" Candy asked perplexed.

"My neighbor," I said, not sure what to call him. "You werewolves, each and every one of you, vow to protect him with your life, or it's no deal."

Candy didn't hesitate. "Deal."

"If I do this, you and others need to be actively involved. You're not just going to point me at him and shoot like I'm a cruise missile. I know you want to stay under the radar on this thing, but I need your knowledge and familiarity with this guy. We would need to work together to review intelligence and plan an attack. If I'm the muscle here, I'd need you to be the strategist and set up the actual event."

Candy nodded in agreement and a look of relief began to dawn on her face.

"Let's meet next week sometime for a planning session. Now, if you don't mind, I have some zoning documents I need to review before this evening."

"Tonight. We need to meet tonight. I'm afraid we'll miss an opportunity if we wait any longer to review details and strategize."

That seemed pretty fast to pull all this together. In fact, the whole thing seemed a bit fast and meticulously well planned. Like a carefully thought out game of chess. I began to suspect Candy had orchestrated this whole thing, vagrant guy and my dog and all.

I nodded in agreement. "Okay, let's meet at The Eastside Tavern tonight then. It's off Route 26, just a few miles east of here. Bring everything you have and we'll see what we come up with."

Candy indicated that she would be there tonight and left promptly.

I put my head in my hands. *How the hell am I going to kill an angel?* I'm assuming demons could. The wars had gone on for thousands of years and we'd managed to hold our own, so we must be able to take them out. Still, they'd killed every single one of us they'd encountered since the treaty. Not exactly good odds on my part. Then there was the pesky problem of getting away even if I'd managed to kill the damned thing and survive.

And Wyatt. Just when things were starting to get better between us, this had to happen. I'd never see him again. Even if I managed to sneak back over, it could be a hundred years or more. He'd be dead of natural causes if an angel didn't bring vengeance down on his head for knowingly associating with me before. I needed to let him know about this, show him where everything was for when I left and what to do if the angels came after him. He was just starting to come to terms with my being a demon, and now I needed to tell him about angels and werewolves. Great.

"Sam, your stupid dog just bit me. Do you think he's rabid? He did get bit by that bear or something. Please tell me you remembered to get him his shots this year."

I lifted my head and saw Wyatt coming around the corner of the house holding his hand. Boomer was trailing behind him looking smug. I jumped up and went to look at his hand.

"Crap, I'm so sorry. I had someone here for a business meeting and I asked Boomer to guard against intruders. He should have known that didn't mean you."

Actually, I wouldn't have liked Wyatt to hear the conversation between Candy and me, but I wasn't going to tell him that. I looked at his hand. Boomer hadn't even broken the skin. Even so, I looked over at the dog and sent a disciplinary burst of energy at him. It was the kind of thing we did to naughty children or household members who got out of line. Boomer yipped and looked at me with big hurt hound eyes.

"Bad dog. No biting Wyatt." I told him.

I looked up at Wyatt and realized that while I had been occupied with his wound and Boomer's discipline he was staring at me with raised eyebrows.

Oh, damn. I was naked.

"I was swimming in the pool and Candy just came by." I trailed off unsure what to say. "I didn't put on any clothes because she's a repressed tight ass and it was funny to freak her out. She doesn't swing that way."

His eyes roved over me with interest and my breath caught. I was still holding his hand. And I was naked.

"I totally forgot why I came over," he said in a rather distracted tone.

I sighed with regret. I was meeting Candy tonight and had to prepare. No time for sweaty heart-pounding sex right now. Hopefully later.

"I gotta meet Candy later tonight about a business deal," I told him, pulling away and throwing on my clothing. "Come with me. There's something important I need to show you."

We walked through the huge glass doors and past the kitchen into the living room. I grabbed his hand and pressed it against a photo of an old farmhouse sending a jolt of energy through the pair of us. I thought he would yelp, or at least flinch, but he just looked at me puzzled.

"This is my safe. I've just keyed it to you so you can open it. Go ahead and put your hand on the picture so I'm sure it works smoothly."

Wyatt placed his palm on the picture and it dissolved into a blur before an open space appeared in the wall.

"If I'm missing more than two weeks, check the safe. I'll have instructions for you and powers of attorneys along with directions on what to do with my assets. I'll also have a list of all my aliases and off shore accounts so you can safeguard them. I'll indicate some way in which I'll contact you."

"And why would you be missing more than two weeks?" Wyatt asked.

"I'll get to that in just a minute," I replied.

I showed him how to close the safe and make the picture reappear then led him over to a large mirror surrounded by cabochons. It looked very shabby chic.

"This is a communicator. It's sort of like Skype with an answering machine. Each of the cabochons represents someone I know, or a member of my household. The blue one here is a kind of 'other' indicator. The white one here is me. If you need to open the safe, take the mirror to your house. I'll light up the white one and try and contact you if I manage to jump a gate into home. All you need to do is touch the cabochon and it will work. If you touch the white one, it will try and contact me at home. Don't ever touch any of the other cabochons, even if they light up."

"The red one is glowing" Wyatt pointed at it.

I touched it to ignore.

"That's Dar, my foster brother. He's a pain in the ass and he calls me all the time. I never call him back."

"Why are you showing me this? What's wrong, Sam?" he asked. He was starting to get angry.

"I'm trusting you to take care of things, to cover for me and make it so I can come back if the shit hits the fan and I need to run for it."

"Sam, what are you into? This is not just some real estate deal with Candy is it? Are you in trouble? Involved with the Mafia or a gang? If you trust me enough to ask me to do this for you, then you need to trust me enough to let me know what you're involved in and what you're up against."

I planned on telling him everything. He needed to know everything so he could be safe.

"There are angels here. They are enemies of my kind. They kill us on sight and have no mercy when it comes to demons. I've been lying low for forty years, now, living as much as a human as I could to avoid detection, but that may have come to an end." I paused, wondering how much background he needed to know.

"Look, I kill zombies for a living, if you tell me an angel is after you, I'll believe you."

Wyatt seemed sincere, and concerned. I didn't realize killing zombies in a video game constituted making a living, but I could see that he was willing to suspend disbelief in this instance.

"Over two-and-a-half-million years ago, my people were

in a very long war with the angels. I don't know what life was like before the wars, but there seem to have always been differences between us and fighting between our races. In the end, there was a stalemate and we divided the realms between us. We demons live in Hel. The angels have the homeland, Aaru, and they also rule this world."

"Is Aaru like heaven?" Wyatt asked.

"I don't know," I told him. "The treaty forbids us from crossing into each other's territory. We take great joy in sneaking here to give the angels the finger before dashing back home, but no angels have ever tried to cross over to our world. We have no way to get into Aaru, otherwise we'd be sneaking over and playing ring and run there too. Anyway, if they catch us here, we're dead. No one has ever survived a fight with an angel. When it gets too hot, we get out of the kitchen. We cut and run. It's about to get really hot in my kitchen. I may have to leave, and I may not be able to return."

Wyatt looked grim.

"Does this have something to do with your meeting with Candy?"

I took a deep breath. He wasn't going to like this one bit.

"Candy is a werewolf and they are being exterminated by the angels. She has enlisted my help to kill one."

Wyatt looked up at the ceiling. I think he was beseeching his god for something.

"You just said no one has ever survived a fight with an angel. So isn't this rather suicidal?"

"I'm special," I replied.

"Special, like maybe stupid? Or reckless beyond all belief? Or with a death wish?" Wyatt was beginning to sound angry. He was right on a few of those points though.

"I don't have much choice, Wyatt. I killed one of them and now I owe the werewolves a service."

"This isn't service, this is suicide," he interrupted. "Tell them no."

"I've been exposed. They know who and what I am and have threatened to bring the angels to my door. I can't hide from them, they can identify me no matter what form I take. I'll never be able to return. This way at least I'll have a chance of staying, or coming back."

Wyatt shook his head, unconvinced. "No. Tell them no."

"If I do this, they'll cover for me, they'll run interference with the angels, they'll make it so I actually have a chance to stay here. Plus, they'll protect you. You're in danger from the angels, too."

"Just because we're friends?" Wyatt asked. "I thought angels were loving and forgiving. They'd really hunt me down and kill me just for being friends with you?"

I didn't want to let him know that I'd marked him. When I'd almost Owned him, I'd left enough of my signature on him that he was clearly identifiable as mine. He could have had a big fucking sign on his forehead and it would have been less noticeable.

"Angels are psychotic assholes," I told him. "They'll kill everyone who has associated with me." Not true, but it might make him feel better. Like he was in good company.

"Sam, how are you going to kill an angel and survive? You can't even stay on your horse."

"I've been locked down pretty tight in this world, so you don't realize the extent of my abilities. Besides Candy is calculating beyond belief. She's an information warehouse, and she's anal about details. I think with her dotting the 'I's and me exploding stuff, we'll make this work."

Wyatt stared at me. He was mad, and worried.

"I'm in on this. I'm coming with you."

"No fucking way. Absolutely not."

"I'm not staying back here like a swooning maiden, safe in

my house, while you ride off and battle angels. You're my best friend. No way you're going to do this without me." He looked me straight in the eye. "I'm not being your proxy unless you include me."

Humans were fragile. Soft and squishy. He'd get caught in the crossfire, he'd be in danger. Plus if an angel saw him with me, then they'd definitely connect the dots on our relationship. I didn't give a flying fuck if Candy got killed, but I couldn't bear the thought of Wyatt dead.

"Sam, the past two years that I've known you have been the best in my life. I should have abandoned my house and run screaming after Friday night, when you explained to me what you were and what kind of things you do to us humans. I know you'll probably eventually do that to me, too, and if I had any common sense I'd never see you again. But, you *are* my best friend. You make me feel alive, like I want to do crazy stuff. I want to do crazy stuff with you. I'm not leaving you to face this thing, friendless and alone."

We stood silent for what seemed like hours. This was beyond stupid, but I couldn't say no to Wyatt.

"Okay, you're in."

CHAPTER 9

I strolled into The Eastside Tavern and grabbed a quiet table out of the way. Some people appeared to have never left the place. Maybe they had a cot set up in the dry goods storage area for naps. The guy with the Rip Van Winkle beard was propping his chair against the wall in a corner and I truly don't think he moved since Friday night. The pretty leggy woman was playing pool this time. I guess there were regulars and there were super regulars here.

I figured Candy for a prompt kind of woman, so I had come a bit early to scope out the place and make sure I grabbed a private table. That way no one would hear us discussing killing angels and think we needed guys in the padded van to come haul us away. Wyatt was to come in a few moments after she arrived. I wasn't sure she'd come in if she saw me sitting with him, so he was back in the banquet area socializing with the staff. As soon as I had plopped into a chair, a waitress sat a cold shot of vodka in front of me and beamed at me happily.

"My name is Kelly, and I'll be taking care of you tonight."

I looked at the waitress. She had to have been over two

hundred fifty pounds with light blonde hair in a pony tail and smooth glowing porcelain skin. She was really pretty, and I thought it was unfortunate for her that fashion right now did not favor a generous build. I wondered what "taking care of" encompassed. Back home, that phrase would have meant she was mine to do whatever I wanted with for the evening, but here those things would be frowned upon. Pity, because I found her very attractive.

She smiled at me expectantly, glancing alternately between my face and the vodka encouraging me to drink it up. The older woman behind the bar was nodding and smiling too. I felt like one of those celebrities in a foreign country that have to eat the raw pig's testicles or they'd insult their host. I wasn't fond of the lemon vodka they'd brought me, but at least it was cold. I raised it in a toast to the woman behind the bar and threw it down as fast as I could. Ugh. Nasty.

"Can I get a Bud Light?" I croaked resisting the urge to suck down my water. I remembered asking for cold vodka before, but I can't believe the bartender would have remembered. She'd barely acknowledged my presence. Of course, I had left with Wyatt, and he seemed to be a bit of a favorite son around here. He must have called ahead for them to have had it chilled like this. It was such a sweet, thoughtful thing to do; I was astounded.

"I'll bring you a piece of cherry pie too. It's homemade," the waitress said before hustling off.

Cherry pie and Bud Light? Maybe she would bring a cup of coffee too and I could have a Twin Peaks déjà vu moment. Where was Agent Cooper when you needed him? Or the log lady. Bet she could kick some angel ass.

My waitress was just putting down my beer and pie when Candy arrived. She raised her eyebrows at the combo putting a large tote bag stuffed with papers on the seat beside her.

"Please bring my friend a slice of cherry pie and a cup of coffee black as midnight on a moonless night." I told the waitress waving my fork majestically as if I were issuing a royal proclamation. Candy shook her head no at the waitress and sent her away without ordering anything.

The werewolf didn't appear to get the reference, which was a shame. Wyatt might, but he'd been a bit young for Twin Peaks. And speak of the devil, there he was in his worn Levis and t-shirt sliding in the chair beside me.

"Look, Wyatt," I said excitedly. "They have cherry pie. You must have some with coffee black as midnight on a moonless night."

Wyatt looked for a second like he thought I'd gone insane.

"I can call you Agent Cooper?" I prodded. "We'll discuss the Laura Palmer case?"

He finally smiled. "Will the log lady be joining us? She was my favorite."

I squealed in delight and planted a kiss right on his lips almost knocking him backwards off his chair in my enthusiasm. Sexy as hell, familiar with cult TV classics, and he arranged to have cold vodka for me. Wyatt rocked. Life would be just horrible without him.

Meanwhile, Candy was looking as if she'd stepped into another universe.

"What is *he* doing here?" she asked, regaining her composure.

"Wyatt will be joining us in our adventures," I told her. She opened her mouth to protest and I told her "my kill, my rules."

That shut her mouth. She glared at Wyatt as he stuffed his backpack under his chair.

"Fine." She dug in her bag, pulling out a stack of glossies and a little box-shaped magnifying glass. "These are photos of the last twenty kills, with ascending order numbers, locations, and dates on them. I didn't include any of the earlier ones. Althean's kills from five years ago back were pretty routine. Basically for offenses against the existence contract like attempting to breed outside our species, assuming wolf form in front of humans or outside the dates specified, not registering, living in a non-designated area without approval, congregating in groups larger than ten without special dispensation, etc."

I was appalled. Who'd agreed to this shitty existence contract? No way would I have put up with that restrictive crap.

"Althean tended to execute in the traditional manner back then, too," Candy continued. "They'd have a tiny wing mark on their forehead as a warning and notice of the justice delivered. As you can see by the photos, the kills have become bloody, and the victims are being genetically altered before death."

If I'd been a werewolf, my ears would have perked up at that one. I didn't think angels could do that. I didn't think any but our kind could do that.

"The DNA markers that indicate loupism, or werewolf species, are removed and replaced with strictly human ones. He is basically turning them human, either before or after killing them."

"They still have the wing marks on their foreheads," I noted.

Candy nodded.

"They mark the victims as deserving of death, of violating the contract in some way," she said. "By marking them, Althean is showing that he believes they truly should die. That his actions are justified."

Why would he turn them human, though? What was the purpose in that?

If this were indeed a genocide, if this angel thought the

whole werewolf species should be wiped out, then I doubted he'd turn them human *before* killing them. Then he'd just be killing a human, plus he'd be removing them from his scope of control. No, I was pretty sure that turning them human happened after their death. But even then, why? Were they such an abomination that even their dead bodies should not be allowed to litter the earth? That all the markers of their species should be removed, to eventually wipe out all trace that they even existed?

I looked at the pictures as Wyatt peered over my arm. They were professionally developed and I wondered if Candy had a photo finishing lab in her basement. I envisioned her stopping in Walmart to pick the gory prints up and snickered.

Candy looked offended, no doubt thinking I found the crime scene photos funny. I didn't care.

"Okay, so what do these people all have in common? They are mostly female, but no one under twenty years old to date it seems. They are from all over the country. Could they have committed the same offense?" I asked.

Candy shook her head. "I can't see that they have anything in common beyond their species."

I frowned. This angel couldn't be just randomly roving around the country killing werewolves. If he were human, I'd suspect the killing locations coordinated with business travel. Maybe we could access the angel's travel itinerary for the next few weeks.

"Any ideas?" I asked Wyatt.

He reached into the backpack under his chair and pulled out one of those tablet computers. I'd seen them in the stores and they looked very cool, but I wasn't sure what I'd do with one. Wyatt swept his fingers over the screen and there was an amazing blur of boxes, shapes and colors. He tapped at the screen, and then waved his fingers around some more. Like Merlin. Without the hat.

"Okay," he said turning the tablet so we could all see it. "I've plotted the last twenty years of werewolf kills against this map and loaded the details into a statistical program. I know twenty years is way outside our window, but a big sample is critical when trending. The bigger the data set, the more accurate the predictions are."

I stared at him. What the fuck? How did my lawn-mowing, eye-candy, neighbor turn into a math geek?

The map was a mess of colored dots, more concentrated in some areas than others. I couldn't make sense of it at all. It reminded me of those ink blot tests. Was it a butterfly? Maybe, a polka dotted phallus? Candy glanced at the map, and then glared at Wyatt.

"Did you hack into my computer and get this?"

Wyatt looked smug.

"Your smart phone communicates with your network, no doubt to synchronize your appointment schedule. I just pulled the network IP address, impersonated your cell phone to get a toe in, and *voila*!"

Whoa. Wyatt did more than kill zombies in his spare time.

"I have passwords, and firewalls! I paid a lot of money to an expert for security from this kind of breach," Candy said, more angry at her security dude than Wyatt.

"Yeah, it looks like Barrett's work," Wyatt commented. "He talks a good line, but he sucks. If his dad wasn't connected he wouldn't get any work at all. I know one company who hired him because they wanted to get in good with his dad, then promptly replaced the whole system. Go with Edmonds Smythe next time. I can still get through, but it will take me a lot more than ten seconds."

"I might go with you, next time," she said to Wyatt.

I admired her ability to take a hit to her pride and move on. And Wyatt was proving to be very useful. Useful beyond moral support and hopefully good sex.

"We have restrictions around where we can live, mainly to keep us from forming large groups and becoming a threat," Candy said, returning her attention to the map. "In cities, we're allowed a greater density. We need to be especially careful in urban areas to avoid detection and a violation of the existence contract. In wide open spaces, we'd be more likely to formulate rebellion and go undetected since we wouldn't need to restrict ourselves so much."

Clearly, the angels liked the werewolves to be confined to the cities, outside their preferred habitat. So they must have been more worried about organized action than public safety. If the angels had been concerned about protecting humans, they would have rounded up all the werewolves and stuck them in some remote area. Like a werewolf concentration camp. Interesting.

"Does the map of the kills reflect the overall distribution of werewolves?" Wyatt asked.

Candy looked again and nodded.

"It seems to. An equal percentage of the population in each area, but of course, we'd need to run numbers just to make sure."

Wyatt turned the tablet back to face him, ran his fingers over it as we watched with bated breath. It took a few moments. I ate my pie and drank beer while he worked his magic. Finally he turned the tablet around. TaDa! The map had been replaced by a spreadsheet showing locations and numbers in descending order.

"Actually, there's a ten percent greater incidence of killing in the smaller cities and rural areas and a seventy percent greater incidence in North America."

Candy frowned at the tablet. "You would have needed to

know the address of every werewolf for that. That information is encrypted on a virtual server. Even I don't have full access."

Wyatt nodded. I was beyond being shocked by any of this. Wyatt was clearly not what he seemed, either.

"Yes, I know. Now if we plot just the kills with the genetic alteration, we see that at this point they are all in North America. Connect them in their order of occurrence and you do begin to see a pattern. If I run a regression analysis and plot that on our map, we can see a prediction of future hits somewhere along this line. Then, I'll just run a second regression on the timeline pattern and it will tell us where in this predictive line he is likely to be by certain dates. If we select where we're interested, I can try and narrow it down with some statistical probability."

I looked at Candy to see if she was understanding any of that. Nope. We'd both been staring at Wyatt as if he'd suddenly began speaking in a strange alien language. I, for one, was turned on as hell. Wyatt was proving to be rather smart for a human. Who knew?

"Why would he kill in this pattern?" Candy asked.

I shrugged. "Angels are really weird about patterns and things weighting out to a neutral state. Who knows why they do these things."

"This accounts for location and timeline," Wyatt continued, "but we still need motive and any other commonality in the victims to better predict his next hit."

"Tell us, oh mighty Oz," I said. "Who will the angel kill next and where? And can I have a heart too, if it's not too much trouble."

He shot me an annoyed glance, then peered at the screen.

"With what we've got so far, I'm betting in the next five to ten days we'll see a hit among this cluster of forty werewolves. If we combine them into household groups, we've got twenty-eight households we need to look at."

"We need to narrow that down," I said, looking at Candy.

It wasn't just the numbers that were an issue, either. Even if we got some indication that there was a kill in progress, we wouldn't get there in time to catch him. We'd need to be pretty confident on a target, then do some kind of stake out. The prospect of sitting outside a house for five to ten days was frightening. Torture would be preferable. I'd be bored beyond belief. I'd be lucky to last a few hours before I went stark raving mad. I wished we could just track the guy down and kill him in a sneak attack.

"I'll dig around and see what else I can do to get a profile on the victims," Candy said sorting through the pictures. "That's the York/Lancaster area, so at least we don't have to go flying halfway across the country to test our hypothesis."

Candy gathered up her pictures, casting another dark look at Wyatt and his tablet, then told me she'd call me in the morning. After she left, Wyatt snuck a bite of my cherry pie and made approving noises while I mulled things over.

"You're a whole hell of a lot more useful than Candy," I told him with admiration. "You've been holding back on me. I thought all you did was kill zombies."

Wyatt shrugged. "You never asked, never really seemed interested in any of the computer stuff I do, so I didn't bother."

I peered at him to see if he was hurt, or angry. He seemed rather cheerful, eating my pie and relaxing back in his chair.

"It's probably the most boring thing I've ever heard in my life," I confessed. "But I'm glad you know all that stuff. It'll probably keep me from getting killed. Thank you for coming."

I meant it. I was glad Wyatt was here. He might get hurt, but everything was a lot more fun when he was around.

Wyatt smiled and saluted me with his fork.

"You are welcome, Sam. I'd do anything to help you out."

Wyatt polished off the rest of the pie.

"Why would an angel suddenly decide to go on a killing spree?" I asked, half to myself. "To begin a genocide? I'm pretty sure they didn't even really want *us* exterminated during the war. They just wanted us to abide by some crazy list of rules. If we'd complied, we would have been in the same spot as the werewolves, but I can't see them offing us just for the heck of it."

"I can't see you or any of your kind complying with those types of rules," Wyatt said, pushing the empty plate away.

"Oh no. Totally against our nature. They were insane even to demand it. If there hadn't been the treaty and the division of the realms, the wars would have only stopped with the extermination of one or both of our races."

I went back to pondering this particular angel. "The genetic alteration thing bothers me, too. That's not something angels do. Plus, the bloodiness of the kills doesn't seem in keeping with them either."

"So, maybe he's not an angel supremacist trying to rid the world of werewolves and preserve the master race. Maybe something happened to him that sent him off the edge of what angels view as acceptable. Maybe he's got something making him crazy, turning him un-angel. Or uber angel."

Or rogue angel, I thought.

CHAPTER 10

It was about four in the morning when my ringing phone woke me up.

"He's hit again. York. Time of death between midnight and three-thirty that we can tell."

Candy, I thought rubbing sleep and gunk from my eyes.

"Two victims this time. A husband and wife. I've asked the local pack to secure the scene until we get up there to look at it. They've already done their sniffing around, but your skills may be able to find something beyond our ability."

"Are you up there now? Do I meet you, or do we ride together?" I asked, still groggy.

"I'll head up there now. If you can meet me up there as soon as you can, I'd like you to check everything while it's still relatively fresh. Besides, the local guys really do need to start cleanup soon, before neighbors notice anything."

York was about a two hour drive. I took down the address, writing it on my pillowcase since I can never seem to find a pad of paper when I need one. Then I quickly called Wyatt and threw on some clean clothes. A shower would have to wait. Wyatt was just coming up the drive when I emerged from my seldom-used front door. He raised his eyebrows a bit at the pillow case I was carrying, but didn't comment.

I wasn't a morning person, but this was the kind of morning to make me want to change my habits. The normal nighttime din of insects had quieted, replaced by early bird-song. It was still fully dark, but there was an expectation of light, an anticipation hovering on the eastern horizon. Everything seemed to be suspended, teetering right on the edge of daybreak. On a razor's edge of becoming. Even Boomer, standing at the corner of the house watching us, seemed to be in transition. As if he were two different beings, one day and one night, on the verge of transformation.

We drove north, taking back roads to Route 15, with Wyatt sleepily navigating through his cell phone GPS. The sun came up with orange and red over the little farmhouses and fields. It was pretty much just us, the early morning commuters, and the cement truck drivers from the plant, although there were signs the dairy farmers had been up earlier. Huge milking barns, long and flat, were lit up brightly before the first rays reached up over the horizon.

We'd made a quick stop at a 7-11 for some coffee and Wyatt grumbled. He was grumpy and the beauty of the morning was lost on him. Evidently, zombie killing last night hadn't gone well, and he'd not had much sleep. He complained repeatedly that he was tired, hungry and hated 7-11 coffee. I was ready to dump his coffee over his head if he didn't shut up about it. I may be a vodka snob, but I'm not a coffee snob. And I don't bitch and moan constantly when I don't get my preferred vodka. Well, maybe just a little. When I got tired of listening to him complain, I pointedly turned on the radio. I had thought about finding some soft rock just to annoy him further, but instead put on blue collar comedy. Wyatt was more fun when he was in a better mood.

The sun was up and Thurmont was stirring with the beginnings of their country rush hour as we passed through toward the highway. Wyatt saw a Sheetz and insisted on stopping, pointedly dumping his previous coffee into the bushes as he walked in. I bought another coffee, too, just so I could compare them. I couldn't tell the difference. They both tasted like cheap generic coffee prepared hours ago and slowly burning on the bottom of the pot ever since.

This area of Maryland was really beautiful. Green-covered mountains flanked the highway, separated from the road by flat acres of fields. Signs indicating directions for various national parks, orchards, and historic attractions didn't detract from the stunning morning view. Route 15 was a scenic route north of Thurmont. Mountains all along the horizon were the backdrop for miles of forests and picturesque farms. The occasional fruit orchard, with the requisite roadside stand, and its manicured, geometrically arranged trees dotted our view.

The coffee seemed to be rousing Wyatt from his sleepy state because just over the Pennsylvania line he looked in surprise at his phone GPS and at the highway marker.

"Why are we going this way to York? Why didn't we go 70 up to 83? It would have been much shorter."

"Rush hour up 70 into Baltimore? And 83? That's even worse. That road sucks when it's *not* rush hour. I'd rather take the back roads and risk getting behind a tractor or some slow poke."

Wyatt fussed over his GPS, not convinced.

"No, Sam, this is really taking us out of our way. We could have gone through Westminster up 27, then through Hanover on 94 if you wanted to take the back roads. We would have gotten there much quicker."

"94 goes smack through downtown Hanover. There are a ton of lights, truck traffic that takes forever each time they stop to try to get back up to speed, and there are two railroad crossings. Two. There is a stupid train taking fucking forever every time I go through there." There was an Utz factory outlet there, though. I had a terrible weakness for Grandma Utz potato chips. They'd be closed this early in the morning, though.

"Even so, we'd save a ton of time going 94. Hanover would put us so much closer to York than this roundabout route."

"I'm not really comfortable going through Hanover, right now," I said.

Wyatt glared at me in suspicion. "You weren't the one who burned down the Hot and Spicy Burger, were you? I really liked that place. Was it an accident, or did they somehow get on your naughty list? Maybe they didn't put enough salsa on your burger?"

"I did not burn down the Hot and Spicy Burger," I protested. "I've never even been there and I don't just go around randomly setting fire to places. At least not on purpose," I added in the spirit of truthfulness.

I really didn't feel like explaining that I'd set loose a couple of those huge holiday inflatable lawn decorations this past Christmas and bounced them down 94 at rush hour. There were a lot of people that probably still remembered me. Especially the ones who'd wrecked their cars. It was so funny, though. Big inflatable Santa flying into the road and cars swerving everywhere. I've totally got to do that again, sometime. Maybe Halloween.

Wyatt looked unconvinced, but didn't pursue the topic further. He continued to pore over his phone, looking up as I exited the highway.

"You're joking with me, Sam. Route 30? You're going to haul down Route 30 from 15 to York? That's forty-five minutes on a good day. It's two lanes, cuts through every tiny town this side of the state line, and will be filled with tractors and hay wagons. What are you thinking of?"

"Do you want to drive? You're so full of knowledge, Mr. GPS, maybe you'd like to drive?" I exploded at him.

Wyatt looked at the interior of my Corvette with something akin to lust in his eyes.

"Yes, I do want to drive," he said.

"Well, you're not." I told him. No way Wyatt was driving my precious car. No one drove my Corvette but me. Only a select few were even allowed in the passenger seat.

We meandered our way down 30 to York with Wyatt complaining under his breath the whole way. I kept turning up the radio volume, but it never seemed to sufficiently drown out his complaints.

I did need his navigation skills once we reached the York city limits, and Wyatt quickly guided me through the outskirts of town to a series of new housing developments. We went past all the gorgeous new homes toward the back, where an older section with fully grown trees hid.

The houses were built in the 70s; row upon row of split-level ranchers and bungalows filled the streets. They were all variations on an identical theme, with their reversed layout and different-colored siding. We parked a couple blocks down so we didn't draw attention to the crime scene. Nothing like an expensive gray Corvette in the driveway to make the neighbors take notice and give everything away. Not that I was the master of stealth. I insisted on driving around the neighborhood nearly five times before I found a place I felt reasonably safe in leaving my car. Wyatt was ready to strangle me. The two-hour car ride early in the morning obviously hadn't done much for his patience.

The house looked pretty much like all the other houses. A split-level ranch with brick on the lower, partially underground level, and white siding on the rest. There was a carport off to the side of the house with a compact sedan parked in it. The house had been loved. The shutters and door were shiny with fresh green paint, and well-maintained begonias hung invitingly in baskets at the edge of the small roof covering the entryway. Carefully edged and mulched beds with newly planted, tiny boxwoods lined the path to the door. The mailbox by the edge of the driveway was cleverly shaped like a windmill and looked recently installed.

Candy met us at the side door, under the carport, her face grim.

"What on earth took you so long?" she asked.

Wyatt gave me a pointed look, but for once remained silent.

We followed her through a small pantry and into the kitchen and dining room area on the upper level of the house. The kitchen had a skillet soaking in the sink, and fresh coffee in the pot. The smell was heavenly. I wondered if Candy had made it when she got here. Thoughtful, but I didn't think you were supposed to make yourself at home in the kitchens of crime scenes.

"It's set to brew automatically at six in the morning," Candy said, noticing my glance. "Looks like all was calm at dinner, and they would have filled the coffee maker and set it right before going to bed, I assume."

The dining room was undisturbed with fresh flowers at the center of the gleaming oak table, and car keys casually tossed into a dish on the matching oak sideboard. We walked past the stairs leading to the lower floor and the front door and headed toward the bedrooms.

"They were killed downstairs, but I want you to see the bedrooms first." Candy noted in a strained voice.

There were three bedrooms. One had been converted into an office and the other appeared to be a child's bedroom. A baby's bedroom so immaculate and organized it looked like Candy herself had staged it. The crib had elephant themed sheets and bumper pad, and a parade of elephants hung from the mobile above it. Wooden elephant cutouts in bright colors danced along one wall. A glider rocker sat against the other with a bookshelf beside it. Stuffed animals were artfully arranged in the crib and along the shelves next to scores of books.

"I thought you said there were two victims," I asked Candy. "What happened to the baby?"

"I didn't know until I got here," Candy said, struggling to keep her voice neutral. "The female was pregnant. Very pregnant. So, really, there were three victims."

My kind breed a lot. It's not uncommon to have over a thousand offspring. Of course, a huge percentage of those never make it past infancy, let alone into adulthood. We don't have any agony over the mortality rate. We don't raise our children or have any kind of familial bond with them. We just form them, and hand them over into a kind of group home for their upbringing. There is no lengthy pregnancy, and once you hand them over you never bother to find out whether they survive, what they turn out to be like, nothing like that at all. We just don't really do the children thing.

At home, there was no particular taboo against killing young, or killing a parent who was in the process of forming an unborn child. This was definitely a terrible crime to angels, though. Did he know she was pregnant? Did he care? Genocide was one thing, but killing a baby, even an unborn one? How could he have done such a thing, violated the precious code the angels live by and get away with it? We get cut down for far less by them.

Wyatt and Candy appeared to be giving the room a moment of silence, so I went across the hall to the master bedroom. The queen-sized bed had the comforter turned down, and one side was slightly rumpled, with the sheets aside. Someone had gone to bed briefly, and then gotten up. I was guessing the female.

"Does it look like she hurried out here?" I asked Candy as she and Wyatt came into the room. "Do you think she heard something going on in the basement and ran to check?"

Candy went over to the bed and looked at it carefully. She pointed to the bedside table where a set of reading glasses and a thick pregnancy guide lay.

"It doesn't look like she raced out of here in any hurry," she said. "Everything looks carefully placed. Glasses on top of the book. Book marked at a spot and placed evenly on the table. If she hurried, I'd expect to see the sheets pulled from the bed a bit and dangling on the edge, and the book tossed aside."

I thought about this as we went downstairs. Had her husband been quietly dead before she went down? Had she surprised the killer and he had no choice but to kill her too? Or had the killer waited for both of them to be together before he made his move?

I expected downstairs to be a bloodbath and I wasn't disappointed. The room itself is what you would expect to see. Couch. Two comfy chairs. Coffee table. TV. There was also a small desk with a laptop on it.

The guy was sprawled on the floor by the laptop. He looked like a human. A human with his head twisted backward and his torso sliced open from sternum to pelvis. The guy didn't have a shirt on, and his sweatpants were sliced at the drawstring waist where the cut extended. The blood appeared to be localized in a pool around him. Not sprayed all over the walls or on the ceiling. I walked carefully around to look at his face. His head was turned at an abnormal degree, the neck clearly broken. Blood had seeped out his nose and mouth. His expression looked placid. He had a pale set of angel wings on his temple, like a birthmark.

"Looks to me like he may have been killed before he was even aware there was someone in the room," I told Candy, wanting her opinion on the matter.

She nodded. "If an angel showed up unannounced in his house, he'd have been partially transformed. It would have been an immediate, instinctual thing. He was clearly dead before he had time to realize the angel was here."

"Maybe he thought it was a friendly visit? If an angel knocked on your door, would you invite him in and serve him tea?" I asked Candy. "Would you automatically think you were in danger? Especially if you hadn't done anything wrong?"

Candy shook her head. "If he'd knocked on the front door, the kitchen and dining area would show signs of late hospitality. He would have put a shirt on out of respect. And she wouldn't look like that." Candy pointed to the figure crumpled against the front wall of the room.

Wow, I thought walking over to the female. This had been a struggle. There was blood sprayed in arcs all around her and over the sofa. A huge smear of blood started high up on the wall, almost at the ceiling, and dragged down to the floor. I couldn't see much of her without touching her, but the heap of pajama clad flesh was torn and burned all over. Claws curled from massive hands, inexplicably at the end of delicate wrists. I saw a pretty white gold chain bracelet with an initialed heart charm and a tiny baby shoe attached.

I turned to Candy. "If it's okay, I need to move the bodies and better examine them."

She nodded, looking at the female werewolf with glassy eyes. Her lips twitched even as she clamped her teeth into them to hold them still. I looked at her and did the math. She looked to be mid-fifties. She'd clearly had at least one child, probably more from what I saw of her body the other day. Her kids would be the age of this young couple. Maybe she was expecting a grandchild. I don't know why her distress bothered me, but it did.

Wanting to give Candy a moment to pull herself together, I asked her to go upstairs and get me a towel. I would probably need one anyway to wipe the blood off myself. She headed up, passing Wyatt on the way as he came down.

"Wow," he said surveying the scene. My thoughts exactly. "I haven't had a chance to look at the computer upstairs, yet. I thought I'd come down here first," he told me.

I nodded over at the laptop. "There's one down here, too. I'm thinking the guy was on it when he was killed."

He looked at the body blocking access to the small desk. "As soon as you clear that aside, I'll take a look at the laptop."

Okay, game time. I removed my clothes, but unlike Candy, just flung them over a chair in a relatively clean corner. Candy came down with a towel and skidded to a halt at the bottom of the stairs.

"*Why* are you naked?"

"I only have the one set of clothes and I don't want to be walking around in blood-soaked clothes all day." Or get it all over my Corvette's seats. "What did you think?"

Candy had the grace to look embarrassed. "Sorry," she muttered.

I thought I'd start with the guy first. I went over to him and removed his sweatpants and boxers. His genitals were intact. The cut ended a good three inches above the pelvic bone. It didn't look like it was done for torture or need to access the organs, which were all there. Why had the angel slit him down the middle like this? The neck breaking action had clearly happened first, and had caused the werewolf's death. Maybe there had been an interruption before the angel could do what he intended with the organs?

I ran my fingers through the body and sent out feathers of energy to explore. There was no energy in it beyond the normal energy that all matter carried. I could feel the DNA signature of the werewolf with its odd mutation. All the other kills had been altered and turned basically human. Why had this one been left werewolf? The angel must have been interrupted before he could finish.

I couldn't feel anything of the angel until I ran my fingers along the burnt edges of the skin. There. There was an energy signature with a faint personal energy note. This hadn't been a weapon, or claws or teeth. The cut had been made by a burning energy, but it wasn't just used to cut the flesh, it was used to explore the victim. Once something is dead, we usually don't mess much with it, so this finding was perplexing. Why would the angel want to explore the werewolf after his life essence left? Why didn't he just do the DNA conversion and hit the road? Was this part of the process he needed to do for the DNA conversion?

I gripped the victim's head on either side, sending feathers into the brain. No one was home, but the brain was intact and free of any angelic energy signature. The angel hadn't been looking for memories. I searched through the circuitry of the connectors in the brain, checking to see if I could access any remnant of the guy's last thoughts. I'm not very good with brains, so I wasn't sure I could gain anything by this or not. I could only find a relaxed sense of comfort. Well, at least he'd died in peace.

Reaching up a finger, I grazed the wing marks on his temple and the energy signature poured into me. Gotcha. This was strong. Very strong. I'd recognize him. I'd have a good chance of sensing him if he was anywhere in a mile or two radius from me and used his energy. Adrenaline flooded me. Fuck, I loved a good hunt. This was the best feeling ever. Better than sex even.

I rolled the body over, away from the desk so Wyatt could reach the laptop. There was nothing at all on his backside. And I checked it very thoroughly just to annoy Candy.

"It was an angel, not an alien," she told me. "I don't think anal probes were involved."

"Best to check," I told her cheerfully, my mind furiously working the angel's energy signature and locking it into my memory.

"I'm done," I told Wyatt as I moved to the female, carefully wiping my hands on the towel Candy gave me. Wyatt leaned over the blood soaked carpet, and carefully picked up the laptop, stretching the cord to a clean spot.

I looked at the female and wondered where to begin. I lay her face down first. Peeling off her shirt, I noticed her back side was surprisingly clean of cuts and burns. She didn't run, didn't turn her back on him, I thought with admiration. There was a significant hole in the back of her head though, with a great volume of blood streaked down her hair and soaking her shirt back.

I stuck my finger in the hole and realized that it was about the size of my index finger in diameter and jagged as if something had been shoved in and dragged upward and out. I looked up the wall, up the blood smear to the round splat near the ceiling. Too high. Grabbing the chair from the desk, I dragged it over and stretched as far as I could. There was a huge nail protruding from the wall. A hefty ten penny nail, which must have originally held some type of heavy artwork. It must have been in the wall pretty tight as it hadn't been removed, and had been painted over. Now it was red with blood. Okay, he was strong enough to pick her up and pitch her high up against the wall where she smacked her skull on the nail and slide down in a trail of blood.

Hopping off the chair, I rolled her over to see the front. Now, this was where the action was. Her hands were massive claws, and her snout extended slightly to accommodate strong pointed teeth the size of my thumbs. Her lips curled up in a snarl and her eyes, even in death, were fierce. She had a burn-edged slice across her right cheek and nose. Her neck and legs were covered in the same burned slices. The huge bulge of her belly was untouched. Interesting. It was as if the angel didn't want to target the area where the baby was. I examined the wounds. They were not terribly deep, but one on her leg had severed her femoral artery. Game over, girlfriend.

Looking at the blood on her claws, I ran my finger over them. I'd never had an angel genetic signature before, since normally I'd be dead if I ever got that close to one. I was kind of surprised to get one from the claws. I'd expected that they'd fought from a distance and she'd not been able to actually cut him. I caught my breath as I processed the unusually long DNA chain. It was the same as the one I carried. Outside of markers for personal characteristics, we had the same DNA. I'd expected them to be vaguely similar. Our races had formed about the same time, and we had some overlap in skills and abilities, but I hadn't expected this nearly carbon copy. How ironic, given our past. I looked up at Candy. Wyatt was furiously typing away on the laptop in a corner of the room.

"I'm thinking the angel came in and surprised the male while his back was turned breaking his neck. I'm conjecturing, but I think he placed the angel mark on the male's forehead, then proceeded to slice the cut in his abdomen with his energy. I'm assuming it's part of that genetic modification he is doing. He didn't get that far before he was surprised by the female. The victims don't have the genetic alteration, so the angel left in a hurry before he could complete the job."

Candy nodded and I turned to face the pregnant body on the floor.

"She interrupted the angel, who shot her at a distance,

taking some care not to cut her where the baby was." I waved at the splatter of blood on the walls and couch. "Those cuts were rather superficial. I think he probably didn't know how to subdue her and get away without causing her and the baby's death. She approached him and actually got her claws on him. He was injured, but I don't know how badly, and he's probably healed himself by now. When she clawed him, he sliced her legs, then grabbed her and threw her against the wall."

I walked over and pointed my finger at the line of blood-soaked carpet. "He hit her femoral artery, and she bled profusely. It flew across the room as he threw her against the wall." I pointed to the wall, near the ceiling. "She impacted with her head against a large nail, up there, and slid down the wall. But it was the cut to her leg that killed her. She couldn't lose much blood with a fetus, and she'd lost too much by the time she hit the wall."

Candy nodded. "That's what the werewolves who were here earlier thought, too."

"I don't think he intended to kill her," I said. "I think he meant to kill the male, and head out without her knowing. Not that that makes him a saint," I added hastily. "He's killed other women by your records, just not any children or pregnant women, which follows their code somewhat. I don't know what peace of mind it will give you, but I honestly don't think he meant to kill either her or her baby."

Candy looked thoughtful. "Is there anything else here we need to see? Do you have enough to maybe track and find Althean?"

"I've got his energy signature, so I think I'm done here," I said slowly, looking at the wing marks on the female's temple.

As an afterthought I ran my finger over them. It would be the same as on the guy since I already had the angel's energy signature. Shocked at what I felt, I jumped about a foot across the room and toppled over on my ass with enough speed to make Candy and Wyatt jump, too.

"There was a second angel," I said in amazement.

Candy stared at me while Wyatt looked off in the distance toward the bookcase with a slight frown on his face.

"The energy signature on this wing mark is completely different from the one on the guy. Two angels were here," I insisted.

"Is the blood from the first angel or the second?" Candy said, her brows knitted in concentration. "Could one angel have killed the guy, left, then another came here, did the weird abdomen cut, then was surprised and killed the female?"

"I don't know," I replied slowly. "I have the DNA signature off the blood on the claws of the female, but that's different from energy signatures. I can't tell whether the blood DNA belongs to the first or second angel." I was so frustrated. I thought I had it all, and here was that big old monkey wrench.

"Let's just watch the video," Wyatt said from over by the bookshelves. He was holding a small round device. "It's a security camera. I have these at my house. This one is active right now and feeding to the computer up in the office."

Jackpot!

CHAPTER 11

Up the stairs we went, with Candy carrying my clothing and trying several times to encourage me to put them back on. Just to irritate her, I ignored her motions and continued to walk around buck naked.

Wyatt quickly overcame the passwords on the upstairs computer and we watched six grainy black and white boxes of video displaying boring images of people walking about, eating, watching TV. The majority of the recording time was just empty blank rooms. Wyatt sectioned out and expanded the downstairs camera, but the resolution was horrible blown up. He reduced it to a more clear size and zipped through the time code stamp on the lower corner of the image. At nine in the evening, the female werewolf clicked off the TV, kissed the male who was on the laptop and said some indecipherable words to him before heading up the stairs.

"The audio on these cameras is horrible, so I don't think we're going to know what they are saying," Wyatt said.

Wyatt fast forwarded slowly until a few minutes after ten, when the male werewolf looked like he was ready to get up.

He stood and stretched a bit, then sat down to do a few more things on the laptop.

"Based on the laptop record, he was just doing some random surfing. News site, clicked on a few links, nothing noteworthy," Wyatt pointed out.

Hmm, no illicit porn surfing, snuff videos, or werewolf revolutionary front chat rooms. I didn't see where this guy could possibly have violated the admittedly strict existence contract. He was squeaky clean, from what I could tell.

A dark shape appeared quickly in the room. "Whoa," Wyatt said, freezing the screen and backing it up a frame at a time.

At ten twelve PM, a dark shape showed at the edge of the stairs, quickly, and silently, approached the werewolf from the rear, and snapped his neck with a smooth, clean motion. He had to have been amazingly strong to have done that, even with the element of surprise on his side. The werewolf fell back and sideways out of the chair as his body attempted to follow the movement of his head. We couldn't see the angel's face clearly from the poor quality of the picture and the angle of the camera, but it didn't matter to me. I had his energy signature; I didn't need to know what he looked like.

The angel paused, kneeling for some time beside the werewolf before bending down and placing his hand on the temple. A blur appeared around his hand and he withdrew it to stare at the body again.

"What is taking the stupid shit so long?" I muttered. "Does he want to get caught or something? I would have been halfway to Baltimore by now."

Finally, he reached down with a finger and a blaze of light traced the cut in the body's midsection. A scream bellowed out of the computer and we all jumped with hearts racing. The whole death had been silent, and I, for one, had forgotten that there was a soundtrack, no matter how shitty. The female werewolf stood at the bottom of the stairs.

Wyatt was forced to move frame by frame at this point to keep everything from being a blur of speed in real time. Crap, these people were fast, fast. The female had screamed, and simultaneously her claws and snout shot out as the angel whirled around, energy flaring. He lashed at her with energy bursts and moved to the side as if trying to push her away from the stairs. She held her location blocking the stairs, but advanced toward him and managed to rake him twice. Once across the face with her right, and a downward strike from his right shoulder with her left.

It was remarkable she'd been able to advance at all with the energy bursts he was tossing around. Reeling from the claw marks, the angel brought energy in a steady stream, a blade shape up from his left, slicing the deep fatal cut into her right thigh. Dissolving the blade, he grabbed the front of her shirt and flung her up against the wall as he dashed from the room and up the stairs. The rest of the video showed her frame by frame sliding down the wall to rest in a crumpled heap of spreading blood. Wyatt paused the video.

"One angel killed them both," he said.

"Yes, but he ran out before she had hit the wall. I wonder if he even knew he'd killed her?" I mused. "And where is the second angel? There is a second angel." I insisted.

Wyatt fast forwarded the video and for a few speeded up seconds we saw the blood pool expand across the carpet, then a whole lot of nothing for hours. Finally, as the time clock showed around one in the morning, a blurred figure appeared.

"Whoa, there he is!" I shouted. As if I was the only one who noticed.

Wyatt backed up the video and we saw the angel descend the stairs to stop at the bottom and scan the room. He was tall and built like a bull. It looked to my eyes to be the same angel as in The Wine Room.

"Do they all look alike? Because I'm thinking that is the one from the bar earlier this week." I asked Candy.

Wyatt paused the video and looked up. "What do you mean 'the one from the bar earlier this week'? You told me you had an angel after you, but you didn't tell me you had seen one up close and personal."

"No, they don't all look alike, although they have similarities," Candy explained. She turned to Wyatt. "That's Gregory," she said pointing to the screen. "He's the angel that kills any demons who cross into this world. We saw him last Friday at The Wine Room."

Wyatt glared at me. He was pissed that I'd neglected to tell him that particular detail when I'd let him know that angels were after me. I felt guilty and it was a weird feeling. I knew what guilt felt like. The humans I owned had all felt guilt many times in their lives, and I had all their memories and feelings stored within me. I didn't like feeling guilty, myself. I'd really been wearing this human form too long and leaning too heavily on human memories. Why would I tell him? It's not like he could do anything to help me out. He'd just worry and do some stupid human macho thing that would get him killed. I didn't know what to say.

Wyatt stared long enough for me to feel even more uncomfortable, then turned around and resumed the video. Gregory walked over to the male victim and looked at him carefully without touching him. He shook his head, but it was hard to read his expression from the poor quality of the tape. He walked over to the female and glanced up at the smear on the wall. Then he bent down over the female.

"Slow it down," I told Wyatt, leaning in. "Frame by frame."

The angel examined her wounds and ran a hand over her rounded belly, less than an inch from the surface. Checking the baby for life? In the slow motion of the frame by frame I saw him reach his other hand to her temple and a flash of light as he left the wing mark.

"Wait," I shouted to Wyatt. "Back it up one more frame." There. Was there a flash of light from his other hand too? I darted from the room and charged down the stairs to the bodies. Pressing my hand against the female's belly, I searched and searched and found. There. An energy signature. A mark of angel wings on the temple of the fetus' head.

Wyatt and Candy reached the downstairs just as I stood up. "He marked the baby," I told them, and I was feeling pretty outraged about it. "He put the angel wings on the baby's head. And on the female's. What the fuck? The mark is supposed to be a sign of guilt. He's covering it up. Althean fucked up and killed an innocent female and an unborn child, and Gregory covered it up by marking them as if they were guilty of a crime. How could an unborn child *ever* be guilty of a crime? It's against their creed."

"They are *all* innocent," Candy said indignantly. "Hundreds of kills in the past five years and we can't tell they've done anything wrong."

"Yes, but they can always twist the contract, find some tiny little detail somewhere to justify it. Nothing justifies this," I gestured to the pregnant female. "Is Gregory in on it, too? Or is he cleaning up Althean's mess and hoping to catch him and set him right before the other angels discover his misdeeds and come down on his head as the boss? Because with this, it's going to be a very short time before Althean finds himself in deep angel doo-doo."

We reviewed the rest of the video, but found nothing else beyond long stretches of no activity punctuated by the local werewolves and their investigative efforts, then us arriving. Wyatt took the laptop thinking he might find something in there that would have caused this couple to be a target, or even be on the angel's radar.

"Do you still have the information on your predictions?" I asked Wyatt. "That repression analysis you did?"

"Regression analysis. I'll add in this data and we should be able to narrow things down further. He's definitely moving faster. If we can identify one or two targets, we'll need to think about how we're going to handle it. Probably some kind of stake out, since alarms and such won't give us enough time to arrive all the way from Maryland and catch him in the act."

Stake out. The thought depressed me.

We drove to a nearby breakfast diner so Wyatt could run his registration analysis and we could all have Moons Over My Hammy with some much-needed coffee.

Candy and I were arguing over my supposedly excessive ketchup use on the hash browns, when Wyatt interrupted us by shoving his tablet in our faces.

"There," Wyatt said pointing at the map. "These three places are very close together and all within the modified predictive line. I'm worried about the timeline though. My model shows two to three days, but I don't have enough recent data points, and it could be as soon as tomorrow."

"Gettysburg," Candy said looking at the map. "Let's head there now, grab the closest hotel room to these three likely spots, and then hit the outlets for a couple changes of clothes and toiletries. We'll reconnaissance the spots today, well before we think the hit will be, then be ready tonight and tomorrow. We'll just pull this straight through. We really need to catch him this week, before his trajectory takes him further away from home and we have to deal with travel."

"Cool, we can go down Route 30," I told her. "It goes straight into Gettysburg."

Wyatt looked at me with disgust. "Not Route 30, again. We just crawled down there, and now we have to go back?"

"It is the quickest way to Gettysburg," Candy told him.

So back down Route 30 we went. Traffic wasn't quite as slow, but it was steady and crowded through all the tiny little towns. As we got closer in to Gettysburg, the small houses in various stages of neglect got closer together and became more interspersed with an eclectic array of businesses. There were used car lots, thrift shops, a sheet metal manufacturer, tile wholesaler, and, oddly, a gourmet tobacco store.

The modern houses gave way to restored Victorian homes as we entered the city limits, then majestic historic mansions and row houses as we entered downtown Gettysburg. The historic knickknack shops, coffee houses, inns, and restaurants enchanted me. Crowds of people peering at brochures choked the streets and sidewalks. At my insistence, we searched the downtown inns only to find that none had any vacancies. A helpful coffee house employee informed us that this was the height of their tourist season and we probably wouldn't find anything this close to the battlefield. He recommended we head back north out of town, closer to the highway, where some privately owned motels may have vacancies.

Hours later, we were tired and grumpy from the endless stream of 'no vacancy' signs when we finally found a place. It was fairly close to the houses we needed to investigate, but was by no means our first pick of sleeping quarters.

Our home away from home was one of those two-story locally owned motels popular fifty years ago. The white paint was patched in not-quite matching colors all over the cement block walls. I hadn't realized white came in so many shades. The doors and trim were a thick red, as if twenty layers of glossy paint had been stacked on top of each other over the decades. Chips along the door and window frames revealed the trim had at times been green, blue, and a lovely shade of baby poop yellow. Judging from the frequency that cars came and left from the parking lot, the motel mostly catered to a rent-by-the-hour crowd.

The guy at the front desk took one look at hot young Wyatt in the company of two middle aged women and made some pretty lurid assumptions based on his expression. He took a bit of convincing that we were indeed planning to stay at least the night, if not several days. Candy begged and badgered, but couldn't get him to give us a ground floor room. I wondered if they were reserved for the hour rentals. People could make quick getaways if needed, maybe out a back window. Plus, ground floor would be easier for the frequent maid service needed with hourly rentals. That is, if they bothered to clean between rentals. Ick.

It had become overcast as we left York. A kind of hot humidity filled the air as it always does in mid August and I doubted whether the threatened rain would cool things off. The old air conditioning units whirred and hummed away, spewing hot air at us as we climbed the cement stairs and headed down the outside hallway toward our room. Ours was the one with the big pool of air-conditioning water spilling across the walk and dripping down onto the parking lot below. I imagined the cold dirty water dropping down on some unsuspecting cheating person as they went in to meet up for an afternoon delight. The inside wasn't terrible, but I could tell by Candy's face that this was a huge sacrifice in comfort on her part. Two double beds with cheap floral bedspreads were crammed in the room with just enough space to squeeze by them and the fiberboard dresser placed against the opposite wall. An old TV squatted on top of the dresser, and the beds shared a painted plywood bedside table with a phone and a cheap alarm clock. Laminated and firmly taped to the bedside table was a sheet indicating various charges for phone calls and pay movies.

"You've got to be kidding me," Wyatt said as he walked over to the TV. I thought he was referring to the age, poor quality, and limited channels of the unit. He reached up and grabbed the remote off the top and I saw it had been drilled and outfitted with a ring which was connected by a long metal chain to an identical ring on the TV. I laughed. All that trouble to safeguard a ten dollar universal remote. If we really wanted to steal it, a good set of tin snips, heck probably a decent pocket knife, could have freed it from the chain. Or we could have just grabbed the TV too.

"What, no mini bar? No room service?" I asked, delighted. I was enchanted by the place. Sleazy sex downstairs, tacky theft prevention. I wondered if the bed vibrated. Yes! There was a coin operated box on the side. I dug around for a quarter and threw myself on the bed to enjoy the ride. Better than the kiddy rides outside Walmart.

Candy was not so amused. She looked as though she was about ready to grab some Clorox wipes and go to town. The expression on her face as I set the bed to shaking was priceless. This was going to be the most fun hunt ever. More fun even than catching that sorcerer for the elves a few centuries back.

Candy pointed to the bed closest to the door. The one I wasn't lying on.

"This is *my* bed. I don't want to see you sleeping in it, I don't want you having sex in it with him or anyone, or even by yourself. I don't want anything involving bodily fluids going on in this bed. In fact, I don't even want you to sit on it. Especially not naked. You too," she added as an afterthought pointing at Wyatt.

"What if I put a plastic bag down first?" I asked playfully.

"I can spray some disinfectant on it afterward to kill the germs."

Candy glared at me. I guess that was a no.

There were some logistical negotiations regarding the shopping expedition. It was silly for us all to go out to buy toothbrushes and cheap jeans, but Candy was afraid to let me shop for her and Wyatt needed incomprehensible stuff at an electronics store. I think he was a little worried about me shopping for him too. He should have been. I purchased more on entertainment value than fashion sense. With me in charge, Candy was liable to end up in a French maid outfit and Wyatt in a bondage harness.

Finally, Candy took down our sizes and preferences and agreed to do the clothing and necessity shopping. She was immersed in one of her lists when I decided that I just had to do something this afternoon or I'd explode.

"Go with Candy," I told Wyatt. "There's got to be an electronics store at the outlets. I'm going to go canvass one of our three potential sites."

"It's starting to rain," Candy noted. "Why don't you wait until I get a change of clothes for you?"

"I'm really fidgety. I can't hang out here for hours and watch network TV or porn." I had to get out of that hotel room and shake the wiggles out or I'd be liable to make poor decisions later. "The one site is only three miles from here and it's not raining hard. I think I'm going to jog."

"Cool, I can take your car then," Wyatt said before the words left my mouth.

"Nope. Nobody drives my car." Like nobody sits on Candy's bed, I thought.

"It will be faster if we don't have to ride together. I swear I'll be careful."

"No."

"Sam, I've known you for two years. You can trust me to take good care of it. I know how much it means to you."

"No."

"You trust me with the key to your safe, to take care of all your affairs if needed, but you won't let me drive your car?"

"No. It's my car."

"So, if you have to flee back to your homeland, am I allowed to drive it then? Or do I have to let it sit and rot wherever you left it last? You'd rather let some redneck with plumber's butt hoist your car onto a flatbed or drag it down the road on a hook to the impound lot than allow me to drive it?"

I thought for a moment. "Well, maybe then," I said, grudgingly. "But not now. You can't drive it now. Or in the foreseeable future."

Wyatt glared at me. This was clearly an issue he would continue to address. I realized that I'd probably eventually have to let him drive my car sometime or he'd harp on it forever. Not now though. Maybe after we'd had sex.

The pair left to run their errands and I was alone in the no-tell motel room. I'd looked at the map and directions on Wyatt's tablet, and he'd set it up on my cell phone so I could use the GPS feature to get there and back if I took a detour. I sat for a moment to prepare myself and bring back up the angel's DNA and energy signature. It was like waving a dirty sock in front of a Bloodhound. I focused and a great anticipation grabbed me. I hoped the angel marked his victims prior to the kill. Scouted out their homes, watched them to see their habits, planned his moves. I had so much on him, if he so much as coughed on a twig I'd notice.

I locked the door, with an actual key no less, and headed out. Thankfully the light rain had stopped, although the humidity would have me just as soaked in thirty minutes. I jogged down the busy four lane commercial route trying to look like I was just out for some exercise. Six blocks, then a left. Two more blocks then a right. The tightly packed houses started to spread apart with more sizable yards, then separated by fields of corn or soybean. A mile down and I turned onto a winding hilly country road that didn't seem wide enough for two modern cars to pass. Heck, two Suburbans would have to four-wheel it, especially with no shoulder on the road. Little clusters of three or four modern houses broke the expanses of crops, hay fields, and cattle pasture. I listened carefully for cars. They'd never be able to see me with the hills and curves in the road until they were almost on me. Jumping out of the way into a muddy ditch or barbed wire would have been my only option on a few stretches.

I quickly realized that running in blue jeans was a horrible idea. They clung to me in the wet heat and the seams were rubbing and chafing. Thankfully I'd worn a supportive bra and a pair of old running shoes, or the situation would have been dire. Still, I was seriously contemplating taking the damned jeans off and running in my underwear. The road was pretty deserted this time of day. I considered it, but decided I'd rather suffer than draw attention to myself when I was on a hunt. That's all I needed was some country boy trying to get lucky with a streaker girl.

I was only a hundred yards from the house when the sky opened up and sheets of rain poured down on me. Fuck, could this get any worse? The jeans were like two hundred pounds of wet sandpaper at this point, and my running shoes squelched water with every stride. This was hell. Not that medieval painting of horned dudes gnawing on limbs and fucking asses. Wet jeans were far worse than chewed up limbs and a sore rectum. I knew this for a fact.

I looked up at the house through the haze of gray rain and wet hair. It was set back from the road down a long driveway. Two story, colonial style with shutters on the windows and vinyl siding. No trees, no deck or patio, no front porch, no landscaping bushes, no cover at all. Just a straight shot until you reached the house where there was a small detached garage and a prefab shed. Couldn't anybody have planted any trees? Or a nice stone fence? Or a privet hedge?

I pretended to tie my shoe and thought for a second. That's when I saw it. There was a drainage ditch running along the driveway about two feet out. It was about two feet wide and eighteen inches deep. This was going to suck big time. Staying bent over, I slithered into the ditch. The downpour was not kind to me. The ditch wasn't full enough of water to splash my way up, but it was wet enough to create a good two inches of mud at the bottom. Where was that rock hard Maryland red clay when you needed it? Did it just stop as you crossed the Pennsylvania border?

I did my best imitation of an army crawl through that muddy ditch. I got to say that, although crawling about twenty yards through mud and rain was physically exerting and dirty business, it wasn't anywhere near as painful as jogging in soaking wet jeans. By the time I reached the end of the ditch at the side of the garage, I was unrecognizable. I couldn't even tell the color of my pants or shirt under the brown sludge. I carefully looked up out of the ditch and didn't see anyone around the house or garage. There were no cars or trucks anywhere, and this guy supposedly lived alone. He was probably at work in a nice warm dry office with all the good people of the world. I was the only fool out here, crawling through the mud in a downpour.

The roof stuck slightly out from the side of the two-car garage and I plastered my sludge-covered ass against the wall, gaining a bit of a reprieve from the rain. Not like I could get any wetter. Wiping my muddy hands on my equally muddy pants proved ineffectual, so I tried wiping them on the side of the garage instead. It didn't help.

I wasn't having any luck sensing Althean, or even Gregory. With Gregory, I only had a dim energy signature. It would be a huge long shot to pick anything up from him, but Althean I should have been able to sense. So either this place wasn't a target in the immediate future, or he didn't do planning or reconnaissance whatsoever before moving in for the kill. I didn't think he was quite that insane, since he'd managed to get away with this so far and a lack of planning will get you caught pretty fast. Still, I thought it might be best to get a closer look in case he was trickier than I thought. I checked around the shed area first and found nothing but an old riding mower and some lawn tools. The back yard revealed that a neighbor's cat occasionally came over to prowl and pee on the sand of the horseshoe pits. That had to piss a werewolf off to no end.

I looped around between the garage and the house. There was simply no cover at all around this place. It looked like a divine hand had plopped a house and outbuildings smack down in the middle of a mowed hay field. If the angel came here, he'd need to be ballsy enough to stride right up the driveway in full view. There had to be an easier target. One with less risk. I wanted to be thorough before I ruled this place out though. Since no one was home, I walked around the house peering in windows where I could. It was a typical house. Decent furniture in a living room, a pile of mail on the dining room table, comfortable looking sofa and a wood stove in the TV room. The yard sloped a bit and the kitchen windows in the back of the house were too high for me to see through. I hooked my hands on the sill and carefully pushed my weight up to stand on an outdoor faucet. The kitchen had a couple of dishes on the counter, a coffee cup on the breakfast table, newspapers piled on a chair.

I managed to ease off the faucet without slipping, but before I could congratulate myself, my other foot sank deep and firmly into sucking mud and I went down on my rear. Well, it wasn't like I could get any more muddy. That was when I heard the familiar click of the safety on a gun. I sat very still.

"Keep your hands where I can see them and stand up slowly."

That was truly easier said than done. Like a game of Twister, I rotated at the waist and onto my hands and knees. The mud retained its firm hold on my shoe and that foot was stuck at an odd angle. I looked up and through my dripping hair I saw a man. A man holding a shotgun. The gun looked like the one Wyatt had back in his gun safe. The guy was in his early thirties, lean and muscled with tan work boots, and a sleeveless shirt advertising a high school sports team. The brim of his baseball cap shaded his face from my view, but I could see a well trimmed short beard decorating his jawline.

"My foot is stuck." I told him.

"Well, pull it out, but keep your hands on the ground," he said unsympathetically.

I braced my weight on my hands and other foot and pulled. And twisted. Finally I tried rocking back and forth and the foot slowly came free. I stood, careful to keep my hands where shotgun guy could see them. He looked me over.

"Who are you and why are you prowling around my house?" The rain had slowed thankfully and he no longer had to shout to be heard above the racket.

"Samantha Martin. I was out for a jog and was just trying to get some shelter from the rain until it stopped." I so wanted to push my wet and muddy hair out of my face, but I really didn't want to get shot. Especially at this range.

"In jeans? And getting out of the rain involves dragging yourself to the house in a muddy ditch rather than walking up the driveway like a normal person? And instead of standing under the garage roof, you sneak around the buildings and look in my windows?" Suspicious kind of guy. He looked ready to shoot first and finish with the questions later. Actually, he looked rather scared. Strange for him to be scared, him a fit werewolf with a gun and me a soaking wet middle aged woman with no visible weapon. There was a good reason for him to be scared, but he wasn't supposed to know about it.

"Is this not the first time you've had someone prowling around your house recently?"

The guy looked at me a moment. "Hold still."

I held very still while he reached down, grabbed the hose nozzle and proceeded to spray me down. It was pretty humiliating to stand there with my hands in the air while some guy with a shotgun blasted me with water. It was uncomfortable too. The water was icy cold and it stung with the force of a fire hose.

"Turn around slowly," he told me.

I complied and had the further humiliation of having my ass sprayed off.

I turned around to face him again while he looked. At least the blast of water had pushed my hair back out of my face. I did my best to look harmless. It was easier than usual since I was soaking wet.

"There were some murders up in York late yesterday night," he said slowly. "They are part of a series of murders, so I'm a bit careful."

There is no way he should have known about that couple. It wasn't common knowledge, and there hadn't even been enough time for the gossip mill to get going. I wondered if he'd been part of the local cleanup crew who discovered the bodies. The tape had been too grainy to easily recognize faces, and I still couldn't see this guy clearly with the brim of his cap so low.

"Do you have reason to believe you may be a target?" I asked trying to give him a significant look. One of us was just going to have to come out and say it soon because all this dancing around was not good for my patience.

"Are you an angel?" There, shotgun guy did it for me. I liked him more and more.

There were all sorts of witty comebacks and innuendos I really wanted to make to a question like that, but I decided to keep with the straight talk program.

"No, I'm the one who's going to kill the angel."

He pushed the brim of the cap up and looked at me in astonishment. Okay, I didn't exactly look impressive right at that moment, but his disbelief was a bit insulting.

"*You're* the demon?"

So not only did this guy know about the murders, and the angel, but he knew I'd been contracted to save their asses. This was a guy I wanted to talk to.

"Have you had anyone nosing around your place but me? Any reason to suspect you might be a target? We think someone in the area might be, but if you could help us pin it down then we might be able to kill this thing."

He looked undecided about whether to lower the shotgun or not. "How do I know you're not an angel?"

Again, I had to bite my tongue. Oh, this was such an opportunity for smart comments. Instead I shrugged. "What do I need to do to prove it to you? I could find the cat that's been peeing in your horseshoe pit and dismember it with my bare hands. Or we could have wild muddy sex here in your yard. I can't see an angel doing that."

Shotgun guy's lips twitched. "You're not of my species. That would be against the rules."

I grinned. "I'm all about breaking the rules."

He grinned back. "Me too actually, but I'll decline your

offer for now." He lowered the shotgun and stuck out his hand. "I'm Craig Stottlemeyer."

Craig was my new best friend. He invited me in, allowed me to drip mud and water all over his kitchen floor, wrapped me in a huge soft towel and gave me a hot mug of tea. I was happy to see his place wasn't pristine. He had a stack of dirty dishes in the sink and piles of papers and old mail scattered around. My tea mug advertised some temporary labor agency and the handle had been Krazy Glued back on at some point. After meeting Candy and seeing that house in York, I was beginning to think all werewolves were OCD neat freaks. What a relief.

Craig was also easy to look at. And look I did as soon as he took the hat off. His neat brown beard matched his ultra-short clippered hair. He had high cheekbones in a thin face accented with an equally sharp nose. The severity of his features was softened by a generous splash of freckles. His eyes twinkled, too. I had no doubt he could dispatch anything that threatened his person or his home, but he looked like he'd do it with good humor and a sparkling smile. He was a cute guy to be a bachelor. I assumed that werewolves had difficulty finding suitable partners since they had to restrict themselves to their own species. In the cities it might be easier, but I could imagine it was slim pickings out here.

We sat at his kitchen table and talked. Craig was well informed of the danger he and other local werewolves were in. From what he'd gathered, the angel liked to strike in people's dwellings when they were alone, which usually equated to night time. There had been a couple of instances when the werewolf target worked a night shift, or was home during the day and they had been killed at that time. Craig was usually at work during the day, but he'd taken off the next few days to prepare a defense. He had hidden his cars down the road at a neighbor's and snuck back quietly staying in a deer blind a good two acres away in the tree line at the edge of his property. There, he ate beef jerky and kept an eye on his house with binoculars. It must have really sucked with the heat and the rain we'd just had. That was really roughing it.

"I figured the freak would sneak around first and plan his attack. I've got a good nose, and I'm a good hunter so I can stay alert in a deer blind for two days with binoculars glued to my eyes. I haven't seen anyone but you since I began at six this morning. I came straight here after we left the Randolphs' house in York. They wanted me to help with cleanup, but I used work as an excuse. I'll be in a good bit of trouble with my pack leader when they find out, but protecting myself is more important than cleaning blood off a carpet."

I agreed. "You got a map? There are some other places around here that are potential targets and I wondered if I pointed out their location and gave you their names you could tell me anything you knew about them and their properties. Anything. The more information the better."

Craig got out an old fashioned map of Gettysburg and circled in red all the werewolf residences he knew. Having some local knowledge was priceless. I dotted the ones Wyatt had indicated were in his predictive line.

"These are the houses he may target, according to our analysis."

Craig noted his place, then traced a finger over. "This is the Smythe place. They're in Hawaii for two weeks. They just left Monday."

Lucky them.

"This one is Robinson. He's a long-distance trucker. He's expected back tomorrow night or the day after tomorrow.

Took a truckload of appliances out to a regional warehouse in Iowa."

Could be Robinson then. That would buy us some time. Or it could be Craig.

"That leaves you," I told him. I felt like I was on one of those dramas where the surgeon tells a man he has an inoperable brain tumor. You have a malignant angel. It will kill you in three days or less.

Craig raised his eyebrows and pursed his lips as if considering his funeral options. "Or, it could be Ms. Staley." He dotted the map in a spot between his place and Robinson's.

I looked at the dot. "According to the master database there isn't a werewolf living there."

Craig gave me a significant look. Ah. Ms. Staley was off the grid. "If she's been able to avoid registration and/or death, then how do you know about her? How does anyone know about her?" I asked.

I watched him take a sip of his tea and look worriedly out the kitchen window. "Sometimes you fake a death, or don't record a birth. It's easy to get human identities and the angel that is in charge of the werewolves doesn't pay much attention to the humans. They are really stupid about most technology, too. It's very difficult though. You can't live as a werewolf. You can't socialize with them, hunt with them, you can't even think of letting your wolf out during the moon. It's a life cut off from your culture, your people, even a part of yourself. You live as a human. You can't mate with a human because it goes against millennia of teaching and culture, but you can't mate with a registered wolf and not blow your cover. There are no records of you as a werewolf. Even the local wolves don't know who you are in case one is tortured or there is a snitch. There are only a few hundred in the world who live like this, but it's important to the freedom and future of our species to have a handful off the grid, just in case.

"Ms. Staley does my taxes. She lives alone. Never mated, never had kids. She's in her mid-sixties. She hasn't changed form in almost twenty years. If she hadn't told me in a fit of loneliness one day I would have never known. She doesn't even smell like a wolf anymore."

Craig looked at me, his eyes no longer twinkling. "That's a horrible way to live your life. Of course, I don't know if ours is much better tiptoeing around, minding our P's and Q's, and hoping our friends don't find our body in the kitchen one day with angel wings on our forehead."

I agreed, but I didn't see how my killing one angel was going to help their case in the long run. I didn't get how the humans got to run amok, breeding like rabbits, taxing the natural resources and driving themselves closer and closer to extinction with their folly, but others like the werewolves were hammered with impossible rules and unnatural restrictions. Maybe just to strike out once would be enough. They'd have the satisfaction of knowing they didn't go gently into that good night.

I shouldn't have cared. If the angels wanted to make life miserable for this species, drive them into extinction, why should I care? It wouldn't make any difference to me. The whole thing bothered me, though. Angels were such controlling assholes. What gave them the right to target a species like this? The werewolves were so outclassed, too. If all of them united they'd never stand a chance against even a couple of angels. Bullies. And the thing with the baby. Hypocrites. Even if Althean accidentally killed the woman and the baby, to mark them as guilty, to cover it up, was deplorable. Fuck, I hated angels.

I asked Craig if he'd mind driving me back to the motel. I was still damp and muddy in spite of the hosing off, and my jeans were beginning to dry into the stiffness of plywood. Even though the rain had stopped, I didn't relish a jog or even a walk back. My legs would have been chewed through to blood and bones by the time I reached the vacancy sign. Craig looked a little surprised as if he expected me to sprout leathery wings and fly back. I could do that, but I was pretty sure I'd be chopped out of the sky by an angel with a sword before I reached my destination. We walked over to the neighbor's house and he motioned for me to get into a little Toyota pick-up. I'd pegged him for a Chevy or Ford man, myself. The Toyota was trashed inside with dirt on the seats, balled up fast food bags on the floor, and a box of shotgun shells spilling out of the cup holder. At least I didn't worry about my muddy ass staining his upholstery. I was more worried about week old barbeque sauce staining my muddy ass.

Craig turned to me even before we pulled out of the driveway.

"So, what do you do? Do you throw lightning, or shoot laser beams out your eyes or something?"

I didn't blame him one bit. I hardly looked like a bringer of death, and the most impressive thing I'd done so far was get my foot stuck in the mud outside his window. Heck, I even had to ask him for a lift. Badass me.

I shrugged. "I can do a lot of things."

It was a good question, though. What could I do? I didn't know what it was going to take to kill this angel. I didn't know what he was going to throw at me, or what he was susceptible to. What if nothing I had worked? What if he ended up being vulnerable to something stupid like aluminum beer cans? Deep down inside, I had a secret fantasy of Owning him. It would be epic to go home and parade around Owning an angel. That was a total fantasy though, and I knew better. Just concentrate on killing him before he killed me. I was thinking that, when I confronted this angel, I should probably start with the basics in terms of my skills and work from there.

Electricity and fire in varying intensities were pretty much gifts at birth. Caretakers had to be fast and proactive around the infants they guarded since babies let loose bursts of energy without warning or provocation. There was just no control at that age, and many would cook themselves, seriously injure their caregivers, or accidently kill a foster sibling. Even the Low managed to master electricity and fire to some degree, although they often couldn't do anything complicated. I'd always been skilled at electricity in all its strengths and forms. I was good at persuading elementals to service too, not that I was aware of any elementals on this realm. My greatest skill, though, was that I could shuffle the periodic table around like a dealer in Vegas. I wondered what a bolt of lightning would do to an angel. Could I use conversion on him? Turn bone to liquid? Harden joints and shatter them? I had thought I might have to fall back on just heaving raw energy at him. Very crude, but when you don't know your enemy it's difficult to be flashy.

Craig didn't look wowed at my vague answer, but he kept silent the rest of the ride. We exchanged cell phone numbers in the hotel parking lot and agreed to call each other if any new developments emerged.

CHAPTER 12

Candy and Wyatt were back before I was. I had to stand outside muddy and wet while Candy carefully laid towels from the door to the bathroom. I wondered if we had any towels left for showers. There was a good possibility they might not bring us any more. This wasn't exactly the Hyatt.

"Take off your shoes and socks," she instructed, "and walk across the towels to the bathroom. There you can shower and dry off. Leave your clothes in the sink. I've already put a clean set in there for you."

"Why don't I just take off my clothes here?" I asked. I'd drip less mud if the clothes stayed on the outside of our room.

"No. I don't need to see anymore of your body, and the other patrons do not need to see your naked backside standing on the balcony here. Just try not to get anything on the carpet."

I obeyed walking the tightrope of towels. Wyatt had wires and plastic things strewn all over the bed (not Candy's bed), and barely grunted a hello. I wondered if he was still mad about not getting to drive my Corvette.

Nothing feels better than a hot shower after you've been wet and muddy for a few hours. Well, except for the parts of my inner legs rubbed into red raw chunks. Those stung like a motherfucker when I peeled off the pants and the water hit them. Hopefully I could stealthily fix the skin before I had to put clothing on.

Even though it was humid and sticky out, being rained on somehow makes you feel cold and damp. I got in with my clothes on figuring I could kill two birds with one stone and get them rinsed of their mud layer. After the water ran clean, I peeled them gently off and plopped the sodden mess in the sink. Candy was considerate enough to have bought shampoo, conditioner, soap, and even some razors. I hadn't even thought of that since most hotels I stayed at had decent supplies in their bathrooms. Of course this one didn't. So their guests didn't take showers after their hour-long rendezvous? Or just rinsed off? Or perhaps they brought their own little clean up bag with them, like I do to the gym. I let the water stream over me thinking about the similarities of Zumba at the gym and sweaty mattress aerobics on the first floor.

My warm feelings toward Candy faded when I saw the clothes she had bought me. A pack of cheap cotton underwear. Okay, no problem. It's not like I needed slut panties for the next two days. Inexpensive jeans. Okay, although I resented that she bought me curvy/relaxed fit. The sports bra was okay. The shirt was just revolting though. It looked like it should have come with a Mennonite cap and a long skirt. It was long sleeved. Perfect for these ninety-degree days we were having. It was pink with little white gingham checks all over it. It buttoned up to a little peter pan collar with picot lace around the edge. The sleeve cuffs were edged in the same picot lace. I put it on and looked in the mirror. There was no fucking way I was even leaving the bathroom in this shirt. I walked out in my bra with the shirt in my hand hoping to see if I could slice enough of it off with my utility knife to tolerate wearing it until I washed and dried the muddy clothing.

Wyatt snickered as I walked out and Candy handed him a folded bill.

"I bet her a twenty that you wouldn't even wear it out of the bathroom. She thought you'd slice it up and wear it frayed just to piss her off."

"You'd have won if I'd brought my multi-tool into the bathroom with me." I told Candy as I tossed her the shirt. "I'll just do the bra thing until my clothes get through the washer and dryer."

"No need," Wyatt said grinning. "I bought you a present."

He handed me a bag. It was glossy pink with an antiqued gold banner and a crest on it. Candy nodded approvingly seeing the designer logo.

I pulled out the t-shirt and unfolded it admiring the bold black and red colors. "Look," I said turning it around and displaying it across my chest. "I'm 'Juicy'."

Wyatt's grin threatened to engulf his whole face and Candy choked a bit.

"It's Juicy Couture," she said, dismayed. "It's a designer brand name."

"Yes, but I'm 'Juicy'," I told her. "Do you think I'm 'Juicy', Wyatt?" I turned to him all innocent.

"I certainly hope so."

"See, it says right here that I'm 'Juicy', so it must be true," I said. "Wyatt, you'll need to have one that says 'Crunchy'. I think that you're probably 'Crunchy'. And Candy can have 'Chewy'. Or possibly 'Tough and Stringy', if they have that one."

"Can I have 'Hard'?" Wyatt teased. "Maybe "Huge and Hard."

I looked at the portion of his anatomy in question. "From this angle, I'd support that. Although I still like 'Crunchy'. I'm very fond of 'Crunchy'."

Candy shook her head in exasperation and neatly folded the shirt I had thrown at her before tossing me a pack of plain white t-shirts she bought for me to wear.

"What did you find on your prowl?" she asked, deftly changing the subject.

I brought them up to speed on my pleasant visit with Craig Stottlemyer, although I left out the part on the off-the-grid werewolf.

"So nothing at his house. The one house is out since they are gone for weeks. We've got some time with this Robinson guy. We could check out his place tonight, get some sleep, and start surveillance tomorrow before he gets back." Candy said, putting the hideous shirt in a drawer.

Wyatt and I agreed. I threw on a white tee so I didn't get rain and mud all over my new Juicy shirt. Wyatt called shotgun as we piled into Candy's car and headed out.

Robinson had a little one-story house that looked like it was delivered on a flatbed. His garage was three times the size of his house, no doubt to accommodate his semi when he was home. The big garage was empty but for a monster-sized Ford 350. This must be where his money went. It had chrome all over, a custom painted Pittsburgh Steelers logo covering the back window, and pink rubber testicles hanging from the trailer hitch. Sheesh. The guy drove a big rig, had a huge truck, I was guessing his dick was the size of my pinky. Since he wasn't home, I covered the ground outside his home in a grid pattern twenty feet out from his walls. Nothing. By the time I was done, I was starved.

"Do you think Althean got freaked out over killing a

pregnant woman and is going to hold back for a while?" I asked, stuffing down a burger and fries at a local diner. "Maybe Gregory caught up with him and has pummeled his ass into submission?"

Candy shrugged. "I don't think he can hold back for long. From the video we saw I think he's snapped and gone crazy. He was pacing all over the place, and didn't act like he was rational and in control of his actions. Still, if we don't see anything in the next two or three days, then we'll have to rethink our strategy. It could be that Gregory has caught up to him and stopped him, but I'm not convinced of Gregory's intentions. It could be that he supports Althean and would only want him to be more stealthy in his kills."

Three days. Shit. I had horses and Boomer, and a zoning hearing. Normally, Wyatt would make sure my animals were okay, but he was here with me. My neighbors weren't on a friendly basis with me, so I called Michelle.

"You read those zoning documents yet?" she asked.

"No, and I'm probably going to miss the hearing. Can you sit in for me?" I asked in my nicest voice. "I'm out of state for a couple days, and I wondered if you'd please go by my place and check on my horses and dog. The horses are in the field, so you won't need to do more than toss a bale of hay at them. Just dump some food in Boomer's bowl. It's in the barn by the tack room."

"Sam, I'm a black girl raised in the heart of Baltimore. I'm not getting anywhere near those crazy animals of yours. Where is Wyatt?" She paused and I heard her gasp in excitement. "Oooo, are you both on a romantic trip? You've *got* to tell me what he's like in the sack. I'll get Darleen to check your farm for you. You just enjoy yourself and call me the minute you're back in town."

"Wait," I said before she hung up. Who the fuck was

Darleen? "Is Darleen your fat friend? The one with the curly hair who sings when she's drunk?"

"She was raised on a dairy farm. Cows are the same as horses, so you can trust her."

Crap, I hoped she wasn't going to try and milk my horses. Especially since they were all geldings. I wondered if I should burst her bubble about my 'romantic' getaway with Wyatt. I was pretty focused on my hunt, and I'd hate to disappoint her with no lurid stories when I returned.

"We're actually up here with Candy on some business. Just wanted you to know that," I said looking at Wyatt and Candy. Maybe I should have waited and had this conversation in private.

Michelle was silent a moment. I squirmed. I might be bad to the bone, but I didn't want Michelle to get pissed at me. She was the best property manager I'd ever had.

"I didn't think Candy was licensed to sell outside Maryland," she said in a very scary calm voice. "And I'm certainly not licensed to manage out of state properties."

"It's a real long shot, Michelle," I said soothingly. "If I buy anything you can open a Pennsylvania office and hire someone already licensed here to manage under you. You're the best, and I'm not about to deal with anyone else. If you would cover for me while I'm gone, I'd really appreciate it. I'll call you the moment I'm back and let you know how things stand so you can get the jump on things." How cryptic was that? I hated stroking egos. It's not a skill I grew up with.

Michelle seemed reassured and chatted on, gossiping about local politics and prominent business owners in town. Finally, she announced she had to go as she had a date with some guy named Javier.

Candy rolled her eyes as I put my phone back. "That girl could be a powerhouse if she ever learned to focus."

"She's young. She's bright. She seizes opportunities and

takes calculated risks; she's got a great future. I don't entrust my business concerns to anyone but the best." I replied. Don't criticize my people.

We headed back to our motel room. Wyatt took a shower while I ran my laundry down for a quick run in the washer. I left it spinning, thinking I'd throw it in the dryer in the morning, and popped back in the room just as Candy was finishing a phone call of her own.

"I love you and I'll see you soon. Call you tomorrow."

"Your husband?" I asked as she hung up.

"No, my son. I've been divorced for seven years now, and we really don't speak any longer. I did see my ex-husband at my son's wedding last year, though."

Wow, I must have caught her in a sentimental mood to reveal this kind of personal information to me. I was even more shocked when she dug in her purse and pulled out a vinyl album of pictures.

"Here's my son and his wife at their wedding. The bridesmaid here is my daughter. She just graduated college this spring and is working up in New York. My son and his wife are in Philly."

She continued to flip through the album. Her kids were attractive, smiling, happy. A lovely family. She even had a shot of the whole wedding party with her husband and his new wife.

"What happened with your marriage?" I asked. Was that a polite thing to ask? Humans asked questions and showed interest in each other's lives, but I never knew where to draw the line.

Candy shrugged. "We were married fairly young. It's not always easy to find a mate, so if you're attracted to someone in your area and they're available, you tend to jump on it and rush into commitment. As we both grew older, I became stronger, more involved in business and in werewolf politics.

Especially after the kids grew up. I think he just wanted a mate who wasn't so dominant, who was less of a mover and shaker, less ambitious. We don't talk, but we're not hostile toward each other. These things happen. I know his new wife. We're not a huge community, so you tend to know everyone, especially if you deal in politics. She's very nice. They seem happy."

Her voice was pragmatic, calm and reasonable. She didn't mourn his loss, but I think she mourned the loss of something. Maybe intimacy? Maybe companionship?

"You never found another mate? Never remarried?" She was on a roll, so I thought I'd ask.

Candy shook her head sadly. "There aren't a huge amount of us, and with our existence contract we're limited in where we can make our home. Even if I wanted to marry someone in, say Richmond, I'd need to petition to move there to be with him, or he'd need to petition to move to my city. Plus, I'm very involved in my business and in politics. It's hard to find time for long-distance dating."

She showed me additional pictures of rounded babies and skinny adolescents. Her kids when they were young. They looked human. Kids with baseball bats, kids jumping in pools, kids making silly faces at the cameras. It was clear that parenting had been one of the most important parts of her life. I wondered how easy it was to move from one phase of your life to another? Candy was successful, but was she happy? Did she long for those days with a husband and her young children again, for a past her?

"I'm hoping for grandchildren eventually," she sighed. "Werewolves live slightly longer than humans. Our average life expectancy is just over one hundred years, and we have a long window of fertility. We need it, because we don't seem to get pregnant easily and we don't always carry a child to term. I was so blessed to have two healthy children, but our numbers are dwindling because our fertility is low. Over the last five hundred years, it's declined dramatically."

"You need some hybrid vigor," I told her. "Cross breed with humans. They are fertile like rabbits, and have a high live-birth rate. You could interbreed with the hybrids then and strengthen your species."

Candy shook her head. "It's forbidden in our existence contract. No breeding with the humans. No sex with the humans at all. It's been that way for thousands of years and it's gotten to the point where we feel repulsed at the very idea. It's just ingrained in our culture."

There was something about that pronouncement that lit a spark in my memory. What was it with angels and cross species breeding with humans? They seemed to freak at the thought.

"Wait," Candy said suddenly, a strange look on her face. "Didn't Wyatt say there was a higher incidence of kills among females? I'd noticed that a few of the early kills had admitted to fertility treatment. I didn't think anything at the time because that's a real gray area in our contract. But now I'm wondering if Althean is targeting the more fertile among us. Can angels discern that sort of thing? It would really hasten our extinction if he picked his victims based on their ability to produce offspring."

"I don't know if angels can do that or not," I said. "Either way, killing an already pregnant woman and her unborn baby is not allowable for them. I could see killing the father, assuming he's the fertile one, and coming back to kill the mother after she gives birth, but not while she's pregnant."

"Do you think it could help us identify who the potential victims are?" she asked.

I shrugged. "I can't sense someone's fertility. I don't think it's going to help us catch him."

I left Candy and scrolled through the TV stations. Candy

had ruled out any porn while she was in the room, so I ended up watching NCIS reruns. Wyatt finished his obscenely long shower and emerged from the steam with sweat pants and nothing on top. The guy had the best chest ever. Slim, but cut and muscular, with arms Popeye would give his eyeteeth for. I stared like a starving orphan. This was going to be the most torturous night of my life. Wyatt pulled the bedspread and top sheet down to the bottom of the bed and tossed himself on it holding the remote-on-a-chain. Damn, that was just sexy.

I was not allowed to change into my pajamas in the room and was banished to the bathroom to disrobe and brush my teeth. Candy had outdone herself on the nighttime wear selection. Normally I just slept in the nude. Tonight I would be sleeping in flannel shorts and a Tinkerbell t-shirt that could easily have contained three longshoremen. Yep, it was that big.

As I walked out of the bathroom, Wyatt caught sight of me and made a choking noise. I pivoted around to show him the entire glory of the Tinkerbell shirt that came well past my knees. I didn't know why I bothered with the flannel shorts since you couldn't tell I had them on under the tent of the shirt.

"Come on, baby, you know you want me," I told Wyatt while posing seductively. I could have been three hundred pounds in this thing and you wouldn't have been able to tell the difference.

"Sorry, Sam, my libido vanished at the sight of that hideous nightwear," he laughed.

I plopped down on the bed next to him and watched Candy take her toothbrush into the bathroom.

"Do you think we have time for a quickie while she brushes her teeth?" I asked Wyatt.

"I heard that," Candy said over the sound of running water.

"That's a no, then." Wyatt seemed genuinely regretful. I wondered if he was still scared of me. I wondered if we'd ever have sex. Hopefully soon before he got old and less attractive. Humans have such short lives, and are not very appealing in the early or late stages of them. Wyatt was very appealing now, spread out on the bed before me like a prime rib buffet. I just wanted to rub my hands up his naked chest. And my mouth. Heck all of me, like a cat against a chair leg. Full of sexual frustration from my imagining, I turned on my side with my back facing him and squeezed my eyes shut trying to sleep.

Candy came out and the lights and TV went off as the others settled in. In spite of Wyatt's claims that he never slept, he dozed right off. I could hear Candy snoring softly too. Just me, awake and horny with my head full of thoughts. How was I going to kill this angel? I didn't know much about them, and Candy only knew a bit more than me. I wasn't sure how to face off something that was at very least my equal and probably much more powerful than me. I'd killed a few of my own kind, but those were accidents. In spite of the propaganda painting us as evil murderous beings, we really didn't battle or assassinate each other on a regular basis. Yeah, there was the occasional feud, but it was over pretty fast. Life was hazardous enough. We're a pretty hardy species, luckily, so it would take a wallop of power to bring one of us down when we were in defensive mode. I'd just have to assume the same with the angel and maybe double it just to be safe. Overkill. When it just has to be dead.

About a half hour into my musings, Wyatt rolled over and grabbed me pulling me across the bed to him, squashing my back up against his chest and wrapping his arm and leg around me. I think they call it 'spooning'. I froze and didn't know what to do. I'd never slept with anybody. We just don't do this sort of thing. It was like being in a straightjacket; one that breathes on you and wraps your legs up too. The whole thing was both uncomfortable and a turn-on. I was starting to get kind of hot having Wyatt wrapped around me like a blanket, and feeling him pressed against me like this wasn't helping me fall asleep either.

It was a long night. I'd doze off, then move into a more comfortable spot only to have Wyatt grab me and jerk me in tighter. Plus I didn't realize that male humans had erections off and on all night long. How the hell was I supposed to sleep with a boner pressed against my ass, reminding me of the enjoyable things I could be doing? It was fucking torture and I woke up to my cell phone beeping, sleep deprived and in a hideous mood.

It took me a few moments to extricate myself from Wyatt's grasp. I thought I'd have to gnaw my limbs off at one point. Of course, my struggles woke him up too.

"What?" he asked groggily as I climbed over him to grab my cell phone off the bedside table. I made sure I smashed my boobs into his face on the way as payback for a night of dick on my ass. I looked at the phone. Craig. His text from a few seconds ago said *"he's here now."* I vaulted from the bed jabbing a knee in Wyatt's stomach and knocking the lamp on top of Candy's head. I had my keys and was out the door before either of them could say a word.

My Corvette screamed along the roads to Craig's house taking up the entire road as I shot around the narrow curves. It was too early for traffic, but I narrowly missed a tractor and a fox. A squirrel wasn't as lucky, and I was relieved to see it flopping around in death throes behind my car as I sped off. At least it hadn't gotten hung up in my undercarriage. At the last moment I realized that I could hardly go rocketing up Craig's driveway smashing into the angel like something from Mad Max. I whipped into the neighbor's driveway, and dashed through their back yard toward the tree line that extended to Craig's deer blind. If they were up, I'm sure the neighbors were startled to see an expensive sports car spinning out gravel in their driveway followed by a half-naked woman darting across their back yard. Not something you see every day over your morning coffee.

My feet were scratched and bruised by the time I reached Craig's deer blind. "Where is he?" I asked breathlessly.

Craig stared at me in amazement. I looked the ruthless killer in my nightshirt with a toddler sized Tinkerbell on the front, bloody bare feet, and bed head. At least my morning breath was fear inducing.

"He's gone. He was only here a few moments around the side of the house. I didn't get a really good look at him, so I can't describe him. He just appeared out of nowhere around the side of the garage, walked over to the house, stayed there for a few minutes, then walked back and disappeared."

"Maybe he crawled up the ditch by the driveway like I did?" I suggested. Stupid idea. I couldn't picture a powerful angel scooting on his belly through the mud. Although it would be really funny to watch one do that. Really funny.

"No, he didn't look rumpled or dirty. Plus, I can see the ditch from here, that's how I saw you coming to the house."

Another testament to my incompetence. This guy probably thought I was a total boob. I was beginning to think I was a total boob.

We walked down toward the house and Craig showed me where the angel came from and where he went to. By then, Candy and Wyatt had arrived, pulling in the driveway like civilized folk. They were dressed, and Candy had even combed her hair, although she had forgone the make-up in her haste.

"We missed him, he was only here a moment." I told them as they walked over to us.

Craig put his hands on either side of a window, then straightened up and walked back toward the garage. "That's exactly what I saw him do. It probably only was three minutes and he was gone."

I looked carefully at the garage and along the path the angel took. Nothing. I looked at the house and at the window. No smudges, no marks, no energy signature, no DNA markers. I stared at the window in despair, and noticed a slight distortion. It was like the window had rippled under heat and a dull prism reflected back. Why would he have applied heat to the window? It didn't appear to be enough to break or even weaken the glass. Was heat a byproduct of his presence? If so, why didn't his energy signature appear to me, and why wasn't the siding where he placed his hands warped or melted even slightly?

I'd done all I could do with my human senses, so I put a hand up and sent a tentative trickle of exploratory energy to the window making sure I anchored it firmly in myself so even the smallest of information would come through. The second my energy touched the window, I felt an explosion slamming me to the ground. Pain seared me, and all I saw was white. White, pain, and a screeching noise like roofing nails on a chalkboard. Was I dead? Was I dying? Or maybe blind and deaf. I wasn't even sure I was still at Craig's house. Definitely not dead since the pain was still excruciating. Pain. Pain. I couldn't seem to find my way out of the sound, light, and pain.

Finally the white dimmed a bit, and the sound began to recede. I realized someone was holding me and stroking my hair. "Sam, Sam." Wyatt murmured in my ear as he rocked me like a human child with a boo-boo. I appreciated his calmness since I was pretty sure whatever injury I'd suffered it hadn't been pretty. Things began to swim into focus around me, and I concentrated to identify where the pain was to cut it off.

Oh my. My left hand was melted up past the wrist. I removed my personal energy from the flesh, leaving it just a blob of melted fat, bone, and tendon. It was as if a wax sculpture had been put too close to a blowtorch. It was pretty dramatic, but it no longer hurt now that I'd isolated it. I must have instinctively shut off my probe or whatever melted my arm would have continued and shot right through me. It would have killed me.

My kind tends to tear ourselves up pretty regularly, what with rough sex and our risky lifestyle. The key is to make sure the flesh has only minimal feeling and that your personal energy is safely away from the areas being ripped or torn, or chewed. Most accidental deaths happened from someone having their personal energy out and about during an unexpected trauma. My personal energy had been extended out and firmly rooted deep to my core. I was very lucky. This could have easily been the death of me.

Wyatt still stroked my hair and I heard Candy and Craig in hushed voices to the side.

"It's going to kill her with one blow. This isn't going to work. Is there some other demon you know? Maybe a better one?"

Great. I was going to be sacked in favor of a 'better' demon. One with red skin, a pointy tail, horns, and a goatee no doubt. They wanted scary? I'd show them scary. I struggled to my feet, pushed back the pounding headache which was fifty percent from lack of coffee, and staggered to the garage. The three followed me. Wyatt at least looked worried.

There was no hatchet to be had in the garage. What self respecting Pennsylvania country boy doesn't chop his own wood? Even better though, I found a hack saw. I smacked my left arm up on a workbench, sending bits of melted flesh flying. Giving myself an inch past the melted part, I started to saw my arm off. It wasn't easy since I hadn't clamped it down first. I had to give myself enough feeling to hold the arm in place, but not enough that it would be agonizing. Still, I made it nice and slow, making sure to stick it in the bone a bit so I had to wiggle the saw blade loose. Bone is usually spongy and hard to cut through without power tools, but whatever melted my hand had made the bone more brittle than usual and somewhat easier to cut. Craig made retching noises; Candy stared with her mouth clamped shut; and Wyatt looked everywhere but my arm. Sorry, Wyatt. I hadn't really wanted him to see this kind of thing. Guess we were back to square one, again. No sex for me.

After I had separated my arm from the rest of my body, I made sure to let it spurt blood a bit over the workbench. I left the melted arm there too. Let Craig clean it up himself, asshole.

Time for a new arm. Like I said before, I could convert myself a new arm in an instant. Wham, new arm. It's not very impressive though to just make an arm appear supposedly out of thin air in a flash of light. I looked at my stump and slowly converted matter around me into a new arm. Bone first, nerves and veins snaking down out of the stump, muscles that grow outward and flesh crawling like a tan plague over the surface. It hurt like a bitch, but it looked horrifying.

"Okay," I said, wiggling my new fingers experimentally in the air. "Let's go back and take a look at that window again, shall we?"

"Don't touch it, Sam," Wyatt implored. "I can't take all this again before breakfast."

I approached the house and held my energy tight to

myself as I looked at the window. I could see it now, clear as day. That's when I realized it wasn't just the window. Whatever coated the window, coated the entire house. It was so clear and obvious, I wasn't sure why I couldn't see it before. I assumed it wasn't made for human eyes, and it was not something I'd ever seen done at home. I looked carefully at the dull rainbow of colors and heard the faint scratching noise. It made a pattern. A pattern I recognized from long ago. Far back in my memories of visits, here.

"It's a hex," I said, half to myself.

"A hex?" Candy looked all over the house and obviously saw nothing. "Like the ones the Pennsylvania Dutch put on the side of their barns?"

I shrugged. "Kind of. The ones around here on the barns are pretty artwork, but they usually don't make any sense from a symbolic point of view, and the makers don't have any power to charge them and create actual wards of protection. They probably had some superstitious meaning a few centuries ago, but they've lost that now. This hex, you probably can't see at all with your eyes. I couldn't see it at first, either, since it's based on color, pattern, and sound. Subtle work that we don't use back home. This one is based on the same ancient symbolic nature that the pretty barn decorations use now. It's a kind of ward to protect and guard the occupants of the house."

I motioned with my hand. "There are a series of circles covering the house. They symbolize eternity and tell me that this protection is meant to last forever. Inside are both five- and eight-pointed stars which carry the protection against evil. Within them is a tulip which is for trust and faith. The symbols add up to an eternal protection from evil that is based on faith. Faith extended from the angel, which is a significant gift." I looked at Craig. "You should feel honored to be gifted this. It's well crafted, and powerful. The main color of the hex is white, which is the energy that powers it. The white is huge. When I touched it, that's all I could see. It practically blinded me. The power behind this is just immense. There are other colors, too. Blue to reinforce the protection, black to bind the hex together as a whole, and a set of reddish purple angel wings like an artist's signature. The wings stamp it as a divine gift. So any idiot who tries to break it knows whose hammer is about to drive him into the ground."

I silently admired the hex a moment. It was just amazing. I couldn't believe the amount of skill that had gone into creating it, let alone the immense power behind it. What angel could possibly have power to just toss into a hex like this? This angel was way out of my league. Way out of any demon's league. The crafting, the level of detail and intricacy of the thing was awe inspiring. I could feel the power humming from it. The whole thing stirred something deep within me. Something beyond admiration. I shook my head trying to clear it of the fascination I felt contemplating this magnificent work of art and its equally magnificent creator.

"In short, it's a protective hex," I told the others. "It guards against supposedly evil spirits, which is why it practically fried me into the ground. I've seen witches do this in the past, but it's not been as powerful and doesn't really do much to keep me out. Those are mainly to keep bad intentioned humans out and as good luck charms. Plus, theirs are visual since the makers are at least mostly human and the protection extends against evil humans who would need to see the warning."

"Why would Althean put a protective hex on the house of a man he was about to kill?" Candy asked, bewildered. "Why bother to protect him against evil spirits when he's planning to kill him in the next day or two? Does he want to make sure no one else gets him first?"

"I'm pretty sure this hex would work against angels as well as my kind and many others. The way it's formulated and how it's activated would keep any angel except the one who placed it from touching the house, and that extends directly to the owner inside or within a certain range outside the house." I turned to Craig. "You could be anywhere within a thirty foot radius, and be totally safe from evil intent against your person, and be safe within your house even if there is no active evil intent. I can stand here and talk to you, but I can't enter your house. And if I decided to do you harm close to your house, the hex would extend out to me. Best of all, Althean won't be able to touch you or enter your house, because it's Gregory who placed this hex."

TaDa! I'd freaked them out with my arm sawing, and now I'd wowed them with my folkloric knowledge. Better not be any more talk of finding someone "better" or I'd have to start chewing limbs and fucking asses.

"Gregory?" Candy looked lost. "Why would he do this? If this is such a powerful and significant gift, then what has Craig done to deserve such protection?"

"I think it's less about Craig personally, and more about trapping Althean," I said. "Gregory knows he's got a problem on his hands. An escalating problem. And he's in charge of these enforcing angels. He's the top dog. It reflects badly on him to have Althean running amok, wiping out innocents. He's got to get him now before there's notice from his higher-ups, or perhaps before you all feel there's nothing left to lose and there's a werewolf rebellion. Think, we've got a couple in Hawaii for two weeks. That leaves Craig and Robinson. He can't be two places at once to catch his naughty boy, so he's safeguarded one, essentially herding Althean toward Robinson. And Robinson isn't due back until late tonight or tomorrow which gives him some time to plan and set a trap."

"So what do we do now?" Wyatt asked.

"I'd propose we do the same. Watch Robinson's to see what Gregory does, then be there when Althean makes his move."

Hopefully, Gregory wouldn't be there, otherwise there would be no move for me to make. No way I was going up against *that* angel. If he showed up, I'd leave him to deal with Althean. If this hex was any indication, he had enough power to kill me with the flick of a pinky. I was going to make sure I stayed out of the range of that pinky. Even if that meant abandoning Wyatt along with Candy and her weregeld and racing for the nearest gate.

CHAPTER 13

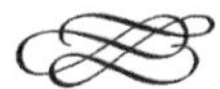

Wyatt and Candy headed over to Robinson's house to watch for angel activity, while I drove back to the motel to put on some clothing. Blood and bits of my flesh had splattered on the Tinkerbell shirt. I felt it was a good look for her, and Wyatt commented that I looked like I'd been to a Disney-themed Gwar concert. Cool idea, but I wanted to get into something less tent like. Plus I was tasked with bringing coffee and donuts.

I didn't want to wear my new Juicy shirt and get it blood covered in some battle. Plus, my street cred was fragile enough without my prancing around proclaiming my juiciness. Thankfully, no one had stolen my t-shirt and jeans from the motel washer. I threw Tinkerbell in the washer, equally confident that no one would steal her either, and proceeded to wait for my choice of clothing to dry. I took my time, grabbing a shower and drying my hair. Remembering the wet hair hanging in my face yesterday, I pulled it into my usual pony tail. Hopefully that would keep it contained and out of my eyes. I walked naked to get my clothes out of the dryer since Candy wasn't there to yell at me, and then headed for coffee and donuts. I really didn't need to get there too early. Robinson wasn't home, so we weren't expecting any action from Althean. He probably wouldn't even try to scout it out until later in the day. Plus, I really wanted to avoid my own personal nemesis, Gregory, who might come to set his own trap and sense me nearby in the process.

The whole stake out thing was boring to the nth degree, sitting there, eating donuts and drinking coffee until I was ready to squirm out of my skin from the sugar and caffeine high. We sat for hours, crouched in the hedgerows, waiting for anything to show up. I played games on my cell phone until the battery was almost dead, then took twigs and leaves and made a series of obstacles for increasingly frustrated and anxious ants.

Finally, just as I was ready to call and have pizza delivered, someone walked up the driveway. Wahoo! Action time! We couldn't see clearly who it was, so I inched along the hedgerow and slowly crawled up behind him pulling my energy up. It was Craig. What a letdown. He was lucky that he heard me with his superior hearing and turned around before I blasted him into bits. I was so disappointed that I almost blasted him anyway. Anything would be more entertaining than another few hours pestering ants behind a bush.

Craig was shaking, his eyes big with fear. And that's saying a lot for a werewolf if Candy were anything to compare by. "An angel came by my house again. I don't care if there's a hex, I'm not staying there."

"Was it the same angel as before, or a different one?" I asked as Candy and Wyatt came from their cover behind a huge forsythia.

"I don't know. They all look the same to me. It might have been the same one, or it could have been the killer. I'm not staying there. I'd feel more safe with a demon who saws her own arm off."

I wasn't sure that was a compliment. I turned to the others. Candy was frowning at Craig in disapproval. Wyatt looked relieved. I couldn't stand hours, possibly all night, of this stake out business. I would go insane if this stretched on with nothing to do but sit and wait.

"Look, I can't take much more of this hovering around with nothing to do," I told the three of them. "I'm an action kind of girl. And I want a beer. I'm going to break into this guy's house and find some booze, and maybe some reading material, anything to entertain me until I can kill something."

I walked over to the door and jimmied the lock in my own special way as Candy argued with Craig regarding his safety choices. Wyatt watched them for a moment then followed me in.

Robinson's tiny box of a house had a small living room, an eat-in kitchen, and a ridiculously narrow hallway leading to two tiny bedrooms. I availed myself of the bathroom and was happy to snag a few naked girl magazines. Too bad there weren't any guy ones, but I was thinking that maybe werewolves were strictly heterosexual. I wasn't, so I'd be happy enough with the girly ones. I also saw some car magazines and a People. I grabbed them too thinking Candy might appreciate some reading material herself.

I was bored and feeling nosy, so I looked through the guy's bedroom. Lots of flannel, and belts with a variety of heavy, picturesque belt buckles. I'll bet *this* guy had an axe in his garage. Whole lot of condoms in the underwear drawer with the tighty whities. I checked the expiration date on them. A few were pretty old. I opened one up for the heck of it and it was a bit dried out. Very careless of him. I wondered who Robinson was getting it on with? He was pretty restricted in his sexual partners with the existence contract. And with the state of those condoms, he'd not just be violating the sex part, but the breeding part also if he were fucking humans. I glanced again at the girly mags and wondered if jacking off to photos of human women would violate the contract. Stupid angels.

The kitchen revealed that Robinson didn't eat much. Or maybe he wasn't home enough to bother with stocking up on groceries. There were some cans of tuna, white beans, and stewed tomatoes along with an almost empty bag of stale chips. Jackpot in the fridge though. It was full of beer. Coors Light, but hey I wasn't going to be picky about stolen beer. It wasn't really stealing anyway. I was going to save the guy's ass, so he owed me some beer. I glanced out the window and saw Candy still arguing with Craig. She waved her finger at him, then walked out of view. I could imagine the conversation now: "Don't you walk away from me, young man."

Wyatt popped open two beers, handed me one and took one back to the bathroom, snagging a magazine out of my hands. There are some things he evidently didn't want to do out in an open field. I hopped up on the counter and sat there drinking my beer. I'd wait for Wyatt, grab a six-pack, or maybe a twelve-pack, and we'd head back to our comfortable spot behind the bushes.

I'd finished my beer, started on a second and was beginning to wonder what the hell was taking Wyatt so long. I'm a get it done kinda girl. Maybe he was at a particularly engrossing part of the magazine and just needed to finish the article. Right. I hopped down from the counter and was about to head over when a boom shook the house practically knocking me off my feet. What the fuck? Did a truck just come through the living room wall or what? I ran to the front of the house, which was all of five steps, and saw a blur of light. The front door was split and sideways on its hinges,

Candy lay in a bloody heap by the door. The light emanated from an angel, who had a limp Craig in the air as he shot some kind of energy through him. Craig looked a lot like a colander at that moment. I pulled up my raw energy and sent a blast at the angel. It would fry Craig too, but he was probably dead anyway.

Craig dropped to the floor as the angel flew back from the blast, smashing through drywall and wall joists into the master bedroom. He narrowly missed Wyatt, who ran down the hall towards us.

"Help Candy," I shouted at him, more to get him safely out of the way than any real concern over the werewolf. I jumped through the considerable hole in the wall and flung another burst of energy at where I thought the angel might have landed. I was a few feet off and blew a hole in the floor as he scrambled for cover behind the bed. I went to dive across the bed at him and just missed having my head blown off by whatever the fuck it was he was throwing around. I rolled away just in time and smacked him with a pillow on the way. Take that, you bastard. He looked confused for a moment, which bought me enough time to roll safely off the bed and avoid another blast. The bedroom was full of holes by this time and drywall dust filled the air.

Lying on the ground, I grabbed the metal frame of the bed and ran a good sized charge of electricity through it, hoping that if he was touching it, he'd at least be stunned. The mattress smoked, but as I scooted around the corner, the angel was alert and waiting. He threw more of the white stuff at me and I tried to duck out of the way. It hit my left hand and I was shocked to see that it blew my hand right off.

"You fucking bastard! I just regenerated that hand!" I shouted at him as he dashed out the door and back to the living room.

I hurtled after him heaving two more chunks of energy

toward him from my right hand and my left stump. One hit, knocking him through the wall and into the kitchen. I saw him slam his back against the island counter, cracking a chunk of the plywood and linoleum off as he slid to the floor. He scrambled to his feet, diving around behind the island. What the fuck would kill this thing? He threw a few more wild blasts at me from behind the island, and out of desperation I blowtorched the whole lot. Maybe fire would do the trick.

Nope. The bastard stood up and tried to make a run for the back door. I wasn't having any of that, so I hit him again with a blast of raw energy and flung him into the fridge. By now, the middle part of the kitchen was on fire, there were holes blown through most of the house, and the fridge door was hanging off its hinges. None of the beer fell out, though. I took it as a positive omen.

He threw more white stuff at me as he struggled to get up from the floor, but it was weaker and his concentration and aim seemed to be going. Maybe I was slowly wearing him down. I took a moment to regenerate my hand while easily ducking his blast. I hate having a stump where my fingers should be.

I saw the angel dive down and guessed that he was going to make a break for the door again. I ran for it and beat him there, blocking the door with my body. That's when he made his fatal mistake. He met my eyes square on. I locked him in place and held him there. It wasn't easy. He still had a lot of power, and he knew his life depended on getting away. He squirmed like a bug pinned to a board, unable to break my gaze as I slowly moved across the burning kitchen toward him. Damn, he was strong, I thought as he kept pace with me, backward through the kitchen and into the living room, past Wyatt and a bloody but alert Candy. Finally, his back hit the front wall of the living room where he kicked and thrashed, his eyes wide with terror.

"I'm not going to just kill you," I told him calmly. "I'm going to Own you so I can keep you with me forever. I'll peel the skin from you one strip at a time. I'll reach up your ass and pull your insides slowly out, gnawing on them and ripping them with my claws. I'll dislocate every joint in your body one at a time. I'll take your bones and heat them, burning bits of you with your own flesh, and just when you think you're dead, I'll bring you back and do it all over again."

I was beyond excited. I *had* him. He was weakening and I was so strong. Mine. I'd be the only one of my kind to Own an angel. I reached him and began to send the mix of raw and personal energy into his body to force him to yield. Oh, this would be so sweet. The raw energy surged within me, and I reached out with the feathers of my personal energy to follow their blazed trail and take what I wanted. I felt him build one last bit of strength within himself to fend me off and smiled as I reached out to touch...the wall. He was gone. Gone. Where the fuck could he have gone? I had him. He was locked in place. No fucking way. Not again.

I shrieked in rage and hit the wall with my fist. That wasn't helping, so I turned around and grabbed the nearest thing, which happened to be Craig's dead body. With a blast of energy, I ripped his arm off at the shoulder and began smashing it against the wall with all of my might.

"Son of a bitch!" I screamed. "Damn mother-fucking cock-sucking son of a bitch!"

I continued to scream curses and smash Craig's arm against the wall with both hands, sending bits of flesh and blood flying around the room and smearing red all over the walls. I kept at it until the arm was a mush of pulp in my hands. Breathing heavy from the adrenaline and the exertion, I realized that I hadn't heard a sound since I'd begun my tirade. I turned my head and saw Candy and Wyatt standing well away from me to the side, staring in horror at something behind me. Turning all the way, I saw a different angel, huge, dark and fearsome, framed by the burning kitchen behind him. I choked a bit and my heart felt like it hit the floor.

CHAPTER 14

The first angel had been tall and thin with blond curls and androgynous features in an oddly stone-like face. I'd not gotten a good look at Gregory from my brief glimpse in The Wine Room. Not much beyond his height and dark red curls. I could see why the patrons had mistaken him for an actor. He was over six feet and built like a champion weightlifter. His crossed arms and chest looked ready to burst out of the navy polo shirt. His legs were snug in the acid washed jeans. I wondered what angel wore polo shirts and jeans? Where was the flowing white robe thingie?

His tanned features were clearly masculine in the odd marble-textured face, almost harsh in their angles with a sharp nose and squared jaw. Dark chestnut curls fell around his ears and one dropped on his forehead. The whole effect would have been terribly sexy had it not been for his eyes. They were black. Black as midnight on a moonless night. They looked at me with a mixture of disgust and hatred. I was so scared that I had to consciously keep my energy at the surface ready for defense. I very much wanted to hide. Maybe if I stood really still, he wouldn't see me. Wouldn't see me here, all bloody, in a wrecked house, holding a mangled arm.

"You cockroach," the angel said, his voice oozing cold fury. He actually hissed a bit when he said it, like a snake. I seriously thought I was going to piss my pants. "I spend my time and energy establishing protection for this man, and you lure him over here and get him killed. What a waste." He shook his head at Craig's body, minus the one arm.

"My carefully laid trap, completely ruined by your impulsiveness. How many more will die now? And you have the gall to think you can Own one of us? The arrogance to think you can Own an *angel*? You miserable, lowly cockroach. I'll squash you like the vermin you are."

He pulled a sword seemingly out of nowhere. A long blade that glowed with a milky iridescence. He grasped it with two hands, and I noticed the guards curved up from the hilt were shining gold angel wings. Was this the sword he used to chop up my kind and reduce us to a pile of sand? Probably. I doubted it was for dicing tomatoes. Either way, I really didn't want to find out what it felt like against my neck.

In desperation, I dropped the pulpy arm and yanked every bit of raw energy I had to the surface hoping I'd at least cause him some pain before he took me out. Even if the sword sucked up most of the energy, maybe there would be enough to knock him sideways and give me a few minutes to try a desperate attempt at escape.

As Gregory took a step toward me there was a deafening roar and the angel shook his head in astonishment. There was Wyatt, his huge gray pistol pointing at the angel. Wyatt, with a combination of fear and resolve on his face, had shot him. With his big gray pistol, he'd had shot an angel point blank in the head. I was torn between admiration at the balls it took to shoot an angel, and a surge of appreciation that

Wyatt cared enough to go head to head with one to protect me.

Sadly, a .50 caliber bullet doesn't seem to do much to an angel. Gregory frowned, the sword disappeared, and he shot one hand out to grab Wyatt's wrist and knock the gun to the ground. The other hand went to Wyatt's throat.

It was a perfect opportunity. Over the decades I had managed to store an immense amount of raw energy. I could have shot it in a stream at Gregory and possibly killed him in a massive blast. It would have killed Wyatt too, but that sort of thing never bothered me before. Demons are not sentimental, and as much as I liked Wyatt, my own personal well being should always come before anyone else's. I shouldn't have thought twice. It should have just been an automatic defensive action. Instead, I dropped the energy back within me and launched myself physically at Gregory. He clearly wasn't expecting it. I knocked him to the ground away from Wyatt who slumped beside us clutching his throat. My stupidity continued as I straddled Gregory's huge chest, grabbed his curls with my hands and whacked his head repeatedly on the ground.

"Pick on someone your own size, asshole," I shouted at him. "Leave him alone. He's just a human, you fucking bully." Brilliant. I was so dead.

The angel looked at me with shocked surprise. Yep, I'll bet he never had a crazed demon sit on him and bash his head on the floor before. He reached up, pinned my arms against the sides of my chest and easily tossed me across the floor like a bowling ball. I slid before coming to an abrupt stop against the wall decorated with Craig's blood.

Before I could get my head to function clearly, he had my arms pinned against my chest again and had lifted me up against the wall with my feet dangling, eye to eye with him. It wasn't very dignified, and I really didn't want to look in those dark eyes. I kept trying to pull my energy up, but he was doing something to me. It felt like my energy had a slippery silicone coating on it and I couldn't grab it. I tried and tried, and it slipped away. He just held me there, silent and staring as I struggled, willing me to look at him. I kept my gaze determinedly fixed at his chin and kept trying to pull up some energy. Somehow I managed to grab a small handful and threw it at him. It was a tiny amount, the same that we use to discipline naughty children or disobedient servants, hardly likely to do more than piss him off further. It was the equivalent of smacking him on the nose with a rolled up newspaper. Bad doggie!

He didn't even budge. Just held me and stared at me until I finally stopped trying to grab my energy and reluctantly looked up at him under my eyelashes. We remained there, looking into each other's eyes while I clenched my jaw to keep from shaking. I wished he'd say something. Something dramatic about what pain and torture he was going to inflict on me or what a horrible nasty cockroach of a being I was. Anything. Anything to distract me from wondering what I was seeing in those black eyes.

"Are you afraid of me, cockroach?" he asked. His voice was deep and oddly seductive. I was far more afraid than turned on, though these two states weren't mutually exclusive for a demon. He didn't seem to want a response. I didn't need to nod. He knew I was scared shitless.

"You should be afraid. You may have been a match for a weakling like Althean, but you are no threat to me at all. You would do no more harm to me than an annoying fly buzzing around my head. I fought in the wars, I was present at the banishment of your kind, I've killed every demon who has faced me since the division of the realms. Far more powerful demons than you have fallen quickly and easily to my sword. Your death would be nothing to me. It would take me no effort at all to end your life, and reduce you to a pile of sand."

He paused a moment and I could feel him exploring me with his power. It burned as it channeled through my flesh and probed my personal energy. I probably couldn't have blocked him out, but I was surprised that I didn't even try. I just let him poke me and turn me over like an interesting rock he was examining.

"You are just an imp, a baby imp," he commented, his tone filled with curiosity. His examination of me lost its rough edge and took on a note of wonderment. Nervously I guarded my stash of raw energy from him and tried to keep his probing closer to the surface. Pinning me against the wall with one hand, he released my shoulder with the other and put his fingers against my temple. I shook a little wondering if I was about to have angel wings imprinted on my forehead prior to my demise.

"A baby. Simple, and unskilled. Lucky perhaps, but not so powerful after all." He suddenly no longer had that hissing sound in his voice and I hoped that was a good thing. I didn't think it was a good moment to argue that at nine hundred thirty-six human years I was well beyond the age of majority, so I kept my mouth shut.

"I have more pressing matters to attend to than sending you to your grave at this moment, and I think you might prove to be of some use to me," he said.

He gave that a few moments to sink in, then abruptly let go dropping me to the ground. I hadn't expected it, and my legs weren't exactly strong at that moment, so I crashed into a heap. The angel turned to the others. He looked at Wyatt in disgust.

"Her stench, her mark covers you like a dog she owns." He shook his head. "You have free will to do as you choose, but what poor choices you make. Stupid human."

He then walked to Candy who stood steady and calm, streaked with blood, her hands and face back to their human form. "You make deals with demons to solve your problems rather than ask other angels for assistance? You have truly lost your way."

She raised her eyebrows and I admired her fortitude. "When have you or your kind ever given us cause to trust you? We have seen none of you, only Althean. Didn't you pay attention at all to what he was doing? Surely you saw his actions, yet you ignored us."

Gregory glared at her. "You should have come to me, or to another angel. Why would you suffer in silence like this? Why would you turn to a demon to help you? We are also bound to work within the terms of your contract, you should have brought this to someone's attention."

"How do we know you don't feel the same?" Candy asked. "We know many think we are Nephilim. How are we supposed to know who to trust? Any of you could feel the same way. Do you blame us for seeking help elsewhere? We rightly assumed that you sanctioned his actions."

I held my breath waiting for Gregory to whip out that sword and proceed to smackdown. Instead, he nodded slowly.

"The Council hasn't decided yet on whether you are Nephilim, and I will not act without their decision," he said, avoiding giving his own personal opinion on the matter.

"We will right this thing," he went on to assure her. "There have been too many innocents killed, and although I deplore your actions, I can see they were made in desperation."

Gregory flicked a hand at the flaming kitchen and the fire died. Instantly. There wasn't even a smoldering coal left. I was willing to bet if I put my hand on the charred island it would be cool. I could do that, but I wouldn't have thought to be so thorough about it. Slowly, he turned and looked at the wreckage of the house.

"Samuel Robinson won't be pleased with the state of his dwelling, little cockroach," he said reproachfully.

Common wisdom says that when you're faced with a being that can kill you three times before breakfast, you should hold your tongue and not aggravate him. So I told him that his friend Goldilocks had done just as much damage as I had. Then I made matters worse by suggesting Robinson use Craig's house since he wouldn't be needing it any more. Candy and Wyatt looked appalled. Gregory frowned.

"It's a much nicer house, he should be thrilled. Plus it's got that amazing hex on it. You did a bang up job on that hex. Melted my hand up past the wrist." Yep, I'd lowered myself to shameless flattery. Next I'd be groveling before him and licking his boots. It didn't do any good. The angel shook his head and actually turned his back on me.

"Unfortunately, the next area will be Waynesboro where there's a sizable werewolf population," he said to Candy and Wyatt. He was ignoring me. Because I was a cockroach. And not even a fully grown one. A baby cockroach with no skills or power whatsoever and not worthy of the slightest notice.

"It will be difficult to drive him into the direction I want with the short time window we have, so I will be using your help," he continued.

He was clearly going to be some time telling Wyatt and Candy what they were going to do for him, so this cockroach decided to see what beer in the fridge was salvageable and if any magazines remained unburned. The beer was less cold than I preferred, but the broken fridge door had blocked the hottest part of the fire from the inside of the refrigerator. I pulled out fourteen of the coldest beers and found a dented roasting pan to carry them with. The magazines were burned beyond recognition, but before I mourned them I remembered that Wyatt had taken one into the bathroom with him. I walked into the living room, past the lecture in progress and down the hallway to retrieve the magazine. I hoped it was a good one. Again I passed by the others without notice, grabbed the roasting pan full of beer and headed out the back door with my stash.

I went all the way down the driveway and around to the spot where we had hidden our cars, then crammed my goodies in the miniscule Corvette trunk, snatching a beer for the road. I chuckled taking a swig of the beer. Evidently, all you needed to do to escape an angel was to get him blathering on about something and just walk right out the door. I wondered if I could make it to the gate near Columbia Mall before he finished talking. I took another swig of the beer, slamming the trunk shut and spinning around to get in and go and smacked my face right into a chest. A really big, hard chest wearing a polo shirt. I choked a little and beer came out my nose and onto the polo shirt. Gregory stood there patiently while I coughed, showering him with beer and snot.

"Shit. Could you not sneak up on a girl like that?" I sputtered, finally able to take a decent breath.

"I think I will need to keep you within my sight at all times, cockroach," he said with a hint of irritation in his voice. "I haven't postponed your execution just to have you run amok burning buildings and desecrating corpses. I have some tasks for you to accomplish before I kill you."

Really motivating speech, I thought, as he took my arm and hauled me back to Robinson's house. I nearly fell, twisting around to lock my car as he pulled me along.

Back in the charred kitchen, a lively discussion broke out about the driving arrangements needed to get back to the motel. Gregory wouldn't let me go anywhere without him. I wasn't driving him in my car, and I wasn't letting Wyatt drive my Vette, so we could all go in Candy's car together. With the driving logistics still unresolved, we began to argue over whether we should spend the night in the motel and head up to Waynesboro fresh, or head up now and hope they even had a motel in Waynesboro where we could shack up. Wyatt had very specific views on what routes we should take to get there. I announced that I had clothes in the washer still, and that I was hungry and wanted pizza. Wyatt offered to pick up pizza in my car, and I told him no. He was *not* driving my car. That was when Gregory made a frustrated noise, ripped my keys out of my hand and tossed them at Wyatt while grabbing me in a bear hug. Suddenly, we were in front of our motel door. Everything spun around me and I was grateful that Gregory still was holding me against him or I would have pitched right over the railing into the parking lot below.

I'd been through gates many times before. I wasn't as talented as Charon, who actually hired himself out to those not skilled enough to find or cross gates on their own, but I could do it solo, and could even manage some of the wild and Elf gates. We didn't make gates. Elves could create some limited ones, but all the big stable gates were created by the angels. Some wild, natural gates existed, but angels were really the masters of this skill. I'd never done any inter-realm gates. I didn't think we even had any, back home. Plus, this was fast. Super fast and disorienting. It took me a while to feel steady, my vertigo probably made worse by my thinking this angel could crush me like a beer can and fling me over the railing before I could take a breath.

"Are you a succubus?" Gregory asked, his deep voice rumbling at me through his chest. It was oddly soothing, that sound. I had a strange, tiny urge to do whatever he asked, but quickly shook it off. "Do you entrance men and women, cleaving them to you as slaves to satisfy your every desire? At first I thought you were just a young trickster imp, but you seem to have this skill."

I snorted. Slaves to satisfy my every desire? Sounded like a great plan to me.

"Oh yeah. The worst succubus in all of eternity, that's me. I've been pursuing that male human for two years now — *two years*, and I'm not even to second base with him. If I were a succubus, my sisters would have had me killed six centuries ago for ineptitude."

Back home I knew several succubi and incubi. There weren't a lot of them, thankfully, because they made quite a stir even among our kind. They didn't have a great amount of power, but what they had was very specialized into sexual desire. Popping over here and enthralling humans was a favorite activity. With barely one foot across the gate they'd have a stream of humans of both genders lined up around the blocks to do whatever they wanted. Even back home they were popular choices for households. They had some influence over our own kind and made good negotiators. Good sexual partners too, although they couldn't withstand some of the really crazy stuff.

How on earth could he possibly think I was a succubus, though? Even my own kind weren't overly interested in me. He'd surely encountered succubi before. Was it possible that he was in some weird way attracted to me and was attributing it to an innate power or skill of mine? I clearly had no such skill, so any attraction he felt would be freely generated from himself. I chucked at the prospect that an angel might have the hots for me. Now that would be funny.

"What level are you then? How many legions do you command?" Gregory rumbled like thunder and velvet against me.

"That's none of your business." I told him, feeling slightly dismayed with myself for not giving him the answers he wanted. I wondered if *he* was some kind of angel succubus. Attractive weird human form aside, he did stir something within me. All that power, and a sort of remote coldness. Like he'd been petrified, and the fire inside him was only a spark, buried deep and waiting to burst into renewal. I wondered if he'd ever been unfrozen. What would he be like with the fire breaking through? Intriguing thought, but no way was he getting my name.

American GIs might recite name, rank, and serial number upon capture, but no fucking way I was going to. Names had power, and the fewer of mine anyone knew the better. My level or current place in the hierarchy would allow him to better know my talents, power level, and possibly even discover one or more of my names. Nope.

Besides, I was beginning to think he knew as little about us as we did about them. He was old enough to have fought in the wars, but so much had changed since then. We no longer had legions. No sense in having a standing army when you haven't had a war in over two million years. Plus, we don't have the temperament for that amount of organization. Need had overcome our inclinations during the war, and we'd also had an Iblis, one of us powerful enough to lead and keep a large organizational structure from breaking down. The Iblis kept us operating as a whole toward one goal. That was a remarkable thing for our kind. We hadn't had an Iblis for a very long time. Even the oldest among us didn't have that level of influence. Or really care to.

Gregory sighed and released his hold on me. "Fine," he said, making it clear that we'd revisit this topic again in the future. "Go ahead and open the door then."

I looked at him blankly. "You took my keys and gave them to Wyatt."

He rolled his eyes. "Are you that much of a cockroach? Do you need keys to open a door?"

Oh. Yeah, that's right. Well I had been acting as a human for forty years after all. I reached over and snaked in the energy to click the lock.

We went in, and I began to gather together our belongings, careful to separate Candy's toiletries as she would have wanted. I didn't need two of my traveling party gunning for me. Gregory looked around for a bit, reading the laminated rate sheet and examining the chained remote with bewilderment.

"Why is this plastic rectangle chained to the television set? Is the zinc-plated chain somehow integral to its operation?"

"It's a remote control for operating the TV and it uses low level infrared signals." I glanced at the remote while stuffing socks into a plastic bag. "The chain is to deter theft."

Gregory frowned and snapped the chain off the remote, breaking a chunk of the plastic off the end with the ring. "How does this deter theft? Any human with a pocket knife could break this."

I shrugged, agreeing with him and resolving to steal the remote just to annoy the management. Candy would probably get charged for it on her credit card, but she was likely to anyway since the angel had broken part of it off.

"If you think that's perplexing, look at this." I stuck a quarter in the bed and sent it to vibrating. Sure enough, the angel looked astounded.

"It's supposed to enhance a sexual experience," I told him.

"Does it actually work?" he asked in amazement, watching the bags bounce their way across the bedspread.

I shrugged. "Not that I can tell. It is a lot of fun though, and it totally freaks Candy out. Maybe if you were in the act of penetration it might enhance the orgasm. I haven't had sexual intercourse on the bed, so I can't really speak from experience."

Gregory shook his head in disbelief at the bed, and then walked around to see if there were any other unexpected human gadgets to examine. I sat on the bed and let it bounce me around a bit so I felt like I actually got my quarter's worth. It was a short ride.

Done perusing the room, Gregory watched me continue packing with his arms crossed in front of him. I felt like a prisoner. I guess I kind of was. After a few moments, he announced he was going down to check us out. "Stay here," he said ominously.

As soon as he walked out the door, I shoved the remote in a bag and proceeded to dig through Wyatt's things. There. The little toddler gun. I quickly stashed it in my rear waistband pulling the shirt over it. It was tiny, and it's not like Gregory would strip search me or even suspect I'd be packing a human firearm.

I'd put all of our belongings into separate shopping bags when I remembered my laundry. The shirt was still damp in the washer, so I threw it in the dryer hoping a few moments on high heat would finish the job. My mind worked furiously. Screw Candy and this whole werewolf thing. I needed to get away from this angel as soon as possible or I'd be dead. Who knows how long he'd find me useful, and eventually this job would be over and he'd finish what he started at Robinson's house. He was fast, he could gate all over the place in less than a second. I'd have to get away from him without using any energy so he couldn't track me and then head to a gate he wouldn't think to intercept me at. He couldn't guard them all. The one at Columbia Mall might be too far, and I was really scared to use that wild gate in Sharpsburg, although it was the absolute closest. Wild gates could rip you apart, and sometimes they had buffer zones where a traveler could get lost and trapped. Sometimes they spit you out somewhere unexpected. Like across the universe unexpected. Not that I knew this from experience. Obviously.

Forty years I'd been here undetected. I was used to living as a human. I'd watch for a chance to get away, then go underground and head for the gate in Philly or maybe the one near Wichita. I mulled my options wondering if he ever slept when I felt myself grabbed by the shoulder and flung against the cement wall of the motel. I hit hard on my left shoulder. Ow.

"What the fuck is your problem?" I snarled, fixing the dislocated shoulder. Gregory loomed over me with menace. What the hell did I do now? Was it against some angel law to dry your clothes?

"I told you to stay in the room," he hissed at me.

"No," I argued, because that is clearly the thing to do when faced with an enraged angel. "You told me to stay *here*. I am here. At the motel. Drying my shirt so we can leave." Idiot.

He was hovering over me and breathing heavy, like he'd run around the building a few times, although I think it was more trying to control himself and keep from killing me. I helped him by continuing to sit on the dirty floor looking up at him. I really wanted to get up and punch him, but my minimal self preservation had finally kicked in.

Grabbing at my arm with the fixed shoulder, he hauled me to my feet and held me a few inches off the ground. "I won't lose you," he muttered half to himself. "You will not slip through my grasp. You will not escape me."

I could see him struggle to gain control when, almost as if with a will of its own, he hissed, "Mine."

It was quiet, but the word pulsed with power. Certain words are more than just words. Certain words can carry the strength of all creation. This was one. I used it when I Owned a being, I used it when I claimed territory, when I created a household bond. I had never used it with such power behind it, though. I felt it slam into me and wondered what he'd meant. In what way had he claimed me?

He managed to finally get control of himself and took a big breath. "I really don't want to have to bind you to me. It would hurt a lot and be very unpleasant."

I appreciated his concern for my comfort.

"No," he said, seemingly reading my thoughts. "It would hurt *me* a lot, and be very unpleasant for *me*. Pain to you would only bring me great joy."

Well, then. "Look, this was all a misunderstanding. See? I'm right here, drying my clothes. I didn't run away. I didn't try to escape your clutches. If you let me go, I'll just pull the shirt out of the dryer and we'll be on our way. Candy and Wyatt should be here any moment and we can head out. You're really scary, and I'm going to do whatever you say." Okay, maybe the last bit was over the top, but I really wanted him to relax and give me enough slack on the leash to slip my collar and bolt.

He looked suspicious, but he did let go of my arm. I grabbed the shirt, and with an angel trailing behind me I went to the hotel room and gathered our things. We went down to the lobby to wait for Candy and Wyatt. What was taking them so long? Did they stop for pizza? Did Wyatt take off on a joy ride with my car? I fretted over the safety of my car. Wyatt might be my best friend, but I'd kill him if he dented my precious car.

We remained in the lobby, air thick with tension, surrounded by the shopping bags. Gregory sat in the little plastic chair placidly ignoring the young girl at the front desk. Probably the owner's daughter, I thought watching her stare enraptured at the angel. I could have stripped naked and done a pole dance with the gumball machine and she wouldn't have broken her gaze. Maybe if she jumped him in an adoring frenzy I'd be able to make a quick getaway.

Candy and Wyatt pulled up and I inspected my car thoroughly for damage. Wyatt looked me over for damage, too.

"Are you okay, Sam?" he whispered. "What can I do to help? You've got to get away from him."

No shit, Sherlock. I had no idea what he could do to help, but I was formulating a plan.

"Just hang tight with Candy," I told him. "Don't antagonize him. I don't want him to kill you."

I was treated to the joy of watching Gregory cram himself into my passenger seat. Corvettes may be sports cars, but they are American sports cars, made for big oversized Americans. Still Gregory took up more than his allocated share of space. I'm assuming he had to buy two seats when he flew commercial. I took the lead and we headed out of town with Gregory silent and brooding beside me. Out of the corner of my eye I could see him staring at me with hostility. Was he still pissed about the dryer episode? Or just pissed in general about my existence?

Gregory's leg was encroaching on the stick shift and I kept grabbing it instead of the shifting lever. It happened a lot, and I swear I was not doing it on purpose. It was like grabbing a block of cement. Still, I couldn't help but be a bit turned on.

I wondered if I could snake my hand up further and get in a quick grope before he removed my arm from my body. I wondered what angel genitals felt like. Did they even have genitals? Maybe they were anatomically like Ken dolls. I hadn't noticed any bulges, even while I was pressed against him through the gate, but I didn't think I was his idea of a potential sexual partner. The thought of sex with me probably left him cold and flaccid. Actually, the thought of sex with me probably hadn't even crossed his mind. Angels probably did it in some ethereal way that didn't involve genitals. Some kind of sterile, esoteric sexual experience. I imagine it was horribly boring. Maybe I could convince him to do it the human way. Or the demon way. I fantasized for a moment about a threesome with the angel and Wyatt. Like *that* would ever happen. This was not a good train of thought for me to be having.

"How did you manage to survive Wyatt shooting you in the head? That would probably have killed me, but you hardly moved. You didn't even bleed." I was curious, and I really needed to get my mind out of the gutter.

He gave me a disgusted look. "You are too imbedded in your physical form, almost like a human. If you hold yourself apart more, these things couldn't affect you. Of course, I wouldn't expect a demon to have the self discipline to do that sort of thing."

Jerk. "Ah, so that's why your form sucks so bad, then. I thought maybe you just weren't skilled enough to create and hold a decent physical form. I wouldn't expect an angel to have the aptitude for that sort of thing."

He glared. "For someone so close to death, you are surprisingly insubordinate."

Yikes. I needed a distraction before I got myself even further into trouble, so I turned on the radio. It may sound weird, but I'm a sucker for 1970s-era love songs, so that's what I put on. I bopped along to Temptation Eyes, then heard familiar opening notes.

"Oh, I love this one," I announced.

Samantha Martin, the human Samantha Martin had a nice set of pipes. She was in church choir when she was young, and was a darned good amateur singer before I Owned her. If they'd have had American Idol back then, she would have at least made it on the show. I Owned an opera singer too, but that skill didn't come up much. I sing whenever I get a chance. In the shower, in the car, karaoke in bars. Sometimes I just sing randomly because it freaks people out. So it was nothing for me to perform car karaoke right now. Even with an angry, pouty, potentially violent angel sitting beside me.

An awesome song came on. It was "Just Remember I Love You" by Firefall. I loved this song. Mushy, sentimental, perfect for serenading an angel. I grinned at Gregory and he looked back at me, a combination of amazement and anxiety on his face. He looked like I'd just sprouted two heads and scales. Of course, *that* he'd probably seen before.

I continued to sing, belting out the chorus before turning my eyes back to the road. Gregory scooted a little away from me, a look of near terror on his face. It's not like he could scoot far, though. He was supersized and my car was too small for distance.

The station was really on a roll. I continued to serenade him with "Band of Gold" and "Don't Pull Your Love Out On Me Baby" but turned the channel when they played "Jackie Blue". I never liked that song.

"I had you pegged for a Slayer fan, cockroach," he commented in a strangled voice, as if the whole experience was more than he could handle.

"Slayer? I can't understand a damned word they are singing. It's all 'bwaa, rhaa, whaa, grrr, grrr, grr'. What the fuck does that mean? I'd rather listen to harpies wail than that shit."

He nodded his head in agreement and I'd swear I saw his lips twitch. No way he could actually be amused. At least I'd managed to put him in a less hostile mood with my unusual music tastes. Good thing as we pulled out of town and onto Route 15 south. I glanced at Wyatt and Candy behind me in the rear view and put the pedal to the metal. In a roar, I had dusted them.

The highway was two lanes each way with a decent shoulder all the way into Montgomery County, Maryland. This time of day the cars were evenly spaced with a good bit of commercial truck travel along the route. I weaved in and out of traffic, honking rudely, darting around cars, cutting off the semis and passing on the shoulder. Today, I wished that I'd bought the red model Corvette instead.

I was glad Gregory didn't know anything about roads, or he would have wondered why I didn't take the shorter way down 116. Wyatt was probably in Candy's car looking at his GPS and bitching and moaning about the extra distance of my chosen route. Route 116 was shorter, much prettier, and there was not much traffic. This way would take us on the busy highway back tracking down into Maryland, then through Emmitsburg to loop back into Pennsylvania on Route 16. I looked over at the angel to see if his improved mood had survived our increase in speed.

"Shouldn't you keep your eyes on the road?" Gregory asked me. He didn't look pissed. He probably thought I was trying to shake him up with my crazy driving. I wondered if he had ever been in a car before. Probably not, if he could gate everywhere. I doubted he'd ever driven, either. That would make him an auto virgin. I laughed out loud at the idea.

"You know, you can't kill me by wrecking your car," he commented in that bored voice. "You'll just destroy your vehicle. I won't suffer more than a scratch. Won't slow me down at all. You're not going to get away from me so you might as well drive like a normal person." He actually leaned his head back and closed his eyes, as if my erratic driving methods were putting him to sleep.

I continued to drive like a possessed maniac. Stupidly, it took nearly five miles before I saw the flashing lights behind me. Good thing as we were almost at the Maryland border. I kept driving a bit, weaving aggressively but trying to keep the speed down so I didn't lose the state trooper struggling to keep up. Finally, I pulled over into an old abandoned gas station, spinning out dramatically with a rooster tail of gravel dust.

"Looks like I'm going to get a ticket," I said. Gregory frowned at me with narrowed, suspicious dark eyes. "I was speeding, you know. Happens to me all the time. It will only take a minute and we'll be on our way."

The Pennsylvania State Police car behind us was a big white sedan. A huge Crown Victoria with the trooper badging all over and the light rack on top. It was a stupid car. If I were a state trooper, I'd make them get me a Ferrari.

The guy behind the wheel took his time getting out. I wondered what in the hell was taking him so long. Did he have to fill out fifteen pages of reports before he even got out of his car? Finally, he opened the door and slid out. He was a young guy. Thin and fit in his gray shirt and dark gray pants. He wore short sleeves in the heat, and the shirt had black fringed thingies on the shoulders. He had a hat on with a chin strap, and I could tell his hair was a short buzz cut underneath. I couldn't really see if he was cute or not, but he had a good body, and looked damned sweet in that uniform.

The cop walked up carefully from the rear of the car, flicking the leather strap on his pistol holster for easy access. He also had a baton, and some pepper spray handy and ready. The baton wasn't a big deal, but I hoped he didn't spray me with the pepper spray. I hate that shit. I unwound the window before he got there, and just as he leaned in, I pulled out my mean and threw it at him while simultaneously pulling the pistol from my waistband and laying it on my lap. I put every bit of menace I had into my voice and announced that he was a fucking pig and I was going to knock him on his ass.

It had the desired effect. The cop leapt back from the car and pointed his pistol at my head screaming "Out of the car! Out of the car and keep your hands where I can see them." I looked curiously at his gun, but didn't recognize it. I was hardly the expert from seeing Wyatt's small collection, but thought maybe I could recognize the caliber. The trooper waved his gun at me, again indicating that I needed to get out right now. Or presumably he would shoot me.

I smiled smugly at Gregory and he glared back at me in open hatred. Carefully, I opened the car door, letting the gun drop to the floor of the car while keeping my hands raised. Gregory got out too, and I realized he was doing something to try and soothe the officer and me. He was talking to the police guy in a low calm rumble and I swear I actually saw the deep blue wash over us both. It pulled and tugged on me with warm persistence, and I wanted to leave the cop alone and get back in the car. I wanted to rub myself on Gregory like a cat and have him look at me approvingly. Fuck no, I didn't want to do any of that shit. No fucking way. I shrugged off the urge and glared at the officer again. The cop looked confused and began to lower his gun.

"You fucking pig," I snarled at him, trying to regain control of the situation. "I've killed cops before and I'll kill you too. I'll blow your fucking head off." I took a few steps toward him.

Gregory redoubled his efforts and the air was thick and sweet with blue. I saw the officer shake a bit, sweat rolling down his forehead. The poor guy would be in therapy for years from this. Fuck, I'd probably be in therapy for years from this. The urge to kneel down at the angel's feet and wrap myself around him was nearly overwhelming.

The cop was slipping from my grasp though and I knew I needed to go all out. I walked up to the officer and slugged him right in the jaw. Not hard enough to knock him out, but enough to override all the calming blue shit. It worked. The guy grabbed me and slammed me face first against my car, yanking my arms behind me to cuff me. In a few moments, I'd be on my way to the police station. I could kill the cop, ditch his car, and be on my way to a gate while Gregory cooled his heels at some local station waiting for me to make bail.

The angel kept pressing his calming influence to no avail. The cuffs were on, and I was halfway to the police car, when Gregory threw up his hands, reached out and grabbed the cop. I felt him let me go and turned to see the angel whispering in his ear. In an instant he had slumped and Gregory held him upright, moving to put him back in his car. I quickly broke the cuffs, and bolted. Plan B.

I like to run. I'm not fast off the block, but I can go forever and keep a strong steady pace. The angel was a huge hulk of muscle. I hoped he wouldn't be able to keep up and I'd somehow lose him. He couldn't find me to gate to me if I kept my energy to myself.

Unfortunately, I only made it about twenty feet before he tackled me from behind. I smacked into the gravel and slid across it with his considerable weight on top, scraping a good layer of skin off my face and body, and knocking the breath out of me. For good measure, he flipped me over on my back and punched me in my stomach.

Looking up at him, gasping for breath, I realized that he'd totally lost control. His face was white and solid looking without pores in the skin, and blackness filled the entirety of his eyes. His teeth were no longer human, but sharp pointed little spikes, like piranha teeth. He actually glowed. Seriously glowed. He was so bright it burned my eyes. There was nothing in him but rage. Not a speck of feeling I could appeal to. Nothing but fury and hate. I grabbed my energy and prepared to empty the whole lot at him. It would probably blow a chunk out of the lower half of the state, but I might as well kill him along with myself. Better than me dying alone.

His eyes widened with the realization of what I was about to do, and he smacked me hard across the face before I could even begin to form the blast. The blow knocked my head sideways and caused my grasp to slip a little. Enough of a slip for him to coat that silicone stuff over my energy again.

"Oh no you don't, cockroach," he hissed at me through those pointy teeth. "Hold still," he commanded, grabbing my arms by the wrists and thrusting them up above my head.

Oh, sure. 'Hold still while I kill you.' Like that was going to happen. I wasn't sure if he was going to execute me straight away or beat the crap out of me first, but I figured it was going to be excruciating either way. I wasn't going down without a fight. I thrashed around with all my strength to see if I could budge him loose from on top of me. I even tried to knee him in the groin, assuming that would do anything. Wrenching one hand loose I flung a handful of gravel and dirt into his face. He shook his head and grabbed, unsuccessfully trying to secure my loose hand while at the same time attempting to pin my legs down with his. I bucked like a wild bull and smacked him with the little bits of energy that I could form. It was all I could manage to break free from the slippery shell he held in place around my energy.

After a few minutes of this, he hissed in frustration, grabbed me roughly around my waist and flung me over his shoulder. My breath whooshed out as my diaphragm smashed against his shoulder and my head bounced on the concrete of his back. While I frantically tried to recover, he began striding off toward the abandoned gas station and my car. Gasping little breaths, I squirmed, kicked and hit and scratched with all my might. Unaffected, he continued on, tightening his grip painfully around my waist to make sure I didn't manage to wiggle free. Wyatt and Candy were far behind us, not that they could intervene at this point. My mind worked furiously trying to find some way to break his hold, to get enough energy to knock him aside, to do anything, for surely I was going to die real soon. I'd tire physically, and without the use of my energy he had all the advantage.

Suddenly, he shrugged me off his shoulder and slammed my back against the cement block side of the building. My head spun again and I felt the warmth of blood sliding down the back of my skull and onto my neck. Without allowing me even a second to move, he pressed himself against me, crushing me between his body and the gritty, pebbled concrete wall. I felt the stone imbed itself into the torn flesh of my head and ground my teeth with the pain. At this rate, I'd be a shredded bloody mess by the time he finished me off.

Slowly and carefully he transferred my wrists to one hand, yanking them above my head and pinning them to the wall. With his other hand, he maneuvered my hips, straddling me and pinching my legs between his own. Within seconds, I was held immobile between him and the building. The only thing still free was my head, so I tried to head butt him and bite whatever part of his face came within range. He was a good foot taller than me, so the best I could do was a light tap on his chest with my forehead before he grabbed my jaw with his free hand and held my head still. At least he didn't have a third hand to whip out his sword. Of course, he could always bring that item out after I was a bloody mess on the ground.

He held me in place and looked at me a moment, hissing with those pointy teeth, his eyes still huge, black, and horrifying. I hurt. I knew my face was a mass of road rash, could feel the blood trickle from my cheeks and down the back of my head in a slow drip. My arms were extended up at their limit with the joints straining uncomfortably in their sockets.

My chest was heaving against his with tiny short breaths, and sharp chunks of concrete dug painfully into my back with the pressure of his body against mine. I was at the point of panic. I was trapped, and there was no way out. My mind helpfully imagined all the ways he could dispatch me in this position. He could rip my arms from their shoulder sockets, crush my jaw, dislocate my pelvis, pulverize my bones and organs against the side of the building, and then shred my flesh with his pointy teeth before finishing me off with the sword. That's how I would do it.

He took a breath, then he wrenched my head to the side facing my left arm, and I saw him out of the corner of my eye as he bent his head down. I felt an odd sense of disappointment that I wouldn't get to see him rip me to bits. Anticipating popping joints and tearing flesh, I took a quick breath and tensed. The feeling that came was like a thousand hot needles as he bit down on me, right on the soft underside of my arm, just in front of my armpit. My shoulders ached, but stayed in joint. This was going to take forever if he was going to concentrate primarily on chewing me up. My faint hopes for a quick death vanished, and I felt him bite down harder.

A burning sensation shot down into my chest and a mixture of vibrations shook me. Was there some poison in his bite? Was it that white stuff that Althean had shot at me? Would my insides dissolve like my hand had? It burned clear through my flesh and into my personal energy, branching out and searing tiny pathways. "This is it," I thought, my mind blurring from the agony tearing through me.

Then unexpectedly, underneath the pain, a far more enjoyable heat surged through me. Pleasure and pain are not mutually exclusive to my kind, and sex frequently involves what humans would consider abuse. Even so, I didn't believe the angel intended to kill me in an act of rough sex. The warmth flooded me and the burning pathways in my personal energy filled with an electric glow. Reddish purple soared through my being. 'Mine' I thought silently as I floated in the stream of color. It was a faint and fleeting thought, without intent or power; almost like an echo from someone else. Strange.

I didn't think revealing my strange state of sexual arousal would do my current situation any good, but I couldn't help the quick gasp and relaxation of my body as tension fell away and I ceased trying to struggle. Well, at least I'd be easier to kill now. And death would be a hell of a lot more fun.

The angel paused for a second, then pushed himself harder against me ensuring I was held fast and continued with the hot needles in my arm. The pain was quickly changing over to pleasure and I wanted to give in to the incredible sensation. Dissolving in a huge wet orgasm at the point of death seemed like an undignified way to go out so I tried to think of things like zoning hearings, taxes, when my next oil change was due. Anything but the red-purple waves singing through me. Shit, I hope he killed me soon, this was taking fucking forever and I was running out of boring things to think of.

Floating in the pleasure, I was halfheartedly daydreaming about useless kitchen utensils when I felt a pull deep within me. Like strings had been imbedded throughout my body and the angel was trying to draw them out. At first it didn't hurt, then the strings stopped moving and Gregory began to yank, pulling with increasing irritation and frustration. Finally, there was an agonizing pressure, like he was digging in on a tug of war contest with all his might. The strings didn't budge, but it felt like my whole body was about to turn inside out. Then there was a crack and snap as everything rebounded into me. It was a good thing I was held so firmly against the building because I probably would have fallen ten feet backwards from the release. I waited for it to begin again, but I only felt a stinging sensation and that familiar warmth as Gregory bit down again.

An eternity seemed to pass before he finally lifted his mouth from my arm. I felt him stare at me, although I couldn't see him clearly with my head held sideways against the wall. "Here it comes," I thought. My bitten arm throbbed. I held my breath, waiting for my death. Slowly, he loosened his grasp and relieved the pressure holding me against the wall. I didn't know what was coming, so I dropped my arms from their achingly extended position and stood there, looking at the front of his shirt and trying to slow my breathing. Finally, he took my arm, the one he hadn't been gnawing on, and walked me over to the police car. That was it? A chewed up arm? Perhaps he was going to continue the job over here?

"Fix yourself," Gregory commanded, pushing me to sit on the ground beside the car while he reached in and finished whatever he was doing to the cop. I was pretty sure the cop was dead. I wondered if he was sticking angel wings on his forehead too. Covering this one up and making it look like the cop had it coming. So much for benevolent messengers of the gods.

I had scrapes down the front from my slide across the gravel; my face was raw, bloody, and was bruised and swollen from his blow. My wrists hurt from the handcuffs, my shoulders ached from being held at that impossible angle, and the bite still burned and throbbed in an enjoyable kind of pain. I was a fucking mess. I wasn't sure I *could* fix myself right now, I was shaking so badly. Why wasn't I dead? And why did he bite me like that? What the fuck was that about?

Gregory put some finishing touches on the cop, who appeared to be asleep in his squad car, then turned to me. He looked me over and shook his head, his face still grim but no longer glowing with pointy teeth and huge black eyes.

"Fine. I really don't care what you look like, or if you bleed all over your seats. You will get in your car with me, and you will drive to Waynesboro. You will obey all the human traffic laws or I will destroy your vehicle and slowly break every bone in your body. Repeatedly. Over the course of several days. Do you understand?"

I nodded. And we drove to Waynesboro in silence. No singing. Fifty-five the whole way.

CHAPTER 15

We sat outside in the parking lot of some local restaurant called The Lamb waiting for Wyatt and Candy. I was hoping from the name that they had Greek food, but it didn't have the usual décor of a Greek restaurant. Maybe they did English food and specialized in mutton? I was starving and we'd been waiting here for quite a while. Candy must drive like a ninety-year-old lady on her way to church because there had been no sign of them. I thought about calling Wyatt on my cell phone, but was trying to be subdued and careful around Gregory. Just in case he was wondering whether to finish chewing my arm off.

"Fix yourself, or you're not going in," the angel commanded again.

Back home, it was typical to see those of my kind looking like they'd had the shit beat out of them. It was a point of pride. When someone higher up the hierarchy chose you for a fun romp, they conveyed their status on the energy signature in your wounds. Displaying them showed your peers that you'd been found worthy of someone higher up the food chain, and that you were tough enough to survive it. The more battered you were the better. Limbs dangling by a tendon, chunks of flesh burned off; all that revealed that you were tough and powerful. Leaving a significant sexual encounter with just a few flesh wounds was embarrassing. It meant that you'd been found to be uninteresting, or too fragile to enjoy properly.

Here though, looking beat up just marked you as a victim. Especially if you were female. A guy could pull it off by implying that the other participant was just as damaged, or claiming to have been in some kind of vehicle accident. No one believed the lies if you were female, though; everyone knew you were covering up domestic violence. Going into The Lamb looking like I did would probably result in the police being called and Gregory taken in for questioning. I liked the idea, but given our last encounter I didn't think it would turn out well. Gregory didn't seem to have any problem taking out civilians when necessary. He'd proven that he wouldn't shy away from murder when it came to thwarting an escape attempt.

I sat there as if all the spirit had been crushed out of me; channeling the submissive, obedient servant. It wasn't easy. I didn't own any submissive people, I liked the fight and challenge too much and submissive humans were boring. Slowly, I fixed myself, taking some time to do it as if I barely could manage even this. It was painful, repairing my wounds this slowly, but definitely in keeping with the wounded, broken spirit I was trying to portray.

"Do your clothes, too," he ordered. "They're torn, dirty, and covered in blood. You're not going in looking like that. It will cause too much attention, and I've got enough to think about without having to enthrall all the humans in the restaurant."

My shirt was a disaster. The jeans weren't too bad, especially since torn and tattered jeans were in style right now.

"I can't do clothes," I told him truthfully.

He stared in disbelief. "What do you mean you can't do clothes? That should be ridiculously simple for you. Even *I* can do clothes."

Implying that he couldn't do much else beyond clothing? So angels weren't good at matter conversion? They were legendary at energy conversion, and they had unparalleled skill when it came to manipulating dimensions and creating gates. I knew they couldn't do the physical form conversion to the extent we did. From what I'd seen so far, their human form was pretty pathetic. I'd just assumed that converting inanimate objects would be a skill they would have. Perhaps that wasn't where their talents lay.

"We don't wear cloth back home," I replied. "If we're cold, we just make ourselves furry or up our metabolism. If we have a humanoid form at the time, it's always naked. We do sometimes skin another creature and wear it like a trophy, but we don't create cloth. Here, it's just easier and quicker to buy it than learn to make it. Especially these weird blends with altered petroleum molecules in the fibers." I looked at my tattered poly blend shirt fondly. Humans were actually pretty clever. I predicted amazing things from them in another hundred thousand years. If they didn't manage to wipe themselves out before then.

He made a motion as if he were going to take his shirt off and give it to me. I wasn't sure how he was going to manage that maneuver in the confines of my car. That I wanted to see. And I did want to see him without his shirt on. Crap, I bet he was ripped beyond belief. Yes, crazy me. The guy pummels me to bits and vows to kill me and I'm all revved up to see him semi-clad. Of course, the shirt wouldn't come close to fitting. It would be huge on me; bigger than Tinkerbell, even.

"They won't let you in the place without a shirt on," I told him reluctantly. "It says there right on the sign."

He paused and looked around the car as if he expected a shirt to appear out of nowhere. Nope, none in the glove box or under the seat either.

"Put on a shirt from the bags you had back at the hotel."

"They're all in Candy's car," I told him. "My trunk is really small and full of beer, so we put them all in hers."

He sat for a moment contemplating his options, then opened his door. "There's a gift shop in there, they've got to have some novelty t-shirts for sale. Stay here." He got out then paused. "In the car," he added, leaning in to look at me sternly. "And the car stays right here in this spot in the parking lot. You and the car don't move."

I had to bite back a smile. He learned quick, this angel did. To hide my amusement, I trembled a bit and tried to look properly cowed. I even tried to squeeze out a tear from big soulful eyes. Gregory frowned at me. "Do you feel sick? Do you need some crackers or something?"

I shook my head at him. So much for my acting skills.

While the angel was doing his shopping, Candy and Wyatt finally pulled up and parked beside the Corvette. Wyatt practically launched himself from the car, running around my car to pull open my door and inspect me.

"Are you okay?" he asked, his face tight with worry. "You're shirt is torn and bloody, what did he do to you?"

"We had an incident," I said vaguely. "I'm okay, though," I lied. I was reluctant to let Wyatt know all the details. My arm still stung from the bite, and it was in a place where I couldn't really see it without a mirror. I was glad it was my right arm, and Wyatt couldn't see it from where he stood. I really wanted to get a look at it first. When I fixed myself, it hadn't repaired. I could feel the red-purple strands of it snaked throughout my body down deep into my personal energy. It worried me. I didn't want to check it out with Gregory in the car, but I was desperate to see what the fuck was up. What *had* he done to me?

"She drives so slow," Wyatt said, looking at Candy with frustration. "You took off, and I knew something was going on. I kept trying to get her to drive faster and she wouldn't."

"She's smart," I told him. "No sense in you both getting yourselves killed in the crossfire."

Wyatt reached in the car and brushed my hair back from my face. I appreciated the gesture.

"Come on, get out of the car," he said gently, as if I were a child or an invalid.

"I can't," I told him. "I have to stay here, in the car, and the car needs to remain right here in this spot in the parking lot."

"What has he *done* to you?" Wyatt asked. I sensed his agitation.

"Wyatt, you need to get out of here," I told him. "I'm going to give you my car keys. Sneak out when we're in the restaurant and get as far away from here as you can. I mean it. Things are getting really bad, and I want you to be safe." He had to know it was bad if I was willing to let him drive my car.

He glared at me. "I'm not leaving you, Sam. I won't abandon you like that."

"You are way out of your league, here," I told him as gently as I could. "Fuck, *I'm* out of my league, here. I'm trying to get away as soon as I can manage it, and I'm really worried that if I slip out of his grasp, he'll take it out on you. I've seen what he can do. He will hurt you, Wyatt. He won't lose any sleep over killing you."

At that time, Gregory came back out of the restaurant with a little bag. I quickly slipped my car keys into Wyatt's hand, and tried to resume my subdued mien. The angel nodded at Candy and Wyatt and seemed pleased to see me with my butt rooted to the seat of the car as when he had left me. I yanked my torn shirt off as he tossed me the bag.

It was a small pink tank top. Really small. You'd think he would have had a better idea of my size from crushing me against a building. I snapped the tag off and unfolded it, pausing a moment when I saw the design. A stylized geometric angel in gold with a triangle body, triangle wings, circle head and a halo was featured prominently on the front, filling the shirt from neckline to waist. I hadn't realized Gregory had a sense of humor. I had to force myself not to laugh as I pulled it over my head. Submissive, meek, obedient, I chanted to myself in my head.

The shirt was outrageously tight. It molded against my breasts and the outlines of my abs. My cleavage burst above the neckline like my boobs were trying to escape the confines of the shirt. I looked less like an angel and more like a Hooters' waitress. Wyatt's eyebrows shot up when he saw the effect, and he glared at Gregory in suspicion and jealousy. Jealousy? Now that was funny.

When we walked into The Lamb, I saw the reason for Gregory's fashion choice. And the reason for the name. The whole gift shop was awash in angel and Christian religious items. I was actually grateful he hadn't gotten me a "Jesus is my co-pilot" shirt, or the one with the blond, blue eyed, Germanic Jesus praying to what would have been my left boob if I'd had the shirt on.

The hostess sat us near the buffet, casting adoring glances at Gregory the whole time. There were crosses on the walls, and scripture verses on the placemats. I wondered if I should oblige them and burst into flames or something. None of the employees seemed to notice the irony of my presence here. It would have been great fun to have Wyatt pretend to exorcise me, but I doubted this was the appropriate time for those kinds of antics. Maybe we'd come back in a week or two. If I was still alive then.

Wyatt and Candy began telling Gregory what they'd discovered on Wyatt's tablet. They'd found a campground nearby and snagged us a cabin; not easy to do since we were at the height of the summer holiday season. Candy placidly avoided looking at me, while Wyatt shot furious glances back and forth between me and Gregory. Great. All I needed now was Wyatt to get testosterone filled and start a cock fight over me. If a .50-caliber bullet didn't harm the angel, I doubted Wyatt's fists would do much except piss off Gregory enough to snap his neck.

"I need to use the bathroom," I announced. Gregory hardly gave me a glance, and the others ignored my statement.

I actually did use the bathroom, mainly to delay looking at my arm. Finally, I could avoid it no longer. I took a breath and pulled the armhole of the overly small tank top down, raising my arm to the mirror. Fuck. The tattoos of angels' wings on the werewolf victims were small and tan. They looked like tiny birthmarks, or skin discolorations from too much sun and too little sunscreen. You wouldn't even notice them if you weren't looking for them. This was over three inches long, in black and deep red-purple. It was vivid and clear; a sword with detailed angel wings curving up as guards from the hilt. Gregory's sword, tattooed in his color. Surrounding it was a round area of reddened raised skin. Like a hickey. I wondered why I hadn't been able to fix the hickey? I wondered if I exploded myself out and recreated my whole flesh from the DNA pattern if the tattoo and the hickey would go away? I doubted it. Besides, a burst that big would bring a furious Gregory barreling into the women's room to beat my ass.

I carefully ran a finger along the hickey mark and the

tattoo, feeling with my energy as well as my skin, and just about dropped to my knees. Lust poured through me and I shook with desire. Great. Just touch it and I was ready to hump the sink faucets. I felt it more gently, trying to explore it without triggering the sexual stimulation. The tattoo, the very color of it, thrummed and vibrated within me. I ran my finger over the hickey and felt the same humming, although it was more flesh centered and not as deep. The hickey mark seemed to have a direct line to my genitals, where the tattoo poured its red-purple streaks down into my personal energy. The tattoo was just as much a sexual stimulation as the hickey mark, only different in that it turned on the non-human, non-corporeal part of myself.

Well, this was just splendid. I now had a super sensitive erogenous zone on the under part of my arm. No need to get in my pants, just run your fingers up my arm and watch me melt. Or lick it. I envisioned for a moment how that would feel, and my whole body trembled. Mmmm. Maybe I could ignore my hunger for food and just lock myself in the bathroom, drive myself to ecstasy for a few hours.

Tempting as that was, I lowered my arm and concentrated on trying to explore the weird red-purple stuff that had invaded my very core. It was like a network of roots, of tiny little hairs driven deep into my personal energy. It was solid, cold, impersonal. I tried to probe it, to feel it out, to determine what it did and how it operated, but couldn't discover anything. It resisted all my attempts to explore it.

Next, I tried to push it out, to gather it together into a manageable mass, or even cut it into sections, to no avail. It just sat there like an uncomfortable alien presence imbedded inside me. I couldn't imagine how I'd ever get it out. I doubted I'd be able to absorb it or neutralize it, and it seemed to resist any attempt at removal. Maybe Gregory could get it out. Not that he'd care. He'd stuck it there and the only way it was probably going to leave was with my death. Which would no doubt be soon.

Pulling myself back to more constructive thoughts, I wondered what the purpose was of the tattoo and the hickey. I didn't think Gregory intended to put a sexual brand on me. He was furious when he'd done it, not remotely in an amorous mood. I couldn't imagine what it did beyond turn me into even more of a horn dog than I had been before. Common sense would lead me to believe that this was either some kind of punishment or a method to track, find, and control me. I doubted even the most ignorant angel would think sexual stimulation would be punishment to a demon, so it must be the latter. Strange, because I really didn't feel like I was under his or anyone else's' control.

Unable to withstand my hunger any longer, I walked out of the bathroom and grabbed some food from the buffet on my way back. It was typical country fare, and I loved fried chicken, backfat green beans, and corn casserole.

Candy remained her placid self at the table, picking at her country ham, but Gregory looked furious. He was practically grinding his teeth and had his napkin balled up tight in a fist. I looked at Wyatt in alarm. Wyatt looked back and shook his head. He clearly didn't know what was going on either. I sat down and scooted my chair a few inches away. Gregory took a deep breath as I sat down, and let it slowly out. I felt him glare at me as he struggled to relax. What the fuck was wrong with this guy? I told him I was going to the bathroom. I didn't sneak out the window, I didn't use any energy, did no conversions. Why was he so mad at me?

"What is your problem?" I asked, unable to resist confronting him. He'd smacked me around, chewed up my arm, stuck a bunch of his whatever into me and added to my already heightened libido. He had no reason to be so pissed at me. "I didn't try to get away, I didn't kill anyone. I was just in the damned bathroom. Why the fuck are you so pissed off?"

Candy kicked me under the table and mouthed "shut up" at me in desperation.

"She doesn't need to shut up," Wyatt snapped at her, coming to my defense. "It's your fault. You and your stupid werewolf problems. And you," he said turning to Gregory. "She's not hurting anyone. Your angel buddy is the one who attacked us. You have no right to treat her this way."

Now I was alarmed. Gregory looked at Wyatt as if he were barely restraining himself from killing him right here in the busy restaurant with everyone looking on.

"I have every right, you miserable demon toy. This is not any of your business. You shouldn't presume to interfere in the affairs of higher life forms."

The angel began to glow slightly and I tensed, ready to dive in front of Wyatt if I needed to.

"Don't believe your silly folk tales," he continued. "Being human is no protection against me. I'm allowing you to live because you are useful to me at this moment. Cease to be useful, or become too much of an annoyance and I will not hesitate to kill you."

Wyatt did not look like he was about to back down. Admirable, but stupid. I knew Gregory fully meant what he said, so I grabbed Wyatt's hand under the table and squeezed it. He looked down at me and I could see him struggling to retreat. I got the feeling Wyatt had never backed down from a fight in his life, and this was terribly hard for him. I could sympathize, but in this instance it was either back down, or die.

Candy distracted Gregory with some discussion on strategy as I smiled at Wyatt and rubbed my thumb on his palm. This was going to be hard trying to stay alive, escaping the clutches of this angel, and keeping Wyatt's knight-in-shining-armor impulses from getting him killed. I needed to keep a lid on my stupid mouth and go back to my meek and submissive routine if I had any hope of success. Somehow I managed this throughout dinner, and even crammed up against Gregory on the drive to the campground.

The cabins were tiny and the ranger wasn't pleased that we were squeezing four people into one. There was no other cabin available though, so he let it go. The campground had winding loops of dirt roads leading to areas for tent camping, RV camping, and finally the cabins. Our section had ten cabins, spaced about an acre apart and surrounded by woods. Each cabin had a grassy patch in front of it, kind of like a lawn that reached from the porch to the road. The road widened in to form a parking area where campers were expected to carry their belongings across the lawn and into the cabin. Worn paths showed where hundreds of campers had lugged their gear back and forth for years.

Rough hewn logs made up the exterior and interior of the cabins. Electricity service ended with the street lights, and Wyatt grumbled that he would need to charge his electronic devices through the cars. There was no television, no phone, no coffee maker, and no vibrating bed. There was no bathroom, either. We'd need to walk down the road about a quarter of a mile to a shared bathroom that thankfully had propane-heated showers. There was a woodstove in the cabin; not that we'd need it in August. Hopefully, the woods would help cool things down in the evenings and we wouldn't miss the conveniences of air conditioning or fans.

As soon as we got in, Gregory announced he had some things to do and left. I was shocked he actually left me behind. Perhaps the meek and submissive routine was working? I doubted it. Of course if the tattoo thing was a kind of homing device, then he wouldn't really need to have me within eyeshot every waking moment. He'd be able to locate me within seconds. The thought was depressing.

No sooner had Gregory left then Candy's placid air disappeared and she rounded on me. "You are going to get us all killed! I manage to get him calm and cooperative, then five minutes with you and he's ready to go on a massacre with that sword of his."

"I'm just trying to keep myself from getting killed."

"If you were helpful and stopped making him so angry, he might let you live."

"What planet are you from? His sole purpose is to kill my kind. And he has a perfect kill-ratio, so far. If I don't get away from him soon, it's game over for me. Do you seriously think he's going to decide I'm not so bad, after all, and let me go? Trust me, it's not gonna happen."

"He's an angel. He's supposed to be merciful and on the side of law and order. If you toe the line, he'll probably just banish you and let you live," she countered. Clearly she'd forgotten Gregory's ominous speech to Wyatt in the restaurant.

"No fucking way he's going to let me live," I told her vehemently. "They don't banish us, because we keep coming back if they do. They kill us, every single time. The only mercy I'd get is a quick death, and I seriously doubt he's got an ounce of mercy in him."

"He's not like you," she insisted. "He's good and you're evil."

"The *fuck* he's not like me. You go ahead and swallow the Kool-Aid propaganda they've doled out over the centuries. He's *just* like me. He killed a fucking cop today just to keep me from getting away. An innocent cop who was doing nothing but his job. He's probably got a wife and kids, and that fucking angel didn't think twice about it." That gave Candy pause.

"You've seen what the angels have done to your own kind — to your werewolves. Althean is on a killing rampage, and Gregory cares only to cover it up and subdue Althean before he gets caught and Gregory gets his ass nailed by some higher up. He doesn't give a shit about humans, werewolves, anyone but his own kind. I killed your pack mate in self defense. I've been here forty years living as a human and you don't see me enacting some genetic cleansing program, do you? I may be a tough bitch, but I'm not killing pregnant women and cops." Well, there was that one cop in Atlanta, but she didn't know about that.

Candy paused, considering my words. "All right, so he's not what popular culture has made angels out to be. He does seem to be more like you than unlike you, honestly. I don't just have my life here to think about, though. I've got the future of my species. I know this sounds callous, but I'm trying to figure out what course of action to take that will result in the best outcome for my kind." She looked at me sympathetically. "He's cleaning your clock, Sam. He may be the better bet here."

Wow, that was brutally honest and I actually appreciated it. I had suspected Candy was calculating and ruthless, and these were qualities I admired. I could hardly fault her for them. Besides, Gregory *was* cleaning my clock. Hell, I'd throw my bet behind him in her place, too. The odds were much better.

"I know this sounds crazy, but I don't think he truly wants to kill you," she added with that shrewd look in her eyes. "I don't think he really hates you, I think he feels something else for you. I think he's attracted to you in his own way," she said carefully.

Well, that wasn't the right thing to say in front of Wyatt who'd been silent up until then.

"I *knew* it. Did he make a pass at you Sam? Is he trying to Own you?"

Angels don't Own, but I got what he was saying. And maybe, in a way, that's what the strange red-purple stuff was. Some sort of ownership mark. "Mine," that voice deep within me announced, silently and unexpectedly. As if I were the one trying to Own, trying to take possession. That was weird. I shook my head and chalked it up to the unnerving events of the day.

"No, he doesn't have any attraction toward me at all," I replied. "He's not trying to Own me. He beat the crap out of me and did this." I showed them my arm, which I had been keeping carefully glued to my side all evening.

They both gasped, and I was taken by the drama of the moment. Candy actually paled. "What does it do?" she asked.

"Is that a *hickey*?" Wyatt said, practically foaming at the mouth. "He gave you a tattoo and a *hickey*?"

"I think the hickey is just a byproduct of the tattoo." I needed to be careful with Wyatt. He was on the verge of going on a kamikaze attack, and I really didn't want to see him die. "I don't know what it does." I lied. I knew one thing it did, which I assumed wasn't its intended purpose. I hardly wanted Wyatt to know Gregory had put a big 'fuck me' spot on my arm.

"It looks like a brand," Candy said. "Like maybe some kind of tracking or homing device?"

That's what I was assuming, but it wouldn't need to be rooted so deeply within me for that. Wyatt came over to look closer and before I could stop him, he ran a finger around the outside of the sword tattoo, right over the hickey. Lust rushed through me in a hot wave. "Don't touch it," I hissed between clenched teeth. If he did that again, I was liable to knock him over and screw his brains out.

"I'm sorry," he said. "It must hurt."

Hurt. If only. I looked at Candy and she had the one eyebrow, wise Spock look going on. Didn't fool her. She might be a total prude, but she knew exactly what had happened when Wyatt rubbed the mark.

Slowly, she walked over and held my arm up to examine the tattoo and hickey closer. "Don't touch it." She'd get the lesbian shock of her life if she did.

Instead, she leaned in and sniffed it. I hoped my deodorant was still working. Not that it mattered with a wolf's sense of smell. Letting my arm go, she looked at me thoughtfully.

"I like you," she said slowly. "You're amoral. You screw anything you can hold still. You don't care about anyone beyond what they can do for you at the moment. You're nasty, irritating, crude, and reckless. You'd sacrifice us without a second thought, even him," she gestured to Wyatt, "to serve a selfish purpose. But in spite of this, I like you. Let me know what I can do to help you get away, to help you live, and I'll do it. Within reason," she added hastily.

Wyatt nodded in agreement. "You know I'll help you anyway I can, Sam."

This was odd. I wasn't used to others volunteering to put themselves in harm's way for me. I could see Wyatt doing it, humans did all sorts of weird things under the influence of friendship and sexual attraction, but Candy had no such motivation.

"There's no way I can make it all the way to a gate with this thing on my arm. I'm pretty sure I wouldn't make it out of town. I'm trying to think of a plan, though. I may just need you to distract him for a moment." I told Candy. "In the meantime, if you could keep him more focused on the trap for Althean and less on beating the shit out of me, I'd be grateful."

I turned to Wyatt. "See? This is why I want you to leave.

You heard what he said to you in the restaurant. He won't hesitate to kill you. Please take my car and go home."

"I'm not leaving you, Sam," he said stubbornly.

I sighed. I had a feeling this wasn't an argument I was going to win.

"Well, at least go out and get me some cold beer. Please," I added. "That shit in my trunk is probably skunked by now with this heat."

Wyatt ran out to get beer for me. He even took Candy's car without pestering me to drive my Corvette. I appreciated his running out for me since I had a feeling I was under house arrest. Besides, I was trying to show Gregory what a good girl I was. See? Branded, domesticated, staying within the confines of my enclosure.

Candy decided to sleep on the couch since she didn't want to share with anyone and there was only one bed. I told Wyatt to go ahead and go to sleep, figuring I'd make some excuse to sleep on the floor later. I couldn't take another night of straightjacket torture, and if he accidently rubbed my arm during the night, then that erection of his wouldn't go to waste.

I sat on the porch for hours listening to the chorus of night bugs, drinking beer, and lining up my empties on the railing. If this tattoo really was some kind of homing device, then Gregory would know it the minute I made a bolt for the border. I'd never make it to one of the major gates before he caught me, and I doubted Althean's killing pattern would take him near a major gate in the next few days. I could try to stall the project. Althean would probably head near a major gate eventually. I didn't think I'd be able to foil his capture for that long, though. Besides, even if I did, Gregory would just decide I wasn't helping, that I was in the way, and I'd be dispatched.

The wild gate at Sharpsburg was about half an hour away

at speed in the Corvette. I didn't think Gregory knew about that gate. I'd heard that angels didn't even sense the wild gates. Normally, he'd never expect me to head there. With this thing on my arm, I suspected that he'd find me wherever I went, and know if I strayed more than a certain distance from him. I needed to somehow get us closer to Sharpsburg so Candy could distract him and I could be through the gate before he knew I was gone. I'd probably be ripped to shreds in that crazy wild gate, but at least I had a chance there. Staying here, I had no chance whatsoever. I'd look at Wyatt's projection of the killings in the morning to see if we circled back down into Maryland. If so, I'd have to work hard to make the trap at Waynesboro unsuccessful. Anything to get us closer to that gate and my last chance.

I finished my beer, and started to put the empty on the railing with the rest. It was a pretty reddish brown color, as most beer bottles were. It had been molded through a rather cheap and sloppy process, and there were a few bubbles and imperfections in the glass. Humans often applied only the minimum of effort necessary to suit their needs. They were satisfied with this beer bottle as long as it didn't stick them with sharp edges, kept the beer contained and temperature consistent, and was fairly sanitary.

Many of my kind were this way, too. Why apply excess time and energy if less would get the job done? The elves were different though. Everything for them had to be perfect and artistically formed. Everything was an opportunity for art and expression. Their homes, yards, stables were filled with intricately embellished functional items. They would never have been satisfied with this beer bottle. Its very presence would have grated on them.

Changing my mind, I took the glass bottle back off the railing, melted the glass and pulled out the air bubbles and tiny bits of debris marring the glass quality. I needed to keep a thin buffer of cool between my human hands and the molten glass as I pulled and rolled. Looking at the blob of clean glass in my hands, I was suddenly inspired, stricken with the urge to create. It was an urge that demons occasionally had. I warmed the glass again, twisting and shaping it. When I was satisfied, I let it cool in my hands. It was now a small brown glass horse in gallop with mane flying and nose to the sky. I ran my finger down the glass muscles in its back and smiled to myself.

"That's beautiful," a deep voice said behind me. Gregory. His tone was that soothing rumble. I got the impression he'd been there watching me for a while as I'd been engrossed in my glasswork.

I looked up at him. His black eyes were hard to read in the moonless night, but at least he didn't appear pissed off. Maybe whatever errand he'd run had allowed him to relax and recover his control.

"Back home, I'd gift it to one of the elves," I told him.

The elves loved art, but they were not often satisfied with their own creations. I thought their art was beautiful and perfect, but they deplored the lack of emotion and feeling. They were always grateful to get something we had made, and they frequently invited us to their social events. We annoy them, but they've always tolerated us like we were crazy eccentric relatives.

"You know elves?" Gregory asked in wonder. "You actually see them socially?"

Oh yeah, the prodigal children. The elves as a race had always been doted on and favored by the angels. They had originally sided with the angels during the war, but became increasingly disillusioned with them as the fighting dragged on.

To everyone's surprise, and seemingly against their own best interests, they ended up pulling themselves from the conflict and declaring neutrality. The angels had been winning before, but after the elves pulled out, we reached a stalemate and thus the division of the realms and the treaty. I'm not sure what caused the elves to come to our turf, but they carved out their own space and refused to enter this realm. The whole reason the angels had created the big stable gates was in hope that their beloved species would come to their senses and join them again.

"Yeah. They ward their land heavily against us, and their adults are kind of stodgy and boring, but their young are fun and playful. They sneak over into our land and play pranks on us, and we reciprocate. It's all in good fun. We sometimes perform services for each other. If we establish a business relationship, then it results in being invited to their social functions."

"Do you go? Are you invited?" Gregory asked, sitting beside me.

"Occasionally. I've performed some services for one of the high lords, and he invites me to holiday functions, and the occasional great hunt. Honestly, I think I get invited to the hunts because I ride like shit and they all get a huge laugh at seeing me hit the ground regularly."

I handed him the glass horse and he examined it carefully.

"I saw you pull the impurities out of the glass. Why did you bother?" he asked, sending strands of himself into the glass to better feel its structural integrity.

I wasn't sure how to respond. Elves would have said that things of beauty should not be marred, that they should attempt to approach divinity in their perfection, that sloppy imperfect work was an offense against nature and the forces of creation. Perhaps the elves had just rubbed off on me?

"I don't know," I replied shrugging. "I didn't have any particular reason, I just did it."

"It's perfect," Gregory handed the horse back to me. "And

it has such feeling and expression to it. That I expected, but I would never have expected this level of detail from a demon. Honestly, I would have expected you to shoot the bottles off the railing or twist them into a horrific mass. Not create this delicate thing of beauty."

"There is equal beauty in the things called horrific. The act of destruction is an expression of beauty, too. I destroyed the bottle to make the horse. Is a pretty glass horse worth the loss of a bottle, but the sound of shattered glass and bits flying through the air isn't? Is transformation only worthy if you approve of the end result?"

Gregory stared at me in silence for a while. I think I shocked him. He'd probably expected me to say "fuck that" and blow up the glass horse or something. Well, I wasn't always a stereotype.

He reached out a hand to me and I tensed involuntarily expecting him to blast me with that white stuff or pop my head off. Unfair, I know, since he was calm right now and we hadn't exactly been arguing. Still, after today, I was leery of his intentions toward me. And it's not like he'd necessarily have to be angry with me to kill me. The whole process could be as emotionless as pinching the top off a dandelion. Gregory paused for a second then gently took a piece of my hair and carefully rubbed it between his thumb and fingers.

"Your human form is perfect too," he said, half to himself. "Down to the last cell. Your energy is so tightly contained. You don't leak like so many other demons."

He leaked. The power flowed off him in waves. It was like sitting next to an open oven. And his form sucked. It was so weird with the strange skin and faint glow. He blurred at the edges sometimes, too.

"You don't have the slightest imperfection in your form," he continued. "I could walk right by you on the street and not know what you are. I could be in the same room with you for hours and not know."

"You did," I told him. "Last week in The Wine Room. I was there when you came in looking for me and I managed to sneak out the back door."

He looked at me in surprise. "You were? I wasn't looking for you. I was there to find Candy in an attempt to gain any information the local werewolves had on Althean. I could sense she was there, but she got out the back door while the humans were smothering me with adoration." He rolled his eyes, as if the reaction of the humans was both amusing and annoying. "I didn't know you were there at all. You were a few yards from me, and I didn't even sense your presence?"

"You weren't looking for me?" I asked. "But you must have sensed me. You were at that werewolf's house a few days later. The one I killed with the electricity."

He shook his head in confusion. "What are you talking about? I had no indication of your presence until you blasted Althean at Robinson's house."

Damn. Candy had lied. She'd made up the whole thing to manipulate me into doing what she wanted. All my panic, this whole madness with Candy had been because I'd thought he was on my trail. He hadn't even known I existed, that I was right there. He hadn't been after me at all. I could have just gone about my life and he would have never known.

He continued to rub my hair between his fingers and I felt him push his energy in once again to examine me. It was pretty rude. He'd examined the glass horse with more consideration. Poking around like this at me was so annoying. I knew I wasn't strong enough to force him out, so I returned the favor and poked back at him with my personal energy. It didn't have the same effect. He brushed me off repeatedly without effort, and certainly didn't get the hint on how disrespectful this sort of thing was. I was nervous he'd find out how much raw energy I had stored within me and tried to compress it tighter, but he was careful to avoid contact with it. The rest of me was fair game though. It was like having someone root through your underwear drawer.

Without warning, I felt him snatch hold of the red-purple within me and pull violently.

"Owww," I yelled and punched him as hard as I could in the arm. It was like hitting a cement block. "Asshole. That hurts. Cut it out."

He stopped and I felt his surprise, but he didn't let go and didn't remove his energy from me. I sat there and braced myself for more pain, but he released and gently pulled back to himself. Silence stretched on between us, but it wasn't awkward. If someone had told me a week ago that I'd be sitting on a porch next to an angel listening to the locusts sing at night I would not have believed it. I was fully aware of his strength and the enormous power imbalance between us, but for some reason I felt a sense of peace.

We continued to sit there in silence for several hours, and then I put the glass horse on the railing beside the empty beer bottles and went in to sleep. My intention was to grab a blanket and curl up on the floor, but I looked longingly at Wyatt snoring softly in the bed. I might not be around much longer. As much as I dislike having someone crush me all night, I really wanted as much closeness with him as I could. I wanted to feel his warm flesh against me. I didn't want to regret missing a moment of that. Filled with longing, I pulled off my clothes and climbed under the covers with Wyatt. He immediately sensed my presence and turned to face me, wrapping his arms tight around me and twining my legs between his. Seconds later and I was clamped against him. There was nowhere I'd rather have been.

I slept some, and woke in the morning to the now

familiar feel of Wyatt's erection against my thigh. As if that weren't bad enough, Wyatt ran his one hand down my back to cup around my ass and brought the other up to the side of my breast.

"Sam?" his groggy voice asked. "Why are you naked?"

I'd forgotten about Candy's presence and her edict regarding nightwear.

"I always sleep naked," I told him.

He caught his breath. "Do you think Candy is a light sleeper," he whispered, his hands roaming across my skin. That morning erection of his had gained focus and was now a hard steel pipe on my leg.

"I'm a very light sleeper," a stern voice from the sofa announced. "And there will be no sex going on while I'm here."

"Can you leave?" I asked her hopefully.

"No. Sam, get up and put some clothes on and go outside while Wyatt calms certain parts of his anatomy down. I've got some bottled water for us to brush our teeth with. We'll wait for our orders from Gregory, and then hopefully we can grab coffee and breakfast on our way."

Candy was very organized for such an early hour in the morning. I would rather have had slow thorough sex with Wyatt then snooze while Candy ran out to fetch coffee and donuts, but that was clearly not going to happen. Reluctantly, I got up and dressed in yesterday's torn dirty jeans and a clean shirt.

When I went out to the porch to stretch my legs, I noticed the glass horse was gone. All the other bottles were still lined up on the porch rail, but there was a conspicuous empty spot where I'd put the horse. I was oddly delighted that he'd taken it. It must have been him. No one else had left the cabin, and it wasn't likely that some prowler had come around, especially with Candy's werewolf hearing. I was glad he liked it.

Hopefully after he killed me, he'd look at it and remember me fondly.

I grabbed the empty bottles and one at a time threw them off the side of the porch against the trunk of an oak. The first bounced off without breaking, so I put a bit of energy behind the next one and was gratified when it shattered with that lovely breaking-glass sound. The others quickly followed, and I ended by blasting the remaining whole one as it lay by the base of the tree.

"I can't quite see how that was a thing of beauty, but I'll allow you to have your differing opinion on the matter," Gregory's amused voice announced.

I turned and was surprised by the incongruity of seeing him holding a drink carrier with Styrofoam cups and a bag. Judging from the smell, the cups contained coffee.

"You brought coffee?" I asked.

He shrugged. "I know humans are basically useless without this morning beverage, and I assumed you'd be the same."

At that moment, we were interrupted by Candy, who burst through the door brandishing a broken remote control.

"I'm not paying for this," she told me, waving it at my face.

I immediately threw the angel under the bus. "It was him," I said pointing at Gregory. "He broke it off the chain and I was just trying to hide the evidence."

Gregory raised his eyebrows at Candy and handed her a cup of coffee.

"Oh," she said in confusion, taking the coffee. "Thank you. I mean, no problem. I'm sure it was an accident."

"No," he told her. "It was no accident. I purposely broke it."

Candy turned bright red with embarrassment and sputtered something about how it was no problem at all, vanishing back into the cabin with her coffee. I grabbed a cup for myself out of the holder and laughed.

"You're mean. I like it. Especially when it's not directed at me."

He handed me the drink holder and the bag along with an address on a slip of paper.

"Meet me at this address in half an hour. We've got a long day ahead of us. If you're late, I'll turn your car into a useless ball of metal."

Without waiting for a reply, he gated away. I assumed that meant the camaraderie was over and we were now back to our former adversarial relationship. The thought made me rather sad.

CHAPTER 16

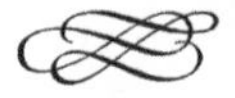

"Do it," Gregory commanded. "Do your thing."

We were at the first of the werewolves' houses and they were away at work. It was a family of three. Father, mother, ten year old son. I didn't know what the hell Gregory wanted me to do.

"Your *thing*," he said impatiently. "Do it."

"What thing?" Was I supposed to fuck Wyatt on the lawn, blow a hole in the driveway, throw a bolt of lightning through the picture window, or strip the skin off some human and forcibly Own them?

"Change," he waved his hand around. "Change into something, then change back. Leave a big old demon energy signature right here on the front lawn to scare Althean away."

Great. He was too lazy to hex the place, so I needed to convert my entire flesh. Did he want me to do this at every house? There were forty werewolf residences in the Waynesboro area. Was I supposed to do this at thirty-nine of them? Fuck that. And what good would it do? Was Althean so stupid, or possibly so insane that he wouldn't realize that that fortieth house, the one without my energy all over it was a trap? Any self-respecting demon would just head elsewhere. Somewhere outside the little regression line Wyatt showed on his computer. Stupid fucking angels. Like a dumb ass lemming.

"You're joking. You expect me to convert my entire form at thirty-nine houses today? Do you realize how much raw energy it would take for that? I'd be drained to nothing," I announced dramatically. I had more than enough raw energy, but I didn't want him to know that.

Gregory raised an eyebrow. "Do it," he commanded. His voice had power behind the compulsion. Huge power. It swept over me with the intensity of a forest fire. I admired his ability to put forth such a huge volume of power, but in spite of it, the compulsion slid over me without effect.

"Fuck you," I told him.

He frowned and I could tell he had expected the compulsion to work.

"Do it now or I will make your human toy into a eunuch," he announced, changing tactics.

Wyatt turned white. He'd do it too, without a second thought. Asshole. Fine, I'd do it, but I wouldn't make it pretty.

I was pissed, so I exploded out everything but my personal energy and stash of raw energy in a rapid blast. Time froze, as it always did when I converted my whole self and I felt the seductive pull of eternity. I could just let the matter go, let it drift on out taking my personal energy with it. I would fade into the fabric of creation, become whole. I forced myself to focus and snap back into flesh. It was like a sonic boom, once out and once in. Crack, crack. Wyatt and Candy were both knocked to the ground. Gregory stood as if untouched, the bastard.

"And she's naked again," Candy said, getting to her feet

and dusting off her pants. "There doesn't seem to be a day that goes by that I'm not treated to the sight of your naked body. Can't you possibly do this without losing your clothing?"

Of course, I'd blown my clothing to bits when I converted, and didn't know how to create new ones.

"Is she always like this?" Gregory asked me, gesturing toward Candy. "No wonder Althean is trying to exterminate the werewolves if they're all as annoying as she is."

"She's alright," I chuckled. "I'll bet she fucks with all her clothes on and the lights off, though."

Gregory looked around, no doubt sensing my energy usage.

"Do it again, over here a bit. I don't think that will be close enough to the house to suffice."

Fuck, this was going to be even worse if I had to do a conversion multiple times at each house. I really would be running low if he kept this up. Was this some way to determine how much I had stored? How much I could do before I collapsed exhausted in a heap? I complained again that this was a stupid idea and that there was no way I was going to be able to keep doing this.

He stopped and looked at me sternly. "Did we not just have this conversation? Let me see. Yes. Yes, it was the same conversation. There was some whining from you, then I threatened to do physical harm to your toy, then you grudgingly complied. Perhaps we can just skip all the middle part and get to the part where you comply? Otherwise, I'm liable to get angry and do all sorts of things I'll really enjoy now and mildly regret later."

I hated this angel.

I walked over closer to the house and again converted myself violently in an explosion of pressure and sound.

Wyatt and Candy stayed farther back this time and managed to stay on their feet.

"I had forgotten about the clothing thing," the angel said as he turned his back on me and walked toward the car. "You'll need to strip each time you do this since we don't have a truckload of outfits for you to ruin."

I glared at him as I followed him, naked, to the car, and noticed him rub a hand over his ear. Blood. That was interesting.

The next house he stood back farther. I smiled to myself and blew everything apart and back with even more force. Candy clutched her head. "Can Wyatt and I be somewhere else for this? If she keeps it up I'll be tossed into the adjacent county. Maybe we can just wait for you all to finish this at a local coffee shop?"

Gregory shot Candy an irritated look, and didn't reply. He clearly had a slight nose bleed this time. "I don't think you need to change your whole self next time," he said rubbing his nose. "Maybe just a portion of you, instead."

The following few houses I experimented, changing just portions of me, using less energy, changing the residents' dog into a rat, which Candy insisted I change back. I can easily convert myself, but I'm not so good at changing other beings. The dog didn't quite go back the same as it originally was. The owners would never be able to tell, but the unfortunate thing would die in a few weeks. I should have left it a rat. At the next house I burned a circle in the lawn with green fire. None of these seemed to have any noticeable impact on Gregory.

"The fire isn't going to have the effect I want," the angel scolded. "The energy signature is too vague and like natural fire. You need to actually change something, preferably yourself."

Men. They always want you to change yourself, why can't

they just like you the way you are? I recreated a foot, but did it with a vengeance. Pop, pop. Candy stuck her finger in her ear, and Wyatt stretched his jaw, trying to normalize the pressure in their ears. And there it was, the light trickle of blood. So it wasn't the size of the conversion that affected him. Was it the pressure change, or the sound, or both?

He stood back further the next time. I was bored with just recreating Samantha Martin, so I decided to experiment with some of my forms from back home. This time I snapped back as a gryphon, making it extra loud. Gregory looked grim as he approached me. He was coughing this time and I could see the specks of blood.

"You can't drive around in the car looking like that. You need to change back into human form."

I didn't wait for him to back away, I snapped out and in with a huge sonic boom. He staggered, then shook his head. Blood dripped from his nose, and trailed down from one ear.

Sound. Everything he'd done with his energy, everything Althean had done had sound or color. Plasma and the usual destructive forces didn't have maximum effect on them, even my raw energy glanced off them with less than expected damage. I couldn't do color, but sound I could do.

"This isn't going to work," Gregory said, turning away from me and surreptitiously wiping the blood from his face. "It's way overkill. You're leaving a huge signature and he'll suspect something."

Well duh, he'd suspect something anyway if he could see I'd been to thirty-nine of forty houses, conveniently leaving one house free with a big bow on top and a 'kill me' sign on the door. I wasn't sure what the fuck Gregory's game plan was with all this. Was Althean's drive to kill the werewolves in a bizarre pattern overriding his common sense? Were we just herding him toward our trap? If so then the overkill wouldn't matter. I couldn't believe Althean would be so stupid, but I really didn't know anything about angels. A demon would never have gone for this. We'd have been merrily killing werewolves halfway across the country if we saw a blatant trap like this being laid down.

"What do you mean it's not going to work? I'm exhausted from all this, and now it's not going to work? Plus we have twenty-six more houses to go," I whined. There was no way we could watch twenty-six residences. Althean had the odds in his favor. He'd strike again and get away, hopefully moving closer to Sharpsburg where I could take my chances of escape through the wild gate.

Gregory paused for a moment. "We'll split up. I'll take ten houses and hex them, and you take sixteen. Just make sure you leave one open. Meet me back at the cabin whenever you're done."

What, leaving me unattended with Wyatt and Candy all day? With plenty of time to escape? And no very specific orders to be here at this time, and there at that time? Did he want me to run, so he could snatch me back out of thin air, deliver a smack down, and teach me a lesson? Maybe he needed some private time. Candy had been annoying as all hell, and spending the day in the company of a demon couldn't have been easy for him either. Or possibly he was just tired of the constant nosebleeds my conversion was causing him. Either way, he had to have some faith that I'd stick around, or that he could find me if I tried to bolt for it.

I puzzled over this and my tattoo as we drove to our allocated houses. Did the mark allow him to find me and bring me to him, or only let him know if I strayed outside a certain distance from him? That kind of constant monitoring would probably require a deep connection, and a sharing of personal energy. If that were the case, then the red-purple inside me could hold a portion of him, and he might have even taken on a portion of me. Oh, that would be unbelievably ironic! My kind does this type of personal energy swap when we breed, but we don't keep the connection to the other person. We just combine their energy with ours to make a new being, then isolate it. There's no desire to carry around a portion of someone else inside you, or maintain a kind of link with them. How much would it irk him if he had a chunk of me inside him, or if his own precious self was tied up inside me? If this were the case, no wonder he was in a crappy mood.

By late afternoon we were down to the last five houses, and I was tired and bored. I'd been riding around naked. I hadn't brought a spare set of clothing from the cabin and had nothing to change into until Candy raced into a Walmart and picked up a pair of jeans and a tank top for me. I refused to wear them since taking clothes off and putting them back on at each house was a pain in the ass. After a long argument, Candy insisted the least I could do was wrap myself in a blanket from her trunk. She claimed it was so we wouldn't get arrested. I'm surprised she didn't put newspapers down on the seat.

I'd gotten creative with my form, doing a goat-lion cross I'd put together for one of the elf parties decades ago, and variations of the stereotypical devil theme from artwork throughout the ages. Wyatt particularly liked the sexy red one with big boobs, and long rope tail that I twirled around suggestively. It looked like something out of *Heavy Metal*. He did not like the muscular black one with the huge two foot phallus and testicles like bowling balls.

We pulled up to a lovely McMansion, with a professionally landscaped yard out back, complete with a grotto pool and hot tub. These werewolves had it good. Wyatt and Candy sat in the air-conditioned car while I took my time admiring the pool. Half the pool was edged in flagstone with a wide set of flagstone steps rising from the water to the naturalized patio. The other half consisted of a man-made cave and a twenty-foot molded boulder with tiny streams of water trickling down the edges. The cave was partially underwater with a ledge to hold drinks and snacks. My pool was the standard issue, and I thought about possibly adding a feature like this. The molded boulder was probably fine by human and werewolf standards, but its fakeness annoyed me. If I did this at my pool, I'd create my own boulder. I missed my pool, and since I was naked anyway I jumped in to do a few laps.

The water was wonderful. They used a saline system instead of chlorine, and the minerals made the water slide like silk over my skin. I explored the little cave a bit and floated around in the water. Candy and Wyatt had to be wondering what was taking so long. Screw them. And screw that pissy angel, too. I'd get done whenever I felt like it. I did a few more laps, swimming low to see the decorative tile work in the bottom of the pool.

That's when I noticed an odd shimmer in the pool wall. Diving down, I took a closer look and just about swallowed the water in excitement. It was a gate. A wild gate. Well, it was actually more like a wild jagged tear. It extended the entire depth of the pool, but it was narrow. I wasn't sure I'd be able to squeeze through it and not leave a chunk of myself behind. It was wider down at the bottom thankfully. I came up for air and went back down again. I couldn't really tell where the gate came out at, but I was running out of options.

This was my only chance. There was no way I could manage to sneak away tonight and come back here. We'd never be close to this house, again. If I didn't go for it with this gate, my only other chance would be the long shot that we'd somehow come close enough to the one in Sharpsburg. This was my bird in the hand, and I needed to grab it. I'd been told my whole life that I took insane chances with minimal regard to my safety, and that's saying a lot coming from my kind. This was the time to prove them right. I went up for air one more time, then swam down and slipped through into the gate.

It was a bad, bad idea, and I realized how bad the moment I stepped in. The gate engulfed me in blackness, snapping shut behind me. It felt like I was encased in black Jell-O. I tried to push through it, but it resisted against me bouncing back. I could rip and tear it, but it was slow going, and it flowed back to itself, leaving no trail of where I'd been. I couldn't tell how far I'd come, but it felt like I'd been plowing through the stuff forever. I had a horrifying feeling that I was going to spend eternity in here suffocating in black Jell-O. It could be worse, I thought.

Never think that. The Jell-O was starting to become sticky and cling to me. I shook it off, trying to push it away and noticed red bloody marks where it had tenaciously stuck on my skin. As if one hickey mark wasn't enough, it seemed I was about to be covered in the things. I wasn't one to give up, so I kept slashing and pushing, making my way each precious inch at a time. Hope filled me as the Jell-O began to soften and liquefy, and a glimmer brightened the darkness. Finally, I thought, I might be reaching the other side of the gate. I hoped it didn't open up into a black hole or something equally deadly. The glimmer expanded and I was blinded by a white flash. I felt something more solid than Jell-O encase me and with a second flash I realized I was underwater. Maybe I had gated into a rock in an underwater cave. I hoped so.

No such luck. As my vision cleared, I realized that the rock was covered by wet cotton fabric. Shit. I should have known. Gregory's grip shifted, but instead of being swept up in his arms, I was dumped over his shoulder like a sack of potatoes as he carried me up the steps and out of the pool.

He had to be furious. I'd had no idea how he'd managed to find me in that horrible Jell-O mess of a gate, let alone get us both out of there. I can't believe he bothered. He must have known what that gate was. If it had been me, I would have said "screw this" and let him die in that thing. Why had he risked himself to pull me out? Was I really of that much use to him? Or perhaps he was too proud to allow me to escape him at all. Maybe he had a need to have absolute control over me and my demise. He slid me down off his shoulder and held me tight against him, my face smashed into the wet cotton of his polo shirt. I waited patiently to be crushed to a pulp. Instead I was held in place, with the angel's ragged breath warm against the top of my head.

"I have no idea how you've managed to survive this long, little cockroach," he said, his voice tight. "How did you make that gate? That was the worst thing I've ever seen in my long, long life. Crippled lobotomized elves with one eye could make a better gate than that."

I didn't know specifically what having one eye had to do with gate creation, but I got his point.

"And you didn't end it anywhere. The edges weren't stable; it didn't really *have* edges. The whole thing was slowly collapsing in on you. I honestly don't know how I managed to find you in that thing, let alone pull you out of it in one piece."

I held very still against him. He didn't sound very angry. I thought he'd be furious, smashing me into little bits for defying him and trying to get away.

"If you're so bent on killing yourself, cockroach, just be patient a little longer and I'll do it for you." He said, sounding as if he anticipated that moment. "I don't know what to do with you. I can't be with you every second, I can't bind you any tighter. Now, I find you can create gates, no matter how terrible and ineffective they are. I should just go ahead and kill you now, you are such an annoyance. Any usefulness you provide is far outweighed by your time wasting and disrupting actions."

Okay, so he risked himself to pull me out of a wild gate only to kill me himself? I guess it was more satisfying if you did the deed yourself rather than have your target die through suicide by stupidity. I could identify. It was so disappointing when your prey fell off a cliff and broke its neck before you could sink your teeth into it and have it die by your hand.

We stood there for a few moments more, then he slowly pulled away and looked me over. I was naked and covered in bloody Jello-O hickey marks. Not exactly a good sight. I risked a quick look up at him. No pointy teeth, no black filled eyes, no glowing, no sword. He actually looked rather bleak. These were hopefully good signs for my continued existence.

"Fix yourself," he said with a sigh, and stepped back to let me work.

I stood and stared at him a moment, sure that I heard him wrong, and that any minute he was going to lop my head off with that sword of his.

"Go on," he urged. "I don't really care, but if we walk back to the car with you looking like that, your toy is going to go insane and try to blow my head off with his little cannon, again. I've killed one human this week; I don't want to kill another. I'm way over my quota for the year, already."

I had an odd feeling the last statement was some kind of angel humor, but I didn't want to ask. Quickly I fixed the Jell-O marks, thinking that Wyatt was going to flip anyway with us walking back together, both soaking wet and me naked.

Wyatt was not happy. He was even less happy when

Gregory grabbed the blanket from Candy's car and proceeded to dry me off, himself.

"Here, put your clothes on," the angel told me. "I'm going to gate you to the last few houses so I can keep you with me. I'll hex them, and these two will follow us in the car."

Wyatt turned red and clenched his jaw, but at least he kept his gun to himself.

It was a slow process. The gating around was fast, but then I had to stand there a moment squished against Gregory to keep from falling over while the world righted itself. Then we had to wait an eternity for Candy and Wyatt to arrive, since Gregory informed me he couldn't trust me to my own devices while he was occupied creating the hex. He told Candy at the first house that she was to watch me and if he found me so much as a foot from where he left me, he'd bash her face into the pavement. I wondered if angels were always this violent or if I was having a peculiar effect on him.

I was a good girl, much to Candy's relief. Besides, where would I go? He'd catch me, and just be more pissed off. Part of me still wanted to try for the Sharpsburg gate, but part of me was really afraid to try that shit again. There were more pleasant ways to commit suicide. That sword of Gregory's probably wouldn't be as bad as dying in a wild gate, but I didn't really want to give him the satisfaction of causing my death. I'd rather suffer horribly.

We finished by dark, and at least three of us were starving since we'd missed lunch. The house with the pool and the wild gate was our intended target. Not that it mattered. I wasn't about to try Jell-O world again, especially if it didn't lead anywhere. We grabbed take-out Chinese and headed back to the cabin to collapse in exhaustion. I didn't even bother with the Tinkerbell shirt, and just wrapped myself up naked in a blanket to sleep on the porch. Candy took her couch, and Wyatt the bed. Gregory sat in the porch chair with his feet up on the railing so he could keep an eye on me. It was rather unnerving having someone stand guard over you while you sleep, but I was worn out and dozed off quickly.

I woke up with my heart racing. It was early, well before sunup, and it took me a moment to realize where I was and what had woken me. Something was here, something I knew, something I wanted to kill. I reached out and felt his presence, about five hundred yards into the woods to the northeast. Althean, stealthily creeping closer.

What in the world was he doing here? Two who are gunning for him are here, and none of his targets. Then it hit me. Candy. Maybe he was ready for his hit, and she was here and sleeping soundly. I'd left no strong energy marks around the cabin, and Gregory hadn't hexed it. We hadn't thought that Candy could be a potential victim, since she wasn't a local. Maybe Althean wasn't going off a database or map, but some kind of sense that located werewolves themselves. That could have been why he'd hit the Robinson house, with Craig and Candy both there.

I carefully turned my head to look at the porch chair. Gregory was gone. I reached out to look for him. I was fairly convinced I could accurately determine his location if he were nearby with all the time I'd spent with him recently, and this tattoo with the red-purple stuff inside me. I couldn't feel him within a quarter mile radius, but I wasn't positive in the outer edges. That left me alone, with prey approaching and no one to interfere with my hunt. My focus narrowed to a laser. I wanted this kill. I was going to die anyway; I might as well have a last supper. Smiling, I slid out of the blanket and tracked my victim, edging quietly around to flank him as he approached the cabin. I wished I could convert into something scary and vicious looking, but I needed to keep this under the radar until the last moment so I didn't scare him off.

Althean's gold curls shimmered in the faint moonlight. He was not trying to be as human in his appearance, and his skin was solid and marble looking with the glow and the blur at the edges. He was naked, which was kind of bizarre. He'd had clothing on at Robinson's. Did the nakedness signify something important? Did he just lose his clothes or blow them to bits like I always managed to do? Of course, I was naked too, and he'd probably wonder the same about me if he saw me. I assumed that his teeth were pointy and his eyes dark. Better keep my arms away from those teeth. One tattoo was enough for me.

I watched him edge toward the cabin. There was a clearing of about fifty feet long between the woods and the porch steps. The best place to grab him would be right at the edge of the woods. He'd pause there to check out the clearing before he made his dash. If I waited until he was in the clearing, he'd be liable to see me and gate out before I reached him. Better to grab him while his attention was on scanning the porch and clearing for activity. Slowly, I trailed him from the side, utterly silent, my heart thudding and adrenaline surging. I had to struggle to keep my energy deep within myself where he couldn't sense it.

Finally, he paused at the edge of the woods to survey the clearing and I made my move. I blew everything out, then back in with a boom of sound. The trees disrupted some of the effect, but Althean dropped to his knees. I jumped on him, knocking him into the clearing and straddling him, and punched him in the face just because I felt like it. It didn't do much except hurt my hand and give him a chance to throw me off and scramble to his feet. I hit him again with another boom of sound, and he staggered. I threw another one at him, knocking him down and giving me a chance to straddle him again. Then I began pummeling him with the sound; he clutched his head. The blood dripped out his nose, eyes and ears, from the corner of his mouth, and even began to seep out his pores. I knew I wouldn't have the time to own him, so I'd have to be satisfied with just killing him. Once he was dead, I'd shred him to bits. I'd roll in the blood and flesh of his empty form. I'd savor the pain and fear of his last moments.

He was struggling less, so I placed my hands against his chest and made ready to hit him hard and loud, when I was grabbed from behind. I knew who it was, so I spun around and threw the blast I had into Gregory instead. He made an *oof* sound and grabbed me in a wrestling hold.

"Stop it," he commanded, covering my energy with that slippery shit, again. I didn't have to look, I knew Althean was gone.

"You fucking bastard," I snarled. "I had him, and now you let him go. He was here to attack Candy."

"I know," he said, sounding oddly affectionate and still holding me against him. "You were just protecting your friend, I'm not angry with you. But you can't kill him. I won't let you kill him."

It was less about protecting my 'friend' and more about making my kill, but whatever.

"Well *I'm* angry. You let him get away. Again! You don't care anything about stopping him, bringing him to justice, or having him pay for his crimes. All you care about is covering your ass by sweeping the whole thing under the rug, protecting your reputation and Althean's. You'll grab him, take him to Aaru, and stick him in some nice office job. Then you'll assign another angel to the werewolves and act like the whole thing never happened."

"What, because that's what you'd do?" Gregory asked. Now he was angry. "You know nothing about me, nothing about how we operate. Don't go making assumptions about our society based on your own twisted lawless nature. You know nothing about us."

"I know enough," I retorted. "I was at the place in York. I know what happened. I felt the bodies, saw the video tape. Althean killed a pregnant woman. An innocent woman and an innocent child died. And from what Candy says, lots of the victims have been innocent. I honestly don't care who you kill, but you have an agreement with these people. They've given up a lot. The least you could do is keep to your end of the bargain. Althean isn't keeping the contract, and neither are you."

"There are subversive factions among us who would bypass protocol and take action. If Althean were just one of these vigilantes, he would be punished harshly. And trust me, prison and punishment among our kind is worse than death. He's wavering in his convictions, though, making him capable of redemption. The last few kills have caused him to go nearly insane with doubt and guilt. The death of the woman and baby have put him over the edge. I know there is something in him still worth saving," Gregory insisted.

"He's not worth saving, and neither are you. You were there in York, too. You covered it up. I saw you put the mark on the woman and the baby, I read your energy signature. Even without the video tape, I know your energy signature very well by now. It was you. You marked them both as if they were criminals. You fucking hypocrite. You'll save Althean, cover the whole thing up, but where's the justice for the werewolves? Their dead have *all* been marked as criminals. A baby, for fuck sake!"

He'd held me by the wrists away from him to look at my face as I ranted. Finding I had a foot free, I kicked him in the shin. It was like kicking a wall with my bare foot.

He looked down at me in amazement. "Marked them as criminals? What are you talking about?"

"The angel wings on their temples," I told him. "I could see it on the woman, and I saw you place it there from the video tape. I got your energy signature off of it, and then I felt the same mark, the same energy signature on the unborn baby. How in the fuck can you justify marking a *baby* as deserving of death? It's not only against the contract, it should be against your very nature. Unless your kind has changed that much in the last two million years, it should be contrary to all you hold dear to condemn an infant, especially an unborn one."

Gregory stared at me as if I'd gone insane. "Criminals? The wings don't make them criminals, they are to convey that someone has paid for any crime they may have committed, that they are clean. They're a forgiveness mark, a blessing, not a condemnation."

I was stunned. What incredible arrogance it was to deign to convey forgiveness on those they killed. I hated these fucking angels.

"So those who violate every rule, every clause of the existence contract, they get forgiveness, too? Same blessing as an unborn baby? Because all of the executions bear that mark."

Not that I thought dead people gave a shit about some pompous asshole angel granting them forgiveness. What the fuck? No wonder we ditched these psychos for our own place. They were so full of themselves, it wasn't even funny.

"Yes, even the worst criminal deserves forgiveness. They've paid their dues with their death, and they should approach their afterlife with a clean slate."

I rolled my eyes. When I finally could resist it no longer and let my entire being scatter throughout the universe, I doubted if it gave a flying fuck whether some angel gave me the thumbs up or not. All were equal in death. Maybe that's what he was saying though in his own full of shit way.

"You'll still cover it up. I know you will. You killed a cop, and you covered that up too. Fucking holier-than-thou hypocrites, all of you."

"I did a lot of things in anger that day that I'm not proud of, but I refuse to feel guilt for that death. I will never let you get away, never let you escape me, and the deaths of a million humans are an easy price to pay for that," he said with determination, finally letting go of my hands.

It was a little unsettling to know that he'd casually plow through a million human lives just to have the pleasure of killing me himself. And they say *we* are evil.

"He's one of yours," I insisted. "Tell me honestly that you'll kill him, that he'll see justice, because I just don't believe that's going to happen."

"Althean will pay for what he's done but *you* cannot kill him. The justice needs to come from our own kind, from someone with the proper authority to deliver judgment."

We stood there a moment as the bugs sang in the woods around us. I wasn't sure I believed him. I suspected Althean would live for millions of years as they plowed through the red tape of who had jurisdiction and what laws pertained to this suspected offense. There was something else I wondered about though.

"Those demons that you've killed, do they get wings too? Are they granted your forgiveness?" I asked, knowing the answer but wanting to hear him say it.

Even in the dim moonlight, I could see a bolt of pain cross Gregory's face before it hardened into a rock like mask.

"Demons are filthy creatures, abominations beyond redemption and forgiveness," he said bitterly. "They don't deserve forgiveness or mercy, either in life or in death."

I shrugged. "Doesn't matter. None of us want your blessing. None of us give a shit about your forgiveness. Like we even care. We return the same. You'll get no mercy from us. No forgiveness, either."

I saw him wince at the last few words.

"None of you has the *capacity* for mercy or forgiveness," he said. He was furious, but at least he wasn't glowing. "Your vibration pattern will continue to diminish, you'll continue to devolve until the lowest worm has more divinity than you. You deserved to be banned from Aaru, to be banished for all eternity. You deserve to be killed on sight with no mercy. I should have killed you the moment I saw you. I should have killed you when you tried to escape me. I should just kill you right now."

That pronouncement should have had me on my knees, begging for that mercy he told me he'd never dish out. But I was pissed, so I taunted him the best way I could think of.

"Then why did you do *this* instead of killing me? What is this you've done to us both?" I asked, running my finger up the underside of my arm and over the tattoo of his sword.

Gregory jerked and clenched his fists. "That," he said. "That is a terrible mistake."

I smiled to myself as he stalked away into the woods. Just what I had thought. He'd fucked up whatever he'd done to me somehow and what the mark did went both ways. If only I could find out exactly what it did and how to work it, I could do to him as he did to me. Whatever that was. Right now, I could turn him on. Funny as that was, I couldn't see how it would work to my advantage in the long run. Hopefully, more useful applications would reveal themselves in the near future. Hopefully, before he killed me.

I turned around to walk to the cabin and my smile faded. Candy and Wyatt had woken up to the booms of sound in the front yard as did many of those in the neighboring cabins. They'd all been an interested audience to the whole exchange. The neighbors must be particularly entertained to see a naked woman arguing with a clothed man in front of the cabin. I also had a depressed feeling that any chance I'd had of a continued relationship with Wyatt was vanishing by the moment.

CHAPTER 17

I woke up rather pleased that I'd managed to get through the last night without damage to my physical person. Candy announced she was making a breakfast and coffee run for us and pointedly left me alone with Wyatt. He sat on the bed and messed with his tablet while I walked around the cabin moving stuff around, and basically hovering. Finally, I couldn't take it anymore, so I scooted up on the bed next to him.

"Please talk to me?" I pleaded. "There is nothing going on between me and that angel. Nothing sexual, nothing romantic, not even remotely friendship. I've been trying to get away from him, and somehow that always ends up with me injured and usually naked. He seems to be less fired up about killing me the past few days, but I've pretty much run out of options. He'll eventually kill me; I'm just trying to stall until I can think of something. There was a wild gate in the pool at that house. I tried to go through and he dragged me out of it. It was a good thing, actually, since I would have died in there. That's how desperate I am, I went into some crazy wild gate with a million to one chance of coming out in one piece and somewhere reasonable. Because a million to one chance is still better than zero."

Wyatt paused a moment, then tossed his tablet aside and gathered me up in his arms. He was still shirtless with his pajama bottoms on and his skin felt glorious against my face and arms. Warm and smooth with his heartbeat against my cheek. He had muscle, but the muscle and flesh had a firm give to it, so unlike the hard rock of a chest I'd spent the last few days being crushed against. I snuggled against him like a puppy and breathed in the scent of his skin as Wyatt tightened his arms around me. It felt so good. I was actually considering giving the straightjacket of sleep another try tonight.

"When he first came after you, I had a knight-in-shining-armor impulse." He laughed. "Stupid, I know. A human can't do anything against a being like him, and you are a thousand times stronger and more capable of protecting yourself than any woman I know. It's horrible to stand back and watch you two go at it, though. It makes me feel worthless, that I'm not worthy of being your friend, let alone anything more. I'm so outclassed, and I'm not used to that. I'm used to being the big fish in the little pond. The one who can get any girl he wants, and could easy smack down any threat or competition. This situation has smashed that illusion to bits. Then every time I turn around you're naked and pressed against him with his arms around you like something from a dime store romance."

I felt him twirl my hair in his fingers for a moment. "I'm making this whole situation about me and my feelings of inadequacy, when it should be about you. You're the one fighting to survive, and I'm pouting about having a supreme being hone in on my woman. I'm sorry, Sam. I'm a selfish jerk. I should be helping you and not having a pity party, here."

I pulled away a bit to look him in the face, and put a hand on his cheek.

"I'd be dead if it wasn't for you, Wyatt. You fucking *shot* him. Point blank, in the head, with that huge gun of yours. I know it didn't kill him like you intended, but it distracted him. If you hadn't done that, he would have lopped my fool head off right then and there. I was practically wetting my pants, and you had the balls to shoot an *angel*. You *are* a big fish in my book. You're clever, fun, hot beyond belief, and you're my go-to guy when the shit hits the fan." That was super hokey, but it was true. And to make my point, I leaned over and kissed him.

Kissing Wyatt has to be one of my favorite things ever. It's soft, then it's firm, then he runs his tongue over my bottom lip, then I run my tongue around the inside of his mouth, then he bites my lower lip, then I suck on his tongue. He dug his hands through my hair and gripped, like he thought I was going to run off if he didn't hold me in place. We made out slowly and thoroughly as if we had all the time in the world. Things were heating up to the point where it was hard to keep activity confined to mouth only. Wyatt let go his grip on my hair to yank my shirt off, and expertly remove my bra.

Now we were both bare-chested. I claimed his mouth with mine again and rubbed my breasts against him, happy for additional skin to skin contact. He rubbed a thumb over my nipple, sending a hot pulling sensation down between my legs. I could feel his hard length just a few thin layers of clothes away as I sat on him. How fast could we move this along, I wondered? If we hurried, we could both be sweaty and spent by the time Candy returned with the coffee. Wyatt bent his head down and ran his tongue over the other nipple, pulling it with his teeth. Fiery sensation washed over me, and I closed my eyes. Coherent thought was impossible and I reveled in the feelings flooding through me. I wanted to get his pants off, but couldn't figure out the logistics of removing them while keeping his mouth on my breasts. If only his pants would remove themselves.

Through the fog of my desire, I heard the door open and a loud "Arrrrrr!"

"Go away, Candy," I said firmly. She sounded like she'd walked in to find dog crap on the floor.

"I left you two to talk and make up, not to engage in sexual relations on the only bed in the place." She complained, showing no signs of leaving.

"Please?" I begged, although Wyatt had already stopped his wonderful exploration of my body and was lying back on the bed taking deep breaths.

Candy took her time getting a donut, and adding cream and sugar to her coffee. "I'm taking my breakfast outside, because it stinks in here, now," she announced, banging the door on her way out.

I threw myself down on Wyatt and scattered frantic kisses up his shoulder. "Oh, let's go for it," I said breathlessly. "You're ready, I'm ready. I'm so ready. You have no idea how ready I am."

I felt the rumble of his laughter against my chest. "I get the feeling that you're always ready, Sam," he said, rolling me over so he lay on top of me. In spite of the promising position, I had a feeling that our opportunity had passed. He gave me a glorious kiss as I ran my nails down his back, then rolled off the bed announcing that he was going to take a cold shower.

"You're killing me, Wyatt," I told him as he grabbed a towel and supplies to head to the communal bathhouse in the campground. "You'll come back and find me shriveled to dust in some female version of blue balls."

"Oh, the drama," he teased, heading out the door. I hopped up and put on my shirt, draping my bra across

Candy's couch just to piss her off, then went to dig through the donuts. Things felt very right with the world again. I grabbed a chocolate cream and went outside, not finding Candy on the porch or in the front clearing.

I just can't seem to leave well enough alone, so I went ahead and sent out a search for Gregory. Casting in a radius around the cabin, I found him surprisingly close. Just around back by the woodpile. So of course I crept around back to see him. Because after making up with my hopefully-soon-to-be boyfriend, it seemed like a smart thing to seek out the homicidal maniac that wanted to kill me and was causing all the trouble with said hopefully-soon-to-be boyfriend. I hoped it took Wyatt a good long time to cold shower his genitals back to a relaxed state, because if he returned to find me behind the woodpile with Gregory, things were not going to be pretty between us.

As I snuck along the side of the cabin, I heard voices and realized that Candy and Gregory were talking. Well, at least Candy was talking.

"She's distracting you with her antics. You would have caught this guy days ago, if you weren't having to chase her down. You can find her any time you want, just let her go. Let her go home. Even if she slips through a gate, no one knows you've seen her except me and Wyatt. We're not saying anything. Althean will be out of the picture, and he's crazy. Even if he says there was a demon, no one would believe him. She's served a purpose, give her a pass. Let her go."

"No"

Well, that was short and to the point.

"She's crazy, she's clearly got some death wish. She'll be back across in a couple of years and you can grab her then. No one back at her place would seriously believe her escaping you. They'd think she was full of it."

"No. I've marked her. Permanently. I'm not letting her go."

Crap. So much for ever getting this damned tattoo off my arm.

"She's living as a human. She has friends, business associates. Humans depend on her. Just let her go on with a human life, then. Take her powers away or something so you feel she won't be a danger to anyone, and just let her be."

Take my powers away? Could he even do that? That would be like blinding someone, or ripping out their tongue. I didn't like the sound of that at all. I think I'd rather he kill me.

"No. End of discussion. I'm going to watch the house. I'll be back."

I scurried silently back around the house to sit on the front porch and drink my cooling coffee. I was grateful for Candy's efforts, but it didn't look like this angel was ever going to let me go unless it was as a dead pile of sand. Probably not even then. I could see him sticking the sand in an urn and putting it somewhere unpleasant just to spite me beyond the veil of death.

I know it wasn't productive to keep harping on my impending death like this, but it somehow kept diminishing in my mind, as if it were truly only a remote possibility. It wasn't. It was real, and I needed to keep remembering in order to stay focused on trying to get away. I wanted to hang around this angel, to be near him when I should be trying to be as far away as possible. He's going to kill me. He's going to kill me. Maybe if I chanted it, I would focus on survival and not on wondering what he was doing right now.

We muddled around the cabin for the morning. Candy had the forethought to bring a paperback to read. I was going stir crazy and my death chant wasn't having much of an effect, so I announced that I was going to buy some more clothes to replenish all the ones I'd ruined so far. Wyatt offered to come with me, but I told him I needed some alone time. In reality, I was going to do something stupid. Fuck, my impulse control was becoming worse than Boomer's. I *was* crazy and clearly *did* have a death wish.

I found the nearest Walmart and blindly threw some jeans, sweat pants, and t-shirts into the shopping cart. Then I found a liquor store. It wasn't easy. They aren't usually open in the morning. All the higher end ones were closed for hours, but I did manage to find a seedy little liquor store with metal bars over all the windows and doors that had proudly opened at eight AM. And if that wasn't testimony enough to their target demographic, their alcoholic offerings clearly were. The only vodka they had was Gilbey's.

I'll admit I'm a vodka snob, but I have nothing against Gilbey's. It burns like Liquid Plumber going down, and you get drunk faster than you can snap your fingers, but at least it's honest. Some of that high end stuff in the fancy bottles was just as brutal and cost five times as much. Still, I'm not drinking it. I'm not that desperate.

The regular clientele of this liquor store clearly *were* that desperate though. There was a whole wall dedicated to various whiskeys. Not a craft beer in the place, although I was pleased to see they at least had Bud Light. It was a bit dusty and behind stacked boxes of Busch advertised for $9.99 a case in huge blue numbers. The wine selection was just as dismal. Lots of Boone's Farm and sweet fruity wines. I wondered what angels drank. I hadn't seen Gregory eat or drink anything, so maybe that was all part of their abstinence routine. The elves drank wine nonstop. I don't think I ever saw one without a goblet in his hand. Angels loved their elves, so maybe they drank wine, too? I doubted they drank Jack Daniels. I strolled around the store in indecision while the clerk looked at me nervously. I'm sure their usual customers were in and out in five minutes flat, while I looked like I was making the decision of my lifetime.

Finally, I grabbed a bottle of blackberry merlot that looked somewhat less rot-gut than the other wines, and paid the clerk the ridiculously cheap price. I just wasn't going to be able to find a decent bottle of anything in Waynesboro at this hour. Maybe it would be the thought that counted.

I drove out to the McMansion, parked my Corvette a block away, quickly locating Gregory. And there I sat for half an hour, almost turning around. Starting the car. Turning off the car. Banging my head on the steering wheel. What the fuck was I doing? Idiot. Should I do it? Should I just go back to the cabin? Maybe I should sit here and drink this nasty wine myself. Finally I got out of the car and made my way as stealthily as I could over to him feeling like the dumbest ass in the whole world.

"Hey," I said. He ignored me.

"Got any bites yet?" I asked, as if he were fishing. "I wonder if he'll make a move today after what went down last night. I walloped him pretty good; you might be here for a long time."

Silence.

"Sitting here staring at a house is really boring, so I brought some wine. I think it tastes like crap, but the elves like it, so I thought you might, too. Actually, I don't think the elves drink this particular wine. In fact, I'm sure they'd think it was crap too, but there isn't much to choose from in Waynesboro at this hour. See, I brought a corkscrew and some little plastic glasses. I'll open it right here in front of you so you know I'm not trying to poison you or anything."

Silence.

I struggled to open the bottle until I realized that the top was a screw off and not a cork. Yanking the corkscrew out, I wondered if I could just pour the wine through the hole I'd made in the cap. The alternative was probably the better choice, so I screwed off the mangled cap and poured a bit, sniffing the glass in what I hoped was a knowledgeable way. The stuff smelled like air freshener. Seriously. Like something I'd hang in my car. Or possibly one of those scented candles that everyone gave me at Christmas.

"Ah, the bouquet," I said, trying to keep a straight face.

I swirled it around in the glass. It coated the sides in a purple sheet and slowly oozed down like a gelatinous monster from a horror movie. If it were any firmer, I'd be having nightmare Jell-O flashbacks from that wild gate yesterday. I'll try anything, so I took a swig.

"I can see why it says 'serve chilled' in huge letters on the bottle," I told the angel, grimacing at the taste. "I'm not a wine critic, but this tastes like grape juice with a couple pounds of corn syrup mixed in. I can smell the blackberry, but I can't taste it at all. Fuck, this stuff is sweet! I hope you brought your insulin. Ugh."

Silence.

I poured him a glass and sat it down by him, arranging myself on the dirt. I filled up my glass and took another gulp, shaking my head at the strange acidic aftertaste.

"I don't blame you if you don't drink it. It might be good for discipline, though. Better than a hair shirt. You should at least give it a shot. Who knows, I could be totally wrong. This could be the best wine ever. One of those secret treasures of the cheap liquor store."

Silence.

Fuck, I was babbling like an idiot. What was wrong with me? I left a hot guy, whose company I enjoy to run over here and bring wine to an asshole who wants to kill me, thinks I'm an abomination, and now won't talk to me. If Wyatt were here instead of this angel, he would be rolling on the ground laughing with me right now. We'd be daring each other to drink the swill, taking bets on who could sip it the slowest without puking. Wyatt was fun. This angel was not. I should just shoot myself because I clearly had no sense left in my head whatsoever.

I sat there beside him, drinking the horrible wine and braiding blades of grass. After a few moments, I dropped onto my back and stared at the thick, dark clouds moving in. He didn't say anything. Didn't even glance at me. He shifted occasionally, so at least I knew he wasn't dead. I thought of all kinds of inane things to say, but I'd made enough of a fool of myself, so I just sat there in silence and watched the storm clouds gather on the horizon.

I'd killed about half the bottle of wine. He hadn't touched his, hadn't spoken to me, looked at me. Hell, he didn't even grunt at me. I plopped my empty glass next to the bottle and his untouched wine, got up, dusted off my rear, and just walked off. I couldn't think of anything to say that wouldn't make me seem like even more of an idiot that I already appeared. I really wanted to bash my head against something. It's not like we'd ended last night on friendly terms, and he'd made it clear in the conversation with Candy that he wasn't feeling kindly toward me. I don't know why I was sort of hurt by all this, why I was at all surprised by his reaction, or lack of reaction, to me.

I drove back to the cabin, and unloaded my purchases. No one was there. I glanced through Candy's paperback, only to toss it down and pace the cabin. I don't deal well with boredom, and there was nothing to do in this stupid cabin. Things were starting to get a bit dark and I heard the distant rumble of thunder, so I went out into a big field by the tent area to watch the approaching storm.

Electricity and plasma are near and dear to our hearts. They are some of our first talents as children, and we always have an affinity for them. Storms here in this realm are just amazing. The smell, the power, the rain, even that strange yellow color the air gets. I was feeling really down and needed a good storm to bring me right again. Was I homesick maybe? Humans are awesome, but there are some things you just can't share with them. Things that would freak them out, or things that are just beyond their understanding. We have such different lives. Our skills, our talents, our culture and society, how we're raised, what we value. Maybe that's why I was tagging around after this angel like a half-starved stray dog. I missed my own kind. And I *was* rusty. Forty years over here and I had an angel beating up on me and one that had twice eluded my grasp. Shameful. Dar would never let me live it down.

The blackness was rolling forward in the sky and I could feel the charged ions above me. I smiled and hummed a bit, waiting for the flashes in the sky to get closer. It was a good storm. The campground lights flickered on in the darkness, and cold hard drops began to pelt down on me. A huge flash lit the sky with an almost simultaneous roar of thunder. It shook hard enough to set off somebody's car alarm, and I laughed as I reached out and called it down to me.

The bolt shot right to me like a lover to my arms. I let some of it dance along my skin, twisting in colored bands of barbed light up my arms and neck, then down my torso and legs. I kept it moving circling and surrounding my flesh, and then flashed it in a disco ball of light around one arm before pulling it into me with a *swick* of sound. I called down another bolt, holding it in my hands in a globe shape, where it flashed and darted about in a prism of color. The next bolt I divided into hula hoops of white, swirling them around my hips and arms. I hadn't had this much fun in, well, in forty years. I hadn't realized how very bleak my life had become.

I called down a huge bolt, shaping it into a giant donut

above my head, then let it rain down around me, causing a ring of fire in the grass.

"Be careful, little cockroach, or you'll set the whole place ablaze," said a soft voice behind me. I was so preoccupied that I hadn't felt him near, but I wasn't startled. Maybe some part of me did know he was close by. I should have known he'd come running the moment I did something like this, no doubt to make sure I didn't burn the whole town down.

I extinguished the ring of fire, leaving it blackened and smoldering, and then called another bolt down, letting it dance along my skin. This storm was fast and violent. I'd probably only have a few more bits to play with before it moved on.

"Gather it closer," the angel instructed. "It's leaking out and the humans in their tents will be hurt. You've got talent, but you're sloppy and lazy with this energy. I know you can do better."

Asshole. It's not like others' safety is ever our priority. Who cared if it leaked out and cooked someone? It's their fault for being in a damned tent during a lightning storm. Still, I pulled it in around the edges just to show him I could.

"Can you work the lightning?" I asked, with the bands still flashing around my arms.

He shrugged. "Most of us can't, it's just not one of our talents. I've been around a long time though, so I can." He called down a small bolt from the clouds and shaped it into a fleur-de-lis with nice tight defined edges. Showoff.

"I used to come with my brothers when the planet was still young and we'd play in the lightning," he mused. "Everything was pretty much plasma and energy then, all these complex molecules hadn't formed yet. We had to manifest in an energy form to hold our being."

"What type of energy?" I asked, curious. That was so long

ago that I couldn't even imagine what the world was like. I felt very young next to him. A baby.

"All sorts," he said vaguely. Then he seemed to make a decision. "I'm most skilled in fire and fire-type energy, so I used to manifest as flame. Smokeless fire, I believe the humans call it. There's no real word for it in their language, though. Sa…my youngest brother," he corrected, clearly not wanted to reveal his brother's name. "He had great talent with electricity and we'd marvel at the things he would do with lightning. I have some talent, but not anywhere close to his level.

"He used to zap us with lightning sometimes, when we weren't expecting it, just to see us jump." He smiled fondly at the memory and turned to me. "You remind me of him, sometimes."

I looked at him in shocked surprise. I reminded him of his brother?

"Was your brother a *demon*?" I asked.

He laughed. "You weren't always demons, you know. You used to be angels. Always different from the rest of us, very different, but still angels."

"Are we no longer angels?" I asked, thinking that his answer meant all the difference in the world.

"I don't know. I thought you had all devolved to a far lesser state. Now, I wonder," he mused.

I stared at him with the lightning still rolling over my skin, waiting for him to say something else. I was afraid I'd break the spell and he'd return to the cold enforcer who was ready to kill me at any moment.

"We were five, my brothers and I," he continued. "The middle three were the least strong, although they have gained in skill and power with time. We've always been close, especially back then, but my youngest brother and I had a special bond."

I could feel a pain and sadness from him. Actually feel it, like it was inside me. Why was he sad? Did he and his brothers no longer have these good times together? Why should an obviously fond memory bring him pain?

I pulled the electricity within my stash of raw energy and looked up at the brightening sky. "These things are so fleeting, always over so fast."

"Yes, they are," he replied, and I realized he was talking about more than just the storm.

I was fairly wet from the big plops of rain. The storm had moved off fast before the downpour could start. The folks about a mile or two down the road were probably getting drenched. I wanted to just walk off and leave him standing in the clearing, or trailing after me. My ego was still smarting from the whole wine thing. Pride isn't my sin, though, so I stood there squeezing the water from my hair.

"Do you work with water much? Can you do this?" he asked unexpectedly as he suspended the water drops I'd shaken from my hair and floated them around me like little opaque balloons. It was pretty cool.

"Wow," I said, genuinely impressed. "Are you using some kind of force to overcome gravity or are you doing something to negate the effect of gravity in an area surrounding the water?"

"The latter." He swirled the little droplets together to make a large sphere, hanging before us. "I'm no expert with water, though," he said with false modesty. I could tell he was showing off.

I shook my head. I'd go ahead and stroke his ego a bit, because this *was* pretty cool. "That's really delicate, technical work; not something we're encouraged to do. We tend more towards big and flashy. Or exploding. Back home, no one would bother spending a lot of time to learn this. I mean, what would the point be if others didn't appreciate it, or it didn't destroy anything?"

I walked over to the globe sticking a finger through the gravity suspension field and into the globe of water. Gregory held it in place around my finger, and maintained the integrity of the shape and field as I withdrew, showing his amazing control over the most minute particle. The guy was really fucking impressive. I'd never seen anything like this before. I stuck my finger in a few other places and he held the field perfectly each time. The sphere didn't even quiver as I moved my finger over and through it. I wondered what else he could do. I'd never been around someone with this much power and control before. I wished I had a few millennia to just trail around after him and watch him work. It would be amazing.

The outside of the water globe began to take on a solid shape and I realized he'd frozen about a quarter inch of the outer water, leaving the inside to swirl about like an elaborate icy snow globe. The outer rim of ice on the globe was as clear as glass with the inside a churning prismatic liquid. Gregory walked over to pluck the globe from the air and handed it to me, placing it gently into my cupped hands.

I carefully ran my hands over the cold surface. It was absolutely clear, perfectly round and smooth. The water inside continued to churn and swirl in a pretty dance. He kept it frozen in the heat of the day, but the warmth from my hands created a slick wet surface as I held the globe. I was amazed to notice that the wet against my hand wasn't cold. Then I realized that he was holding the cold tightly against the surface of the globe, and the wet was actually a created buffer between my hands and the ice. I suppose he did this to keep my hands from sticking to it? Or possibly to keep my hands from being cold? Whatever his motive, it was a skilled piece of work to differentiate the temperature so cleanly and sharply in such thin layers. He made it all seem so easy. Fuck, he was *so* damned impressive. Damn it all, now I was even *more* drawn to this asshole.

I wasn't sure what I was supposed to do with the globe. Just admire it? Stick it in my freezer and save it as a souvenir? Instead I sat it in the grass in front of me and tried to raise it. I could shoot it with a burst and blow it across the grass, but I couldn't get the darned thing to float at all. I kept messing with it while Gregory watched and continued to keep the globe contained and frozen. I attempted different methods to see if maybe I could move it sideways instead, since up seemed beyond my talents.

"How long have you been here, on this side of the gates?" he asked, abruptly changing the subject.

"A little over forty years," I told him, getting the globe to rock a bit. No sense in lying at this point.

"Wow, I guess that makes me rather incompetent," he said, as if the idea amused him.

"It's not like I came in with guns a-blazing." I tried to get the globe to roll further to no avail. "Before this, I'd do like everyone else and pop over to wreak havoc and party, then dart back across the gates. This time I intended to stay, so I was very careful in cloaking my energy signature when I arrived. The biggest thing I've done before this week was Owning this flesh, and assuming its form. It was risky, but she was an ideal candidate for a long-term identity to assume."

"How did you manage that without detection," he asked with interest. "We should have been on you fairly fast after an Own and a full body conversion."

I shrugged. "I don't know. I was surprised, too. Humans have made a perfect environment to conceal small energy usage," I told him. "Cell signals, microwaves, X-rays, power grids. If you're careful, it's easy to stay within the parameters of the existing power flow. For big stuff, you can mask under an electrical storm, or blow out a power grid in a surge. The really big stuff is impossible without detection, but you can still get stuff done and run under the radar. I have no idea why you didn't catch me back then, though."

He stared at me, fascinated. It's not like I was giving any big secrets away. No one would have the slightest desire to repeat what I'd done, and I'd either be dead or unable to return. I might as well spill the beans.

"Forty years. Why would you *want* to do that? To live so hindered?" He seemed truly perplexed. "What appeal could this possibly have, to live without the use of your power? To live as a lowly human? You're a being of spirit. You're so much more than this."

"I have my reasons," I replied vaguely.

"Can you not return? Will you be killed? Are you a runaway servant?"

"No," I said indignantly. "I have status, and a household awaiting my return." Not that my household was big. I was just an imp, after all. And everyone had someone gunning for them. That's just the way life was in my world.

"Is it the human you've marked as yours? Do you stay for him, for love of him?" he asked with a strain in his voice.

Was he insane? That I could love a human? That I could love at all? Wyatt was my best friend, and I did want to stay here to be with him. But love?

"He amuses me," I said slowly. "I know he's only a human, but he amuses me. The chase, the sexual tension. He's fun, and I really enjoy his company."

We stood there and the silence stretched on between us. I could feel that pain in him again, as if my words bothered him. His dark eyes bore into mine searching for something.

"Go home," he finally said, as if the decision caused him agony. "I won't come for you, I won't stop you. I'll ensure you have safe passage through the gate near Baltimore, the one in the mall in Columbia. It's the most stable gate on the north-east coast, and the safest. It will put you out near the elf border."

You would have thought I'd be gone in a shot, but I remained there with stupid indecision as my hand crept up my arm, stopping just shy of the tattoo. I didn't want to leave Wyatt. I didn't want to leave this angel. I didn't want to go home.

"Why? Why are you letting me go now after telling me you'd slaughter millions before letting me go?" I asked.

"I can't kill you," he said, a hint of desperation in his voice. "I'm afraid if you stay, that I will kill you, that I'll find myself in a situation where I have to kill you. I can't go through that, again."

"But what about this?" I asked, touching the tattoo lightly. I was bound to him, his demon.

"I can't remove that," he said. "With some study, I may be able to eventually dull some of its effects, but it's there permanently. I don't know how you're going to explain it when you return home. I'm not usually so rash. I'm sorry."

Wow, an apology. From an angel. Pigs truly do fly. I didn't know what to do or say, so I wandered in a daze slowly back to the cabin and put my bags back in the car. Candy and Wyatt still hadn't returned, so I sent Wyatt a quick text and headed out. I didn't see Gregory again.

CHAPTER 18

It was about seventy miles from Waynesboro to the gate. I know I went down through Emmitsburg, then took Route 140 up to Westminster, but I honestly don't remember the trip at all. I was very close to home, but couldn't bring myself to go there. Wyatt would take care of everything for me, and be a rich man for his troubles. I hoped it helped make up for me not saying goodbye in person. I had turned off my cell phone to avoid his calls. I just couldn't talk to him right now. I just couldn't tell him in person that I would never see him again. I tried to keep my mind off of him and off Gregory as I drove numbly down the road. The back roads from Westminster to Columbia were beginning to fill with late Saturday traffic, but I was driving in the opposite direction and thankfully didn't hit any gridlock.

Columbia was a well manicured suburb outside of Baltimore, filled with expensive homes in wooded subdivisions, consultant and technology offices down tree-lined avenues, and winding, well maintained streets. The place had an overwhelming air of neat, liberal money. On the surface, it gave flashy lip service to environmentalism, but underneath it was as shallow and selfish as anywhere else in the world. It was as fake as a boob job and acrylic nails. A very expensive boob job and acrylic nails that people lied about and claimed were real. I shopped here a lot.

I always got a bit lost trying to find the damned mall. All the streets looked the same, and the buildings and signs were artfully hidden behind maples and oaks. I know this seems like a strange place to put a major gate between two dimensions. It's not like the angels intended to put a big gate at a mall. Heck, they didn't intend it to be anywhere near civilization.

When the gates were first built, they were in remote areas where it would be easy to see anyone coming and going, and to guard them. The humans are like ants though, breeding like crazy and spreading themselves over every surface of the planet. For some reason, all the major gates ended up engulfed or near big cities and, unfortunately for the angels guarding them, tended to be in high traffic areas. The one in Columbia was no exception.

The universe clearly had a sense of humor, for a mall had grown up around it. A big, upper-middle-class shopping haven complete with a Nordstrom's and Macy's. You didn't want to cross during the night, when the mall was closed, but during the day it was open season. The poor gate guardian had the worst job ever. If you hit it during Labor Day or the weekend, the place was teeming with people. Through some weird design fluke, the gate moved around the mall area, but once you located it, you just blended in with the teens and harried soccer moms and slipped right through. Because it was so popular and well used, the gate had to have a full-time, alert and powerful guardian. He constantly changed his appearance, and he didn't take prisoners.

I parked my car safely on the outer edges, even though I'd

never see it again, and walked in the Nordstrom's entrance. The gate was clearly not in the shoe section, and I checked it thoroughly. Nor was it anywhere near the rhinestone-studded Ralph Lauren belts. I hoped it was in the Sephora store. It wasn't, but a really cool shade of MAC lip gloss was. I was now accessorized with a little bag as part of my shopper disguise. Clearly, no one would suspect me with a cosmetics bag, although I had no idea what I was going to do with lip gloss back home. Most of my forms there didn't even include lips.

I spent several hours weaving my way through stores, looking for the gate. I hoped it wasn't on the outside of the mall today. It would be harder to slip in unnoticed while in the parking lot. Not that I needed to be unnoticed this time, since I had my handy dandy get-out-of-jail free card from Gregory, but old habits die hard. I had made it down to the food court, and was contemplating buying a smoothie when I heard a voice call me in a name that should never be spoken this side of the gates.

"Azi Niyaz!" a voice said, with a tone of relief.

I froze. Two of my names. Crap, it's a wonder the idiot didn't go ahead and spew out the others. I turned carefully around and saw one of the Low behind me. He was in the flesh of a thirteen-year-old boy, which was disturbing in and of itself. I don't like to Own children. They don't have a lot of life experience, so it's really a waste of time. Plus, they make foolish decisions in regards to their willingness. It just felt wrong, but they were easy prey so it was something the Low did if they got the chance.

The form he took had floppy brown hair in a mop around his face and ears and pale skin with blue eyes. His jeans hung practically off his hips, and his t-shirt advertised some kind of surfboard. It was a well put together form, but the eyes gave him away. They were incorrectly formed and like rat's eyes darting around under the curtain of brown bangs.

As soon as the Low said two of my names, he sputtered to a stop, realizing his error. He cringed back from me and corrected himself.

"I mean El. I'm so sorry, El. I welcome your punishment."

Yeah. I could hardly flay him or remove a digit here in the food court. Punishment would be in order back home, not just for saying my names this side of the gates, but by addressing me that way in general. There were titles of respect you used for those above you. Names were for peers and above only. This guy was Low; he wasn't even in the ranks of the hierarchy. He really shouldn't even have been addressing me at all. Using the title El was a good call, though. El meant "Mighty Being" or "Powerful One" and was a title used far above my pay grade. He was flattering me to make up for his mistake. He should have used Baal, which means Lord, and is more in keeping with my level.

I waited for him to proceed. He must be desperate or he wouldn't have come within twenty feet of me, let alone speak to me. He shifted from foot to foot, keeping his eyes fixed on the ground right before me. The guy clearly knew his manners.

"My apologies, El, for disturbing you with my presence. I am unable to find the gate and would be glad to offer my person to the lowliest of your household in return for assistance."

Wow. It was way above his station to ask me for assistance. He truly was desperate. He can't have been a total idiot. Beyond his initial error, his etiquette was impeccable. I would have been offended if he offered himself to me, as I was above his station. To offer himself to the lowest rung of my household was fitting, but the service he was asking was far beyond that gift.

I looked at him closely. He probably saved for centuries to purchase assistance crossing the gates on a long-awaited holiday, and now found himself stranded by his guide and unable to return. I wondered if Gregory would even bother with someone so low, or if he would have one of his minions dispatch him. The angel seemed to take some pride in doing it himself, so maybe this guy would rate.

"Did you pay Charon for passage, or some other guide?" I asked.

The Low let out a huge breath in gratitude, keeping his eyes firmly on the floor in front of me.

"Oh no, El. I could not afford Charon's fee, so he advised me to try another guide. The journey here was uneventful, but it's been two days since he was to meet me and I fear I am stranded. I don't have the skill to find the gate on my own or avoid the guardian."

Great. He probably paid Phlegyas or one of his flunkies. Phlegyas was good. He wasn't as good as Charon, but he could activate the gates and get someone safely back and forth. He was very untrustworthy, though. It didn't matter how much you paid him, he was liable to forget about you or just not bother. The Low should have withheld partial payment, and had someone back home ready to beat Phlegyas to a pulp if he didn't return as expected.

Two days. He must be starving and scared. He was so Low, a human could probably kill him with bare hands. I wondered if he'd been sleeping in the parking garage with the homeless people. He didn't look very dirty. I wondered if he could even convert, or if he'd had someone else do it for him. His form was pretty good for the level he was at and his speech and manners were good. Maybe he had some unrecognized talents. I should send him home to see if my household could use him. If not, they could play with him a bit and set him loose. Did my get-out-of-jail-free card include a Low?

"Follow me. Remain at least ten feet behind me at all times. Try to act as if you're not following me." I spun around and headed out, knowing that the guy would rather slit his own throat than lose me in the crowd.

Finally, I found the gate — by the carousel of all places. It was a few feet in front of a bench parents used to watch their children go round and round on the plaster horses. The humans walked by and through it without the skill to activate it. Humans could fall through some of the wild gates accidently, and the elf gates were sometimes set up to snag unwary humans like a carnivorous plant and bring them over, but the angels had done a good job. Their gates were complex and perfect creations. Many of us had the skill to activate them, but an equal number could not, resulting in a thriving guide industry. Some guides were on the level, and some would take your money and get you killed.

I popped into Starbucks and sipped on an iced latte while looking casually around for the guardian. I assumed the Low was still following me. I didn't check and I certainly didn't offer to get him a coffee. Normally, I would have roamed around here for hours excluding people and narrowing down the loiterers until I identified the guardian, but not today. Tossing the remains of my latte in the trash, I walked right up to the gate and placed my left hand upon it. Before I had a chance to activate it, my wrist was in the surprisingly firm grip of a tiny elderly woman with purple hair and a wildly patterned dress.

"You should not touch that, dearie," she said in a pleasant voice. I saw a flash of sharp little piranha teeth as she smiled.

"You should not touch *me*, dearie," I replied, turning my other arm to show her the tattoo.

She jumped like I'd stung her and stared at the mark. It

would have been one thing if it were just the tattoo, but that damned hickey was still there too. And I had the feeling that it wasn't supposed to be. She better not try and touch it or I'd punch her across the floor. Then I'd get arrested for assaulting a little old lady. I wondered if I could call Gregory from jail and have him come down and make bail for me. I didn't think he had a cell phone. Even if he did, I doubted he'd bail me out.

The gate guardian peered closely at the tattoo and I held my breath, fist ready. Finally she released my wrist, and looked me up and down, shaking her head in disbelief.

"Well, I'm certainly not one to question my superior's actions or decisions," she said in a rather sarcastic voice. Then she went on to question them anyway. "That's plain *wrong*. I've seen bound demons before, but not that. That's just insane, that's what that is. What was he thinking? Not that it matters. You're walking dead anyway, and the bond will break once you're killed. I've been told to let you cross, which I had to have him repeat twice. I've *never* been told to let someone cross. And why he'd let you cross with *that* on your arm, I have no idea. Why would he want you walking around the other demons with that? Perhaps he just wants to freak them all out and send them into a state of panic."

I wondered what it was about the mark that would send my kind into a state of panic? Would they be alarmed that one of their kind had been bound and not killed like we normally were? Would they suspect me as a spy?

"This has been a very enjoyable conversation," I told her. She seemed rather insubordinate for a guardian. Maybe all the years hanging around teenagers at the mall had affected her attitude. "Can I activate it now and go, or are we going to discuss this over salad and an iced tea first?"

"So what has he compelled you to do?" she chatted on. "Are you going to bring back a hoard of demons for him to exterminate? Act as a go between and negotiate something with the elves? Maybe blow up your entire realm? Usually it's building stuff, but you don't seem the type to put up temples, bridges or pyramids."

"Do I look like I'm compelled to do anything? Do I *seriously* look like anyone could compel me to even bring them a coaster?"

She looked me over again. "You look like you're compelled to cause trouble, but I doubt that's the boss' directive."

"Can we get on with this, then?" This guardian was a pain in the ass.

"Oh no, you can't activate the gate. I have specific instructions that I must activate it for you. In fact," she dug around in a large purse, "I took notes."

She pulled out a brown fast-food napkin with writing on it and read from it.

"Do not let her activate the gate. She is liable to close it in on herself halfway through. Then I'll need to come back here to pull bits of her crushed body out, and that will cause me to work months restoring the gate. Activate the gate for her. Also, make sure she doesn't accidently drag in dozens of shopping humans and the kiddie carousel with her to the other side. It's never happened before, but she'll find a way."

Ha, ha. So funny. Gregory the angel comedian. "Fine," I told her, flicking my wrist for the Low to approach. He darted over to stand silent looking at the floor in front of my feet.

"Oh no," the guardian protested. "He told me you, not you and some sniveling worm. You can cross. I'll take care of this one. He's not significant enough to bother the boss with."

Well, that answered that question. I put some steel into my gaze and hefted the weight of my raw energy to the surface in a flash, just to show her what I was packing. She didn't even budge.

"How disappointing," I sneered. "I will just go back to the angel and let him know that I was unable to complete the task he *compelled* me to do because the guardian would not allow me through with my servant. He'll have to leave the pressing matter he is dealing with to accompany me back here."

The guardian clearly didn't like that idea, but I could see her weighing if it was a bluff or not.

"He's not even high enough to be considered a being," she said grudgingly. "I could see where maybe the boss didn't notice his existence. Still, I'm going to activate the gate, and go get some sweet and sour pork. As far as I'm concerned, you crossed alone."

Good compromise. She activated the gate along with a repel perimeter to make sure I didn't accidentally drag in any humans then headed off to the food court.

One step and I'd be home. Back to my household, my own kind, the life I'd grown up with. The time I'd spent here wasn't much when compared to my life so far. Just an extended vacation. Time to end it and get back to business.

Time to do something reckless and impulsive. I turned to the Low and took his hand. With a flash of energy, I twisted his hand completely around, breaking the wrist and facing it palm up on the arm. I'll give the guy credit, he didn't even flinch. He might be useful after all.

"Go to the steward of my household and show him this. He will have you pay for the service I've rendered. Whatever payment he deems fitting." I motioned to the gate, and the Low crossed, ducking his head in gratitude but never raising his eyes. Then I closed the gate, dismissed the repel perimeter and walked out the nearest mall exit.

CHAPTER 19

Of course, the exit I took was at the opposite end of the huge mall from where I'd parked. I walked all the way around the exterior of the mall, including the parking garage, to the outer edge of the lot by Nordstrom's with my little bag of lip gloss. I wanted to make sure the guardian didn't see me. As far as she knew, I was gone. As far as Gregory knew, I was gone. I hoped the bond wouldn't register if I kept my energy usage to zero and I kept my distance. It's not like he'd be looking for me if he thought I was over the border. I'd have to be even more careful about my energy than before. I'd also have to make sure I avoided any proximity with those of my kind over here. If Gregory showed up to get them, he'd sense my presence nearby and know I'd remained.

Could I possibly be free? Free to take the assets I'd hidden and start a new life. I couldn't assume a new form, but I could use the human methods to gain a new identity. They were very clever about their forgeries, if you had the money to pay them. I'd contact Wyatt and have him meet me. I'd have to get a new identity for him, too. He could still kill zombies with a different name.

I took the highway home, slogging through traffic, then pulled down the road past Wyatt's house. I should feel happy. This was my choice. I felt just as miserable as before, though. I looked over at Wyatt's house, thinking of his broken fridge door, and shooting guns in his back yard. I wandered about my yard, patting Boomer, dipping a toe in the pool and watching my horses in the field, grazing peacefully. My eyes were getting misty, which was a human thing, not typical of my kind. I went inside, and saw the blinking button on the answering machine. I hit play, thinking this would be the last time I'd hear this person's voice. It was Wyatt.

"Hi, Sam," he said sounding miserable. "You're not picking up your cell phone. I don't know if you'll stop by your house, or even listen to your messages before you leave. Probably not, but I wanted to leave a message just in case. You must have shook up Althean pretty bad, because he killed someone outside of Hagerstown today. He bypassed Waynesboro entirely. We're heading down to Sharpsburg which looks to be his next area. There are only a couple werewolf residences there, so I'm hoping we can nab the guy and wrap this up.

"I'm tagging along with Candy to help her out for a couple of days. If this thing isn't resolved by then, I'll probably call a friend to come pick me up and I'll head back. I know you said Michelle was arranging for your animal care. I called her to make sure she'd cover for the next few days until I get back. I want you to know I'll go right to your safe and follow all your instructions. I'm hoping you'll find a way to come back, although it doesn't look like that's going to be possible. If you ever make it back in the next sixty years or so, I might still be alive. I'd love it if you looked me up, even though I understand we'd hardly be able to pick up where we left off."

There was a few seconds of silence on the tape before he continued. "Sam, knowing you made all the difference in my life. Everything is different when I'm with you, risks are fun, amazing things are possible, anything can be overcome. I was never a serious person, but with you I really saw how humorous and fun life could be...if I only took a chance. I'll always remember you. I know you're immortal, and that your time with me was a grain of sand on the beach of your life, but I hope that knowing me meant something to you, too. Good luck, Sam."

I really had been away from home, living as a human for too long, because my eyes were leaking all over the place and my chest was heaving air out in choked bursts. It was very unpleasant.

I cried until I felt like I didn't have any more in me to cry. Didn't make me feel any better and I looked like shit. My face in the mirror was red and blotchy with puffy eyes, and I couldn't breathe through my nose. I missed home, missed my own kind, but wasn't ready to go home and deal with the politics, the power struggles, the stupid breeding petitions. I liked my life, here. When it got boring, fun was within arm's reach. Humans were plentiful, and very entertaining. And Wyatt. I really liked being with Wyatt.

There was no logical reason for what I was about to do at all. I was staying here in this realm, but I wasn't going to run off and hide under a new identity either. I couldn't really go back to the way things were before this week. I'd just have to make the best of what lay ahead. What I was doing was a leap off the cliff, trusting in my instincts that things would somehow be okay. I got a much needed hot shower, changed my clothes, packed a small bag and headed west toward

Washington County and Sharpsburg. Whatever happened, happened.

Sharpsburg was a dot on the map. A series of country routes led there from the highway around the mountain and through Boonsboro. I prefer the steep winding narrow roads right over the mountain and down into the heart of the little town. With less than a thousand residents, it's got that typical small, one street town kind of feel. The place would have faded into oblivion except for the fact that it saw the bloodiest day of the Civil War right on its doorstep. Over twenty-three thousand dead, wounded, or missing. That's pretty impressive, even by demonic standards. The historical folks did a decent job with the battlefield site, too. It had scores of informative plaques, monuments, and some cannons. It would have been far more impressive to have tens of thousands of mannequins posed for battle, bloody and shot to bits, and scattered around the fields so visitors would walk amid the carnage and really get a feel for the action, for the scope of the slaughter. It's a shame preservation groups didn't take these things more seriously.

It was such a tiny town. I searched for Althean, trying different vantage points to make sure I covered the whole area. I wasn't sure what I was going to do, now that I was actually here. Should I wait for Althean to show up, and then swoop in dramatically? Should I text Wyatt, letting him know that I hadn't left? Should I search for Gregory? Maybe not. I wasn't sure what he'd do to me since I had not crossed the gates as he told me to. I knew I was going to have to face him, eventually. Either way, I knew he wouldn't be pleased. No, I really didn't want to find Gregory. Not yet. I searched again for Althean, then went to the General Burnside Tavern for a drink. I was not really good at this waiting thing.

The bar was small. One room with a few tables and a couple of dart boards. Some guy with a guitar played in the corner with his case open for tips. It didn't have a lot of money in it and I suspected what was there was placed by the guitarist himself in an effort to prime the pump. Everyone ignored him. There were four guys at the bar drinking beer and watching football on TV. It was too early for the pro season or even college. Did they show football re-runs in off season? The best of last year? I plopped down next to them and ordered a Bud Light. I knew better than to ask for vodka in this place.

Part of my thoughts went to a constant scan for Althean. That was a boring activity though, so I drank my beer, eyed the patrons and wondered what I could do to entertain myself until I could kill something. The four guys at the bar were riveted to the game on TV. There were a couple of guys playing darts. The guitarist started up again bellowing some ballad about love and tulips. One of the guys at the bar glanced at him in irritation and turned the captioning on the TV. I didn't realize they close captioned football games. Huh.

"What's the guitarist's name?" I asked the bartender.

"Bob Burrows," he told me, glancing over at the singer. "He annoys everyone, but the owner's sister knows him so we have to let him play."

I took a swig of beer and looked over at the guy. He was skinny, with a short beard and longish brown hair. Mid-twenties. His hands on the guitar were rough and calloused with a wedding ring on his left hand. He had that far away look in his eyes of a man whose dreams have been derailed by reality. The guitar was second hand, but in decent shape. The case battered with some band stickers that clearly were not placed there by the current owner. His sheet music was propped up in the lid.

"How often does he play here?" I asked.

The bartender shrugged. "A couple times per week if we're lucky. He works construction. Went to Shepherd

University across the river for a year for music, but got married and dropped out. His wife gets irritated if he's out here too many evenings."

I got up and walked over to the guy. "Are you Bob Burrows?" I asked.

He looked at me, clearly noting I was not one of the regulars, or even a local in this small town. "Yes."

"I'm a private investigator out of Hagerstown," I told him. "I'm doing surveillance in a divorce case. I just wanted to let you know that your wife is fucking the propane delivery guy. His wife hired me to get proof after she found some naked pictures of your wife on his phone. You seem like a nice guy, and I just thought you ought to know."

I never saw a man scramble up his guitar and case so fast in his life. He raced out the door and a few moments later a truck roared out of the parking lot. His wife probably was cheating on him. Loser was so hung up on what could have been that he can't have been very present in their relationship.

I turned around to see the patrons staring at me. Even the four football watching guys had torn their gazes from the television to look at me with their mouths open.

"You wanna play darts?" a short wiry guy asked me.

Althean was still nowhere nearby so I played some darts and ordered the hot wings that were on special.

The hot wings were good, but they didn't improve my dart game. I finally gave up and started tossing darts into the various decorations on the wall holding the dart board. My favorite was in the nose of the mounted deer head. It was very amusing to see a lovely cluster imbedded in the deer's left nostril. The patrons and bartender started to look at me warily. They probably were beginning to think they had been better off with the guitarist. Much to everyone's relief, the bar finally announced last call. I'd filled the deer head and a painting of some military guy with dart holes, and was trying to convince one of the drunken guys to put a stalk of celery in his mouth in a William Tell-style feat of accuracy. The bartender managed to shoo us out the door before I impaled the guy.

Still no Althean. It was two in the morning and I was getting bored with walking the one street town. I could go to the all night Waffle House up the road, but I was worried it would be too far to get an accurate fix on my target if he arrived. Everything was closed in this town. Crossing the street, I made my way again to Burnside Bridge Road, where a small gas station occupied a corner.

The gas station had closed hours before, but there was a soda machine humming away outside the garage building. I only had change enough for one soda, so I used a small trickle of energy to dislodge the rest out of the machine and wasted some time shaking them up and pitching them against the gas pumps. The minimum wage attendant would get quite a shock when he opened in the morning and found the pumps sticky with dented soda cans strewn about.

Finally, I couldn't take any more boredom. I texted Wyatt letting him know that I had decided not to leave anyway, and that I was in Sharpsburg vandalizing a gas station. I told him that he should come down and bring some beer so he could drink with me. Then we could pitch the bottles into the road.

Maybe I should just pick up Wyatt and go back to our houses. If I wasn't allowed to kill Althean, then the whole thing was going to be pretty snoozeville. Although, I did want to watch and see what Gregory was going to do to him. I could learn a lot from that guy. Wyatt called back immediately.

"Sam? You're really still here?" he asked in a hushed tone.

"Yeah. Why are you whispering? Where are you? What's going on?" I asked, whispering back.

"Gregory wanted us both to leave, to go home and let him handle it, but Candy insisted she needed to stay. I think she wants to make sure it's truly resolved before she goes back. I'm still here because I have the computer models, and I don't have my truck so I don't have a way back. We're holed up at one of the werewolf houses off Burnside Bridge so Candy doesn't get attacked separately again. Gregory has been gone for hours. He's in a horrible mood. Seriously horrible mood.

"Sam, why didn't you leave? What are you doing still here? You're not safe, here. I don't know what he'll do if he knows you're still here. He's a sanctimonious jerk; I don't think he's going to tolerate you living over here now that he knows about you. Plus, the mood he's been in this evening, he's liable to just kill you on sight. You really need to make yourself scarce."

Sanctimonious was a good word. I had no idea Wyatt had that kind of vocabulary.

I didn't know what I was doing, either. What was I trying to gain from this? Why didn't I just scoop up Wyatt and go back to the house? Because I was a stupid idiot and couldn't keep away from this damned angel. I needed to see him, needed to know who he really was inside. Candy wasn't the only one who needed to see this through. I had to see if Gregory would deliver justice or just cover it up. I shouldn't really give a shit, but I needed to know if the angel was a hypocrite, to know what his moral framework was, to know if he lived by the inflexible code which fractured our races so long ago.

"Where are you?" I asked Wyatt. "I just want to make sure you and Candy are safe. Don't worry about me; I know what I'm doing." Lie, lie, lie.

Wyatt told me the address, somewhere off Burnside Bridge Road. I told him to stay tight, and that I'd call him in a bit.

I went out again, casting around for Althean without success. Dreading what I was about to do, I drove to the outer portion of town, as far away from where Wyatt and Candy were as I could get and converted every cell of my being in a huge pop of noise. I hoped it was far enough away to not scare Althean, but close enough to jar Gregory's exterminate instinct and bring him running.

It was barely a second later before something large and rock like flashed an inch from me and knocked me to the dirt.

I slid across the ground for about three feet. "Damnit, I just took a shower and put on clean clothes."

"You!" the angel said. He closed his eyes, and then opened them again, as if I were an illusion that would disappear. "The guardian *saw* you cross. She told me she saw you go through the gate with her own eyes. How did you get back here?"

I wasn't about to narc on the guardian. "I have mad skills," I told him.

He looked at me blankly.

"I am a being with many diverse talents," I explained. The guy really needed to work on his modern slang.

"I know what 'mad skills' means, I just don't see what that has to do with anything," he said. "Why? Why did you come back? I go against the council decree that I should kill you on sight, then actually allow you to freely return home and you not only come back to this realm, but you come here and bring yourself to my notice less than twenty-four hours from when I let you go."

He took a deep breath and let it out in a whoosh. "When I want you to stay, you practically kill yourself trying to get away, and when I want you to go away, I can't get rid of you. You, cockroach, are truly my worst nightmare manifested.

What was my sin that I am punished by having you constantly around, messing things up, thwarting my plans?"

Thwarting his plans. It sounded like some bad guy in an old western. All he needed to do was twirl a long handlebar mustache and chuckle deviously.

"Yes, well dastardly villains like you deserve thwarting," I joked.

"How do you think I'm a villain?" he looked confused. "Do you still think I won't punish Althean? Or is it because I killed that human law enforcement officer? That was unfortunate, but I was not about to allow you to escape me."

"It was a joke. You know, because you used the word 'thwart' and it's such a cliche word. Oh, never mind." He had to have a sense of humor somewhere in that thick head of his. Or maybe not. "I came back because I need to see this to the finish. I owe Candy a blood price for killing one of her pack mates and my taking out Althean was the price. I don't want it said I go back on my contracts, on my word."

"You know I will not allow you to kill Althean. So your contract is void. You are simply unable to fulfill it. Candy will have to renegotiate another blood price with you. Why are you really here?"

I could hardly tell him I was obsessed with him and that he better get used to me stalking him like a creeper in a white van.

"I have OCD," I told him desperately. I don't know how my mind made the jump to that. Maybe because I'd been thinking of Candy and I was fairly certain she had all the symptoms in the diagnostic manual.

He sighed dramatically. "Okay, please enlighten me as to what this OCD is."

"Obsessive Compulsive Disorder. It's a mental condition some humans have where they do repetitious behavior, or actions that are driven by compulsion and not the logic of the situation. So you see, I have OCD and cannot quit in the middle of this. I just need to see the hunt through. If I can't kill him, then fine, but I need to see it through to the end before I can move on. Or I'll go crazy and wind up in an institution somewhere."

That was the stupidest excuse ever, but maybe he'd believe it.

He scowled. "You are the worst liar in all of creation. I have no time for any more of your ridiculous falsehoods. You've drawn me away and even now Althean may be at the house attempting to kill while I stand here bantering with you"

I'd been scanning constantly since I had arrived. "No, he's not there. I can sense him and track him if he's within a couple miles radius. That's how I knew he was at the cabin in Waynesboro. Will that help you? Maybe you can use that skill of mine?"

The angel paused thoughtfully. "I can't sense him until he uses some energy, so your skill would possibly help save a life. If you try to kill him or hinder me in any way, though, I will not spare you. Don't think that because I let you go once that you have special privileges. You are a cockroach and I won't tolerate your interference."

I nodded. "If you're not with me, let me know how I can contact you. You don't have a cell phone number I can text you on, do you?" Damned angels were so backward about human technology I wasn't even sure he could use a walkie-talkie.

"No, I don't. Your energy use is how I sense you. If you convert something or use your energy to call me when he's near, Althean will be tipped off and flee. You've nearly killed him twice. I doubt he'll risk fighting you again."

It was really wicked, I know, but I ran my finger over the tattoo. "I can call you this way," I teased.

He ground his teeth. "Will you stop doing that? Stop messing with it until I can find some way to disable that unfortunate feature?"

"Is it always this strong? Does it fade with distance or time? If I'd crossed the gate, could we still feel it? Would it even remain?"

He rubbed his face and ran his hands through his chestnut curls. It was a very human gesture. "It will always remain and time won't do anything but maybe make us more used to it. I don't know what effect distance will have on it. Perhaps it will be weaker. Perhaps I won't sense you at all if you're far enough away or across the gate. The original binding that it's based on, that it was supposed to be, is meant to summon you no matter what realm you're in or how far away you are; to know your location when I want to find you and be able to gate to you; and to compel you to do as I command."

There was that compel thing again. He must have fucked that part up too because I didn't feel particularly compelled to obey him.

"So, you mean you didn't intend to put a two way erogenous zone on my arm?" I asked, running my finger over it slowly. It felt amazing and I found myself wondering again if angels had genitals. He'd probably kill me, though. I got the feeling angels didn't do sex.

"No," he ground out. "And if you don't stop that, I'll remove your hands from your body."

"Then I'd be forced to use my tongue," I said, rather breathlessly. That sounded like an even better idea.

"I'll remove your tongue, then. Repeatedly. Until you get tired of growing it back."

He seemed very serious, so I reluctantly stopped. Besides, it was difficult teasing him when I myself was getting turned on twenty times what he was.

"You will remain near me and tell me when he's close." Gregory said, in a voice that sounded suspiciously commanding. I was okay with what he was proposing, but the whole compel thing had me a bit on edge, so I decided to pester him a bit more just so he wouldn't get any ideas that I was compelled to do stuff.

"We'll be joined at the hip," I told him, wiggling my eyebrows suggestively. "Or maybe joined at other parts of our bodies."

"Not going to happen," he said. "Although I may be tempted to drag you by your hair."

"I might like that."

He shook his head in exasperation. "Are you sure you're not a succubus? You seem really obsessed with the sin of lust."

"It's a good sin. I like gluttony an awful lot, too. Sloth has its moments, but I just don't understand acedia at all. I mean, what the fuck *is* that anyway? Oh, and greed is good, to quote Gordon Gekko. Anger, envy, and pride," I ticked them off on my fingers. "I don't often have much use for them. It's a shortcoming that I'm hoping to correct in the next millennium or two. I'm not very old; I can't be expected to have mastered them all yet."

"I think you've worked too hard on some of those," he said dryly. "Maybe you should switch over to virtues instead. Give yourself a much needed break."

Virtues? Yeah, right.

"Virtues are too difficult," I told him, shaking my head. "Look how old you are and you've hardly made a dent in them. I'll admit, you seem to have zeal nailed, as well as faith and temperance. Self control? I've got my doubts based on your recent actions. I'm not seeing the kindness, love, or generosity, either. That humility thing seems to be pretty far beyond your reach, too. Really, really far. I'm sorry to tell you this, but from what I can see, the sin of pride is a major component of your character. Dude, you're fucking old. You should have these things pretty well ticked off your shopping list by now. I'm seriously disappointed. Seriously."

He stared at me, his face unreadable. I wondered for a brief moment if I'd pushed him too far, but he didn't seem angry. Crickets chirped in the background, like an old cliché, but I just met his gaze and refused to break the silence.

"I can hardly wait until this is over," he finally said. "Then I never have to spend another moment with you for the rest of eternity."

He turned and walked away, and I followed him, feeling rather relieved.

We gated back to the target werewolf house. Gregory stood there, patiently holding me upright while I got my bearings. It didn't seem to take quite as long this time, but we did gate a fairly short distance. Less than five miles.

The house was a beautiful single-story log cabin nestled in the woods. The driveway actually had a small bridge to cross over the creek to get to the road. Pines flanked the driveway and formed little oases among the hardwoods, with their tall dense canopy. Underneath, their orange needles cushioned the ground like a soft mattress. I knew I'd get sap all over my jeans, but I couldn't resist sinking to sit on them and breathing in their fragrance.

Gregory sat beside me in silence while I continued to cast around for Althean. It was early morning, and I could see a faint lightening of the sky to the east. It would remain dark in these woods for quite a while, though. Sunday wouldn't bring any early sounds of workday traffic, and we'd have hours before even the earliest church goers headed out.

"I know you think Althean is capable of redemption, so you're probably not likely to kill him. Are you going to punish him yourself, or lock him away in some jail?" I asked him the question that had been on my mind for days.

Would he change his mind and kill Althean? Would he banish him? Was there some kind of rehab for angels who went crazy? Electroshock therapy or something?

"Why didn't you just let me kill him the other times?" I continued. "You've got to admit, your actions make it look like you really want to take it easy on him."

Gregory sighed in exasperation. "You just won't let this go will you, annoying little cockroach? No, I don't want to kill Althean. I'm hoping I can save him, that we can rehabilitate him. I know why he is doing these things, and there are others among us who feel the same way. I don't want him to become a martyr to his cause. If that happens, the council will have a whole faction to wipe out instead of just a few random extremists. Looking at things with a long term perspective, it would be best to keep Althean alive and convince him to change his mind on these matters."

I shivered in the warmth of the summer air. I had no doubt about this angel's methods of changing someone's mind. I think I'd rather be dead.

"This is bigger than just a few dead werewolves," he told me, rather heartlessly. "There are subversive groups in Aaru who wait to pounce on any opportunity for political gain and possible overthrow. We keep a very tight leash on these groups, but a martyr would benefit their cause. The issue with the werewolves has been going on without resolution for a long time, and people feel strongly on both sides of the issue. Opposing factions would love to seize on this as their banner."

He looked over at me, and then quickly looked away. "I won't allow you to kill him, little cockroach. I know you desperately want to, and I'm sure you have the skill and power to do so. If you did, you'd be signing your own death sentence. The council would never allow your continued existence if you killed an angel."

I sat for a moment in silence. "You're going to kill me, anyway, why do you care if the council decrees my death or not?" Not that I even knew what this council was.

"I'll kill you when I'm ready to," he assured me. "That is the directive, and you will eventually die. I have discretion on when and how I dispatch demons that enter this realm in violation of the treaty. I usually kill them on sight, but I've bound you to me and you are under my authority and control. The council won't interfere with my decision in this matter. But if you were to kill an angel, I doubt I could protect you."

He looked grim and I got the feeling he would fight tooth and nail to protect me. I had no idea why. What use could I be to him beyond tonight? Did he really feel it was worth it to keep me around and tolerate my annoying behavior? Was there something else he had planned for me that would make this all worthwhile?

The lights came on in the cabin. Wyatt and Candy were probably up. I wondered if the other werewolves, the ones who actually lived there, had managed to go to sleep. I wondered how much they knew about what was going on; what danger they were in. I glanced at Gregory, sitting like a brooding statue beside me. It didn't take much of my attention to continuously cast for Althean, so my mind wandered. At least Gregory didn't intend to kill me right away. That was a huge relief. Maybe we could actually hang out together sometime. Perhaps hang out for a few decades. At least until my usefulness was over. I knew that was a ridiculous fantasy, but I still indulged myself in it.

To keep my hands busy I grabbed a nearby pinecone, and stuck some sticks and needles into it creating a bizarre prickly and sap covered animal while I daydreamed about playing with lightning beside this angel, or possibly fire. Maybe he'd teach me to manipulate water and make that cool globe. I eyed my needle-covered pinecone animal. Great. In my boredom, I'd been reduced to creating children's campfire crafts. My hands were covered with sap, and the stuff just didn't come off. I ended up coating them with dirt so at least they were no longer sticky. If this stupid crazy angel didn't show up soon, I was going to go out of my mind.

Finally, as the morning sun had fully risen, I sensed him. Good thing, since I'd stacked my loose change into little piles, had a whole stable full of pinecone animals, and was now making little pine needle haystacks for them to eat. I was covered in sap and dirt.

I tugged Gregory's sleeve and indicated with my hands that our target was at two o'clock, about fifty feet away and moving slowly in. He frowned at me uncomprehendingly and looked with astonishment at my pinecone menagerie. I guess he didn't watch too many spy movies, or experiment with nature crafts. I pointed and went through the motions again, carefully whispering this time.

He nodded. "Stay here. Don't move. Don't do anything. Don't say anything. Nothing. I want your posterior rooted to this spot."

I nodded in agreement. I lie and I don't follow directions well, so as soon as he left the little pine tree shelter, I got up and followed him. I had to stay a good distance back so he wouldn't hear me. He edged up closer to the house, and waited a moment before walking into the tiny yard of cleared trees in front of the house. It had to have been only fifteen feet from tree line to tree line.

I edged up behind him, staying behind a pin oak, hopefully out of sight.

Althean appeared at the edge of the tree line directly

across from Gregory. It was like the scene from High Noon without guns or tumbleweeds.

"Have you finally leashed your dog?" Althean said derisively. The nervous glances he was casting around gave his bravado less credibility. "I thought you were neutral in this, but I now wonder after you had your demon practically tear me apart."

"She is not easy to control," Gregory confessed. "I *am* neutral in this. The council has not given its decision though, and you cannot run around like a vigilante delivering your own personal brand of justice. We are sympathetic to your views and understand why you've acted the way you have, but you must cease and return to Aaru."

Althean paled. "So you can imprison me? So you can bring me back to 'sanity' and obedience? I am not the only one who feels this way. The council is taking too long in their decision and the time to act is now. You can bend me to your will, rip my mind apart, but others will be right there to take my place. They are Nephilim. You know that."

"We do not know that for a fact," Gregory said. "The council will not exterminate a species — will not commit genocide — until we are certain they are Nephilim."

"The council is committing genocide through attrition," Althean countered passionately. "The existence contract is so restrictive that the werewolves are slowly dying out. In a few millennia they will no longer exist and the council can walk away with clean hands and claim innocence. Cowardice. Have they become so weak they are afraid to shed blood? Afraid of delivering justice and hard mercy? There are still angel renegades that escape them, Nephilim still walk the earth. It is clear to many of us that the council is incompetent and unfit to rule."

Gregory barely restrained his anger. "You are not privy to the workings of the council, and are not in any position to pass judgment on their fitness to rule! Would you lead a war against them? Attempt a revolution? It would be over very quickly, I assure you. And the result would not be to your satisfaction."

He paused to calm himself and continued. "I will offer you the chance to live, exiled among the Fallen ones whose path you have mimicked. Or you may choose to return to Aaru for redemption," Gregory said.

Fallen ones? Did he mean us? He'd banish Althean to our realm? We'd eat the guy for lunch within ten seconds of crossing the gate. Dude would be better off choosing to fall on his sword, instead. It would be a far more pleasurable way to die.

"You would send me to the demons?" Althean asked in horror. "Clearly, your vicious reputation is deserved if you would consign me to that eternal torture. I will return with you to Aaru, but be aware that my 'rehabilitation' will not even put a bandage on the seeping wound of this division within us."

Gregory walked toward Althean, who had bowed his head in submission. I felt something within me pinch with alarm and knew what was coming long before Althean even began to formulate the blast. It seems Althean decided to go out like a man. Impossibly fast, he threw a stream of that white energy right at Gregory.

Before it even left his body, I had darted out in front of the pin oak and shot my own bolt of raw energy at him, curving it to loop around Gregory and leave him untouched. It was a tricky piece of work, especially since I was doing it on the fly. It hit Althean just as his bolt of energy left, cutting his blast short and knocking him solidly to the ground. Gregory jerked to the side, either in anticipation of Althean's blast or in reaction to my looping energy. The white stuff the angel had shot missed him by inches and unfortunately smacked me right in the chest, throwing me backwards into the pin oak where I slid to the ground.

Fuck, this stuff hurt. This was the same shit that took my hand completely off back in Gettysburg, so I was a little alarmed. I pulled my personal energy safely inside and started to regenerate. It must have been a smaller blast than the one before because it hadn't blown through me. It did leave a nice hole in my right lung, destroying the ribs and tissue and leaking blood all over the place. I sealed off the blood vessels, and explored the damage. I'd had worse.

Gregory looked over at me in surprise. He took in my injury and exploded in anger. His vaguely human looking form disappeared in a wash of bright light and power. He shone so bright in his fury that they had to have seen him all the way to the road. "Oh, fuck," I thought in panic. "I've disobeyed him and he's gone insane with rage. He's going to come over here and finish me off."

Instead he strode over to Althean who was trying frantically to get upright. I must have hit him pretty hard, I thought smugly.

"She's just a demon!" Althean said in panic. "You can't kill me over a stupid, worthless demon!"

Gregory picked him up by the throat and held him, his feet dangling from the ground. "She's *mine*," he hissed. The word sang with power and ripped through the air in a wave, trembling the earth and raining pine needles to the ground. The morning bird sounds stopped abruptly and the silence was eerie.

Althean began to shake. "No," he choked out. "You cannot. She's a nasty stupid cockroach. She's not worth it."

Gregory tightened his grip and Althean's words ended in a gurgle. "Mine," he hissed and began to shake the smaller angel.

I covered my ears as a high pitched screeching sound, like

nails on glass filled the air. Althean convulsed and he tore at Gregory's arms frantically with his hands. I saw what appeared to be dirt falling from him, then realized that it was sand. Slowly, Althean was dissolving into a pile of white sand from the feet upward as I watched. The process was agonizingly slow; Althean kicked and shook while Gregory continued to hiss and stare at him with those merciless black eyes. In minutes, only his torso and head remained and the sand rained down upon the ground. Gregory kept at it until there was nothing left but a pile of the white grains. He stared at it, grim-faced, and then proceeded to wipe his hands casually on his jeans.

As I watched all this with interest, part of me was getting worried. The white energy was having the same kind of slippery effect on my raw energy that Gregory had when he touched me. I was able to regenerate small portions of myself with the bits I could grab, but the white stuff was eating in deeper and quicker than I could fix. Giving up on regeneration, I concentrated my efforts on getting the white stuff converted and cleared out of my system. It was persistent and multiplying fast. If it destroyed too much of me, it might reach my personal energy. Or I'd be too dissolved to hold in the massive amount of raw energy I had stored within me. Releasing all that energy would be like a bomb going off.

Gregory turned from the pile of sand to look at me, his expression becoming alarmed.

"Fix yourself!" he commanded, an edge of desperation in his voice.

"I'm trying, you asshole," I replied.

I felt hands on my side and realized that Wyatt and Candy were there. Candy looked worried and Wyatt was trying to apply pressure to the wound. I looked down at Wyatt's hands and saw that the blood oozing between his fingers was becoming streaked with an opalescent white. Crap, the raw energy was leaking out and causing me to lose form. I didn't want that to happen with this stuff eating its way through my flesh.

"Hold on, Sam," Wyatt said, applying more pressure. He needed to stop or the raw energy would burn his skin like acid. "Is there anything human doctors can do? Should we call an ambulance?"

I shook my head at him and kept trying to convert bits of the white stuff into nice neutral carbon based molecules. If I could just grab enough raw energy, I could dispel the whole lot of it, but the slippery coating was only allowing me access to a tiny bit at a time. I had to fight for every little bit. Meanwhile, the remaining white stuff expanded faster than I could negate it and was dissolving several important organs. The body I was in was on the verge of failure.

Fuck. I put my hands to the ground and started to slowly trickle raw energy out into the earth. If I could release some of this, then maybe I wouldn't blow half the county up when I went.

"You need to get out of here," I told Wyatt, bubbling blood up from my ruined lungs. "You and Candy. Fast and far. As fast as you can."

"I won't leave you, Sam," Wyatt insisted.

"I'm not joking. You need to leave right now," I told him, enunciating as best as I could.

Wyatt continued to protest and I looked at Candy.

"You promised to protect him, to keep him safe. Get him out of here." I told her and she nodded grimly.

I didn't have time to argue with Wyatt any longer. I turned to him and put every last ounce of strength into pulling out my mean. "Get the fuck out of here right now," I snarled at him.

He jumped back and looked hurt. Candy seized the

moment and grabbing him by the arm dragged him as fast as she could toward her car.

I gave up trying to stop the white stuff and began concentrating on dumping as much raw energy as I could. The ground around me was beginning to smoke. The whole thing was an exercise in futility. It would take me nearly two months at this rate to dump my stash of energy. I looked up at Gregory, who just looked back at me.

"Now would be a really good time to get that damned sword of yours out." I told him, trying to speak the words as clearly as I could with all the blood I was spitting. I needed to say this before my lungs totally gave out. "I'm assuming it collects our energy as you kill us so you don't blast half the planet apart. How much capacity does it have?"

He told me, pulling the sword out of thin air. It wasn't enough. The sword would hold about half my energy. If I could dump another two percent before I croaked, then maybe it would be enough to limit the destruction a bit. He'd probably die, so I wasn't about to reveal the limitations of his sword to him. I didn't want him changing his mind and gating out of here to save himself, leaving me to blow a huge chunk out of the ground. I wondered if the sword would survive the blast. If not, then we were back to square one. Not that we had any other options.

"Do it." I told him.

He paused. "How much raw energy are you packing?"

I rounded down. Way down. Like ten percent of what I really had, down. He raised his sword and began chanting something. I closed my eyes. I don't have any problem facing my own death, but I simply could not look this angel in the eyes as he killed me. The chanting stopped and I held my breath; then it started again.

"Would you hurry the fuck up? I don't have all day here," I told him, keeping my eyes closed just in case.

The chanting stopped again and I heard him whisper something under his breath. I tensed, waiting, but instead of my head rolling on the ground I felt myself pushed onto my back in the blood-wet grass. I risked opening my eyes and saw Gregory kneeling above me, shining white with his black-filled eyes and sharp teeth. What the hell was he doing? If he killed me this way, then everything would most likely be blown to bits. His eyes met mine.

"I'll surely burn for this, but I seem to be heading down that path anyway," he said as he leaned down into me, shoving his hand into the hole in my chest, and placing his lips on mine.

I thought it was a pretty inappropriate time for him to be getting his freak on, even by my standards, but who was I to judge? I opened my mouth to kiss him back and winced as his hand dug deep within my ruined flesh. Just like sex back home, I thought. I felt a vibration humming through me and realized that Gregory was slowly dragging the white energy out of my body and into his hand. It hurt terribly as the stuff burned and ripped its way out through my flesh. Another sound, like bells with his red-purple energy tinged in gold, was spreading out from his mouth across my flesh in a wave of regeneration. He was trying to heal me. I appreciated the effort, but I was really far gone and the hold on my raw energy was severely compromised. Desperate, I tried to shove some into him to hold.

He accepted a good sized chunk, so I proceeded to transfer the entire lot to him. Ridiculous, I know, but I wasn't thinking too clearly at this point. I heard his quick intake of breath, as he realized the volume of energy and attempted to block the transfer. Things were getting fuzzy around the edges of my consciousness, and I was frantic to unload this energy before I croaked. I shoved it back at him more firmly, and he again blocked it. We continued this game of hot potato, with my slipping through additional chunks here and there as he was distracted trying to resist the largest portion. I knew it was too much for him, but I couldn't help it. I could taste his blood filling my mouth as I continued to overload him with raw energy. Finally, with a massive effort, he crammed the largest portion back, shoving it deep within me and yanked with all his might on the remaining white stuff. The pain was intense and everything narrowed in to black....

When I came to, I realized that I was breathing with both my lungs. Gregory lay on top of me, with his weight thankfully on his elbows and knees. His face was turned away from me, but I could hear his ragged breath. Everything seemed to be in the right place. Personal and raw energy, flesh, bone, most of my blood. I reached up a hand and twirled one of his chestnut curls around my finger, tucking it back behind his blood crusted ear. His human form really sucked, but the hair was awesome. Soft and shiny, dark coppery red with a hint of brown. The curl sprang free from behind his ear and back onto my hand. So pretty.

He turned his head to look over at me, yanking the lock of hair free from my fingers. His eyes were still dark and his teeth pointy. He was covered in blood, both mine and his. "You *lied* to me," he hissed.

He was really pissed. He had a reason to be since I'd nearly cooked him from the inside out. That said, this whole "save me, then want to kill me" pattern seemed to be an ongoing theme in our association.

Gregory grabbed me by the shoulders and thumped me gently against the ground. Very gently. With great restraint. I was starting to rethink my assessment of his lack of self control.

"You *lied*! You have fifty, a hundred *times* the energy you said you have. My sword couldn't even have absorbed it all, and it was created to take out the most powerful demons with room to spare. There is no way you can hold that much energy and be stable. No way you can carry that around long term. Nothing can do that."

I just looked at him. What was I supposed to say? We don't need to carry around energy back home, it's plentiful around us. I had been surprised at the amount I'd been able to hold over here. I was actually a bit depleted with all the conversions I'd done this week. I didn't think telling him that would reassure him though.

He smacked me on the ground again. "Angels cannot hold raw energy. The sword can absorb it, but it needs to change, to *become* something before I can attempt to hold it within me. You were killing me by shoving that much into me. Couldn't pass up on an opportunity to be free of me at last, could you? You attempted to kill me while I was trying to save your life."

"I didn't intend to kill you," I told him. It was kind of the truth. "If I had died, there would have been a huge explosion from the release of all that raw energy. I was trying to find a safe place for it. How am I supposed to know you can't hold it? I don't know anything about angels."

He stared in disbelief at me, his face so close to mine. "I should have killed you the first moment I saw you. I should have let you die just now. You will never be anything but a worthless disgusting cockroach. But no, against council decree, against all common sense I healed you. I've let you go free, I've saved you from death, and I've healed you."

"Are you not listening?" I shouted. He was inches from me, but I was pissed. "What fucking alternative did I have? Let's review the options here: One — I die from Goldilocks' blast and release my raw energy, killing you and a whole stinking bunch of humans. Two — you absorb some of my energy with the sword and kill me. I release less raw energy and kill a smaller bunch of humans and hopefully your sword doesn't blow up, too. You may or may not die. I don't fucking know. Three — you heal me, but I lose control and release enough raw energy to still kill a bunch of humans and possibly you, too. Or four — you heal me and help hold the energy so it doesn't blow anything up. Wow, four sounds good to me. How the fuck am I supposed to know you can't hold it? Fuck you."

He glared down at me. I kind of wished he'd get up. Having an argument this close was really disconcerting.

"And why does a little cockroach like you care one bit about human death? Why would you care at all if an angel lived or died?"

"I don't know," I shouted. "I don't fucking know. Now get off me, you asshole."

Abruptly he stood up and continued to frown at me while I scrambled to a seated position.

"You need to go home. I'll take you to the gate myself and see you through it. Stay there and don't come back." His voice sounded flat and hard. This was clearly not negotiable.

"No," I told him. "I want to stay here. I have a life here and I'm not leaving. You can shove me through the gate, but I'll be back. You can't watch them all, and I'm very good at sneaking through."

Gregory sighed and ran his hands through his hair.

"Fine. In the interest of my sanity, I'll agree to let you stay as a bound demon. But there are rules. No Owning. No killing humans. No breeding. I see any plagues, asteroid strikes, or another ice age and I'm going to rip your head clean off your neck. Got it?"

Sheesh, like I could do any of those last things. I was just an imp, after all.

"Scouts honor," I said. "Totally. Absolutely got it."

He frowned. I was lying, and he knew it.

"Cockroach, do not push me on this. If you're too much trouble, I can always take you back to Aaru and drag you around on a leash for the other angels to pet."

Yikes. The idea of being a demon slave in Aaru was truly frightening. I nodded and tried to look sincere.

"Hey, can you gate me back to my car before you go?" I asked in what I hoped was a friendly tone. "I left it, like, five miles from here."

He gave me an incredulous look. "What am I, your taxi?"

"It will just take you a second. I mean, I *was* helping you tonight. I *did* save your life after all. It's the least you could do, you know."

He shook his head and with an exasperated noise, gated away. Asshole.

Figuring I'd have a better chance hitchhiking if I cleaned up a bit, I walked down to the creek and tried to wash off as much blood as I could from my shirt. My bra was hysterical. One whole side was missing and it had been hanging in tatters under my destroyed shirt. Taking it off, I hung it on a tree limb and left it. I looked rather scruffy, braless with a backward torn shirt, but hopefully some hung-over local would give me a ride.

As I walked down to the main road, I saw Wyatt coming toward me. We walked casually toward each other as if we'd had a chance encounter while out on a walk.

"I told you I wouldn't leave you," he said, smiling as we met.

"What did you do, leap out of Candy's car? Smack her on the head with a box of wet wipes?"

"I threatened to shoot her if she didn't let me out," Wyatt said. "I would have done it, too. She told me she hadn't promised to protect me from my own stupidity and let me out."

Candy and I were going to have words.

"Aren't you going to ask me if I'm okay and feel me up for flesh wounds?" I was hopeful he'd get the hint on the feeling-me-up part.

He grinned. "You're up and walking around. You don't have a huge angel sword sticking out your back. I've learned that means you're okay."

"I get to stay, Wyatt," I told him. "If I can manage to behave myself, then I get to stay."

Wyatt nodded, his eyes warm on mine.

"Well then, let's go find your car, go home, put some steaks on the grill, and get you a shower. Naked. With a loofa," he teased.

"I'm very injured and will need you to help scrub my back," I told him.

"I was planning on it," he said, putting an arm around my shoulders as we walked side by side down the road.

I was going to go home. My earthly home. The one here in Maryland. Where I intended to stay as long as I could. With Wyatt. Hey, I'd be able to catch the Monday Zumba class tomorrow morning. Cool.

EPILOGUE

The sun was at its highest point, offering no relief for any creature foolish enough to be out midday. Iguanas, normally basking on rocks, were nowhere to be seen. The goats that climbed along the seaside cliffs were hidden away in caves.

The angel stretched his wings over the red dust, watching it cling to the taupe-colored flight feathers. The feel of the heat, the dry, red, sandy dirt reminded him of somewhere else. Of course, he could never be in this form there. The blasting winds would tear apart this soft flesh even before the radiation cooked through skin and bone.

This place was enjoyable. Even though he never fully committed himself to a corporeal form, he could still feel the bake of the sun on skin, the scrape of rock on his wings, the bright light causing his dark eyes to water slightly. He frowned, wondering for a moment how the demons could stand it. How could they endure the constant onslaught of sensation that a deep physical form brought? He could barely endure this.

He looked up to see a man approaching him. It was

another angel with dark spiked hair and wings of pure white. He looked down at his own wings with their swirling colors of cream and taupe. The scars were barely visible after all this time. He could feel them though, aching deep beyond the muscle and bone to the spirit part of him. It had been so long ago, but the scars still felt like fresh wounds.

"Brother," the dark haired angel acknowledged as he walked up to the seated figure.

Gregory rose. "Brother."

The dark haired angel shuddered slightly as he took the offered hand and clasped it. Shimmering, he shifted into a female form, although still with the short dark spikes of hair.

"Female?" Gregory asked.

The woman grimaced. "You're very much to the right at the moment, and it is uncomfortable not to have balance between us."

Gregory frowned. Was he? He was often accused of being too far to the right, but not so much that he caused such discomfort that others to feel the need to change. It was her. She was so very far to the left, and he'd just gotten used to balancing in her presence.

"Brother, what are you doing?" the woman asked, sitting down on a large rock. Gregory sat too, in a silent agreement that this would be an informal family meeting and not a confrontation.

"What kind of horrific binding did you do with that demon? Why didn't you kill her? And now you've killed Althean. Brother, you are creating enemies left and right. You're lucky everyone is too scared of you to take action."

Gregory smiled. It wasn't a nice smile. He was well aware that his three remaining brothers were happy to stir the pot and spread doubts about his competency, about his sanity.

"I'm also lucky that I have such loyal brothers to watch my back," he said

"Seriously," the woman urged. "Why didn't you kill her?"

Gregory shrugged. "I thought she'd be useful in hunting Althean. They have skills. I think I may use her in some other projects before I kill her. I might as well since I took the time to bind her."

At least he lied better than that irritating cockroach of a demon. She'd surprised him, acted very un-demonic in protecting her human toy by jumping on him and smacking his head on the ground. It made him curious about her. No, it made him wonder with a fleeting hope if maybe there was some spark in them, something left of the angels they used to be. It was a whim he'd indulged in, with horrible consequences.

"Brother, there are rumors about the binding. Rumors that it is too in the flesh, tied to sensation, that it binds you as much as it binds the demon," the woman said.

"She was not easy to bind," Gregory interrupted. He paused, realizing that he sounded defensive. "I haven't bound a demon in ages, and I was very angry at that moment. Yes, the binding is flawed. I will fix it as soon as I have the time."

Angry was a mild word for what he was at that time. It wasn't the first time he'd let his temper get away from him with disastrous results. He'd always struggled with anger. And pride. It seemed over the ages that he been giving in far too much to sin and too less to virtue. Funny how that happens.

"But if you, too, are bound, Brother?" The woman let the question hang in the air.

"No. She's just a baby, and far too Low to have any idea of how to use a bound angel," he insisted.

But she wasn't Low. All that raw energy, and that perfectly formed human flesh with her spirit imbedded deep and tightly contained. Such potential hiding in a dirty little cockroach. It was a shame she'd not live long enough to realize that potential. Not that it mattered. Even if she did somehow manage to survive, she'd never bother to expand her knowledge and skills. Demons only wanted to roll around in the muck of sensation, and play frivolously in the physical world. Such a waste.

"Besides," Gregory added. "I don't plan on having her live more than a year or two."

"What? You don't plan on walking her around Aaru on a leash, like a pet?" The woman laughed.

"She'd just pee on the carpet," Gregory said, amused.

The woman waved her hand. "Enough about this filthy creature. Why have you not formally reported on Althean's death? The longer you wait, the more the factions accuse you of wrongful murder."

"As soon as I am able," Gregory assured her. "I gave Althean a chance to return on his own, or be banished to Hel with the demons and he refused either option."

The woman laughed. "You seriously gave him the option of being banished with the demons? Like he was going to choose that? Wow, you *must* have been pissed. Still, I can't believe you actually killed him."

Gregory couldn't believe it, either. Again, it was anger. Blinding, white hot anger — not that Althean attacked him, but that he'd so injured the little cockroach. Just thinking of it brought up the urge to pulverize something, smash it into the rocks.

"Althean attacked me," he replied.

"Come on." The woman grinned. "You could have subdued him, taken him down. You dusted him."

"He would not back down," Gregory insisted. "I had no choice. He was determined to be a martyr for his cause."

Probably. Not that Gregory had given him a chance.

"Was it the demon?" the woman asked. Gregory stiffened. "Did she kill Althean? Are you covering for her?"

"No. I told you she is Low," he said.

They sat in silence for a few moments. The dark haired angel let her eyes trail along Gregory's outstretched wings, shifting her own white ones so they swept the red dust in a pattern of lines. Picking up a wing, she admired the red dust clinging to the bottom edges.

"We cannot go back in time, Brother," she said sadly, affection in her voice. "Even if we could, I'm not sure it would be right. What's gone is gone. They are not angels anymore, they are demons, and we cannot bring back our loved ones by indulging in reckless fantasy."

Gregory nodded, looking out along the shore. His brother was right, but encasing himself in stone, trying to petrify the hurt inside hadn't helped either. Still, something deep inside him felt like it was chipping away at the hard edges. Like it was trying to get out. He wasn't sure if he should let it. When he meditated on it, he saw a laughing imp playing with lightning, or sometimes his younger brother, also laughing and playing with lightning. But she was not the brother he still mourned. That was foolish thought.

The red haired angel stood and stretched his wings once more.

"There will be no reckless fantasy," he assured his brother before gating away.

ALSO BY DEBRA DUNBAR

The Templar Series:

Dead Rising

Last Breath

Bare Bones

Famine's Feast

The Imp Series

A Demon Bound

Satan's Sword

Elven Blood

Devil's Paw

Imp Forsaken

Angel of Chaos

Kingdom of Lies

Exodus

The Half-Breed Series

Demons of Desire

Sins of the Flesh

Cornucopia

* * *

Imp World Novels:

No Man's Land

Stolen Souls

Three Wishes

Northern Lights

ACKNOWLEDGMENTS

A huge thanks to my copyeditor Jennifer Cosham whose eagle eyes catch all my typos and keep my comma problem in line, and to Damonza, for cover design.

Most of all, thanks to my children, who have suffered many nights of microwaved chicken nuggets and take-out pizza so that Mommy can follow her dream.

ABOUT THE AUTHOR

Debra lives in a little house in the woods of Maryland with her sons and two slobbery bloodhounds. On a good day, she jogs and horseback rides, hopefully managing to keep the horse between herself and the ground. Her only known super power is 'Identify Roadkill'.

debradunbar.com

Printed in the USA
CPSIA information can be obtained
at www.ICGtesting.com
LVHW091455120724
785340LV00032B/173

9 781733 06919